Louise Tondeur was born in Dorset in 1972, and grew up in Bournemouth. She now lives in Cambridge. Her first novel, *The Water's Edge*, is also published by Review.

Praise for *The Haven Home for Delinquent Girls*:

'The smell of plum puddings, mince pies and marzipan wafts through Tondeur's delicious second novel . . . this novel compellingly explores female friendship and insatiatable human appetite' *Manchester City Life*

'Louise Tondeur breezes t quite work out what they *Elle*

'A story of confusion, love ⟶ ⟶ this book is very readable' *Buzz!*

'Tondeur has researched her material well, and instantly evokes the atmosphere of other times . . . the struggles of the women are all the more moving for what's left unsaid' *Diva*

And for *The Water's Edge*:

'Tondeur writes with a mischievous eye for description . . . a fresh and gentle book of awakenings, discoveries, connections and love' *Time Out*

'Fascinating . . . dark secrets jostle with the dust beneath the hotel beds' *Guardian*

'An engaging debut. This author is so good at portraying real life' *The Times*

'An utterly charming, strange and subtle love story' Emma Donoghue

'Full of surprises, twists and turns . . . while the story is compelling, it is really the quirkiness and quiet beauty of its characters that makes this such an unusual debut' *Big Issue*

Also by Louise Tondeur

The Water's Edge

The Haven Home for Delinquent Girls

Louise Tondeur

review

First published in Great Britain in 2004
by REVIEW

An imprint of Headline Book Publishing

First published in paperback in 2005

2

ISBN 0 7553 0143 9

Typeset in Minion by Palimpsest Book Production Limited,
Polmont, Stirlingshire

Printed and bound in Great Britain by
Clays Ltd, St Ives plc

Headline's policy is to use papers that are natural,
renewable and recyclable products and made from
wood grown in sustainable forests. The logging and
manufacturing processes are expected to conform to
the environmental regulations of the country of origin.

Headline Book Publishing
A division of Hodder Headline
338 Euston Road
London NW1 3BH

www.reviewbooks.co.uk
www.hodderheadline.com

Orsino: But died thy sister of her love, my boy?

Viola (as Cesario): I am all the daughters of my
    father's house,
    And all the brothers too: and yet I know not.

                    Twelfth Night, William Shakespeare

1

November 2004

The room at the top of the stairs had its own smell. It was sweet, like sick can smell sweet, and it was stuffed full of junk: furniture, clothes, bedding, various household objects and sacks full of rubbish. The bin bags which hadn't split were swollen, as if they had their mouths full and were refusing to chew. The black plastic shone in the light from the window as it stretched over whatever was inside them. I imagined the contents trying to fight their way out as soon as I turned my back. Some of them had been jammed in between the piles of things and the rubbish was spilling out like guilty secrets, just as it was downstairs in the hall. Bits of food packaging, mouldy bread, half-eaten cake, blackened carrots, plastic bottles of cordial and the odd dirty can were arranged between the debris and the old clothes, rotting where they had fallen.

Eve climbed around the curve of the stairs behind me, a cigarette stuck between her teeth. She removed it with a thumb and index finger.

'Disgusting, isn't it?' she said. I nodded. She looked through the doorway with me. The junk had been thrown in randomly. Under an upside-down coffee table, mixed up with an old sheet, were bits of what could have been a rocking chair, some orange peel, furry with mould, and a bottle full of lumpy grey milk.

'This room is your job, right?' she said after we had gazed in

1

silence for a while. She glanced at me sideways to see if I would complain, but I didn't reply. The window on the far side still had its flimsy yellow curtains. Through it, reluctant streaks of daylight picked up the dust which hung around like it was waiting for something to happen. The walls were covered in peachy-coloured paper which was faded where the light had hit it and falling off in places. There was so much stuff that I couldn't get a sense of how big the room was, although, next to the window, and covered in trash, I could just make out a single bed, with an iron head-rest and feet like dragon's paws.

'Some of it you can save,' Eve said, the cigarette drooping from her mouth. She grabbed hold of a leg from a pile of dining-room chairs. They were balanced one on top of the other, near some dirty cardboard boxes. 'Like these for instance,' she said. 'Anything broken, chuck it out. Plus anything useless. Just put it in the skip.' She waved her hand at a doll's pram which had lost its hood and was orange with rust. It was leaning to one side because a tower of magazines had collapsed onto it.

'And the clothes,' she said. 'They can go too.' There was an old red coat nearby. It was thick and rough with brown buttons and something had eaten through one of the pockets. A large wicker laundry basket was full of vinyl records which were spilling out into a washing-up bowl. Some Marigolds had stuck themselves to the side of Kate Bush's *Greatest Hits* like a pair of giant pink limpets. Eve turned to go back down the stairs. 'Oh, and the rat man hasn't been yet, so be careful.'

With the mask and gloves Bernie gave me, I made my way through the piles like an explorer. I had my own thick plastic sacks for the most disgusting stuff and cardboard boxes for anything I thought could be rescued. At first, I worked quickly because of the smell, but after a while, with each object I picked up, I began to wonder what the old man had used it for and why he had kept it. All the objects must have stories attached to them. They were silent and told me nothing, so I had to guess. I bought that in Spain on the day I met my wife. A priest gave me those beads in Bognor Regis one summer. That was the umbrella I carried to the job interview in Margate. I imagined I was one of those people who will dig things up in a thousand years' time. This shoe tells me that the man who wore it ate only vegetables and worshipped the moon. But eventually I got pissed off with all the stories flying around my head. There were too many of them and Eve came upstairs and told me I was slow, so I picked up the objects without thinking about them. I arranged bigger savable things along the landing, a footstool, a crate of vases, some china plates, but mostly I carried armfuls to the skip: old books, newspapers, dolls' heads, broken table tops, bent picture frames.

By teatime, Eve and Bernie had cleared the hall and I had made a path to the window, which I heaved open, so that the autumn air could rush into the room. When I stuck my head out I could see the driveway and below it the lake, surrounded by nodding trees. Turning back round, I noticed through the rubbish that there was a fireplace in one wall, clad in green tiles. I was also beginning to uncover the bed, which still had its unmade bedclothes as if its owner had risen in a hurry and returned to find his room full of things.

That was the day I found the sign under a pile of damp cupboard doors, by the low wall in the driveway. The wooden posts that used to hold it up had rotted and were covered in green mould. Once I had shifted the doors, I turned the sign over, dislodging several woodlice as I did so. The wood hadn't rotted at the top, probably because of the paint and varnish. *The Haven*, it said in bold writing across the top, but the rest of the paint had chipped away. The only other words I could read were, *founded 1849*. I showed it to Eve.

'Is that the name of the house?' I said.

'Yep,' she said, putting down her mobile so she could examine it.

'What does it mean, "founded"? I thought the rubbish man lived here.'

'He did. Before that it was a home. We might be able to save it. Put it by the wall.' My gloves had turned green with moss from holding it up and there were woodlice running backwards and forwards along the top, but I did as she said anyway.

'What? An old people's home?' I said, going back over to the car.

'No. Don't be stupid.'

'What sort then?'

She looked at me and grinned. 'A home for girls like you,' she said and her mobile began to ring.

After I had cleaned the sign up a bit, I went back up the stairs and looked out of the window of the top room again. The sunlight was gone. A mist had come in across the lake and had settled around the house. It was like we were sitting inside a cloud.

As we had driven round the hill in the rain that morning, I had noticed that the horse chestnut tree at the end of the house had turned half golden. I couldn't remember if it had been like that the day before. Half its leaves were still green, but those nearest the house glittered like dim torches in the mist that clutched them. When I opened the window and leaned out, I could just see the outermost branches as they reached beyond the house like fingers. If I were outside on the road now, I thought, the mist would cover me too and I might not be able to see the tree at all. I felt as though it might come into the room, like smoke, and cover everything. Perhaps it would circle around me and carry me off somewhere and I could be a genie for the night.

2

February 1959

The bakery was closed. Frankie Lymon and the Teenagers were singing on the radio and Alex was in the kitchen with *The Modern Motor Car* open in front of her.

'Citroën, Fiat, Renault, Mercedes,' she said to herself as she wrapped strips of puff pastry round the insides of three white dishes. A sweet wine and peach sauce was simmering on the stove. It smelt spicy and made her want to dip in her finger and try some. She had just switched off the heat when she turned and noticed a woman in a green hat knocking on the window. Alex leant through the door into the shop, mouthed, 'We're shut,' and went back to the table to slice apricot for the flans.

'Chevrolet, Bentley, Studebaker,' she murmured, imagining a line of shiny cars driving past the bakery. She had begun to dip the pieces of fruit into the sauce and arrange them in a spiral pattern on the base when she saw that the woman was still there, knocking on the window again and waving. She was wearing a long green coat that matched her hat, and shiny black shoes. Alex went out into the shop, because Mr Sabre was drinking the tea she had made him in the back room with a coconut fancy.

'We're shut,' said Alex through the window. The woman said something she couldn't hear, and didn't go away, so Alex went to get the long key from the hook. The picture of Edith smiled down at her from the wall above the loaf trays. Under the photo were three certificates in frames. 'Edith and Michael Sabre', the first one said, 'Butlins Quiz Champions 1951'. The Q and the C were in green curly letters. The second and third were the same, only these said 1952 and 1953. She picked up the key. On the opposite wall were three more: 1955, 1956, 1957. Alex knew that in 1954 they had been beaten by a question on petunias and a suspect judge. The certificates were signed personally by William Butlin.

She opened the door.

'I simply must have some custard tarts,' said the woman. Her voice was thick, like the cream Alex piped into chocolate éclairs on Saturday mornings. She sounded so desperate that Alex stood back and let her in.

'Custard tarts. Do you have any?' the woman said, taking off her gloves slowly, one finger at a time. Her hands were smooth and white.

'I'll go and see.'

Mr Sabre had cleared away already, so Alex had to go back into the kitchen. 'We have vanilla and pineapple,' she called.

'Good,' said the woman.

'How many?'

'Three of each, please,' she said. Her shoes tap-tapped as she walked to and fro across the shop floor waiting for her pastries.

After the latecomer had gone and the flans were turning golden in the oven, Alex got the laundry basket and set up the ironing board in the shop, because there wasn't room for it in the kitchen. She started with one of Mr Sabre's shirts, the white one with a pink collar and blue cuffs, smoothing it with her hand. It was cold and damp and the arms stretched along the board as if someone had been squashed flat then forgotten about.

She sighed and looked at the pile of clothes still waiting to be washed. The green drainpipes he had bought after the funeral were hanging off the side of the washing machine as if they were about to run away.

After Edith died, Mr Sabre did two things. First, he bought himself a whole new wardrobe; second, he walked past the

6

homeware showroom on his way to make deliveries every day and looked in at the window like people do when they are choosing cakes. Now the new washing machine stood like a smug white monster in the corner of the kitchen and reminded him that Edith wasn't behind the counter in the shop any more. He had Alex, the machine and a heap of new clothes instead.

Alex thought of the Creature from the Black Lagoon from the poster above her bed. He opened his mouth to say something but then changed his mind. Since she had seen the film three years ago, the Creature would sometimes appear inside her, cross-legged like a conscience or an ugly prophet, telling her what to do, predicting what might happen, dishing out advice when she didn't want it, kicking her hard when she felt guilty about something and sometimes even having a go at answering Mr Sabre's questions for him.

Alex sighed and moved on to a pair of red slacks. As she watched the iron moving to and fro and the steam rising, she thought about what it would be like to slip her own legs in between the thick straight fabric. She put down the iron, lifted the trousers from the board and held them up against her blue dress as if she were in a shop trying them on. One day the feeling would burst inside her like seeds bursting out of an exploding flower, and she would pull on the clothes one after another: shirt, trousers, jacket, shoes. Then she would look just like Elvis in the *Jailhouse Rock* poster above her bed.

She heard Mr Sabre shuffling along the corridor. He came in holding his empty cup and crumb-covered plate. Michael Sabre was fifty-five and almost fat, with red cheeks and a scarred pincushion face. His hands were pastry-coloured and made Alex think of yellow frogs on the side of a pond. He took his cardigan from the peg by the door and wriggled into it.

'What is special about the 1956 Renault Dauphine?' he said in a serious voice.

Alex thought for a moment. 'It has its engine at the back.' She picked up another one of his shirts to iron and pulled it straight on the board. This one was her favourite. It had colourful vertical stripes and musical notes on the collar.

'When was the first mass-produced car made?'

She hesitated, closed her eyes and tried to picture the page with the cars and the years in the book.

'1902?' she said, opening her eyes and hoping she was right.

'1901. One wrong,' said Mr Sabre. 'What was it called?'

'Um.' She screwed up her eyes again.

'Do you want to be a quiz champion or not? The Curved Dash Runabout made by the Oldsmobile Company in the United States. One out of three,' he said. 'Next, planets.'

'Have you got a book?' she asked, loading his clothes into the basket.

'Look in the cupboard when you take those up.' Mr Sabre's encyclopaedias, atlases and dictionaries were arranged on the bookshelf in the back room. The ones that wouldn't fit were stacked in his cupboard and rotated twice a year, at Christmas and Easter, when he would curse because his back hurt, say, 'Help me carry these, will you?' and swap the books over.

Alex put the clean washing down on the bed and went over to the cupboard. Inside, it smelt of leather and socks. His clothes were hung up neatly: shirts together, trousers together, cardigans, jackets. Belts, braces and ties were on the wardrobe door. The white overalls were downstairs on the hook in the kitchen, so that in the privacy of his bedroom, Mr Sabre might not have been a baker at all. There was no sign of flour or butter or yeast apart from a faint musty smell which hung about the whole of the upstairs of the bakery like a lodger with long hair who refuses to leave. She felt around inside the cupboard and pulled out *A Professional Guide to Angling* and *The Norton History of Britain* before she saw the book on astronomy.

As she reached in to get it, she touched a pile of things lying crumpled at the bottom of the wardrobe, which she hadn't noticed before. There was a red dress, a matching handbag, a shawl and shoes. It was one of Edith's outfits. She rubbed the material between her fingers. It smelt dusty. The handbag undid with a faint click. She thought about the times when Edith must have opened it and delved inside for lipstick or a handkerchief or a pencil. Alex closed her eyes and pictured her back in the kitchen breaking an egg into a bowl. When she opened her eyes again, she saw the photo of Edith holding a green rosette staring at her from the sideboard where the alarm clock stood. Alex felt suddenly sad. She stuffed the clothes back where she had found them, took out *Wandsworth's Astronomical Companion* and ran downstairs.

On her way home Alex had to walk through the cemetery. After she had pushed open the gate on the other side and had stepped back out onto the street, she paused at Mr Bradley's house and looked over the wall. She took in the dark green and red bushes which had thin fingers and looked as if they had been covered in icing sugar, then moved quickly away and soon the street of tall red terraces stretched behind her, like soldiers in their uniforms.

When she got in, her parents were in the front room with food on trays on their laps so that they could watch the new television. She sighed and wished she was back at the bakery making fruit loaf. Through the door, she saw her father, who grew wider every day, almost bursting out of his armchair. When he sat in Mr Bradley's car seat, he was too big for it and bits of him stuck out either side. Once, when she was younger, she had tried on a pair of his trousers and they were so big, she could have fitted into them three times over.

Alex's father had just been promoted.

'He gets a new uniform and everything,' Alex's mother had said proudly. 'With a hat.'

'Driver,' her father said, trying out the word. He mimed steering the wheel and smiled.

'Chauffeur,' her mother corrected him.

'Who for?' said Alex.

'Mr Bradley of course.'

'Wow,' said Alex. That was the day when he went out and bought the television set.

Mr Bradley was the cinema man. He owned the Rio in town and Alex's father had been a security guard there since before

9

she was born. It had been his job to weed people out and escort them from the theatre by the elbow. There were five main types of misbehaviour: entering without a ticket, throwing sweet wrappers, talking loudly, wearing a large hat, and hanky-panky, which her father told her meant too much kissing. When she was small Alex used to imagine him shining his torch into people's faces as they watched the films.

The first ever film she saw was *White Christmas* and the day afterwards Alex went into the bakery while her mother was in the grocers nearby. She had been sent to pick up some doughnuts. It was cold and sleet had fallen in the night, so the streets were icy. In those days, her eyes were about level with the top row of coconut fancies, but if she looked up, she could see Edith's hot sagging face looking down at her. In front of her were several plum puddings, a whole stack of mince pies and two beautifully iced cakes with Santa skating merrily across the top as if they were frozen white ponds.

'Can I have one of those?' Alex said, pointing at a marzipan snowman by pressing her finger into the glass, but Edith ignored her.

'Come into the kitchen, I want to show you how to make Christmas cake,' she said instead. Alex followed her.

'We went to see *White Christmas* at the cinema,' she said as she stirred a wish into the sticky mixture.

'You need more nutmeg,' Edith replied. 'It's in the bag. Really? Did your father take you?'

Her mother often sent her on errands to the bakery and she gradually got to know more of Edith's recipes. Inside the shop she witnessed the changing seasons. In March there were rabbit-shaped biscuits and chicks sitting in marzipan eggs. In the summer there was pink coconut ice. In October there were pumpkins and witches' brooms decorating the cakes, and for bonfire night, apples rolled in a gluey toffee. Then it was Christmas again and the shop was filled with the smell of spice, icing and Edith Sabre's sweat.

In those days, Alex had to sit with Mrs Rodgers, the ice-cream seller at the cinema, after school every day until her father was ready to take her home. The ice-cream seller didn't like Alex's father. When Alex asked her mum why, she said it was because Mr Rodgers had wanted the job as security guard, but Alex's father told her that the two of them had been sweethearts at school and he had let her down. Once Mrs Rodgers cornered Alex's dad by the popcorn and called him a rotten egg.

It was the bakery that rescued Alex from the ice-cream seller. That day, the coconut ices were sitting on their trays behind the glass cabinet and the air was so hot it felt as if the day was melting.

'I don't like waiting at the cinema,' Alex told Edith.

'Free films, as much ice cream as you can eat,' Edith said. 'What's wrong with you?' She was folding clothes into a neat brown case in the back room.

'Mrs Rodgers hardly ever gives me any,' Alex said. 'Apart from when she cleans out the tubs. And I only get to see films at Christmas.'

'Pass me those shoes.'

'Where are you going on holiday?' Alex picked up a skirt and wrapped a sleeve round her wrist.

'Skegness. Put that down. It's for a special occasion.'

'Is it someone's birthday?'

'No. We've got through to the general knowledge finals.' She took the skirt and re-folded it.

'Can I have one of those iced buns?' Alex said. Edith carried on folding for a while as if she was making up her mind.

'OK. There's some in the kitchen that didn't come out right. Don't tell your mother.'

'Mrs Rodgers has wet hands,' Alex said when she came back from eating her bun. 'And she smells funny.'

Edith looked at her as if she was seeing into the future.

'What do you want to be when you grow up?' she said.

'I don't want to work in the cinema like my dad and Mrs Rodgers. I hate Mrs Rodgers,' she said sulkily.

'I'll teach you to make cakes then,' Edith said just like that, and went back to folding her skirts. Alex sat down in Mr Sabre's armchair and watched her and felt pleased, as if something important had been decided.

'After school every day,' Edith said when the case was full.

'Instead of Mrs Rodgers?'

'Yes. Fetch your mum in and I'll tell her.'

There was a sound of clapping and music from the new television.

'You're late today,' her mother said, without taking her eyes from the screen.

'I did his ironing for him.'

'Again?' she said. Alex's father laughed. He was still wearing his chauffeur's uniform. His fat shoulders shook. She wasn't sure if he was laughing at the ironing or at the television. Alex shifted the book on the universe under her arm, feeling frustrated because they wouldn't turn round and look at her.

'He misses Edith,' she said.

'Six times quiz champion, that woman,' said her father. Edith and her father had lived on the same street when they were younger. Still neither of her parents turned round. They could have been talking to someone on the TV.

'Amazing mind. Full of facts,' her father said. He tapped his forehead.

Alex was relieved to finally climb the stairs to her room. She lay on her bed with her book. Her posters smiled down at her from the walls: *The Creature From the Black Lagoon*, Michael Landon from *I Was a Teenage Werewolf*, and a big one of *Jailhouse Rock*. She closed her eyes and imagined she was Elvis in the poster then opened the book on astronomy and saw the planets zooming into space in front of her as if she had created them herself.

3

Alex was pouring a little more milk into an almond slice mix when Mr Sabre came into the bakery kitchen with another bag of laundry and hung his new jacket on the peg by the door. It was the green one with the wide lapels he had bought the day after the washing machine had arrived.

'The icing on the buns isn't thick enough,' he said. He wrapped his apron string round himself twice and went into the shop.

'Mercury, Venus, Earth, Mars,' Alex said under her breath. Behind her were the pastries she had made earlier, filled with apricot pieces and nuggets of lemon rind, and the date slices, which were thick with dark brown sugar and molasses.

'And hurry up with those slices,' he called, turning on the radio. Elvis was halfway through 'All Shook Up'.

'Jupiter, Saturn, Uranus, Neptune, Pluto,' she murmured. When she looked up from the solar system, she saw that the woman in the green hat had returned. Alex poured the mix into its tin and watched to see what the woman would buy. Macaroons, she thought, sliding the cake into the oven, but the woman pointed to the apple turnovers, which Alex had folded in sugar that morning. She had tried one herself after they came out and the sugar was golden and sparkled on her tongue. She smiled at the thought of it, wiped her hands and shook out the bag of washing. Then the woman, holding out her money, hesitated, looked again and chose two almond-topped macaroons as well. Alex was pleased with herself and watched as Mr Sabre wrapped them.

13

She had begun to feed clothes into the top of the washing machine when the elegant woman looked through the kitchen door at her and Alex saw her eyes properly for the first time. They were brown, like a mixture of mud and laughter, or something secret that Alex didn't know about. She turned back to the baker's dirty clothes and the woman left quickly.

After they had closed for the day, Mr Sabre shuffled around in the shop for a while, straightening the empty cake trays and certificates on the wall, then he came into the kitchen and hung up his apron.

'What planet is nearest to the sun?' he said, moving a damp sweater out of the way so that he could sit down on a stool to pull off his shoes.

'That's easy. Mercury.' She carried on mixing her batter, lifting it from the bowl to check the thickness.

'Planet nearest to earth.'

'Mars.'

'Fifth planet from the sun?'

She counted on her fingers. 'Saturn.'

'Wrong. Two out of three,' said Mr Sabre, nudging his feet into his slippers.

'What's next?' she said.

He thought for a moment. 'The names of the oceans.'

By the time she went to get her coat that afternoon, she had arranged drying clothes on stools and over the doors and on a line from the mixer to the sink. She heard the creak of the baker's feet on the stairs. As she pulled on her duffel coat, she noticed that he had pinned a chrysanthemum to the lapel of his new jacket. Mr Sabre came in, smelling of aftershave, and shrugged into it. He was wearing the shirt with the blue cuffs. His stomach was hanging over a pair of jeans which Alex hadn't seen before and he had slicked his hair down so it stuck greasily to his head.

'I'm going over to the shop on Carling Street with some choux buns,' he said. 'Do the ironing before you leave, will you? Fold the collars down this time.'

Alex sighed and took off her coat again. Mr Sabre wrapped a

14

scarf round his thick throat, picked up the tray of buns and headed off into the afternoon.

Half an hour later, Gene Vincent was singing 'Be-Bop-a-Lula' on the radio as Alex slipped off her dress and pulled on the stripy musical shirt and the green drainpipes. She stood admiring herself for a while, then she ran upstairs to Mr Sabre's bedroom to find some shoes and a tie. The curtains were drawn. She wanted to pull them open and let the daylight rush into the room like a dog, but instead she went over to the cupboard. She put on a pair of white socks and the red leather brogues with creases in the toes and smiled as soon as she caught sight of herself in the mirror. Kay Starr began singing in the kitchen so she grabbed a tie and ran downstairs to dance. She was tying the tie carefully like her dad had shown her once, when she realised that the kitchen door was slightly open and someone was looking in through the shop window. It was dark outside, but when the figure pushed her face to the glass, she saw it was the woman with the green hat and the white gloves. She knocked on the window and waved. Alex grabbed her dress and ran out of the kitchen. She sat in the armchair in the back room staring at the cabbage-coloured curtains, wondering if the elegant woman would tell Mr Sabre.

At nine o'clock the next day, on her morning off, Alex walked across the foyer of the Rio. Mrs Rodgers was cleaning her implements in the small sink by the sweet counter and was wearing pink rubber gloves. Her face was drooping, as if it had begun to slide off the edge of her skull because the glue wasn't strong enough. Alex was thinking about the woman in the green hat when the man on the door nodded at her. She got in for free because of her dad.

'Going up in the world, your dad,' said the man. 'Driver, eh?' He mimed a steering wheel. She smiled at him and sat near the back, with her duffel coat wrapped round her like a blanket, because the heating didn't come on until midday and going to

15

a show in the mornings was like stepping into a toffee-flavoured larder. There were only three other people there: a couple in the front row and a man with a hat pulled over his face so that Alex wondered how he could see the film. The lights went down and the music started. Today it was *The Blob* with Steve McQueen. Last week she had seen *Invasion of the Body Snatchers*, but the best films were the ones with Elvis in them. She had watched *King Creole* and *Love Me Tender*, memorising the outfits he wore so she could push her face into her pillow at night and think about trying them on herself. Steve McQueen's face filled the screen and she settled back to watch. But all the way through the film she was thinking about the woman with the green hat tapping on the window, unable to get her out of her head.

When the woman with the hat came back later that week, Alex was learning the creation and Elvis was singing 'I Want to Be Your Teddy Bear' on the radio. Alex had propped her father's tattered brown bible from home against the scales so that she could read it. The bible was so old the pages were falling out and she had been worried that the word of God would fly away down the street as she walked to work or fall into a sponge mix and get baked with all the other ingredients, so people would have to spit it out, like people who didn't like cherries who bought a cherry sponge by mistake. Some of the pages were marked with butter or chocolate fingerprints because she had turned them quickly between folding the chocolate fancies.

'Day one, day and night, day two, heaven, day three, earth,' she said to herself, looking to see if she was right. She had been watching the shop, too, for the last hour, because Mr Sabre was in the back room with a Chelsea bun and a cocoa.

She was about to wipe her hands and close up when the elegant woman came in. Alex stopped rubbing her hands and stood against the wall in the kitchen for a second, wondering if she could ignore her, but the woman rang the bell on the counter and tapped her feet impatiently. Alex didn't want Mr Sabre to hear. She took a deep breath and went out into the shop.

'Can I help you?' she said, looking at the floor.

The woman chose three squashy meringues, a cherry pastry, and a slice of gateau, pressing her white-gloved fingers against the glass as she made her choices, without saying anything. When Alex had wrapped her cakes for her, the woman gazed at her with the mud and laughter look.

'You looked very handsome,' she said. Alex blushed, stared at the toffee wafers and didn't reply. 'Don't worry, I won't tell anyone.'

'We're closing now,' Alex said. She turned, dusted her hands on her apron, and took the long key from the hook as Edith looked down at her.

'Well, I had better go.'

'Yes,' said Alex, feeling relieved, but the woman hesitated and looked over towards the kitchen door.

'I would love to see where the cakes are made,' she said.

Alex was surprised. She took the woman over and showed her. The room was cream-coloured as if they were inside a vanilla sponge mix with a light on. Alex looked awkwardly at the spot where she had stood in Mr Sabre's clothes while the woman took in the table, the ovens, the mixer, the flour and the shelves of ingredients and clapped her hands together.

'It's wonderful,' she said. She walked over to the table and inspected some coconut bites which Alex had taken out of the oven an hour before.

'Try one, if you like,' said Alex, because she could see that she wanted to. The woman picked one up and put it whole into her mouth.

'I would love a cup of tea,' the woman said. Alex looked at her uneasily, but she half wanted the woman to stay.

'OK,' she said. She filled the kettle and put it on the stove. 'Mr Sabre is in the back room.'

'Is that the old man?' She looked around for a chair, found two stools by the door, and pulled them over to the table, then she ate another coconut bite, whole again, opening and closing her mouth like a fish.

'Do you do the baking?' she said.

17

'Some of it. Mr Sabre does some at night.'

'I would like to watch you,' said the woman. 'I can't imagine how these cakes are made, they are simply divine.'

Alex put a mug of tea down in front of the woman, who was clearly used to a cup and saucer, but she didn't say anything about it.

'I have to do fruit buns now, actually,' said Alex. 'You can watch if you like.' The woman clapped her hands again.

'I won't tell anyone, you know,' she repeated.

'About the cakes or about dressing up?' said Alex.

'Dressing up,' said the woman. 'I shall tell everyone about the cakes.' She looked at her slyly. 'You know, there's the most wonderful café where you can dress up,' she began, but Alex interrupted her in alarm.

'You can test me on the creation,' Alex said, washing her hands in the little sink and taking out a bowl.

The woman laughed. 'Why?' she asked.

Alex flicked the opening pages until she found the beginning of Genesis and passed the woman the brown bible.

'Mr Sabre is going to ask me about it today. He was quiz champion.'

'I'd rather just watch.'

'Test me on the days.'

'All right. Day one,' she said.

'Night and day,' said Alex. She weighed out flour for the buns carefully and sieved it into a large bowl.

'Day two,' said the woman, as Alex shook out the sugar and sliced the cold yellow butter. She chopped the butter into small pieces quickly with a blunt knife.

'Raisins,' Alex said, waving behind her to the shelf in the corner.

'No,' said the woman. 'Not raisins.' She laughed.

'Pass me the raisins,' Alex said, turning to look at her and pointing at the wooden box. The woman's eyes were still sparkling with leftover laughter but she got up anyway and found the box of wrinkled brown fruit.

'What's your name?' said the woman.

'Alex.'

'Aha,' said the woman. 'And how old are you?'

'Nineteen, nearly twenty,' Alex lied.

'Are you sure?' said the woman.

'Yes. What's your name?'

'Isabelle,' said the woman. 'But people call me different things. Isabelle doesn't suit me.'

'What do people call you?'

'Indigo, Innocence, Irene. Anything beginning with I, really.'

'The heavens,' Alex said. 'God created the heavens on day two.' She stirred the mixture with a wooden spoon and felt like making a wish as if it were Christmas. I wish, she thought, but she didn't get any further.

'Day three,' Isabelle said. Her voice sounded calm, thick and serious, like syrup.

'Day three is earth, sea and plants. Day four is sun, moon and stars,' Alex said, hoping she sounded smooth and cold like Isabelle did. She put her hands into the bowl to rub the flour and butter together.

'Day five,' Isabelle said.

'Day five is birds and sea creatures.' Alex wiped her hands on a tea towel and turned to face Isabelle. 'Day six is animals and Adam and Eve, and day seven is rest.'

'Very good.' Isabelle laughed, but then her mud-coloured eyes were suddenly serious. 'Put the clothes on again for me,' she said, almost in a whisper.

'What clothes?' said Alex, pretending not to understand.

'You know.'

Alex didn't reply. She stirred the bun mix too much, watching the spoon going round and round. Isabelle got off her stool and came over to look into the bowl, but then they heard Mr Sabre moving around in the back room.

'I'd better go,' Isabelle said. She hesitated, put her hand on Alex's arm and traced the line from her shoulder to her wrist. 'Perhaps I can come back again.'

Alex carried on stirring for a moment, then she made up her mind.

'All right,' she said. 'On Thursday he's delivering cinnamon swirls and maple fingers to the new shop on Carling Street.'

'On the other side of town?'

'Yes,' said Alex.

Alex went through the graveyard and took the path towards home as usual. When she looked over the wall into Mr Bradley's garden she was amazed to see it was full of hundreds of green tulip buds which had pushed themselves up from under the soil since she'd last looked.

Her parents were eating sandwiches and watching *Double Your Money* when she got in. Hughie Green's voice was rising and falling excitedly. Her mother held her sandwich halfway between her plate and her mouth, like a statue. Alex could only see the back of her father's wide head and shoulders, but he didn't move either. She wondered if Medusa had turned them to stone.

'Hello,' she said.

'Hello,' they called, coming to life. Then they turned back to the television.

'Hold on,' said her father, when she was about to go upstairs. He reached into his fat brown bag, pulled out a poster and waggled it at her.

'Got that for free,' he said. She took it from his hand and unrolled it. *Teenagers From Outer Space* it said along the top. Alex grinned.

'Thanks, Dad,' she said and kissed him on the forehead.

'Hasn't been released here yet,' her father said, turning his thick neck back towards the television. 'You're lucky to get it.'

'What are you giving her more rubbish for?' said her mother.

'It's not rubbish, Mum.' But her mother ignored her.

'She doesn't need any more posters.'

'Give it a rest.'

'Have you been flirting with that ice-cream seller again?'

Her father fiddled with the collar of his uniform uncomfortably and didn't reply.

'You have, haven't you? You are unbelievable.'

Alex slipped out of the room miserably. The argument continued below as she climbed the stairs with her new poster. They didn't notice she had gone.

When Isabelle knocked on the door on Thursday, Alex was mixing flour and butter and learning the wives of Henry VIII. She went and let her in.

'What are you making?' Isabelle asked.

'Cheese scones,' said Alex. She moved a tray of date slices over to the side to make room for Isabelle to sit down.

'Can I help?'

'You can grate some cheese.'

Isabelle looked perplexed for a moment. Then she sat down on the stool, took off her gloves and rolled up her sleeves. She began to grate the big slab of white cheese that Alex had ready on the table. After a couple of minutes, she was bored and put the cheese down.

'What are you reading?' she said.

'Do you like tulips?' said Alex. 'Only I saw some tulip buds near the graveyard. They'll be out soon.'

'Graveyard? Yuk,' said Isabelle. 'I hate the places.' She leant over and picked up the book about Henry VIII, leaving the rest of the cheese ungrated.

'*Tudor England*,' she read. She looked around to see if there were any new biscuits for her to try and then, when she didn't find any, at the kettle. 'Shall I make tea?' she said bravely, as if she might not know how to do it.

'I'll make it,' said Alex. She filled the kettle with water. 'There are flapjacks in that box if you want one.'

Isabelle got up, reached into the box and ate one of Alex's syrupy flapjacks.

'Good?' asked Alex.

'Divine. Shall I test you again?'

'Yes. Henry the Eighth's wives. Make up questions.'

Isabelle walked up and down the kitchen behind Alex, her lovely shiny shoes clipping across the red tiles.

'How old was Jane Seymour when she died?' she said, as Alex handed her a mug of tea.

'I don't know. That's not in the book. How old was she?'

'I haven't a clue.'

'Ask questions from the book,' she said.

'You told me to make them up. All right. Who was his second wife?'

'Anne Boleyn.'

'What happened to her?' She sat down on the sack of flour near the wall and flicked the pages.

'Beheaded.'

'When did he marry Marie Antoinette?'

'Never. He didn't marry her.'

'Joan of Arc? Elizabeth the First? Jane Eyre?'

'Elizabeth the First was his daughter.'

'Aha. What about the other two?' Alex felt Isabelle get up and come over to her. When she was so close Alex could feel her breath, Isabelle lifted her hand up and touched her neck. Alex felt how warm she was behind her. She carried on mixing the scones.

'Joan of Arc is a saint and Jane Eyre is a heroine,' she said. 'They aren't in the book either.' Isabelle still had *Tudor England* in her hand.

'Katherine of Aragon then,' she said, running one of her fingers down Alex's neck.

'I don't know. I can't remember.'

'Put the clothes on again for me,' Isabelle said in a whisper. Alex turned round with the tray of date slices in her hand.

'No. I can't. I don't want to,' she said, even though she did want to.

'I'd like to kiss you,' Isabelle said gently. Alex thought about it for a moment. It wasn't how she thought her first kiss would be. Her first kiss was supposed to be with Julia Adams in the sequel to *The Creature From the Black Lagoon*, when she had saved her from the monster, but maybe she could practise with Isabelle first.

'All right,' she said at last.

Isabelle made her wipe her hands on the tea towel and led her over to the space between the giant mixer and the sacks of flour. They leant against the wall. When Isabelle kissed her, Alex felt as if she was putting her hands in cake dough. Isabelle tasted of flapjack. Suddenly the air smelt too sweet and yeasty and the flour dust caught at the back of her throat. Alex felt dizzy. She pushed Isabelle away.

'We shouldn't do that here,' she said. 'Mr Sabre will be back soon.' Isabelle pressed her head and back against the wall so that she could feel the cold of it on her skin.

'Where then?' she said.

'I don't know where,' Alex said. She went back over to the tray of date slices standing in rows like a sweet brown army. They had watched the kissing from beginning to end. Each one was soft dark brown, with a date arranged on top, and just mouth-sized. She picked up the tray again. Isabelle had sunk down next to the wall now and was crouching, watching Alex move around the bakery kitchen.

'Come out with me at the weekend. I know the most perfect café,' she said in her smooth, creamy voice.

'No,' Alex said, sliding the date slices onto a shelf. 'I can't.' Then they heard Mr Sabre opening the shop door with his empty trays. Isabelle got up and kissed Alex neatly on the cheek before he came in.

'Hello,' she said gracefully, walking into the shop, her shiny black shoes tap-tapping. 'I felt faint and Alex very kindly made me a cup of tea.'

After Isabelle left, Alex made more apricot turnovers, the most beautiful she had ever made, with sugar like tiny golden hail that faded into her mouth when she ate one afterwards.

'Who was Henry the Eighth's fourth wife?' Mr Sabre asked, stacking the trays by the door. Alex got a clean bowl out.

'Jane Seymour.'

'No. Anne of Cleves. How many Catherines did he marry?'

Alex counted on her fingers. 'Three,' she said.

'Correct. Who was queen when he died?'

'Um. Don't know.'

'One out of three,' he said, helping himself to a coffee prof-
iterole.

When she got home, Alex ran up the stairs past the television
and her parents and lay on the bed with an atlas, trying to learn
the rivers of Latin America, but instead her head was full of the
kitchen, the mixer and the woman with lots of names leading
her by the hand gently, pressing her against the wall to kiss her.
She felt like a flower bursting. She saw the seeds spiral away as
if she was blowing on a dandelion clock; she sensed the cold of
the wall on her back and saw Isabelle crouching against it to feel
the cold of it herself, watching her with her mud-coloured eyes.
The Teenagers from Outer Space looked down on her as she fell
asleep with the atlas across her chest.

Isabelle came into the shop the next day and pointed to the
éclairs.

'Three please,' she said.

Alex flushed. She turned and wiped her hands.

'I enjoy watching the cake-making,' said Isabelle. 'I'd like to
do it again.'

'No,' said Alex sharply, worried that the bursting flower inside
her would get too much and she would have to run out of the
bakery and into the street. She packed three éclairs into a box,
without looking at Isabelle. 'Anything else?'

'A jam roly-poly, please. I know a wonderful café,' she added
softly. 'Where you can dress up. And nobody cares.'

'Anything else?' said Alex. Her hands were sweating. Two more
people had come into the shop, one of them had a cat in a basket.
'No animals,' she said, trying to stay calm. She hoped they hadn't
heard what Isabelle had said.

'Yes,' said Isabelle. 'I'm having a tea party. A small loaf and a
cherry upside-down cake, please.' The remaining customer in the
queue sighed impatiently, while Alex hurriedly wrapped the cakes,
even more desperate now.

'Anything else?' she said again, wishing hard that Isabelle would
leave.

'Three of those macaroons and a banana turnover.' Isabelle took her purse out of her bag and when she gave Alex her handful of coins, there was a piece of paper with them. Alex put it in her pocket and turned to serve the next customer. Isabelle left quickly.

Later, Alex washed her hands, put on her apron and made curly pastries with sticky butterscotch paste and tried to think about the rivers of Latin America and not about Isabelle and her piece of paper. She concentrated on the butterscotch instead until Mr Sabre came into the kitchen.

'What's the longest river in South America?' he said.

'Easy. The Amazon.'

'How long is the Orinoco?'

'One thousand six hundred miles.'

'Very good,' he said. 'Longest river in the world?'

'Um.'

'The Nile.'

'That's not in South America.'

'Be prepared for trick questions,' he said. 'Two out of three.' Edith Sabre, six times Butlins quiz champion, watched her through the open door.

That evening, Alex sat on her bed and took the piece of paper out of her pocket. It had a neat blue line round the edges and across the top it said: 'The Memory Lane Café'. Underneath that: 'Members & Guests. Dress code: 1920s and 1930s. Live entertainment nightly'.

4

The first time she saw Rachel, Alex was peering through the window of the Memory Lane Café. From the outside, it looked uninteresting, a brief break in the factory wall which ran all the way along the road, curving with it. You could stand in the street where the café was and see no one. You would just hear the sound of metal meeting metal in a factory a few streets away or an engine coming to life somewhere.

When Alex got there, the only car was parked right outside: a dark blue 1957 Ford Thunderbird. She recognised it from Mr Sabre's book. There was no name over the door, just a sign saying 'Open'. In the window was a picture of a man with black hair and a black moustache standing next to the same car that was parked a few feet away. Underneath, it said 'Rufus Immanuel' and something in Spanish she didn't understand. Alex watched as a tall thin couple came round the corner and went through the door. As they paid and disappeared, she noticed the young woman in the ticket booth. She was a few years older than Alex, with bouncy blonde hair and pink eyelashes like fairies. Alex thought she was the most beautiful woman she had ever seen. She wondered if she knew that she shone like a star. When the ticket seller flicked her eyes up to look at her outside the door, Alex felt as if she had been knocked over and was still standing up at the same time. She flushed and turned away.

The second time she saw Rachel, it was a Saturday. Alex was wearing Mr Sabre's green drainpipes, the stripy shirt with the musical collar and the red shoes and had told her parents she had to help with the bread. She took a deep breath and pushed open the door. As soon as she went in, she could hear the music. She recognised it from the radio programme called *Nostalgia at Teatime* which Mr Sabre listened to on Wednesday afternoons with a Venetian sponge. She couldn't look at the woman with bouncy hair in the ticket booth for too long because she made her feel like she was falling off something like the diving board at the swimming pool. The beautiful ticket seller took in Alex without smiling and tapped a sign which said 'Strict 20s and 30s dress code' with her pink fingernails. Then she went back to counting the coins in her little wooden drawer.

'This is all I have,' said Alex nervously. The woman looked up again and patted her ponytail.

'All right,' she said. 'I don't care.' She held out a pen and let Alex sign her name and pay her money. As Alex took the pen, she brushed her hand accidentally and it was like an electric shock.

'My father wouldn't let you,' the young woman added. 'Don't let him see you or he'll throw you out. You're probably too young anyway, aren't you?'

'Who's your father?'

In answer, she pointed a pink fingernail at the photograph of Rufus Immanuel in the window. 'Through the curtain,' she said and went back to her coins.

Alex backed away quickly before the ticket seller could change her mind. She walked down the steps into the smoke-filled room and looked around for Isabelle but she couldn't see her. A woman in a long dress and pearls brushed past and waved to a friend. The jewels on her wrist sparkled. She looked as if she had slipped into her costume like a fish slipping into its scales before emerging from its egg. Gazing past the people by the steps, Alex saw that there were candles on the tables which made the glittered silver surfaces shine. The air smelt perfumed and was full of the sound of voices. There was a red light coming from somewhere, though she couldn't tell where.

A man at a table near the steps was sipping lime and water.

He had round glasses and straight blond hair. The bubbles in his glass could have been made by tiny fish who had forgotten how to breathe and were slowly drowning. She watched the bubbles rise to the surface, up and up and up. The man saw her looking and raised his glass in a toast. She still couldn't see Isabelle. She felt worried now. She moved away so she could look for her. There was an empty trapeze swinging low in one corner and, at the front, a woman in a sequined blue dress and a feathered hat played the piano, her arms rising and falling, her sharp elbows lifting quickly.

As her eyes got used to the light, Alex noticed dancers on the far side of the piano and waiters and waitresses. Trying to calm the nervous feeling in her stomach, she watched them moving between the customers, turning their hips and arms this way and that to get past. Every so often the barman would disappear behind the curtain next to the bar and then re-emerge with trays of food. The dancers were moving their arms and feet together and smiling widely at nothing.

Alex picked up a menu with curly handwriting from the nearest table. The piano player was called Melanie. Alex saw it on the back of the menu, as if diners could order her to go with their drinks. Melanie. Her name sounded like the music she played. Alex scanned the list of cocktails. 'Over the Moon,' she read, 'peach schnapps, vanilla ice cream and shredded coconut. Jiminy Cricket: peppermint ice and vodka. Tipsy Penguin: orange liqueur, hot chocolate and marshmallows. Uncle Arthur: ice cream, brandy and maple syrup. Armadillo: black coffee, cherry brandy and cream, served with a plate of coffee beans.' There were four pages of them. 'Prohibition,' it said at the end of the list, 'the Memory Lane's famous hangover cure.'

She looked around again for Isabelle, from one side of the bar to the other, but she couldn't see her. She felt even more nervous. Whenever the curtain by the door swung open, her stomach somersaulted, because it made her think about the ticket seller. She wanted her to come down the steps so she could see her again but she was scared in case she did. A man with shiny black hair pressed his thin ringed fingers sharply into Alex's shoulder so he could get by. More people pushed past her, lifting their drinks in the air to avoid spilling them. She saw a man in a fur coat abandoning a table, so she took a deep breath and made her way towards it through the crowd.

'What would you like, son?' said a waiter smoothly. His voice was like milk, right next to her ear. His breath was warm and smelt of biscuits. She looked quickly at the menu again.

'Chocolate,' she said.

'You mean a Huckleberry Finn?'

'Um. Yes,' she said, trying to sound older than she was. The waiter smiled and moved over to the bar.

'Henrico?' he called to the barman. 'Huckleberry for table four.'

Alex watched as the barman mixed her drink quickly. She saw him tip in whisky and cream and stir it with a long spoon.

Another song began. The dancers slowed down and swung to and fro like bulrushes by a pond. Melanie's voice surrounded them like paper. The waiter put Alex's drink down and waited for her to pay. She fumbled nervously with the coins and then watched the dancers sway.

The song was sadder now. They hardly danced at all. Melanie's elbows rose and fell, like breathing. She had her eyes closed and she sighed as she sang. The people in the café were shuffling from foot to foot, catching each other's eyes and waiting, because they knew that the next song would be fast and happy, like a car going down a high street too fast, heading for a cliff, about to tumble over the edge into the sea, or maybe it would land on the beach if the sea was out. It would turn over and over and over and twist out of shape. The next song would be furious and full of red light like the café, and happy too as if the too fast car was a lovely thing. To swirl and dive over the cliff like a heavy bird, to crash into the rocks was wonderful. But first they had to wait for the slow, sad song to finish.

Melanie sighed and lowered her arms, and the song finally ended.

Alex stirred her chocolate and tasted the sharp whisky taste. Her head felt lighter already. She still couldn't see her new friend anywhere. She watched as the barman poured peppermint brandy into a glass with his eyes on the dancers' pointed feet. Then suddenly she saw Isabelle at a table in the corner with four other people. She was leaning over with a pack of cards in her hands. The man with rings and shiny hair who had squeezed past her earlier was sitting next to her. His lips were set in a thin line. The red light cast a shadow over all the players. People passed by the table, and the next time Alex saw them, the man with black hair was looking seriously at the other players, who sat back in their chairs and sighed. As Isabelle began to shuffle, Alex got up and pushed her way through the crowd towards them. The chocolate drink was making her feel braver. As she got closer, she touched a man with a brown moustache on the arm. He turned, raised his eyebrows and took a cigar from the ashtray near to him.

'What are they playing?' she said.

'Happy Families,' said the man and he laughed loudly.

'Snap,' said someone else and joined in the laughter.

Alex squeezed past a large man in a smart dinner jacket and put her hand on Isabelle's shoulder. Isabelle turned round.

'Alex,' she said and smiled. 'This is Alex, everyone.' The players looked up from their cards for a moment and took her in.

'She's young,' said the man with shiny hair. Alex felt like a sponge cake that had sunk in the middle.

'Yes,' said Isabelle.

'Couldn't you get her some better clothes?' When he said it, he curved his lips into an ugly expression, as if he had tasted something he didn't care for. Alex's cheeks flushed and she wanted to click her fingers and disappear, but she stayed rooted to the spot, looking at Isabelle, hoping she would defend her.

'I think she's charming.'

'Quite,' said her friend and turned back to his cards. Isabelle looked up at Alex.

'Why don't you have another drink while I play?' she said.

'All right,' said Alex uneasily, wishing hard that she hadn't come. Isabelle flicked her eyes elegantly at a waiter.

'Chocolate,' said Alex. 'I mean, Huckleberry Finn.'

'And ask Henrico for some more Banana Sunrise,' said one of the other players. Alex saw that the jug on the table was empty. The waiter nodded and headed towards the bar. Isabelle caught her eye for a second and Alex felt her stomach twist and knot itself when she remembered the kiss in the bakery kitchen.

'Aren't they lovely?' Isabelle said, nodding at the dancers.

'Yes,' said Alex. 'Lovely.'

'Hold on. What are we playing for?' someone asked.

'The loser digs the winner a pond,' one player said.

'I already have a pond,' said Isabelle. The man next to her reached out and ran a hand over her shoulder. Alex shuddered as if he had touched her own arm instead. She felt terrible.

'You might not win,' said the shiny-haired man. Isabelle smiled.

'Have I introduced my friend Miranda?' she said. To her surprise, Alex saw that the player next to Isabelle wasn't a man but a woman, dressed in men's clothing like she was, although Miranda's suit was very smart. She gazed down at Mr Sabre's clothes and thought how stupid she must look to Isabelle's friend.

'I also already have a pond,' said a serious man with a neat white beard near the end of the table.

Alex gasped. The young woman who had taken her money at the door was bringing over the jug of Banana Sunrise and the chocolate. As she moved towards them, each bit of the ticket woman curved. Even her blonde hair curved. It curled out from her head like springs. When she handed Alex her chocolate, their eyes met for a second.

'What's your name?' Alex asked.

'Rachel,' she said. Alex looked into her round face and felt as if she was falling into her, in the way someone might fall off the Empire State Building into the air. She was frightened of losing control, of suddenly grabbing Rachel round the waist and sweeping her onto the dance floor, where everyone would move out of their way while they spun around and around. She made herself fix her eyes on her shoes.

'On my bill,' said Isabelle. Rachel wrote quickly in her notebook.

'Rhododendrons?' said someone. 'Does anyone have rhododendrons?' The players shook their heads.

'The loser plants the winner a rhododendron tree,' said someone. 'Come on. Let's play.'

Isabelle was about to start the game, when she noticed Rachel still hovering by the table. Alex saw her blush and pat her hair with her hand.

'Can I get you anything else?' Rachel asked.

'Olives,' said Miranda.

'Cashew nuts,' said someone else.

'I haven't the right kind of soil for rhododendrons,' said the man with the white beard. Miranda smiled and stirred the jug of Sunrise with its long wooden spoon.

'When I last played, the winner chose someone else as their prize,' she said smoothly.

'Another player?' said the bearded man. Alex looked at them all in disbelief. Isabelle was ignoring her completely now.

'Of course,' said Miranda as she poured the pink liquid into Isabelle's glass. The players looked at each other.

'A marvellous suggestion,' said Isabelle.

'We all put a token on the table to show that we agree,' said Miranda. She undid her bow tie. 'Olives and cashew nuts,' she said sharply to Rachel who still hadn't left them.

Alex watched her back as she walked away. As she did so, she had the white-hot feeling she got when someone had given her bad news. Only this time it wasn't bad, it was exciting and dangerous, like swimming in treacle might be dangerous.

Isabelle took her silver earrings from her ears and pushed them into the middle of the table. The game began.

Alex could see the numbers and pictures on the cards, but she didn't recognise the game. The backs all had the same curvy S shape printed on them. Isabelle put down a card with a picture of a green spider running across it. Miranda had a prince with a green hat and a flower. 'The Prince of Grass' it said in funny letters at the bottom, with 'III' next to it.

Another, faster song started. Isabelle stopped playing for a moment and clapped her hands. People around Alex joined in, but she was following Rachel around the room with her eyes, wishing she could go and talk to her. When she looked back, Isabelle had draped her arm across Miranda's shoulders and was mouthing the words of the song. The music stopped and the dancers sat down for a rest at a table near the front. Alex had lost sight of Rachel.

'Six Armadillos?' Alex heard the waiter say as he handed round their drinks and the little plates of coffee beans.

Melanie hit the keys hard, looked up and smiled right around the room, as a man on the dance floor swung his head back and opened his mouth. The woman he was dancing with did the same so they looked like a giant flower with curling petals. She was wearing a scarf with a giraffe pattern. Alex could feel the whisky swimming around somewhere between her eyes. The woman on the dance floor seemed to turn into a giraffe herself and tower above everyone else in the room, her long nose rooting for leaves. Isabelle looked up towards her and giggled into her drink.

Then there was Rachel again, smiling at the man with round glasses and straight blond hair. Alex watched as she went over to his table. She glanced around, took his hand and led him over to the piano. Alex looked on miserably. She wasn't surprised that Rachel liked him. His blond hair made him look like an angel. Suddenly a man Alex recognised from the photograph next to the door appeared. It was Rachel's father, Rufus Immanuel. As he came over to the dance floor, Melanie ended the song abruptly. The swaying couples stopped to watch. Rufus pushed the reluctant table of dancers away from their Armadillos and back onto the dance floor.

'What am I paying you for?' he said, snapping his fingers at Melanie. He turned to address Rachel.

'Just like your mother! What are you doing? In front of the customers. You are supposed to be a waitress. *¿Quieres que piensen que eres una puta? ¿Qué diría tu mamá,* eh?'

'My mother's not here.'

'Don't talk back to me. *¿Que he criado? ¿Una puta?* A hussie? Eh?'

'We were only dancing.'

'*Igual que tu mamá.* Same blonde hair. Same free and easy life. Huh?' He took his daughter's arm and pulled her away, while the barman guided her dancing partner back to his seat. The people sitting near the front who had overheard shuffled uncomfortably in their seats for a second, then began talking again. The dancers organised themselves chaotically. Melanie called out the name of a new song and they nodded. She began to play again and soon it was as though the music had never stopped. Alex had been despondent when she had seen Rachel dancing, but now she had disappeared she felt even worse.

She looked into her drink. It was nearly gone. She felt queasy. Isabelle saw and waved to the waiter, who brought her another drink with a smile. Alex's eyes went back to the circle of people playing the game. Within a few moments Miranda laid the winning card.

The new tune was soft and pillow-like and the dancers seemed to lean forward towards her and then away from her, like dolls on springs. She could only just hear the song over the sound of the people's voices. As they sang, the words echoed around the bar and fell around Alex's shoulders like a spirit haunting her. As the room moved round and round, Alex looked back towards the table and saw Isabelle kissing Miranda. Alex's face creased into a frown. She suddenly felt hurt and confused in spite of the drink. Isabelle saw her looking, untangled herself and waved to her. Reluctantly Alex put her drink down and went over, the room still spinning.

'Alex,' she said. 'Did I introduce you to Miranda? I'm her prize.' Miranda smiled and held out her hand. The chocolate danced around in Alex's stomach and she felt as if she was going to throw up. She backed away through the crowd of people and heard Miranda laughing. Isabelle called after her.

'Oh, Alex, I'm sorry. Come back.' But when Alex looked round, they were kissing again. Miranda held Isabelle's face in her hand like she was clutching a flower.

She stumbled towards the stairs and the velvet curtain and nearly collided with Rachel. She had to reach out and hold on to her elbow because the room was spinning so much. Rachel turned and frowned. Her hair bounced away from her head in coils. Her breasts curved under her uniform. Alex looked into her eyes and wanted to kiss her, but Rachel peeled her fingers from her elbow. She waited for a moment, but when Alex didn't say anything she went away through the crowd with her tray. Alex wondered if love was like having angel wings in your head, because that was how Rachel made her feel.

Alex felt sick again. She pushed herself back up the steps, through the swing doors and into the fresh air outside. The sound of music and the voices stopped. Thin rain wet her face. She threw up onto the pavement and dark brown chocolate-coloured sick ran down the kerb into the gutter. She rubbed her eyes and then her breasts under her shirt for comfort. As she stumbled along the pavement, she nearly ran into a young man holding a yellow leaflet. A group of people, huddled like tardy carol singers, approached the door to the café. Alex and the young man stared at each other for a few seconds. Then he gave her the leaflet.

'God bless you,' he said. He put a hand on her shoulder, but she pushed past and stumbled off down the street towards home, thinking about Isabelle's laughing face and Rachel, the beautiful waitress with bouncy hair and the way she moved through the red light. Behind her, she heard someone come to the door and curse the people who looked like carol singers.

'Get lost. Go to hell. *¡Vete al diablo!*' It was Rachel's father. When Alex turned to look, she saw one of the men with the group press a yellow leaflet into his hand.

'*Vete al diablo*,' Rufus said again, but he folded it and slipped it into his pocket. He wouldn't drop litter outside his own café. When the group finally began to walk away, he bent to pick up the other leaflets which had fallen like square autumn leaves in front of the swing doors.

Alex crept into the house. The sitting room was dark and her parents were in bed. She was relieved that she didn't have to face them. It seemed strange to come in when the new television wasn't on and the house was silent. The rain on her face had woken her up, as if the Memory Lane Café and Isabelle and the waitress called Rachel and the fiery chocolate drink were a dream, but the sleeping house spun as she tried to climb the stairs quietly and now her head hurt as well. She stumbled over a pile of Mr Sabre's atlases and quiz encyclopaedias and lay down on her bed, thinking about how beautiful Rachel was and how she shone like a star. As she looked up at the Creature from the Black Lagoon and asked him what she should do, she realised that her face was wet with tears as well as rain.

She still had the yellow leaflet the young man had given her. 'Be sure your sin will find you out,' it said across the top. Alex screwed it up and threw it across her room. Then she pulled off her clothes, stuffed them under the bed and got between the sheets. Isabelle and Miranda's laughter filled her head and she wiped the tears from her face. She closed her eyes and there Rachel was, smiling at her from inside her head. Alex wished she could see her again, but she didn't know how she would talk to her. She felt stupid for not speaking to her properly when she had the chance. She turned over onto her front so that her face was in her pillow. Three faces swung around her head: Edith Sabre with a rosette, Isabelle laughing into her cards, and Rachel as she peeled her fingers from her elbow. She would go back, she thought, and they would look at her and they wouldn't laugh and she would make Rachel love her.

5

'Where's the Acropolis?' said Mr Sabre as he ambled into the kitchen. He had his new jeans on and a bottle of Old Spice in his hand. Alex was icing buns and thinking about what had happened at the Memory Lane, but she was ready for him.

'Athens.'

'Correct.'

She carried on pouring the warm white sludge over the bread fingers in front of her, while Mr Sabre shook some aftershave into his palm and slapped his cheeks, looking pleased with himself. He saw her watching and cleared his throat.

'The Temple of Apollo?'

'Delphi,' she said.

'You're drowning them in icing,' he said. He put the bottle down and slid into his comfortable shoes. 'People don't like sticky fingers.'

Alex was annoyed and wished he would go into the shop, but she slowed her pouring. The smell of aftershave hung around her head. She hoped the buns wouldn't taste of it.

'I'm going over to Carling Street with some pastries later,' he said, 'so put them out for me. And I'm out for lunch, so you can close up today.' He came over to the table and pointed at one of the buns. The smell of Old Spice got stronger.

'You've hardly covered that one at all.' He took the pan from her and carefully poured out icing.

'Who are you seeing for lunch?' Alex asked.

'Never you mind,' he said, but he smiled to himself. 'Who is Apollo's twin sister?'

'Artemis.'

'Three out of three.' He went over to a tray of tarts waiting for fillings. 'Make sure these get enough jam, they were a bit dry yesterday. Someone might complain.'

Alex thought of her blackberry jam tarts with exotic pools in the middle and crumbly pastry on the outside. She opened her mouth to protest but Mr Sabre had gone into the shop and was sliding back the bolts on the front door.

'The tarts were lovely,' she muttered to herself.

Mr Sabre had just finished cleaning the glass cabinet where the cakes sat when Isabelle came into the bakery that day.

'Alex,' he called. He stood up, dusted off his trousers and picked up a jam finger. 'I'm having a cup of tea with this. Care to join me?' he said to Isabelle. Mr Sabre's idea of being polite to posh women was to offer them tea and cakes. There was an awkward silence.

'No thank you, you're very kind, but I have to be somewhere,' Isabelle said.

'Well, if you change your mind,' he said, and shuffled off through the kitchen.

'Alex,' Isabelle said, when he was out of earshot. The way Isabelle said her name made it shine like glass. It sounded beautiful and not like her name at all.

'What can I get you?' said Alex, pretending Isabelle wanted to buy something.

'Were you so very upset?' Isabelle said. She tried to look into her face.

'No,' said Alex. She screwed up her fists. She wanted Isabelle to go, but she wanted to ask her about something too. Isabelle put her hands on her shoulders.

'Don't be like that,' she said. 'How did you like the café? Divine, isn't it?'

Alex paused for a moment, checked Mr Sabre was really gone and took a deep breath.

'I like the waitress.' She said the words before she could change her mind. Isabelle smiled slowly, like sun-coloured butter was spreading over her face.

'That's wonderful,' she said. 'Which one?'

'The one with the blonde hair.'

'Rachel?'

'Yes. Rachel.'

Isabelle picked up Alex's hand and patted it. 'Go on a Tuesday,' she said. 'Rufus stays in bed all day on Tuesdays. It's his day off. And it's very quiet. Not like Saturday.'

When she had gone, Alex went into the back room with Mr Sabre's cup of tea and found him in front of the mirror. He was smearing Brylcreem into his hair.

'The pastries for Carling Street are ready,' she said, handing him the cup. He narrowed his eyes at her.

'Have you put greaseproof paper on top?'

'Yes.'

'Don't forget the scones,' he said. 'Don't use all the sultanas, I'm making a fruit cake at the weekend.'

'Why?' said Alex. 'I can make one on Monday.'

'Not for the shop, for . . .' He stopped.

'For the woman who works behind the counter at Carling Street?'

'Yes.' He put his cup down. 'There's some washing upstairs for the machine.' He shuffled off towards the door.

Alex's mother was in the hallway looking flustered when she got in, as if she had been out in the wind. Her father was in his armchair. He was still wearing his uniform and peaked hat. The television was on and can-can girls were high-kicking their way across the screen.

'We've been invited to a party,' said Alex's mother.

'Fancy dress,' called her father, who didn't turn round.

'By Mr Bradley.' Her mother's eyes sparkled with excitement.

'Really? That's great. Can I come?'

'No,' said her father. 'You're not invited. Adults only.'

'Oh.' Alex sat down on the stairs, deflated. 'When is it?'

'Tuesday. There's going to be TV people there and everything,' said her mother. She leant against the wall and patted her hair.

'Tuesday?' Alex's eyes lit up. 'Really?'

'Yes. Why?' said her mother.

'No reason. I might have to help with the bread again, that's all.'

'He's a slave-driver, that man.'

'What are you going to go as?' Alex said.

'I don't know.' She looked anxious.

'Your mother's worried about it.'

'How come you got invited?' Alex said.

'Privileges of the new job,' said her father.

'Is there a theme?'

'The theme's Noah's ark,' said her father. Her mother turned so she could stand in the doorway and watch the screen.

'Can you make us some dinner?' said her mother over her shoulder.

'OK. Sausage pie and veg all right?'

'Please. Do some of your nice sage and onion gravy again.'

Alex hesitated. 'I think Mr Sabre went on a date today.' It made her mother giggle.

'Silly man,' she said. 'How do you know?'

'He left before lunch to see the woman who works behind the counter at Carling Street. All dressed up.'

'He'll never find another Edith,' said her father. 'She knew her stuff.' The camera turned to reveal a group of flamingos in front of the stage where the can-can girls were dancing. Alex's mother clapped her hands together.

'Flamingos!' she said. 'We'll go as flamingos.'

'I'm not going as a flaming flamingo. Don't be daft,' her father said, without taking his eyes from the screen.

'Pink feathers, some make-up, a pink evening dress,' said her mother, going over to the sofa so she could carry on watching. 'It'll be so glamorous.'

'Don't be stupid. How much money are you planning to spend?' her father said.

'Enough. And don't call me stupid. Are you still here, Alex? Go and put the dinner on.'

'I'm not wearing pink,' her father retorted.

'So you'd let me be the only person at the party without a decent costume, would you?'

'I didn't say that but I don't want you spending.'

'You're just trying to show me up.'

'Me in a ruddy pink outfit's going to show you up. I'll go in a suit.'

'You'll go in a suit over my dead body.'

'Don't tempt me.' The argument about flamingos continued as Alex disappeared into the kitchen to find an apron.

Alex went with her mother to the fancy dress shop at the far end of the High Street to look for costumes. She hadn't been inside before. It was bright with artificial light and smelt of cloth. The shopkeeper gave them a clipped smile as they came in and then went back to his paper and his cigarette. Alex wandered amongst the outfits. Some were displayed on manikins: a pirate's coat with a hat and a hook, a ballerina's tights and white shoes, an explorer's hat and binoculars. Others were on racks. She browsed through the jackets, rubbing the fabric between her fingers, while her mother tried on some pointed slippers. She had just got to a sign which said 'Historical: Men' and found Henry the Eighth, with a hat, waistcoat and gold chain, Merlin and Abraham Lincoln, when her mother called to her.

'Find something for your dad,' she said. 'He says he won't wear pink.'

Alex looked through the animal section. There was a donkey's head, a green frog suit with a monocle and a felt hat, and a cockerel sweater with brown and orange feathers. The one she liked best was a huge shaggy coat. It was golden with a fringed hood. The tag pinned to it said 'For men. Lion'.

'How about this one?' She held it up. 'It's a lion.' Her mother was walking up and down in some pink shoes, smiling to herself.

'Try it on,' she said. 'So I can see what it looks like.'

41

When Alex struggled into the heavy sleeves and pulled up the hood, she was almost lost inside it. She held up her arms. The ends of the sleeves drooped over her hands. It was warm and soft inside and it even smelt animal-like.

'It smells furry,' she said.

'It's perfect,' said her mother, pulling off the pink shoes. She came over in her stockings and began to feel the mane around the hood and thread the buttons into their holes so Alex felt like she was being fitted out herself.

'Shouldn't you both go as lions? If it's Noah's ark?'

'That doesn't matter. Look. There's trousers too,' her mother said, picking them up from the rack. 'Take it off and find him a tail to go with it.' Then she went over to the section marked 'Evening Wear: Women' and flicked expertly through the dresses until she came to a pink silky one with a wrap and a pair of white gloves, while Alex searched through a bin at the back of the shop, which was full of tails. She picked up a long rope with a bushy brown tip and looked over to her mother amongst the evening wear. By the door where they had come in, she noticed more signs above the racks with dates written neatly in black ink: Authentic 1900s, Authentic 1910s, Authentic 1920s, Authentic 1930s, Authentic 1940s. She looked to see if there was a men's section with dates too. She found it on the other side of the shop, near a jewellery cabinet displaying fake tiaras and turbans on a row of heads.

'Have you got one yet?' said her mother. Alex held up the tail and went to look at the men's evening wear 1920s section. She looked through the jackets and trousers quickly, admiring the cut and the smart black material, wishing she could try them on, and told herself she would come back after work one day that week.

'These and the lion for my husband,' her mother said, dumping all the clothes she had found on the counter. 'Come on, Alex.'

'Hire or buy?' said the shopkeeper. He put down his cigarette and began to fold the dress carefully in tissue paper.

'Hire.'

Alex made her way over to them and put down the tail.

'You'll have to buy the tail. We don't hire tails.'

'Fine. And we need some feathers. Pink ones.'

The shopkeeper went into a wooden drawer and found some. 'You'll have to buy the feathers too,' he said, glancing back at his paper.

'Fine. How much?' Alex's mother got out her purse while Alex gazed at the 1920s evening wear and thought about Miranda laughing in her smart black suit.

6

In Alex's bedroom, books were arranged untidily across the floor: *The Atlas of Everything*, *Mercer's Universal Compendium*, and *Everyman's Advisory*. There was an empty bag from the fancy dress shop at her feet and the yellow leaflet from the church people was still crumpled in a corner where she had thrown it. She stood in front of the mirror wearing a pair of authentic thirty-year-old black trousers. She examined the cut from the front and from the side: the way the material curved over her thighs and between her legs. She looked at her skin and the way it travelled over her breasts and up into her neck. She pulled on a white evening shirt. She looked at herself for a while, the shirt hanging unbuttoned. She pushed her arms into the jacket, which had long lapels and was made of a material that caught the light as she turned to and fro.

Alex opened her shirt so she could see the curve of her breasts again and ran her hand over them. Seeing herself in the clothes made her glow. She undid the buttons on the trousers and pushed her other hand into her knickers so she could feel the rough patch between her legs. All the while, she kept her eyes fixed on the mirror, at the place where the unbuttoned shirt met her skin. The glow inside her grew bigger. She pushed harder with her hands until she couldn't stand up any more. Instead, she lay on her bed, with her knees raised, and moved her hands backwards and forwards until she felt the usual urgent feeling and the gentle orgasm rolling over her like a wave. She lay still with her hands inside the trousers for a while after it was over, pushed her face into the pillow and thought about Rachel's lovely green eyes. Then she heard her mother climbing the stairs. She panicked, jumped from the bed quickly and pulled off the clothes. She slipped the shirt off just in time. Her mother put her hand on the door as she was stuffing the clothes back into their bag. As her mother came in, Alex was on the edge of the bed in her knickers, slipping her dress over her head.

'Come downstairs. I'm making cheese on toast,' she said.

Alex was worried. Her mother only cooked when she was upset. 'I'll do lunch,' she said hopefully, but her mother ignored her. 'And I've got something you might recognise.'

'What?' But her mother wouldn't reply. She just looked at her curiously and headed off downstairs again. When Alex ran down to the lounge, her mother handed her the stripy shirt with the musical collar. There was no sign of the cheese on toast. Alex swallowed hard, unsure for a moment if she had been found out.

'This was mixed in with your washing,' said her mother. Alex stood in the middle of the room wondering what to say.

'Where did it come from?' her mother asked when she didn't reply. 'Does it belong to some boy you've been seeing?'

'No,' said Alex in alarm. 'Mr Sabre lent it to me. When it was chucking it down the other day. I got soaked.'

'Weren't you wearing a coat?' said her mother. 'Why didn't he lend you an old jumper of Edith's?'

Alex sat on the sofa and put the shirt down carefully as if it might wake up and start telling its own story if she made any sudden movements.

'Very brainy, that woman,' said her father as he came in. He had only heard the last part of the conversation. He dug a thick hand into his brown bag, took out an album and waved it at her. It was the soundtrack to *The King and I*.

'Free, that was,' he said.

'Are you sure it's not some boy?'

'No.'

'What boy?' said her father.

'There isn't any boy.' Alex put her head in her hands, but she would rather they thought that than knew about Isabelle, Rachel and the café.

'This was in her room,' Alex's mother said, holding up the shirt.

'I'll deck him,' her father said angrily, about to get up out of his chair again, but his wife waved a hand at him.

'Sit down and shut up, for God's sake.'

'I was wet so Mr Sabre lent me the shirt,' Alex insisted.

'If you're lying to me, Alex, you'll be in trouble,' her mother said. 'I can ask him.'

'Ask him then,' Alex snapped and ran from the room.

On Tuesday, her mother stood in the hall, Mr Sabre's shirt forgotten about. Her father was outside checking Mr Bradley's car, which he had borrowed for the evening.

'Hadn't you better get ready, Alex?' her mother said. 'Bread-making, remember?'

'In a minute,' Alex said.

'We'll drop you off if you like.'

'No, it's OK. I'll walk.'

'Through the cemetery? It's dark.'

'I'll walk,' Alex said sharply as her father came in.

'I can't drive like this,' he said. He pulled off the yellow mittens Alex's mother had persuaded him to wear.

'How do we look?' said her mother excitedly. She was wearing pink lipstick and blusher and the feathers tottered drunkenly on her head. As well as the hooded coat and trousers they had found for him, her father was wearing black wellington boots. Alex's mother had coloured his nose black with eyeliner and given him lines for whiskers. He looked like a golden Eskimo with a red face.

'Great,' said Alex. 'When will you be back?'

'Late,' said her father.

'Midnight,' said her mother, opening the door so that a blast of cold air rushed in. Alex suddenly thought of her mother turning into a pumpkin as the clock chimed. She stood in the hallway watching the slice of night in the frosted glass window until she was sure they had gone. Then she ran upstairs and got changed herself.

When she arrived at the Memory Lane, the church people were there again with their leaflets. She had to wind her way past them to get through the door. The man in the ticket booth hardly looked at her and let her in straightaway without tapping the sign as Rachel had done.

'Nice outfit,' he said.

'Thanks,' she said, feeling pleased with herself. A tulip bud opened gently inside her chest.

'It's Tuesday,' he said when she tried to pay. 'Free.'

The café was almost empty. A few people sat at tables talking. Rachel was leaning against the bar talking to Henrico the barman, who was chopping limes. She looked a hundred times more beautiful than the picture of her Alex had in her head. She felt suddenly hot and had to turn away. She sat down at the nearest table and played with the menu. There was no music; the piano stool was empty. Alex looked over at the table where she had seen the card game, but there was no one there. Henrico had disappeared into the kitchen, so Rachel flipped open her notebook and made her way over. Alex felt suddenly devastated that she didn't have anything interesting to say to her.

'Yes?' she said.

'A glass of water please,' Alex said. She looked at the way Rachel's hips curved out from her waist as if she was a cello.

'What are you looking at?' said Rachel, looking down at her waist herself.

'Sorry,' said Alex. She blushed.

'Just water?'

Alex tried desperately to think of something to say to keep Rachel there next to her. 'And olives,' she said, hoping she sounded as smooth as Miranda had when she had ordered them. 'Where's the piano player?'

Rachel patted her hair. 'She's late. Have you been before? On a Saturday night?'

'Yes,' Alex said.

'You were a bit tight,' Rachel said, remembering.

'A bit,' said Alex.

'You look different. Nicer.'

Alex looked down at the table.

'Thanks.'

'You know Isabelle, don't you?' said Rachel.

'She comes into the place I work.' Alex couldn't think of anything else to make her stay. Rachel nodded and made her way back over to the bar, just as Melanie tottered down the steps, swaying slightly. She was dressed in canary yellow. Rachel went to meet her. Melanie handed over her coat and sat down at the piano.

'Make me a pro, Rachel,' said Melanie a little too loudly as she opened her music case. Melanie played classical music instead of singing songs. The notes were as light as water.

A waiter delivered Alex's order, while Rachel sat next to Melanie on the piano stool. Alex watched Rachel longingly. She could see that Melanie was teaching her how to play. She loved Rachel's pink fingernails and the way she had to raise the end of her fingers slightly to keep them out of the way while she played.

But then to Alex's dismay the man with the blond hair came in again. He cleaned his glasses and sat down. Rachel got up from the piano and led him onto the dance floor again. They danced in silence, while Melanie played a waltz with her eyes closed.

Rachel and the man moved closer together, pressing their bodies into each other as the music slowed. Their cheeks were touching and Alex wondered what it would be like to dance with Rachel and feel her cheek brush her own, gently and softly.

There was a lido in the smart part of town, where the water was cold and leaves from the trees that hung above it crisscrossed on the surface. Alex went to swim there in the summer when it was very hot. The lido was so long and so deep that she was exhausted after she had swum just one length, with the summer leaves caught in her hair. Watching Rachel dance was like falling under the water at the lido, too exhausted to swim any more, sinking down with the leaves circling above her and the taste of the pool in her mouth. Then she would come up to the surface again and feel the sun on her face and swim so hard her chest hurt. That was how Rachel made her feel. Her chest ached, but she carried on watching.

Melanie smiled and started to sing, while Rachel and the man swayed to and fro and began to kiss each other easily and deeply. Alex felt as if there was an acrobat in her stomach, dancing frantically. The kissing was slow and careful and they carried on swaying as they did it. The acrobat was jumping around inside Alex like he was on a trampoline. After a while, Henrico came out from the kitchen, saw them and said something sharp in Spanish. Rachel stopped and said something back. Henrico disappeared again. As her dancing partner went back to his table and Rachel ran through the curtain by the bar to argue with Henrico some more, Melanie carried on playing a sweet, sad song. The customers at the front, who were still waiting for their order, shifted in their seats uncomfortably. Eventually Rachel came back out and moved plates and glasses around as if nothing had happened, deliberately not looking over to where the blond-haired man sat.

'Bit different from a Saturday,' Rachel said, lifting the pepper pot from Alex's table and wiping underneath it absent-mindedly. Alex swallowed and looked down at her menu.

'Can I get you anything else?' Rachel said, as the man she had been dancing with disappeared up the steps. She sighed at the empty chair and glass he had left behind.

'That's Gabriel. Did you see us dancing? What do you think? Do we go well together?' Her pink fingernails curved around her notebook as she stared at the exit. 'We're in love.'

The public cemetery looked as if it had shaken off its mourning clothes now that it was spring. If Alex stood still for long enough, she could smell the leaves and hear the birds laughing in the clear air. When she got to the place where the gravel path divided into three between the gravestones, she sat down on a bench and watched as the low afternoon sun shone on the thin sycamore trees. Further down, blossom-filled branches stretched over the stones like wedding guests made of confetti. Behind her, a bush covered in red flowers hummed with the sound of the birds hidden inside it. She listened to them and thought about Rachel and the café.

Alex didn't go back to the Memory Lane for a while after she saw the kissing, but all the same, Rachel fizzed inside her. If she tried to stop thinking about her, she could feel her fizzing somewhere else instead of her head: in her foot or in the back of her hand. She imagined diving into the lido with her, under the leaves, and thought about what her hair would look like if it was wet. She would wipe the water from her face, she thought. Then, because the sun was sinking in the sky like a melting orange ice lolly, she got up and made her way towards the peeling gate. When she looked over the wall of Mr Bradley's garden she saw that the tulip buds were still clenched like fists. She could see a little bit of colour at the tips but that was all. She wondered if Rachel would like the tulips.

After that, Alex thought about Rachel every day: as she sat in the cinema and watched *The Thing From Outer Space*, *Monster on Campus* and *Attack of the Fifty-Foot Woman*; as she walked past Mr Bradley's garden and through the gate into the cemetery; and as she stirred her cake mixes and added lemon juice. She thought about her when she ran to the shops to buy extra icing sugar before they closed, when she reached up to lift raisins off the shelf, as she broke eggs, as she served in the shop. She learnt her off by heart instead of memorising the states of America and the mountains of Nepal for Mr Sabre's questions. She dreamed about her as she looked up at Julia Adams and the Creature from the Black Lagoon. When she thought about her, a warm feeling started in her toes and crept slowly over her body as if she was sinking into a huge bowl of uncooked syrup fancies.

7

Tunnel forward in time, past trays of cherried Belgium buns with sweet sultanas and rows of sticky flapjacks, past crumby plates and damp mouths, past teatime after teatime, and imagine someone comes into Alex's bakery eighteen times, chooses several macaroons, eats them with tea at home on a table covered in a lacy white cloth, wipes away the crumbs, washes cup and plate, looks out of the window and thinks about the rest of the day, week, month, year streaming out in front of him or her like a handful of fruit-coloured kites blowing in the wind day after day after day. In the time it took for the man or woman you imagined to eat the macaroons and wash his or her plate eighteen times – sometimes it was a strawberry tart instead, and once there were three, because the person you imagined invited friends – in the time it took for the man or woman with the lace cloth to pick flowers, smile at them, arrange them in a vase, top them up with water, watch them wilt and turn into brown moulded sticks, throw them out, pick another bunch to smile at, in the time it took for a tray of white rolls to get forgotten and sit and turn stale, then grey-white, then green under a shelf in the bakery, in the time it took for Easter to arrive, for Alex to help Mr Sabre swap over his quiz books from the cupboard to the back room, so that volumes like *The Norton History of Britain* and *Wandsworth's Astronomical Companion* were arranged in full view next to the fireplace and *The Encyclopaedia of Everything* and *The Evolution of Clothes* were hidden at the back of the wardrobe:

that was how long it took for Alex to decide that she didn't care about the man with blond hair or the kissing and that she would go back to the Memory Lane to see Rachel again. Ten trays of Belgium buns and flapjacks, eighteen dirty plates, cups and saucers, thirty-three macaroons and three strawberry tarts, three friends, one handful of kites, two bunches of flowers, one mouldy tray of rolls later, Alex peered over the wall into Mr Bradley's garden in amazement. All the buds had disappeared and the space was full of dark purple tulips. She wanted to pick big handfuls of them and give them to Rachel.

The garden was so crowded, there was no room for anything else, not even for another tulip head to push its way up from the earth. They were all the same dark colour. Alex wondered what would have happened if just one sunny yellow or deep blood-red flower had opened in the middle. From above, she could see right into the mouths of the flowers to their black and yellow furry tongues. She reached out a hand to touch the petals of one of the flowers nearest to her. She was thinking about Rachel surrounded by the tulips as she walked home, and how she would like to pick the flowers so that she could stroke the petals for a while longer. She closed her eyes so that she could keep the colour of them inside her head.

Much too early, before her parents were up, Alex woke. The thought of the tulips and of Rachel came into her head as soon as she opened her eyes and saw the early morning sunlight pouring in through the window. She wanted to see her again more than anything. She imagined giving her the flowers and dancing with her next to the piano and suddenly it was too much to bear.

She went quietly out of the house and ran along the road. When she got to the garden next to the graveyard, she didn't stop to think about it. She reached out her hand and began to pick Mr Bradley's tulips, until she had a whole armful. When she looked down, the damaged place where the flowers were missing looked like a row of demolished houses. Where the green stems were snapped and bruised, white sap oozed out. She felt sorry but it was too late. No one in the house moved. It was still asleep with its curtains drawn.

Alex turned to run. She ran through the peeling gate of the cemetery, past the new graves with the garlands, and didn't stop to catch her breath until she was next to the bush covered in red flowers and humming with birds, but then she thought about Mr Bradley and was suddenly frightened. She ran under the blossoms and the tree with the hugging branches, along the gravel path to the High Street, past the early morning shops and in through the bakery door, with the tulips in her arms. Once she had got her breath back, she found a vase from one of Mr Sabre's high cupboards and arranged them next to the fireplace. She sat down in the armchair, pushed the guilty feeling all the way down into her feet and looked at the beautiful petals and the dusty green stems.

As she sat with the tulips on her table, a waiter she had seen before came to take her order.

'Expecting someone?' he said, looking at the flowers.

'Yes,' said Alex.

'I wish someone would bring me flowers,' he said and put his hand over his heart. 'What can I get you?' he asked when he had finished dreaming.

'Lemonade,' said Alex, because it was the first thing she spotted on the menu. Rachel was nowhere to be seen. Melanie was at the piano playing a quick sharp tune. Her fingers chased each other along the keys and back again.

The waiter returned with her drink.

'Where's Rachel?' Alex said. The waiter looked at her for a second.

'Friends?' he asked hesitantly.

'Yes,' said Alex.

He went behind the bar again and bent down to rummage in the rubbish bin. When he came back over, he had something screwed up in his hand. It was a yellow leaflet. He spread it out, put it down in front of her and pointed at a name on a list of addresses at the bottom.

'There,' he said.

Alex's stomach flipped as if someone was tossing pancakes inside her. A juggler with a frying pan in each hand was tossing them, one way then the other, in time to Melanie's urgent music. When the waiter had gone back behind the curtain to the kitchen, she read the leaflet properly for the first time: 'You can be saved from drink and gambling,' it said. Then it was all about God, on both sides. Right at the bottom, there was a paragraph in smaller print. It said: 'The Lord has especially called us to save young women who have fallen. Local homes for delinquent girls and women, which have been blessed by the Lord.' Then there was a list of addresses. The name the waiter had pointed to was about halfway down. 'The Haven Home and Day School for Delinquent Girls, Eade Village', it said, and in brackets, 'Housed in ruins of former church'. Alex wondered for a second if it had a roof. It was the home nearest to the town. She knew from when she had had to learn names of local villages for Mr Sabre's questions that Eade crouched in a bend in the coast as if it had been left and forgotten about. She had never been there, but she thought of it as a sad place, as if the village itself was lonely and sat in a corner sucking its finger with a grey face. She picked up the leaflet and the tulips, went over to the bar and found the waiter again.

'Why has she gone there?' she said.

The waiter moved his hand in a curve in front of him. 'In the club,' he said.

Alex was stunned. 'What?' she said, not sure if she had heard him properly.

'You know,' he said, gesturing in front of his stomach again.

Alex handed him the tulips. 'These are for you,' she said.

'For me?' she heard him say as she ran away up the steps and through the velvet curtain. 'What about your drink?'

That night, she lay on her bed and stared up at the Teenagers from Outer Space, Julia and the others as if they might tell her what to do. Then, when she had fallen asleep, the Creature from the Black Lagoon opened his seaweed-flavoured mouth and came up with a wonderful idea.

*   *   *

54

On Saturday, when Alex went into the café, the room was full, just like it had been the first time she had come, and red light skulked about with the cigarette smoke like strangers in an alleyway. The church people were outside the door again. Rufus Immanuel strutted around the tables in a white jacket and bow tie. Alex watched him nervously. She ducked out of the way when he went past and sat at a table near the door. Melanie was in her full feather and sequin costume but she wasn't playing for the moment. She perched on the piano stool, sipped a glass of something lime green and talked to a man in a black dress. Alex remembered Rachel playing tunes with her, the time she had seen her kissing Gabriel, the way she had lifted her pink fingernails away from the keys as she played, and her smile as she had turned to Melanie and laughed.

There was a band at the front next to the piano, made up of three men with a trumpet, a cello and a clarinet. Rachel's father nodded at them in approval as he walked by. They played Gershwin's 'Summertime', very slowly and rhythmically, as if someone with tired thighs was walking up a spiral staircase into the sky, one step at a time. The dancers swayed backwards and forwards, like hypnotists with beads round their necks. Alex felt tense. She searched the faces in the room, hoping she wouldn't find Isabelle or Miranda amongst them, but neither of them was there.

She longed to see Rachel again; the empty space she had left behind in the café was horrible. It made Alex want to go back out into the street and try to find her by herself. She felt uncomfortable, as if her clothes didn't fit or she was at a party she hadn't been invited to. She couldn't wait to get out. But she had made a plan and she was going to carry it through. She ducked again as Rufus went past and waited until the waiter she had given the tulips to approached her table.

'It's you,' he said. 'Thanks for the flowers.' He put his hand over his heart.

'Pleasure,' she said, trying to sound calm.

'My name's Evan.'

'Alex,' she said. She suddenly felt more nervous than ever, as if Rufus or the waiter or Melanie might look into her head and see what she was planning. She realised that Evan was waiting to take her order.

'What can I get you?'

'Huckleberry Finn, please,' she said casually, expecting to be asked if she was old enough to drink, but Evan was still thinking about the tulips.

'Sure,' he said with a smile. She drank her chocolate quickly and ordered another one. After her third drink, she noticed Isabelle coming down the steps, wearing silver sequins. The back of Alex's hands, her arms and neck went prickly with fear, but Isabelle didn't see her. She weaved her way between the tables, saying hello to the people she knew. Alex followed her with her eyes as Isabelle sat down at a table near the piano and ordered a drink. Alex's heart was beating fast. She was drunk enough to do what she had planned to; now she needed to find the courage to do it. She watched as Isabelle got her cards out of her bag and shuffled. A man nearby saw Alex following the card game and pointed with his fork.

'That's Scrummage,' he said. 'I wonder what they are playing for.' The room began to spin around inside Alex's head with the whisky and chocolate. The drink was making it easier to find her courage, as she had hoped. She felt dizzy.

'Sometimes they play for each other,' said the tulips waiter, hearing what the man had said as he went by.

Finally she couldn't stand it any more. Taking a last glance at Isabelle, she slipped out from the table.

'Going so soon?' said the man. When he smiled, Alex could see he had silver jewels on his teeth. She went up the steps to the curtain. The pretend carol singers were peering anxiously through the door, clutching their leaflets to their chests like children.

'Religious nuts,' said the woman in the ticket booth. Her mouth turned down sourly.

Alex went out into the evening. She approached the little huddle of people with leaflets and stood in front of them. The world was swinging backwards and forwards and she felt sick, but she stood up as straight as she could.

'I'm a girl,' said Alex, too loudly, with the whisky behind her eyes. The group watched her to see what she would do next.

'She's drunk,' said one person. Someone else broke off to press a leaflet into the hands of a man and woman who were leaving, but they waved him away. Alex held up a hand and began to count on her fingers.

'I dress up as a boy. I drink. Chocolate and whisky. I saw *Creature From the Black Lagoon* when I was thirteen. I stole some tulips from Mr Bradley.' Then she got to the end of her fingers, so she couldn't say, 'And I kissed Isabelle next to the mixer but then I watched her play cards when she was the first prize and I've fallen in love with a waitress and it's like I've fallen into a cold swimming pool full of leaves.' The church people didn't understand what she was talking about. They began to move away from her. More people were coming out of the café. She realised she had to make them listen.

'No. Wait, you don't understand.' They had all moved away now and were grouped around the door again. Alex pulled one of them by the sleeve.

'Tell my parents to stop watching television and to send me to the house in the village with Rachel,' she said.

'God bless you,' said the man whose sleeve she had grabbed. He gave her a leaflet.

'I've got a leaflet already,' she said, holding his arm more firmly because the world was swaying so much. 'I think I'm delinquent.' She said the word carefully because it was difficult. 'How do I get to go there?' She pointed at the back of the paper where it said 'The Haven' in black letters.

'When you're not drunk,' said the man, 'come to church.'

'But I want to go to the delinquent house,' Alex said. The man was ignoring her now and she was left on her own in the street which was shining from the recent rain, as if there were stars inside it.

That night, like a returning prophet, the Creature from the Black

Lagoon spoke to her again, spitting seaweed out of his mouth as he did so. In the dream, she sneezed and he turned into the man with the yellow leaflet who said, 'God bless you,' then back into the monster again. He picked up Julia Adams with one hand and waved her around his head. 'Come to church,' he said, put Julia down carefully, and smashed a green fist into a little white boat.

When she got in from Mr Sabre's that Monday evening, she sensed straightaway that something was wrong. Her mother and father were waiting for her in the front room. Her father was standing up and her mother was perched on the edge of the sofa nervously.

'Your mother's upset,' said her father.

'You've been lying to me, Alex,' her mother said, looking at the blank screen of the TV in case it might spring to life.

'No I haven't,' Alex said, suddenly caught out. The window she had built in her heart for Rachel to climb through shut suddenly. She wanted to nail it up with thick planks of wood, but it was too late.

'Oh. Only I bumped into Mr Sabre and he didn't know anything about you helping with bread-making or lending you shirts in the rain.'

Alex shrugged, pretending she didn't care. She was picturing the hammer and the wood, and making a box around the bit of her where Rachel was.

'He must have forgotten,' she said at last, realising it was a weak excuse as she said it.

'Really? Well, I've had the fancy dress shop on next door's phone.' Her mother sounded even angrier now. 'He said can he have the authentic 1920s gentleman's trousers back. What does he mean?' The wood and nails splintered and cracked and the window in her heart flew open again. She couldn't help it. She could feel the curtains fluttering.

'Have you been seeing a lad behind our backs?' her father said. He pushed his fist into his palm like he used to when he was confronting ticketless cinema-goers.

'No,' Alex said, shaking her head and wishing they would leave

58

her alone to think. She sank down on the sofa, miserable because she was unable to explain.

'So it's you that's been wearing gentlemen's trousers?' her mother said. There was silence for a moment as the question hung in the air above their heads.

'A couple of times,' Alex admitted because she didn't know what else to say. The Creature from the Black Lagoon, appearing like a buddha in her head, told her to tell her parents everything and show them the yellow leaflet with the houses, but she was too frightened now.

'A couple of times! Where did you go in them?'

'A café,' she said.

'What kind of café?'

'Just a café.' Her parents looked at her with big worried eyes. She wanted to say: there's carol singers outside and a woman with a giraffe pattern and funny cards with pictures and Melanie and a band and hot chocolate. I gave a waiter some tulips and there's a beautiful waitress called Rachel. Only she's not there any more and I've got to go and find her. But she couldn't say it. She sat with her head in her hands instead. Her mother and father looked at her as if she had turned out to be from outer space and not their daughter after all.

'So you've been going to a café?' her mother said between her teeth, as if cafés were the most evil places in the world.

'Yes,' Alex said, standing up again to confront them because she wanted them to understand. But her mother was going out of the door.

'I'm making cheese on toast,' she said as she went. She began to bang plates about and Alex was left standing awkwardly in front of her father. He played with his fist against his palm as if it was a baseball in a glove. Then realising there was no lad-behind-his-back to sort out, he scratched his knee thoughtfully.

'Can't see anything wrong with borrowing a pair of trousers,' he said after a while. They looked at each other in silence for a moment. Then he delved into his brown bag, took out a rolled-up poster and handed it to Alex.

'Free, that was,' he said, scratching his knee again carefully. 'From Mr Bradley.'

Alex unrolled it. *Attack of the Giant Leeches* it said across the top.

'American,' said her father in a low voice as if the poster was a holy thing that not everyone deserved to know about.

It was odd to walk through the graveyard and along the High Street when the closed shops had put on their Sunday clothes. The bakery was shut, with its blinds drawn. Alex imagined Mr Sabre inside with *The Thornwise Book of Facts* and a fig roll, and maybe the woman from Carling Street in there with him, but instead of opening the door to the bakery and going in to find her apron, she went into the chapel opposite. Its brown doors were open wide, like a Cyclops whose single eye opened only once a week. She wasn't wearing a hat, so a solemn man by the door handed her a headscarf from a box and made her tie it under her hair before she entered. She saw the man who had given her the leaflet outside the café and one of the young women, who had a guitar. They didn't recognise her, because she was wearing her sky-blue dress instead of her dancing clothes.

Alex sat on a wooden chair with her chin resting on her hand while the people around her sang songs and prayed. No one said anything to her, apart from the old man who was the only other person sitting in her row.

'You work in Michael and Edith's bakery,' he said loudly during the space left for silent prayer. She blushed. She didn't want to be recognised.

'Lovely lemon buns,' he said. He reached over and patted her knee. He smelt of urine. Then the man who had given her the leaflet stood up and began to talk. He talked about love. He talked about a love so big that it surrounded the whole world. Not just the world. The universe. Mercury, Venus, Earth, Mars, everything. This love, the man was saying, is as big as the oceans, as big as the mountains, bigger than anything. It made Alex think about what it would be like to kiss Rachel by the mixer. A feeling like lemonade travelled into her hands and her stomach. The Creature from the Black Lagoon roamed around her head, bashing boats and cracking eggs. She thought about Rachel's bouncing hair. Then she sensed the man with sagging trousers at the end of her row moving closer to her and realised that the preacher was telling them to hug the person they were standing next to. The saggy man was standing with his arms open. She stood up and hugged him. The smell of urine mingled with a musty mouldy bread smell that she remembered from one time in the bakery when she found a forgotten crate of rolls. The man grinned at her and sat back down again.

When she was the last person sitting on the wooden chairs, and the woman who played the guitar had packed up and left, she took the folded yellow leaflet out of her pocket and looked at the list of addresses on the back. The preacher came over to her.

'We're locking up now,' he said. 'You'll have to go.' She saw that the solemn man who gave out scarves was by the door with a key.

'Sorry,' said Alex.

She stood up. Then she took a deep breath and sat down again. 'Can I talk to you?' she said.

'I've got five minutes,' said the man hesitantly, looking at his watch.

'I need to go to the Haven,' she said.

'Sorry?' said the man.

She showed him the back of the leaflet and pointed. 'I think I'm delinquent.'

'Why?' he said. 'You're not pregnant, are you?'

Alex didn't say anything. She just looked down at the yellow leaflet.

'Perhaps you'd like to speak to my wife. She's a nurse.'

'I'm not pregnant. I kissed a woman in the bakery,' said Alex. The man opened his eyes wide and moved away from her slightly. She took another deep breath.

'I'm only sixteen but I drink. Whisky,' she said. She looked up at him and thought about Rachel again. Her five minutes were nearly up, but she had to keep trying. 'Can you talk to my parents for me? Today?' she said. She thought about it for a moment. Her parents didn't have a phone. 'I'll write my neighbour's number down.' She took out a pen, scribbled on the leaflet and handed it to him. He looked at her with his mouth open, but she got up, put her scarf in the box, and ran out of the door before he could tell her to stay.

She waited in the cemetery by the red bush full of birds for ages before she went home. When she got back, her mother and father were pacing up and down in the sitting room. Her mother had been crying. Her father's neck was thicker than ever. He looked uncomfortable. He moved around uneasily with his hands in his pockets.

'We've had the religious nuts on next door's phone and your mother's upset,' he said as Alex came in.

'Why didn't you tell us?' her mother said.

'Tell you what?' said Alex nervously.

'About the woman in the bakery,' said her mother. 'They said you was seduced. They said that it was being around the cakes that did it.'

'I always thought you was normal,' said her father, scratching his leg and looking at her as if he was trying to work out what wasn't normal about her.

'The religious people said it was because we didn't bring you to the church,' said her mother. She sat down on the sofa.

'They said there was somewhere you could go away to for a bit to make you better. By the seaside,' said her father. 'I wish I could go to the bloody seaside. Do you want to go to the seaside place then? To see if they can fix you?' he said.

Alex sat down on the sofa and rested her head in her hands. The Creature from the Black Lagoon roared around her head. Then she thought about Rachel and imagined dancing next to the piano with her while they pressed their cheeks together, softly and urgently.

'Yes,' she said at last.

8

November 2004

I pulled into the services, locked all the doors and spread my money out on my lap. After I had looked at it for a while, I rummaged around in the glove compartment amongst old tapes and sweet wrappers, swearing under my breath. Eventually I found the scrap of newspaper I was looking for. I smoothed it out on my leg, stroking it like a cat. The words that had attracted me to the job advert, right in the middle, were *live in.* There was no phone number, just an address and *send a CV to.* Kitchen assistant, I thought. Assistant meant that you would be helping someone who knew what the fuck they were doing. I put the advert on the dashboard, stuffed the money in my pocket and went inside.

The lights were bright and artificial and as I walked across the squeaky grey floor, I thought about how the services and the motorway and the car park I had just left my car in had all been going on for the last two years. The people walking, the sticky drinks, the babies and guide dogs, games machines, the expensive coffee had all been happening and I had known nothing about any of it. I stood in the brightly lit shop and gazed at the cuddly toys and the rows of CDs. Two years of scraping blue chairs, burgers, paper hats, letters on army paper from Neil, road maps, Little Chef Olympic Breakfasts, keys in locks, footsteps in corridors, dinner in rows at grey tables, pens on clipboards, psychiatrists' reports, cappuccinos, tinny music, cleanest toilet competitions. I picked up Barry Manilow's *Greatest Hits*, feeling hypnotised by it all, and turned it over to read the back. As I swapped Barry Manilow for a gift edition of *Abba Gold*, I thought about how two sets of things can happen side by side and no one in the first thing knows about anything in the second. It's not just two things, I thought, putting Abba back, millions of things are all happening at the same time, like the universe is a giant hedgehog with stories for spikes going off in different directions. I gazed at the rows of horoscope books while I thought it. They were next to the ones that promise to sort out your life in twenty-four hours. Out in space a star exploding. On earth babies being born at the same moment who will never meet each other. Shops, schools, roads, jungles, deserts, brothels, alleyways, all with things happening in them and none of them knows about the others. I went to look at the pick 'n' mix. Perhaps the brothel and the desert did have something in common. One thing. A person who has been in both, who knows someone whose brother went to the same school as the woman who works in the shop, who passed a hitchhiker in the road who had been trekking in the jungle and had been bitten by a malaria-carrying mosquito. So he goes mad and has hallucinations like those he gets when he injects himself in the alleyway with his friends. I was pleased with myself for making up a story, but then I saw the security guard look at me suspiciously so I raised my eyebrows at him and walked over to the pile of leisure wear. All the things that had been happening, the mosquito, the hitchhiker and the brothel, crowded around my head. I let them whisper in my ears and went up to the counter to buy a map, a new sweatshirt and some trousers. I swung my bag as I went past the security guard and walked into the toilet of the year which smelt of the sort of bleach I used to use in the hospital.

After I had changed into my new clothes, I crouched above the seat to piss, and when I washed my hands, I had to dry them on my hair because the hand-dryer didn't work. There was a whiteboard with a pen attached to it on the wall for cleaners to write on when they had done the floors and checked the toilet roll. I wrote 'Shit' on it for a laugh and went up the steps to the service station café.

It was positioned halfway along a bridge over the road. The M1. I bought some coffee and sat down next to the window, so I could see the cars zooming past underneath me, thinking that if the floor hadn't been there with the chair, the dirty tiles and the coffee, I would have fallen down onto the white lorries. I looked into my drink, as the undissolved granules disappeared slowly. Then I gazed out of the window and watched the road for ages and the cars dashing past into the night to places I didn't know about.

I closed my eyes and thought about my favourite fantasy: I am tired and someone else is driving, someone I am in love with. I tried out the words in my head again. In love with. It made me think of two people inside a big sack of sand. Anyway, whoever is driving, the bloke I'm shagging, isn't saying anything. We're a long way from where we're going. It's dark and maybe it's raining. The journey is going to go on and on for ever. I am watching the dark night and the rain, the headlamps and the orange street lights.

When I opened my eyes, I sipped my coffee again but it was going cold and the cup smelt of industrial-strength dishwasher soap anyway so I looked into it like a fortune teller instead and I thought I could see faces, like the hitchhiker or the woman who owned the brothel, but there were too many of them for me to be able to tell which was which. I felt the money from my savings in my pocket. I had about enough to stay in a hotel for one night. After that I would drive to the address on the advert. I knew it was crap but I had no other plan.

9

By the time I got to the house the next day, it was dark and raining steadily like someone climbing up stairs. I got out of the car and ran to the front door. I banged loudly, hunched under my coat in the rain, but there was no answer and when I tried the handle, it was locked.

It was really dark now, because there were no street lights this far from the main road and there was a thick tree pressed against the house on one side. I stood back and looked up at the grey building, which loomed above me like a storm cloud. Rain was bouncing off the roof. I shuddered. It looked like one of those haunted houses off the telly.

I was annoyed at myself for thinking that I was going to be able to spend the night there. I tried to force the front door, but I couldn't. There was a crumbling green gate in a wall to one side, which swung open when I pushed it. Inside was a dark overgrown garden, but no visible way into the house. I told myself I didn't want to sleep inside anyway, it was too frightening. I was wet through and exhausted so I lay down under my coat on the back seat of the car. I suddenly felt lonely because I realised I had nowhere else to be. To send myself to sleep, I thought about the time my dad taught me flying matches. I wouldn't let myself tell the story. I wanted to save it up like someone saves a cream cake to go with their tea because they want to enjoy it, sinking their teeth into it, letting the jam and cream and icing ooze over their tongue. As I drifted off into a fitful sleep, I dreamt uncomfortably of the hotel room of the night before.

I woke to the sound of someone pulling into the drive. When I opened my eyes I saw a truck with a skip on the back of it parking next to my car. I grabbed the advert from the dashboard and turned the words over in my head one last time: 'Kitchen Assistant Required by Catering School. Live in. Experience of cake-making and working with people essential'. I'm a good liar, I thought to myself.

The driver of the truck came over and banged on the window. He was a middle-aged man wearing a woollen hat. He frowned at me with his face almost touching the glass.

'We don't want none of you here,' he said.

'I've come about the job,' I said, opening the car door. I waved the scrap of newspaper at him.

'Oh, I see,' he said. 'Sorry. Thought you were one of them rough sleepers.' He looked me over. 'I'm Bernie,' he said.

'About the job?' I said. I got out and tried to smarten up my slept-in sweatsuit.

'You better talk to Eve about that.' He began to walk back to his truck. I quickly grabbed my coat and followed him. It was very cold. I pulled the coat round me and stuffed my hands into my pockets.

'Is Eve in charge?' I felt nervous all of a sudden.

'I work for her, yes. She'll be here soon. Tea?'

'Yes please.'

He got a flask out of the van and poured me a cup thought-fully.

'You been in catering long?' he said and examined my face for an answer.

'Yes,' I lied. 'Fancied a change, you know?'

'Right.' Then another car approached up the hill and pulled into the driveway. It was a black Nissan Princess. A woman, who I took to be Eve, wound down her window.

'Who the hell's this?' she said to Bernie. I noticed a cigarette in the hand which still gripped the steering wheel.

'She's come about the job,' he said before I could answer. The woman pulled on the handbrake and got out of the car. She was shorter than me and thin from smoking. Her hair was boyish and black and she had eyes like ravens that darted backwards and forwards as if they were looking for something to hook on to.

'You're keen, aren't you?' she said.

'I was passing and I—'

'You were sleeping in your car,' Bernie interrupted.

'Never mind,' she said and walked off towards the door, fishing in her pocket for a key as she did so. 'Come on,' she said impatiently, glancing at me over her shoulder. I followed her, leaving Bernie to climb back into his truck and turn on the radio.

When Eve opened the door, the smell was overwhelming. The house was full of rubbish, some of it in bags, but most of it just piled up against the walls or spilling out across the floor.

'As you can see,' she said, 'there's a lot of work to be done.'

'About the job,' I said.

'Yes,' she said, taking a step back from the smell. 'Got your CV?'

'Er, no, I . . .'

'References?'

'No. I can get them.'

'Well. No one else has applied. How much experience have you had?'

'Two years',' I lied.

'Doing what?'

I started on my story although I didn't get to tell all of it. 'Working in a café.'

'What sort of pastries do you make?'

'Pastries?'

'Cakes then.'

I thought wildly and a Mr Kipling's fruit sponge came into my head just in time. 'Fruit cake mainly.'

'Qualifications?'

'Oh. GCSEs. NVQ Level 2,' I said, picking qualifications for myself at random.

'I see. Can you start straightaway?'

'Yes.'

'OK.' She looked me in the face seriously and then lit another cigarette. When she flicked her lighter, the flame danced in front of me and the knot I had in my stomach tightened but I tried hard not to show it.

'What's your name?'

'Erica. Ricky.'

'Hello, Ricky. I'm Eve. Have you had breakfast?'

'No.'

'Good. First job. Go in and make us all a bacon sandwich. I'm starving.'

'In there?'

'Yes. Or didn't they teach you that in your café?'

I looked in through the front door at the rubbish with a pathway cleared down the middle.

'Go straight through,' Eve said as if she was directing me to the toilet. 'The stuff's in there. The gas is on and we've got the water sorted out but there's no lecy yet.'

'OK,' I said uncertainly.

'Put your jumper over your face. It helps.'

I struggled out of my coat, took off my jumper and did as she said. The smell was so bad that I thought I was going to be sick. Eve came in behind me and opened a window but she left again straightaway.

I ran into the kitchen and opened the back door and all the windows. I stood leaning on the sink. Outside in the garden I could see more rubbish bags. The last thing I wanted to do was cook. The years at the flat when I had looked after my dad and my brother seemed like centuries ago. I wasn't sure if I could remember how to cook more than beans on toast. I told myself not to be stupid and made myself look around the kitchen.

There was no fridge. Next to the sink there was an old-looking and very dirty gas cooker. On the side, there was a bottle of ketchup, a box of matches and a tub of Flora in a Tesco's bag. A frying pan rested on the hob with bits of egg stuck to it. There was one cupboard with a door still attached. The others had lost their doors, or they were hanging off forlornly. I looked in the cupboard with the door and found an empty egg box, some rashers of bacon and half a loaf of Tesco Value bread, so I set to work.

After I had scraped most of the egg from the pan with a spoon I found in a drawer, I fried the bacon in some Flora. When I lit the match, a quick flame started somewhere in my stomach too. Soon the rubbish smell in the air blended with the cooking bacon. Even though I wanted to get out of the house and out into the open air again, I leant against a broken cupboard until the bacon went crispy as I liked it, then I squirted ketchup on the bread, found a knife and plates, and ran back through the house.

Eve and Bernie ate their bacon sandwiches in silence with more tea from the flask.

Away from the sick smell I felt hungry again so I ate my sandwich quickly, sitting in the driving seat of my car a distance from the others, wondering if I should risk running out of petrol and just drive away from the strange woman and her rubbish-filled house, but then I remembered that I didn't have anywhere to go.

'Next job,' said Eve, coming over to the car, 'is clearing this place. Up to it?'

'Yes,' I said.

'OK,' she said, seeming surprised. I wiped my hand across my mouth and got out of the car.

'Let me give you a tour,' she said, screwing up her eyes at me, as if she was trying to work out whether I really was going to stay.

We held our jumpers to our faces again. Bernie had gone to start clearing the garden. In the hall the black bin bags were stacked five or six high and stretched from wall to wall. Most of them held their shape and bulged like hamsters, but some had split open and their contents crowded around the floor.

'Nice of him to bag it up, eh?' said Eve as we looked.

'Who? The person who used to live here?' I said.

'Yep. He died. I bought it cheap,' she said matter-of-factly, as if dying was like popping round the garage for a packet of fags.

'Oh, I see,' I said, trying not to sound bothered. 'Where did it all come from?'

'The guy who was living here was funny in the head. He hoarded it.'

'He lived here with all of this?' I said, looking around in amazement.

'Yep. Unbelievable, isn't it?' She went into a room to the right of the front door. It was long and thin and inside the rubbish continued although I could see that they had begun to clear it, because some of the stuff was packed into boxes.

'Why did he keep it? What happened to him?' I said, examining a broken toaster. 'You'd think he'd be ill.'

'He was. He snuffed it, didn't he? Help me move these,' said Eve. She waved at a couple of wooden crates. 'The rubbish man died and we have a business opportunity.'

'The rubbish man?' I said, as we shifted the crates over to the window.

'It's what the people in the village called him,' Eve said, delving into one of them, which was full of old notebooks.

'I found these in the office yesterday,' she said. 'Thought they were worth keeping. They go right back.' She opened one at random. The date written in careful black handwriting inside the front cover was 1 July 1923.

'Wow,' I said.

She opened another couple and as she flicked the pages to show me, I saw that they contained lists of names. My new employer reached into the box again and pulled out another, a green one this time. The date of the first entry was 1954. She turned the pages: 1955, 1956, 1957, 1958 and, near the end, 1959. I read a couple of the entries: *Doris Evering (stealing), Marjory Makepeace (foul mouth)*. The names continued but I didn't have time to look properly before Eve snapped the book shut and put it back in the crate with the others. I wanted to sit down on the floor and go through the whole crate to find out what the notebooks were about, but I didn't want to show that I was interested.

71

'Come on,' Eve was saying. 'I'll show you the rest of it.'

When we went into the lounge, the bin bags stopped. Instead, there were books piled up everywhere. There was a space by the fireplace framed by a sofa, which was also covered in books, and a couple of armchairs. If you had been sitting by the fire you would have been frightened that the books were going to swallow you up.

'This was where the rubbish man died,' Eve said, going over to the armchair nearest to the fireplace. She pointed at a smashed window. She told me that the police had had to break it to get him out and that they had made a pathway through the hall to the front door but had left the rest. Eve had bought the house in an auction. The person who taught her everything she knew about baking had heard about it coming onto the market. The whole thing was Eve's friend's idea. I stopped listening and while she told the rest of the story, I looked around at the dusty towers of yellowing books which were waist high. Against the walls, some of the stacks were taller than me.

'Did these belong to the rubbish man?' I said, picking one up, so that I got dust all over my hands. The pages were glued together with damp, so that when I tried to open it, they ripped. All the books were like that.

'No,' said Eve. 'About twenty years ago, when Mrs Burns the librarian died, Rachel got rid of a lot of old books. The story goes that in the morning, the skip was empty. He'd brought them all up here. No one knows how he did it.'

'Like Stone Henge.'

'What?'

'I saw it on the telly. No one knows how they did that either.'

'If you say so.'

'Who's Rachel?' I asked.

'Rachel Immanuel,' she said. 'At the library.'

'Who?' But I didn't get a reply because Eve had gone over to the fireplace.

'Seems like he was burning them in the end,' Eve said, lifting the cover of a red hardback out of the ashes.

*   *   *

72

In the room at the top of the stairs I had made a path to the fireplace and was squatting next to it so I could examine what I had done so far, when I noticed that some of the dirty green tiles around the hearth were loose. I pulled away a couple and was probing the empty space underneath when Eve came upstairs to talk to me.

'Where are you sleeping?' she said.

'Er. I don't know,' I said nervously. I didn't want to spend another night in the car, but I was frightened that she might suggest I sleep in the sick-smelling house.

'You can stay at the library with me. Rachel won't mind.'

'Who's Rachel?' I asked for a second time. In answer, Eve got out her mobile and pressed a couple of buttons.

'Rachel. Hi. Yes. It was hard work. I've offered someone the job. Yes, really. Can we both stay with you tonight?' The whole conversation lasted about thirty seconds and I wondered if Rachel had said anything at all.

It was dark before we finally filled the skip and Bernie hooked it up to his truck and took it away. I was very tired and very dirty. I stood and looked up at the stars as Eve went into the house with the torch to find some matches because her lighter had run out.

'We'll go in mine,' said Eve, emerging from the house again, so I left my car where it was and got into Eve's black Princess, wondering who Rachel was and why she lived in the library.

10

We went in through the brown arched entranceway. There was a door to the left and one to the right. We took the one on the left. It opened into an apartment where Rachel was waiting for us. She had skin like she had been carved out of wood, short hair and green eyes like a witch. They were the sort of eyes that linger on you for just long enough to make you think they are casting spells. She had positioned her wheelchair next to the fireplace and was sitting in an armchair nearby.

'So this is the new cook?' said Rachel. The room at the back of the library was comforting after the house full of rubbish. It was small. The sofa and chair took up nearly half the space and there was a fire leaping around excitedly in the grate. I watched it for a while.

'Yes,' said Eve. 'This is her.'

'Kitchen assistant,' I corrected them, feeling worried by the word cook, which sounded too important.

'What's your name?' Rachel said to me and when she glanced at Eve, her eyes danced like crystal balls.

'Ricky,' Eve replied for me. Rachel stared at me as if I was a painting and she was trying to work me out.

'Why do you live in a library?' I asked her for something to say.

'Why not?' she said. She laughed like a train going past.

'She's the librarian,' Eve said simply.

'That's right,' said Rachel, still gazing at me with her witchy eyes.

74

'Would you like to see the Millennium Kitchen?' Rachel asked, once we had all had a bowl of tomato soup. She had lifted herself back into her wheelchair so she could wash up and now she came back into the lounge, wiping her hands. Before I had time to answer, she wheeled herself over to a door which led into the library. I hesitated for a moment.

'Go on,' said Eve. 'What's wrong with you?' So I followed. We passed some bookshelves and an enquiries desk and went down a ramp to an extension, which was built like a conservatory with a big glass wall.

Rachel flicked a switch and the fluorescent strip lighting blinked into life. I looked around me. A counter for tea and cakes was suddenly lit up. Behind it was a coffee machine and a price list. There was also a row of computers along one wall and tables and chairs, a bit like garden furniture, arranged here and there.

'The Millennium Kitchen,' Rachel said. She spread her arms as if she was a magician who had just sawn his assistant in half. 'The lottery paid for it.' She pushed herself over to the French windows. 'Look at the patio.'

The library extension and the strip lights were reflected back at us in the glass. I pushed my face up against the door so I could see out. It had been raining and puddles had formed on top of the tables and the paving slabs in the little garden.

'Don't people get coffee on the books?' I said, turning away.

Rachel tapped a laminated piece of card nearby. It said, 'The Millennium Kitchen. No Smoking. No drinks to be taken past the ramp. Please take care with books when you are in the Kitchen. Customers will be asked to pay for any damage. Internet 50p for ten minutes. Members of the Silver Surfers' Club free. No downloading. No offensive sites. Enjoy Your Visit.'

I put it down again and examined a poster advertising children's story time and an over-sixties book group.

'The crumbs can be annoying but I've only had one serious spillage in four years,' Rachel said. 'A cappuccino all over *Pride and Prejudice*. But the man was very nice. He gave me extra for another copy of *Persuasion* as well.'

I turned back to the window. The moon was making the little garden blue and grey and lighting up the white chairs like sudden sculptures.

'Go out if you want. There's a water feature.'

'Like off the telly?' I said.

'It was on the telly. We had TV cameras, Charlie Dimmock and everything.'

'Really?' I said. I pushed the handle so I could go out. Rachel followed me. She wheeled herself over to a big white planting trough along one side.

'You might have seen it. They repeated it last year.'

'We didn't have a . . .' I began, but then I closed my mouth again. Rachel was busy pointing to different things in the garden.

'They put herbs in over there because they said they were doing a disabled garden for me and that meant being able to smell stuff. I told them I wasn't blind, I've got arthritis in my legs, but they put them in anyway because that's what you get if you have a disabled garden apparently,' she said, sounding proud.

'Blind people might visit,' I said.

'That's what Charlie said.' She put her hand out to touch the mint.

We had had a blind woman in the hospital where I was a cleaner and once I held her arm while she found the toilet because the nurses were busy with a man who thought he had been arrested and was in a police station. The WRVS woman with the library trolley had got her a special talking book with headphones, although the only one she could get hold of was *James and the Giant Peach*. When I asked her about it, she said it was very short notice.

I stopped thinking about the hospital and I went over to join the librarian so I could smell the herbs. The air smelt damp and clean because we were near the sea. Then I saw something wedged between Rachel's knees and the side of the wheelchair. It was a silver case with a pattern carved onto it. The moonlight caught its surface and made it shine.

'What's that?' I said.

'Oh, I meant to put it back,' she said a little too deliberately, as if she had wanted me to see it. She picked it up and opened the clasp. The insides were lined with thick black cloth. 'It's a card game.' She held out the top card. It was decorated with a picture of a girl in a brown dress and hood with a Roman XIV underneath it. I looked at it in amazement, but Rachel was staring at me again, not unkindly, as if I was one of those complicated puzzles.

'I'll show you how to play sometime,' she said and closed the case without further explanation. I followed her back through the library and into her apartment, where Eve was getting ready for bed.

'Eve's staying in the spare room until she can move into her new flat,' Rachel said.

'Soon, I hope,' Eve called from the bathroom.

'Aren't you going to live at the house?' I asked her.

'No. Only room for one member of staff to live in,' she said briskly.

'You can have the sofa,' Rachel said to me and she went to find a duvet. 'Once Eve moves out, you can have the spare room,' she said when she came back, 'until the house is ready.' She grinned at me and I was suddenly suspicious of her generosity but I didn't say anything.

That night I slept the most comfortable sleep of my life. I moulded into the sofa and the cushions Rachel had given me and I wondered whether she had sprinkled sleeping dust on them because they smelt musty but I fell asleep straightaway.

11

Loud banging had been going on below me all morning. I had added a chest of drawers, a pair of bathroom scales and a peeling hat stand to the savable things which lined the hallway as if we were suddenly hosting the *Antiques Roadshow*. I had just returned from dragging an old Hoover out to the skip when I saw Bernie had left a penknife next to the fireplace. It was perfect. I pocketed it before I could think about it any more. Eve rounded the bend in the stairs and stood in the doorway.

'Bernie's been sorting out the kitchen,' she said. It sounded as if he was demolishing it. She took a cigarette out and patted her pockets. I watched her looking for a light. I thought I knew what would happen next. She would say could I see some matches by the fireplace in there? And I would bring them out to her and watch as the little pink head of the match exploded like a hand unfolding or like a tiny sun. I would see the flame leap just for a second as Eve lit her cigarette. Then she would wave her match hand and the flame would go out. But that wasn't what happened. Instead, she pointed at the matchbox and said, 'Pass me those. We're having a bonfire.' My heart skipped.

'What? Here?' I said, handing over the box.

'Yes,' she said. 'Don't you know what day it is?'

Bernie heard her and called up at us from the hall below. 'Fifth of November,' he said. 'Bonfire night.'

'I thought we'd make a party out of it,' Eve said. 'We need your help.' She headed off round the bend in the stairs again. I was about to follow when I noticed that she had left the crate full of old notebooks on the landing with some other savable stuff. I found the small green book that I had seen on my first day and scanned the lists of names. *Andrea Jones (feeble-minded), Jessica Dean (vandalism), Rena Finlay (petty arson), Harriet Neil (homosexual),* and overleaf the list Eve had shown me: *Doris Evering (stealing), Marjory Makepeace (foul mouth), Joyce White (backward).* When I read the last entry on the page, I stared at it in astonishment: *Rachel Immanuel (pregnant).*

'Are you coming?' Eve shouted impatiently.

'Was Rachel at the house?' I called back.

'Yeah. Common knowledge, I guess.' Eve sounded surprised.

I sat down with my back against the wall. The next book I picked up was dated 1917. I turned the pages and read the names to myself. I could only just decipher the first on the list because it had been crossed out with a neat black line: *Sally Worthing,* it said. Then: *Mavis Free, Jemima Faraday, Elaine Brooks, Doreen Hutchinson, Amanda.* The last entry on the page had no surname although there was something in brackets next to it. The writing was smudged because damp had wormed its way between the pages. I lifted it closer to my face. It said: *Amanda (sixteen, runaway).* Overleaf, there was another list of names. I read the first, *Wilhelmina Dearing,* but the others were too faded. I could hear that Eve was still talking to Bernie about the bonfire so I searched about in the box for something else. I picked up a book which was different from the others. It had tiny flowers drawn on the front and, in careful loopy handwriting, the same bible verses written over and over again. First: *for the love of money is the root of all evil, which while some coveted after, they have erred from the faith, and pierced themselves through with many sorrows.* Then: *the wages of sin is death but the gift of God is eternal life through Jesus Christ our Lord.* There was a signature on the last page: *Doris Evering.* One of the girls from Rachel's list. I rooted around to see if I could find any others that contained more than just lists of names.

'What are you doing now?' Eve called from below me. I didn't answer for a second. The book I had come across was red and slightly larger than the rest. I flicked through it and realised it was more of a journal than a notebook. I began to read: *I had a dream about a chain of tiny blue flowers*, but then I heard Eve coming upstairs to find me. I dropped the journal back in the crate and jumped up.

'For God's sake,' she said from halfway up, just before the stairs bent round towards the top room, 'stop dawdling.'

'Sorry,' I said. 'What do you want me to do?'

'All those piles of books in the sitting room are useless,' Eve replied as we went downstairs. 'We need to get rid of them. And the stuff from the kitchen.'

Bernie held out a Tesco's bag and showed me the sausages and rolls inside with a few bottles of beer, but I leant against the wall and jammed my hands into my pockets.

'What's wrong with you?' he said.

'I don't like bonfire night much,' I said.

'It's all right, we're not having fireworks or anything. Just the fire,' he said. 'We should get on with it. Start passing stuff out.'

I worked my way across the lounge, shifting the piles of books, while Eve shouted instructions and Bernie arranged the forlorn hardbacks around the unlit bonfire which he held together with planks and a door. As the number of the books in the lounge diminished, I became more anxious. I wasn't sure if I would be able to sit and watch. I wondered if I could make an excuse and slip back to the library and I was worried in case Eve wanted to burn the old notebooks, too, before I had had a chance to look at them more carefully. Once the hardbacks were all outside, I ran upstairs with the torch and grabbed the red journal from the top of the crate where I had left it. Then I went outside. The night had thrown itself over the hillside like a blanket. Bernie was bending over a stack of things he was creating in the driveway to throw on later, and I saw my chance. I switched off the torch and tried to creep away back down the hill to the library, but I nearly collided with Eve halfway across the drive.

'Where are you going?' she said.

'Nowhere.'

'Good. Take these to Bernie.' She put the matchbox in my hand. 'I'm going inside to get the hot dogs.'

I sat a distance away on the low stone wall, the journal stuck under my coat because it was too dark to read it, forcing myself to watch as Bernie carefully lit the corners of the fire. Some bits of cupboard had paint on them and they spat at us viciously because they didn't want to be burnt, but soon the books were blazing. Now I was transfixed by it. I hugged myself and tried to look away but it was hard. The flames were like a hypnotist with a swinging gold pendant. It seemed as though all the words from the books were shooting up into the sky as tiny fireworks or merging with the smoke and air and going back into the atmosphere to become part of people and the insides of their heads. I felt them dancing in front of me like I had real flames in my eyes and not reflections.

'Want some?' said Bernie, walking up from the shadows and waving a bottle of beer. He startled me.

'What? Oh, yes please.'

'Cold?'

'No,' I said, even though I was. I rubbed my arms. I didn't know how long I was going to be able to take it.

'Why don't you come closer if you're cold?'

'I said I'm not cold. I like it here.'

'Suit yourself.' Bernie sat down next to me and passed me a beer. 'Only a couple left. Make the most of it.' His face was in shadow. 'I know how it is,' he went on. 'I feel safer in the van myself.'

'What?' I said.

'They don't like any kind of burning.'

'Who doesn't?'

'Spirits,' he said and grinned at me. I shuddered. Eve came out with a plate of sausages and onions and heard what he said.

'Gets rid of them then, does it?' she responded.

'Perhaps it does,' said Bernie, still grinning. 'Maybe it'll bring them back. Or make them angry. Some people in the village say that's why he filled up all the space with rubbish. To keep them away.'

Eve looked at my frightened face and laughed. 'Stop telling stupid stories, Bernie, and get the table. You're frightening her.'

I looked around at the dark shapes in the garden behind me and shivered again.

'I'm not frightened,' I said.

Bernie trotted off to get a fold-up table from his van to hold the pile of hot dogs.

Once the table was up, she began cutting the buns down the middle efficiently. She handed me the ketchup and mustard as Bernie threw more books on the fire.

'Right,' Eve said. 'You finish these. I'm going to get Rachel. She said she'd join us for supper.'

I finished arranging the onions and mustard on the hot dogs and sipped my drink, watching the bonfire spit and the flames blowing this way and that in the wind. I still had Bernie's knife in my pocket. I touched it with my fingers for reassurance. Sometimes the flames seemed to be coming closer, their hands reaching out towards me; other times they bent away from me. I didn't think I could stand it for much longer.

'Have you got the torch?' Bernie said.

'Oh. Yeah.' I passed it to him.

When Bernie went inside the house with the torch to find more beer, I made a run for it, the notebook under my coat. I went across the grass and down the hill, past the library and down to the harbour where the chippy was. I sat on the edge of the quay, and looked out at the lighthouse, gripping the knife and letting the notebook rest next to me on the concrete. I timed the beam, five seconds, and the darkness, ten seconds, like someone breathing slowly in their sleep. Apart from the moon-light on the water, the darkness was thick when the sudden glare of the light from across the rocks faded. As I watched the purple shapes of the boats bobbing in the treacle-coloured water, the cold night wrapped its arms round me in a hug.

Fixing my gaze on the lighthouse, I rolled up my sleeve,

revealing the neat line of scars already there. Pressing hard, I drew the blunt knife across the top of my arm. It didn't even bleed, it was just a graze, but straightaway I felt better. I hid the knife in my pocket again, pulled down my sleeve because I was cold and watched the beam of light advancing and retreating. I counted: five then ten, five, ten, five, ten. Then I flicked open the pages of the notebook and concentrated on the words. I could only read them when the beam came because my eyes didn't have a chance to get used to the dark.

It went like this: *I had a dream about a chain of tiny blue flowers twisted around each other, with the sun playing on them. In the dream I lay next to R by the lake, under the trees.* Ten seconds of darkness. I was just making out the words in the moonlight when the page was illuminated again. I was dazzled for a moment and then: *She was talking about lots of things and I was falling asleep, listening to her words.* Ten seconds of darkness. *In my sleep I said 'I love you' and I rolled from side to side and Doris heard, and she told Joyce, who told the attendant* Darkness *so now I've been locked in again. She says I have to stay in here and think about everything I did: the mixer* Darkness *the mixer, the café, dressing up and imagine a big X crossing them out. I tried it but it didn't work.* Darkness. This time I looked out at the boats and counted to ten. *I feel the same as when I stare at the wall. Blank. She says I shouldn't have had a job and that's what turned me into a man. She says anything can turn you bad, cakes can do it too.* I wondered how cakes could make someone bad. I thought for a moment it meant cakes can make you fat, but that didn't account for the bit about being turned into a man. I was also wondering who R was, but as soon as I read the next line I found out. I could only just read it because it had been scribbled out. It said: *I wish Rachel was here and we were locked in together.* There was the librarian's name, illuminated by the yellow glare of the lighthouse. I wondered what it meant, but I was too cold to carry on reading. I picked up the book and made my way up the road so I could call at the One Stop shop.

By the time I got back to the house, the fire had died down a little and Rachel and Eve were there, eating hot dogs. Rachel was shaking her head.

'Still don't know how he brought all those tired old hardbacks up here,' she was saying.

'Where did you get to?' said Eve when she saw me approaching.

'Went to the shop,' I said. I held up the bottles of beer I had bought on the way back.

'Great,' said Bernie, rubbing his hands.

'OK.' Eve eyed me suspiciously. 'Come and have some food then.'

I slipped away again for a moment and stood out on the hillside, holding the red book close to my chest, letting the darkness bunch around me like a crowd of friendly people. I looked up at the sky. It was full of stars. Then I looked back at the spitting fire and the three figures grouped near it. Bernie was right, I thought. The spirits from the books were leaping back to heaven one after another.

Eve's voice interrupted my thoughts.

'I found a crate of notebooks in the office. Some kind of record of admittance, I think.'

'They'll be useful,' Rachel said. I wondered what they would be useful for.

'I'll bring them down to the library,' Eve said. 'Where's Erica? Ricky. Get the torch and go and find that box of notebooks for Rachel.'

I went into the house, shining the torch on the imaginary ghosts that sprang up on either side of me as I climbed the stairs. But before I shifted the crate, I went into the top room, put the matches back and hid the journal under the loose tiles of the fireplace.

Back at the library later, I pulled off my jumper and examined the new scratch on my arm. I figured I would have to make myself come to get to sleep. I pushed my head into a cushion and put my hand inside my tracksuit, but when I closed my eyes, all I could think of was the bonfire. I pulled my hand away and tried to think about the story in the red journal instead but the fire kept coming back, so I screwed my eyes up tight and made myself think of a dancing candle flame.

Once when I was small and scared of the dark, I climbed onto my dad's bed. He put his arms round me and said that I had a candle burning inside me and that if I closed my eyes I would be able to see it and I wouldn't be scared any more, so I closed my eyes and looked and there was the candle, just as he had said. When I woke up the next morning, my dad had carried me into the room I shared with my brother and had folded me into the covers. If I ever had trouble sleeping after that, I thought of the candle. I imagined the matches, the rough edge of the box, the sudden flare and the smell of the smoke, and the yellow flame twisting its hips and grasping the wick with its feet. So, lying on Rachel's sofa, I imagined there was a candle burning next to me, its tiny flame dancing one way then the other. Soon I was dreaming about candles, flying matches, lighthouses, purple night-time boats, red books, hot dogs and the huge orange flames of a bonfire that I had started myself.

12

Frost was covering the ground outside when Rachel woke me up with a big mug of hot chocolate and marshmallows. In the library extension, I could hear water running. It was Monica, washing up. Monica lived next door to the library at the Old Vicarage and worked in the Millennium Kitchen serving cappuccinos.

'I've made you a Tipsy Penguin,' Rachel said. I asked her about the name but she just grinned at me.

We were looking out of the window at the white hillside when Eve came in from the library, carrying her own mug of chocolate.

'We'll have to put this on the menu,' she said. 'What's in it?'

Rachel looked at her slyly. 'Secret,' she said.

'Be like that then,' said Eve. 'I'll work it out.' She had a brochure in her hand. She waved it at us. 'This just came.' She showed it to Rachel and I peered over her shoulder. On the front there was a picture of the house. 'The Haven Baking School' it said in the sky above it. 'Learn how to make perfect cakes for all occasions every time. Beginners welcome' was written underneath where the grass was. *Every* was underlined. There were dates and prices and a map showing people where Eade was. Each room was a different rate. On the back was an application form for the students to fill in and a big star shape with 'Special Offer. Opening Weekend Half Price' written inside it.

'Why aren't you dressed yet?' Eve said, pointing a cigarette-clad finger at me. I felt uncomfortable.

'Um,' I said.

'Count yourself lucky you're still here,' she said. 'No references. No CV. And still in your nightshirt.'

'Shut up, Eve, for goodness sake,' said Rachel. 'Don't you know what day it is?'

'Sorry,' Eve said.

'Now,' said Rachel, handing me her cup to put back in the kitchen. 'You two are going to have to help me, because today's the day.'

Eve turned serious and stood up so she could pace up and down across the room.

'Put some clothes on, Ricky,' she said.

I pulled on my tracksuit bottoms and an old hooded top Rachel had given me over the nightshirt, then I squashed my feet into my trainers. Eve muttered something about personal hygiene, but I ignored her and rolled on some Mum that I kept next to the sofa.

'Where are we going?' I said when I was ready, but neither of them answered me. I wriggled into my jacket.

'Bring those,' said Rachel, pointing at some flowers she had in a vase near the fireplace. She was already wheeling herself out of her front door with Eve behind her. I grabbed the flowers and ran after them. The wind was blowing outside. The trees by the lake were bobbing around like drunk people trying to wave at each other. We hurried up the road. I could see my breath as we went and could still taste the marshmallows in my mouth. Eve pushed Rachel's chair because we were going uphill, past the overgrown front garden of the Old Vicarage. We came to a stop at the steps up to the little church with the thatched roof.

'Now you'll have to help me,' Rachel said, putting on her brakes. Slowly, she stood up and we positioned ourselves either side of her. Then, bit by bit, we went up the steps together, looking like three friends in a football team posing for a photo. Rachel felt warm and soft leaning against me and she smelt of the library.

'Get the chair,' said Eve when we got to the top. Rachel rested against the wall while I fetched it. She sat down again gratefully.

'Give me those,' she said and grabbed the flowers from my hand. Then she wheeled herself along the path, while we came slowly behind. She paused in front of one of the slightly newer-looking gravestones. It said, 'In Memory of James Burns 1898–1954', and underneath that, 'And also his wife Billy Burns 1900–1986, much loved Eade Village librarian from 1919'. Rachel divided the flowers into two bunches, reached forward and laid one bunch on the ground. After a moment she turned herself round and went further down the path without saying anything to us.

I tried to follow her, but Eve put her hand out to stop me. We watched from where we were while she stopped by another stone and put down the rest of the flowers. After a while, we went over to join her, with the cold morning wrapping itself around our faces like scarves. Rachel didn't look up or even show that she had noticed us. Eve wouldn't let me stand too close. I could just about read the name on the stone. 'Annabel Immanuel' it said and there was a date underneath which I couldn't make out. I wondered who Annabel was.

'Stupid old woman,' said Rachel to herself and wiped the tears from her eyes angrily. Eve nodded to me and we wandered into the church porch to sit down out of the wind.

'Is Annabel a relation?' I said.

'Rachel's daughter,' Eve said. I gasped and looked out at Rachel in horror.

'What happened?' I asked, but Eve didn't answer straightaway. She thought for a moment.

'I think she'll tell you if she wants to,' she said carefully. I felt awkward and didn't know what to say. Part of me wanted to ask more questions but it was too hard to watch Rachel by the grave-side. I stared at an old sign on the wall instead which said, 'Please close this gate and door lest a bird should enter and die of thirst'. Lest was a funny word, I thought, it sounded like vest, rest, best, nest. I knocked it around my head.

'What does lest mean?' I said eventually because I didn't want to think about Rachel and her daughter.

'Just in case,' said Eve. She looked out at Rachel.

'Oh. Right,' I said, but I was still puzzled.

'It almost happens, but you do something to stop it.'

'It could happen or it nearly happens,' I said, thinking it was weird that such a small word could mean so many things.

'Just in case is better,' said Eve, hugging herself because she was cold. 'There are lots of things that could nearly happen. Think of it as just in case.' We didn't close the door, but no birds flew in while we were there. I couldn't hear any birds at all.

Rachel turned and saw us in the porch.

'What are you doing in there?' she said. 'Come on.'

We went back down the steps doing the same football photo pose and returned to the library, where a queue of people with books in their hands had formed.

'Can't a woman have a bit of time off?' said Rachel under her breath, fiddling in her pocket for the key.

We left her behind the enquiries desk swiping people's cards with her bar-code reader like she was waving a new kind of magic wand, and headed up to the house.

The top room was appearing like a jigsaw. When the bed was uncovered, I sat down and wondered about the last person who had slept in it. Maybe it was the old man who used to own the house. I thought about getting out the red journal and reading it, but I was planning to save it for after Eve had left. I had been making up the next bit of the story in my head all day.

After I had shifted the last cardboard box out to the skip and dusted off the final dining-room chair, I stood in the middle of the floor with my hands on my hips and looked around. It felt strange now that the room was so empty. If I closed my eyes, I could imagine the stuff was still there, all around me. The sweet smell still hung about, even though the window had been open all day. I looked out at the hillside. The curtains were blowing in the autumn breeze. It had stopped raining and the afternoon sunlight was playing with dirty floorboards. I turned and saw that the only thing left apart from the bed was the matchbox next to the fireplace. I stuffed it in my pocket, telling myself that then the room would be empty. I was about to lift the loose tiles and retrieve the red book when Eve appeared, cigarette in hand.

'Are you going to get those references for me?' she said.

'Yeah, sure,' I lied. 'Just need to send a couple of emails, that's all.'

'Fine. I'm off now.' She was about to head downstairs again. I didn't mean to ask her but suddenly I did, in spite of myself.

'Why did you take those notebooks to the library?'

'What? Oh, Rachel wants them for her research.'

'Research?'

'Into the history of the house,' she replied. 'Girls who came here and other stuff.'

'What other stuff?'

'The stories that the house is haunted.'

'Like Bernie said?'

'Load of rubbish. But you can ask her about it if you want.'

I shrugged. 'I'm not bothered about stories,' I told her, but after she had gone, I carried the red journal down to the lake and sat under a tree with spreading branches so I was completely hidden. This is what it said next.

It was dark but I've worked out how to open the shutters. I got Doris to steal this notebook for me from the office so I would have something to do while I'm in here, because I felt like I was going to float away the last time. My head feels funny. I wouldn't let myself think about what she said at first. But I must have done something wrong or she wouldn't have shut me in here.

I tried to imagine Doris, the author of the book of bible verses, stealing the red journal I was holding. Then I carried on reading, gripped by the book as if it was one of those thrillers with a murder every other page. There was a list next.

Here are the things that are wrong with me. 1) I'm funny in the head. 2) I love R the same as when I look up at the sky and see the

*stars. 3) drinking. 4) dressing up. I'm not supposed to love girls so
I have to stay up here and think about being a young lady.*

I snapped the journal shut. The person writing in the book
had been in love with the librarian.

Suddenly feeling like I shouldn't be reading it, I looked up at
the branches of the tree which were making a latticed window
with pieces of dark blue sky in between their fingers. I remembered an article I had read on the front of the *Sun*, which said
'Lesbians Stole My Baby' and had a picture of two women smiling
at the camera. A woman I shared with once in prison was a lesbian.
She had a picture of Sigourney Weaver in *Alien*, though she never
tried it on with me. I couldn't stop myself opening the journal
and turning the pages again.

*I feel dizzy. I'm not allowed any food until I go and tell her. She
says I am deviant but that I can get married and be normal again
and that I have to learn to say it: deviant, married, normal. But I
don't want to say it because I don't feel like a chain of words. I feel
like spreading my arms wide and flying away. I thought about kissing
Isabelle next to the mixer and I'm not supposed to do that. I lay
on the floor and looked up at the ceiling for a while. There's a crack
in one corner that looks like a monster's face. She says I won't be
able to keep it up for long. Stage one is saying the words, she said.
Stage two is changing and becoming a young lady again. I feel like
a Danish swirl that's been left too long on the shelf and has gone
stale around the edges.*

It had started to get dark and I could hardly make out the
words any more. The first bit of writing stopped abruptly and
now there was a new entry in a different kind of pen. I held the
book close to my face so I could see it.

*I fell asleep after that and dreamt that I kissed Rachel in a tent.
There was a musty-smelling blanket. It was completely dark so we
couldn't see each other. I had to go into her office. I said the words
under my breath, deviant, married, normal, so it sounded like the
breeze had taken my words away. She said that's better and let me
have a sandwich. But then . . .*

It was too dark to carry on. I leant against the tree trunk and jammed my hands into my pockets because I was cold. My fingers met the box of matches from earlier. Just like the matches that had got me into so much trouble. I closed my eyes and there I was with Neil, waiting on the stairs. Me with a hair slide and a cuddly mouse, Neil with his Action Man. There was the smell of burnt toast in the air and there was the beige carpet under our feet as we looked down at the front door. I was clutching my mouse tight round the neck and willing the doorbell to ring. That day at Kevin's was the first time I did it. I had stuffed the matchbox into my pocket then too.

I remembered going on and on about having my own room until my dad said I could have the box room by the bathroom. At the weekend, he painted it and moved my bed in there. The next day I came home from school and lay on the bed for a while thinking how great it was. My brother had to walk home the long way with his friend's mum. I heard her bang on the door and then open it with the spare key when she didn't get a reply.

'Where's Dad?' my brother said when she had gone.

'I don't know,' I said. My dad was usually cooking us cheese on toast and beans for dinner by now and we'd all eat it round the small table in the front room. Then the phone rang. I picked up the receiver and performed my celebration dance at my brother who had got there too late again. I flashed my flat chest at him, moved my bum around and stuck my tongue out. He hung around to find out who it was.

'Hello,' I said into the phone, trying to sound grown up.

'Is your mum there?' a voice said.

'My mum doesn't live with us. She lives with Kevin. We go and see her on Saturdays but we can't stop there because Kevin's not got enough room. Kevin's got three boys,' I said without stopping for breath. The voice on the other end of the phone paused.

'Your dad's in the hospital,' it said. 'Can your neighbour drive you over or can you get hold of your mum?'

I thought about Mr Jeffers our neighbour who never wore

shoes. He had a hearing aid and waved his stick at anyone who came to the door.

'Our neighbour is too old,' I said.

'Your mum then,' said the voice patiently. 'Have you got your mum's number, pet?'

I read out Kevin's number from the back of an envelope. Underneath the word 'Kevin' my dad had written, 'The arsehole.' I thought it was funny and I giggled into the phone.

'Dad's in the hospital,' I said to my brother after I had replaced the phone carefully.

'Has he broken his leg?' my brother said. Someone in his class had broken his leg by falling out of a tree. But I had forgotten to ask.

My mum arrived to pick us up half an hour later. We waited for her on the stairs. I had packed my school bag with emergency things: my favourite hair slide, my toy mouse and my Etch-a-Sketch. My brother had stuffed a pocket full of toy soldiers and was holding his Action Man and a tank tightly in his fists.

After we had seen my dad in the hospital, we arrived at Kevin's flat and sat on the sofa. Bonny the Alsatian padded up to me and put her head on my lap, so I could stroke her ears. Kevin's three sons, all ginger-haired like their dad, stood and gazed at us. They looked like mini-Kevins, or stairs, standing next to each other in height order, top, middle, bottom. Someone could have used their heads to climb up to somewhere.

That night I fed Bonny chocolate biscuits from the cookie jar in Kevin's kitchen which was shaped like a plastic chef, with a moustache, a white hat and chequered trousers. It made noises like a pig when you lifted the lid. It reminded me of the birthday card I got when I was ten, which sang 'Happy Birthday' when you opened it up. If you did it really quickly over and over, it sounded like hiccups. I put the cookie jar on the floor and Bonny stuck her nose in it and ate the biscuits one at a time, crunching them with her teeth so loudly that I was frightened my mum would hear, but she didn't. No one stirred, so I sat with my back against a cupboard and played flying matches for a bit. Then I

93

tried the new game I had been planning. I held my hand over the flame to see how long I could do it. I made myself cry and I had to hold my palm under the tap afterwards, with Bonny licking my leg, but I counted five seconds: one, two, three, four, five. That was the first time.

I looked up at the bits of star-filled sky framed by the lattice of branches. It almost seemed as if the stars were fruits hanging just above my head or part of a stained-glass window strung across the tree. I was freezing. I ducked under the branches and ran back up to the empty house. It was very dark, but I climbed the stairs to the top room and hid the book under the tiles again, telling myself I wouldn't read any more, like a teenager promising not to masturbate.

13

When I got in that evening, I noticed a yellowing piece of paper on the table. I rubbed my arms against the cold and picked it up. It unfolded like a map. It was old, and the folds had almost worn right through. I laid it out in front of me carefully. The writing was hard to make out because it was old-fashioned. *Deed of Sale*, it said along the top in curly letters. Underneath that: *John Brown, Farmer, 3rd March AD 1832. The Grey Farm House, Eade Village. Built on remains of St Mary's Church.* I scanned the rest of it. There were details about land and equipment and signatures at the bottom. Just then the door opened and I heard someone shouting goodbye. Rachel was coming in with her shopping. I quickly refolded the document and went to help her.

I watched her carefully as she fiddled with the bags in the kitchen, thinking about the red journal.

'What are you looking so serious for?' she said.

I examined her face and didn't say anything. I couldn't bring myself to ask her about what I had read under the tree. I thought of the front page of the *Sun* again: 'Lesbians Stole My Baby'. Rachel didn't look like one of the women in the picture. I worried for a moment about staying in the apartment with her in case she was waiting to make a move on me, but then I told myself not to be stupid. If she was pregnant when she was at the house she must have shagged some bloke so she couldn't have been one then, could she?

When the shopping was put away, Rachel lifted the crate of notebooks onto the sofa.

'These are wonderful,' she said, shaking her head in disbelief. I wandered around her lounge, feeling awkward and strange. The moon was hanging above the lake, yellow and beautiful. Suddenly, I could feel Rachel coming up behind me. She grabbed my wrist and I jumped.

'What happened to you?' she said lightly, looking at some new scratches on the back of my hand.

'Oh, doing the garden. I got scratched,' I lied. I didn't look at her while I said it.

'There's some antiseptic in the bathroom. Dab some of that on it.'

'OK,' I said. 'Thanks.' I took my hand away.

She went over to the coffee table and began to flick through a couple of notebooks. 'Which ones have you looked at already?' she asked.

I showed her, fishing the books I recognised out of the box. She looked at the bible verses Doris had written as if she was reading a letter from someone special.

'Doris,' she said. She tipped her head on one side as if she was struggling to remember. 'She was small and she liked to knit.' A sad, slow smile spread across her face. 'And which one am I in?' she said, eager as a little girl.

I smiled at her. I couldn't help it. I picked up the small green one and found the page with *Spring 1959* at the top. She read it quickly: *Harriet Neil (homosexual), Doris Evering (stealing), Marjory Makepeace (foul mouth), Joyce White (backward), Rachel Immanuel (pregnant).* There were arrival and departure dates too in a neat column at the edge of each page. When she turned the page, I could no longer see the book because she lifted it close to her face. Whatever it said made her sad. There were tears in her eyes.

'Stupid old woman,' she said to herself and snapped the book shut. Then she suddenly became cheerful again. Without saying anything else about it, she started rooting around, opening books at random and exclaiming at the dates.

'Shouldn't we give them to someone?' I said.

'Like who?'

'I don't know. Whoever was in charge.'

'It was run by the church but they employed women who lived in the village.'

'So there isn't anyone to give them to?'

'The librarian is usually the best person,' Rachel said, beaming at her own joke and patting herself on the chest as if someone had just made her a prefect.

I was so enchanted by the notebooks that I had forgotten about my arm. My sleeve was pushed back slightly, revealing more scratches, as if I was some kind of weird piece of art that was being uncovered bit by bit.

'You really hurt yourself badly doing the gardening, didn't you?'

'Yeah,' I said. I pulled my sleeve down over my hand again as she fetched a box from next to the stereo that I hadn't seen before. It was full of papers.

'I've got all this to go through,' she said when she had shifted herself onto the sofa. 'And now the notebooks as well. Keep me busy.' She looked at me sideways. I could tell she wanted me to help. I stared at the wall for a while instead, pretending not to be bothered about what she was doing, but eventually I became too curious not to ask.

'What is all that?' I said.

'Funny you should ask,' said Rachel, beaming at me because she had been waiting for me to say it. 'Make me a cup of tea and I'll tell you about it.'

'I'm not bothered,' I said automatically, but I went into the tiny kitchen and filled the kettle anyway.

'And bring me some of that apple cake,' she called. 'It's in the tin.'

'I'm making a display about the house,' Rachel said when I handed over her tea. I took a bite out of the apple cake and it was one of the most wonderful things I had ever tasted. I stared at it in surprise.

'For the library?'

'Yep. Bits about its history. That kind of thing.'

'Can I look?' I said in spite of myself. I peered over her shoulder. She was holding the map-like document I had been looking at earlier with *Deed of Sale* along the top. I had a closer look this time. Rachel dusted away the crumbs and spread it out over the coffee table so I could study it.

'It's amazing,' I said. I felt as if I was looking at history all of a sudden.

'He owned all the land down to the lake and more behind it,' Rachel said. 'Look at this one.' She unfolded another large sheet. I leant over it so I could make out the words: *6th November AD 1849. I, John Brown, bequeath my house to the church for the upkeep of unfortunate or feeble-minded girls in memory of my daughter, my land to become common land.* There were the same details of the house and its equipment as before. One phrase stayed in my head: *unfortunate or feeble-minded girls.* The words sounded foreign and exotic. I imagined the girls at the house: in the hall, on the stairs, in the top room, the kitchen, the garden, and the lounge where all the books had been.

'Interesting, isn't it?' said Rachel, glancing at me slyly.

'What else is there?' I said, looking at the pile again. Rachel pulled out a postcard with a really old picture of the house, taken from the bottom of the hill near the lake. I was astonished for a moment because it looked almost the same as it had when I left it that afternoon. It was so still and silent, just like it always was.

'That's about 1920. Something like that anyway,' Rachel said. 'What's it say on the back?'

I turned it over. '1922,' I read.

'There you go then,' she said. 'I expect you're bored now.' She began to collect the papers together again just as I was about to ask her if I could look all the way through. I shrugged and leant back against the sofa.

'I'll tell you all about the house sometime,' Rachel said.

I held on to my cuffs and looked at my lap. 'What it was like when you were in there, you mean?'

She looked at me intensely for a moment. 'Not just that.'

'I'm not bothered, like I said,' I told her and went back to my cake. 'This is gorgeous,' I said. 'Did you make it?'

'Yes.'

'Is it out of a book?' I said. I remembered as I said it that I was supposed to know about cakes, but Rachel didn't seem to care. She reached up to one of her shelves and handed me a scrapbook. It contained page after page of cake recipes, all written out by hand, starting from the most simple sponges to ornate pineapple and cherry brandy puddings or chocolate and coffee desserts. Sometimes they were splattered with food, as if someone had intended to make tiny illustrations of the ingredients.

'Did you make this?' I said, looking at a page with step-by-step instructions for banana bread.

Rachel smiled and sipped her tea. 'No, it was a friend of mine. You'll meet her,' she said eventually. 'And she gave you the book?' I said, turning the pages.

'Yes,' Rachel said. 'It was a long time ago now.'

'What's your friend called?'

Without saying anything else, she put down her tea and wheeled herself into the library. I heard her going down the ramp into the Millennium Kitchen. While I was waiting for her, I flicked through the cake book, thinking that if I could somehow memorise the recipes, then I wouldn't need to worry about the references, but I realised I was being stupid. I was going to be found out as soon as Eve asked me to hand her a whisk and a sieve and to beat up an egg.

When Rachel came back, she had a CD ROM and a large brown book similar to the cake scrapbook in her lap. She handed me the CD. It had pictures of several lighthouses on the front, merged into each other artistically, and the words *The Lighthouse Foundation World Encyclopaedia* in a smart purple box. I turned it over and read the back. 'For the protection and preservation of lighthouses and those who work in them,' I read, 'fascinating information on lighthouses from all over the world. System requirements: suitable for use with an Apple Macintosh OS 9 and above. Launch in browser.'

'Is it good?' I said, wondering why Rachel was showing it to me. She was beaming like the Cheshire cat from the children's corner and sipping her tea again. Her eyes were dancing.

'Look who it's by,' she said.

I looked right at the bottom at print so small I had to hold it close to my face to read it.

'Graphic design and programming by—'

'No. Not that bit. Under that.'

'Picture and text research and compilation: Alexandra French.'

'That's her. The same person who made me the cake scrapbook. We're good friends.' She held up the old brown book. There was a picture of a lighthouse on the front. 'The lighthouses used to be in books before they were on CD,' Rachel said. 'These encyclopaedias came out every few years and were compiled by Jemima Faraday.' I was sure I had heard that name before but I couldn't remember where.

'Jemima died in the sixties. When she was younger she had a thick ginger plait down to her waist,' Rachel was saying. 'She got Alex the job at the Lighthouse Foundation.' She turned the slightly crumpled pages, revealing more photographs. 'It was the old lighthouse encyclopaedias that gave Alex the idea for making the cake book.'

I wondered if Alex the lighthouse researcher, who had once put together Rachel's cake book, was the same wayward girl who had written in the red journal. Hadn't she mentioned cakes? Cakes can make you bad and turn you into a man, something like that anyway.

'Alex does the CD ROM and teaches cake-making?' I said, trying to piece it all together. What kind of weird person would do that?

'Yep. Look.' Rachel opened the green notebook and found the list which included her own name. She turned to the page that had brought tears to her eyes earlier and showed me. *Alexandra French (homosexual).* I didn't know what to say.

We heard banging in the Millennium Kitchen.

'Silver surfers night,' Rachel said by way of explanation. 'Eve will be back soon.'

100

I suddenly felt awkward hanging around with Rachel. I wasn't sure why she wanted me to know about all of this stuff but it made me feel funny. I stood up and waved the CD in the air.

'Can I have a go on this?' I said.

'If you like, none of the surfers have turned up yet.'

I went down into the Millennium Kitchen. Apart from Monica behind the counter, there was no one there. I sat down in front of one of the computers and I slipped the lighthouse CD into the drive. An index of countries arranged by continent filled the screen, with little maps for illustrations. *Click to view further information*, it said at the top. I scrolled through the lists until I got to the Eade Village lighthouse. I clicked on the link and a picture appeared. It looked as if it had been taken a long time ago. I scrolled down for the date: *1959. To see inside, click here.* I clicked again and the inside of the lighthouse appeared in front of me. This time the pictures were more modern. I looked at the iron staircase and then at each room. There was a foghorn, a kitchen and bunk beds and then finally the lamp which perched on top of a revolving plate like an eye. I was staring at the screen and thinking of Alexandra the lighthouse researcher, locked in a room with her pen, dreaming about Rachel, when Eve came down the ramp.

'You're in here,' she said. 'Looking at Alex's CD? Good, isn't it?'

'Yep,' I said. I wanted to ask her if Rachel and the lighthouse researcher had had some kind of thing together but it wasn't the sort of question you could just come out with.

'Dinner's ready,' Eve said when I didn't say anything else.

'OK.' The curved rooms inside the Eade Village light were flashing on the screen. Just then, three silver surfers came in and began chatting to Monica.

'Sent off for those references?' Eve asked as we went into the sitting room.

'Er. Yes, of course,' I lied.

That night when I fell asleep, I thought about Alex writing in the red journal and making the recipe book for Rachel. I imagined I was under the tree with latticed branches again, but this time I began to dream about my dad and me outside in the summer, my brother with his football, the flare of the first match and my mum and dad arguing through the walls.

14

I set off for the house just as Rachel was letting the first borrowers in to choose their books. I was still thinking about my dad as I climbed the hill. When I got there, I couldn't stop myself going over to the fireplace and checking that the red notebook was where I had left it, as if it contained my story and not someone else's. When I heard Eve's car pulling out of the drive later, I moved the tiles away again, lay on the bed and read the next few pages:

She said that's better and let me have a sandwich. But then I had to come up here again. I am supposed to think about what it means to be a young lady. Duty is the first thing I had to think about. I have to tell her what it means. I tried to paint the word on the inside of my head. Duty. I thought of the Queen, sitting on a throne surrounded by flowers, rabbits, grass, loaves of bread. I thought about being in a car and gazing at a map of the countryside, trying to decide where to go next to see hedges, old twisted trees, cows in fields. I thought of my mum and dad in the front seats, not in front of the television, my mum pointing out the way, my dad's thick red neck, the pretty white flowers outside the window. My hands smelt of soap. Next to me was the picnic hamper. Through the window, I saw a ruined country church with a tall spire and wondered if God was still living inside. When she asked me again, I said: the Queen, the country, my mum and dad, God. She smiled and I got soup and crackers. I've told R how I feel about her and she . . .

Eve got back sooner than I thought she would. Reluctantly, I pushed the book back into its hole next to the fireplace and pretended that I had been cleaning the window. When Eve came upstairs, I was looking out at the mist. I turned round to find her inspecting one of the walls. She was holding a plastic wallpaper steamer.

'Daydreaming?' she said.

'Thinking,' I said.

'Same thing,' she said and handed me the steamer.

'But the electricity isn't on yet,' I said.

'Bernie's going to run a cable from the generator on the back of the truck,' she said. 'Fill this up with water. Then plug it into the extension lead and chuck the cable out of the window.'

I felt as if I was hatching an elaborate escape plan and was going to abseil down the side of the house as I tossed the lead down to Bernie. Either that or Bernie was the witch and I was Rapunzel letting down my hair.

Soon there were bits of wallpaper all around my feet. I kept going, scraping and peeling, unwrapping the room as if I was inside a parcel. When I pulled a big piece off one wall, I stood back in amazement, because underneath was a blue and red painting. I quickly peeled away more paper. Some of the paint had come away, but I could still see the lines which were meant to be the sea. There were fish swimming under the water, little boats with sails and the lighthouse with the sun setting behind it. I called to Eve and Bernie to come and look, feeling like one of the people on the telly who find cave paintings. They stood and shook their heads.

'The things you find,' said Bernie. He wiped a hand across his face and went back downstairs, just as a van pulled up outside.

'It's the electrician again,' Eve said. 'Coming to turn us on. Finally.'

After all the wallpaper was in bin bags, I lifted the paint out of Eve's car boot. I left the lighthouse and the sunset picture until last. I worked from one side of it right the way round the room to the other, because I was hoping Eve would tell me not to paint over it, but when she came up to watch me, she folded her arms and said, 'Give that bit an extra coat to get rid of it.'

'OK,' I said and closed my eyes so I could think about what the room would be like when it was full of furniture.

'What are you doing?'

'Nothing.'

'Well, wake up, because I'm taking Bernie with me into town to the showroom to look at cookers. I want the undercoat done by the end of today.'

After the Nissan had pulled out of the driveway, I finished the painting. Then I took the red journal with me and went down to the kitchen to have a break. The sink was standing on its own, looking lonely, with all its pipes revealed like private parts. Everything else was gone. At least the electricity was working now. Out in the hallway I found a socket for the kettle Eve had bought, lined up tea bags, milk, sugar, cup and spoon next to it in a row and made tea. Then I remembered something. I ran out to my car and opened the boot. I found the photos, more than one film's worth stuffed inside a single Boots envelope. I took them back into the house with me.

It was getting dark already, so I turned on the lights. I left the journal unopened on the floor and looked through the pictures while I drank my tea. My mum and Kevin in Majorca, my dad, Bonny, my brother in his army uniform, me and my school friends, a stupid one of me pulling a face. I spread the photos out so I could see them better. There were over fifty of them, some of them blurred and with the people caught before they could pose, or with red-eye or too close to the camera. I sat with them around me like a skirt. I still had the box of matches in my pocket. I struck one and watched it burn. After one had gone out, I lit another. I did it three times, then I was ready.

I struck another match, waited until it was burning steadily and held my hand over it. My eyes watered but I kept it there, playing the game I used to play when I was a kid to see how long I could stand it. When the match went out, there was a red mark in the middle of my palm, as if someone had picked me as the murderer in wink murder. I pulled off my jumper, lit another match and held it under my arm this time. I did it four times, so I had four red marks in a neat line, one after the other. I couldn't feel it any more after the first two. It was heady, like smoking a joint or jumping off a diving board.

Afterwards, I leant back against the wall with my eyes closed and held on to the feeling for as long as I could. I was still sitting there, with the photos around me, when I heard the Nissan pull up outside. I swept the photos together so that they hid the red book, jumped up and pulled on my sweater. I was stuffing the matches into my pocket when they came in.

'Looking at photos?' Eve said mildly. Bernie was behind her.

'We've ordered an oven for three weeks. Should give us enough time,' he said.

'Have you finished the top room?' said Eve.

'Yes,' I said. 'It's done.'

'Good,' she said. She and Bernie went into the kitchen and they stood surveying the space. Eve pointed out what would go where and they talked about it in low voices.

'So imagine the cooker is there already,' Eve was saying. 'The fridge will have to be where?'

I put my hand out to touch the photos and reassure myself that the journal was still there. Then I leant back against the wall and let the voices in the kitchen murmur around my head but after a while the burns got too much, and I ran upstairs, taking the journal with me. I ran into the bathroom to hold my arm under the cold tap. I kept it there until it went numb.

'What are you doing, Ricky?' Eve called. I heard the front door slam.

'Nothing.'

'Your photos are still on the floor down here.'

'OK.'

'Bernie's gone and I'm going back to the library now. Are you coming?'

I didn't want to hang around with her and Rachel, I wanted to be on my own, so I made an excuse.

'I forgot to clean the fireplace. I'll walk home after I've done it.' There was a pause from the hallway below. When she answered, she sounded surprised that I was volunteering to stay but she bought my excuse.

'Oh. OK. See you later then.' The door slammed for a second time and I was on my own again.

I wandered into the top room and sat down next to the already clean fireplace. I rested my chin on my hands before I flicked through the red book, but I didn't read any more. I stared at the pages but the words just danced out of my way. My head was full of me as a little girl, the flat, the garden, my brother's football, my dad and the flying matches. I had been promising to tell myself this story and now I did, as if I was writing in the red book myself.

I think my dad liked me best when I was small. He used to tell me things. One hot midsummer afternoon when I was nearly eight, he took me out onto the grass in front of the flats where my brother was doing keepy upies with his football. The world was dry as an old skeleton. We sat down on the concrete path and he got a match out of a box and held it in front of me.

'A whole forest of thousands of trees can go up just because of this, Ricky,' he said. 'See them fireworks the council put on?'

I nodded. I remembered them swooping up into the air like birds on fire in a desperate final flight.

'One of these,' he said, waving the match. Then he lit a cigarette out of habit and I saw the match that could burn down forests and make fireworks fly shaken out in his big hand. The blue smoke curled around our heads. The day was so hot it felt as if it was standing completely still. My brother had forgotten about his football now and had gone back up the stairs to the flat to ask my mum for a can of Coke.

I waited to hear more while he took another drag and I looked at the tattoo on his arm as he raised his hand to his lips. It was a tiger with its mouth open, because he was born in the year of the tiger. My mum said he should have been born in the year of the rat after she found out he was seeing the woman in the hairdressers', and that she might take him down to get the other

arm done with a rat on it, but I didn't know about any of that
then. I looked at how the faded colours blended into his arm
under the hairs. Above us, my brother was running along the
balcony, pretending to be a rock star. He was mixing together
the words he could remember from 'Size of a Cow' and 'Altogether
Now', songs on the *BP Big Hits* album my dad had got free at
the garage.

My dad put his cigarette out on the path next to him. Then he
struck another match and sent it tumbling over and over in a
smooth triple dive. It fell gracefully and singed the grass around
it before it went out. We watched in silence. As the heat and the
singing went on above us, he clutched my small wrist and helped
me to hold my own unlit match. He showed me how to move
my thumb and finger and send it tumbling over itself. At first
they landed around my feet, but then one took flight and sailed
away from me into the air, so he held my hand while I lit one,
and I did it again. I watched the flame fly across the grass and I
laughed. My brother began another chorus, as if he was hovering
above shepherds on a Christmas card. I heard the door open
above us just as my dad was helping me to strike another match.
My mum leant over the railings.

'Your dinner's ready,' she said.

My dad clamped his hand on my arm to stop me but it was
too late, I had already let the match go and it went tumbling over
the grass to join its friends.

'Get inside, Neil,' she said to my brother. The singing stopped.
'What the hell are you doing?' she said.

Reluctantly my dad and I climbed the hot stairs and went into
the flat. They rowed about the matches all through dinner.
Afterwards it turned into a row about the second-hand washing
machine my dad had bought and how it didn't work unless you
kicked the door a few seconds after you closed it. Neil was outside
with his football again. I lay on my bed and thought about the
tumbling lights, while their voices went up and down through
the thin walls.

*　　　*　　　*

The first time I saw my dad do it was a few years later, when I was twelve and my mum had gone to live with Kevin. My dad was holding a match under the palm of his hand to see how long he could stand it.

'Don't tell your teachers,' he said, and he looked worried, as if I had caught him reading porno. I often fell asleep thinking about the look on my dad's face when I caught him with the porno matches.

Worse was the time just after my dad's accident. We had a home help called Janet who said she could only come once a fortnight because of Margaret Thatcher, which made me think of Maggie ill in bed while Janet cooked her shepherd's pie and did her hoovering. I told her that she was wrong because John Major was in charge now and she said she was going to speak to social services to see if she could come more often and it wouldn't be long. While Neil was out at cadets, she taught me things like how to heat up frozen pizza, how to mix up egg and cheese to make omelettes, how to defrost a ready meal and how to pour powder into the washing machine. I felt grown up. I showed her how you had to count to five after you pressed start and then kick the door. I did the sideways karate kick from the telly that I had been practising on Neil.

The day it happened Janet had come round to tell me that social services had cut back and she had lost her job so we couldn't have a home help any more.

'Get your mum to come in and help, love,' she said to me sadly and patted my face. When she had gone, I went in to find my dad.

'Janet's not coming any more,' I began. Then I saw that my dad was sitting in front of the mirror with his sleeve rolled up. He had been running a kitchen knife lightly over his arm. He turned round when I came in and then looked at me with frightened wet eyes. I ran out of the room and went and lay face down on my bed and cried. I wasn't sure if it was about Janet or about the kitchen knife, but I cried anyway. He came and stood in the doorway with his sleeve still rolled up.

'It's all right. Don't tell anyone,' he said, but I wouldn't stop crying, so he went away again. I heard him fumbling in the bathroom with the TCP. Later I got up and cooked frozen pizza and hung our clothes out on the plastic dryer, like Janet had told me. My dad came into the front room but Neil was there in his cadets uniform, so he didn't say anything.

After dinner, I took some candles into my room and a box of matches. I lit them, made two pools of wax on my bedside table and made the candles stand up in them, so I could sit on my bed and watch the patterns they made. There was smoke, a thin trail of it, which started at the top of the flame. If I blew them gently but not too hard, the little lights danced like ballerinas. I watched the flames until my eyelids were tattooed with them and I had to blow them out because I was falling asleep.

Whenever I felt upset about my dad being ill, I would get the matches and light the candles so that I could watch the ballerinas dance. I spent my lunch money on candles sometimes after we had run out so that I could keep the dancers by my bed. They were like my guardian angels. And after that, when my dad did something stupid or if the dinner had gone wrong and got burnt or when my dad laid into my brother, or sometimes just for fun, I went back to the tumbling match game that my dad had taught me. I sat on the floor with my back against the bed and my knees hunched up and I flicked one match after another until a whole box had gone. I watched them tumble over and over like dying fairies.

15

April 1959

The wind had been tearing about the hillside all afternoon, weaving in and out of the trees by the lake, rushing down to the beach, past the church with the thatched roof, the Old Vicarage, where Mrs Johnson the dog breeder lived, the library and out towards the lighthouse. The sea itself was jumping around excitedly like a child waiting for presents. That morning Doris had been into the office next to the front door to search for pencils. She found a silver one and was holding it to her chest in delight when she opened a drawer and saw a stack of notebooks. And there, spread out on the desk, was the record book where the names were written. She closed the drawer with a snap, read *Doris Evering (stealing)* and flipped the book shut without reading any more.

Still clutching the silver pencil, she walked out onto the curve of the hill to see if she could spot the car approaching. She watched the trees bending their heads like mourners by the lake and the surface turning murky as it reflected the sky. It was a deep metallic grey, almost purple. It looked like a cauldron full of magic spells. The wind made her feel alive. First thing, when she woke, she had seen a rainbow arching across the dark sky in the distance and the few rays of light had turned the clouds silver. She looked around to see if the rainbow was still there, but now there was no sunshine. No car came either. She went back inside again to hide her new pencil under her mattress, her wind-bitten eyes shining. Then she sat on her bed and returned to her knitting needles, wondering with each stitch what the new girl would be like.

Before lunch, Joyce had been in the kitchen garden, picking tulips from under the sycamore trees to make an arrangement for the table. She looked up at the sky and it felt as if it might fall on her head. She stood with her mouth open, her tongue stuck out ready and her arms stretched. Her auburn hair touched her shoulders lightly and she grasped the flowers tight in one hand, waiting for the rain to fall on her face. But her face stayed dry and now the wind had died down to a whisper and the air felt warm and moist, as if someone had wrapped her in an invisible blanket. She hurried back inside with her flowers, disappointed. It felt as if they were waiting for something important to happen but it was only the new girl, whose car still hadn't arrived.

After lunch and the dishes, she sat on the stool in the kitchen and looked out at the afternoon with her hands on her lap, so that when the rain did start she could run outside again and tip her head heavenwards.

She was still there later when, in the lounge, Marjory stacked up all the wood they needed for the next two days by the grate and watched the flames wrapping their arms round an old log, hugging it with fiery love. When she and Doris had lit the kindling that morning, the wind had rushed down the chimney and blown the smoke about so that it made her cough and she was frightened the flames would shoot out of the grate, but now the wind was ominously quiet. Marjory wondered if the new girl would wait out the storm and come tomorrow instead. She added another log and watched it be embraced, the hugging orange and yellow arms carefully squeezing and burning, just as rain began to throw itself against the windows of the house.

'Bugger it,' she said, because the noise had startled her. The rain hit the grass, the stone path that curved round the hill, the roofs of the houses in the village and the tin-coloured surface of the lake like thousands of tiny wet soldiers with parachutes, and the first crack of distant thunder rattled across the sky. The lightning had been far out to sea but the next time it would be closer, darting about the top of the lighthouse and illuminating the brown rocks for a moment in a purple glare. Mrs Brown wasn't about so Marjory went over to the armchair with the hollow seat and felt around inside for her radio. She fiddled with the controls, trying to find some music to drown out the rain.

Meanwhile Harriet, who was the oldest, was looking out of the window in the little yellow office when the sky broke open like an egg. She thought the thunder sounded like someone banging a fist into the ground. She watched the rain with a solemn face.

'I knew there was going to be another storm,' she said sadly to her misty half-reflection in the window, which was almost a mirror with the silver-grey sky behind it. 'We'll never get to go out to the light if it carries on like this,' she continued. She banged her fist down on the desk next to her so she could hear if it really did sound like thunder, just as a bolt of lightning turned the window purple and her own miniature thunderclap was echoed by another, like God answering her prayer.

'The new girl will get caught in it,' she added, as if it was a prophecy, turning back to her reflection and thinking about magic mirrors that could tell people how beautiful they were.

'Am I beautiful?' she said to the hazy image of her face with the storm behind it and the rain running down the pane. Then she banged her fist on the desk again.

It was only the middle of the afternoon, but it seemed like evening already as the storm took Eade Village by the shoulders and shook it. At the Old Vicarage the dogs howled; at the library, Billy Burns the librarian pulled the curtains shut and wedged a woollen scarf in the crack under her door, to stop the cold getting in, then she went to make herself and her pregnant assistant a cup of hot chocolate, so they could sit behind the returns desk with their book-mending tape and listen to the rain drumming on the roof like a bored man with a hundred thousand tapping fingers.

Just then the pastor's black car swung round up the hill towards the Haven. The rain was lashing against the windscreen and Alex didn't see the house until she was really close to it. It peered out at the dark afternoon like a frightened owl. More lightning came as she quickly said goodbye and climbed out of the car. She counted silently as she had been doing ever since the storm started. One, two, then the thunder sounded. The storm was almost directly overhead.

Hugging her coat round her, she ran towards the green gate the pastor had told her about, with Entrance painted on it in white letters, unfastened it and went inside. It opened onto an overrun walled garden. Creeping roses, big flat green and red leaves and spiky flowers were being blown about fiercely. As she ran along the stone path, she saw that here and there in the garden there were bits of ancient grey masonry and Alex remembered what the yellow leaflet had said about church ruins. A vine crawled over the wall and she saw that there were crumbling gravestones along one side. The path took her to another high gate, leading into a paved courtyard. A circle of stones enclosed a thin tree covered with bright leaves, which were getting tossed about in the wind. She was soaking wet now and wasn't sure where she was supposed to go. There was an outhouse at one end, meaning that the courtyard was completely enclosed. Then she spotted a door leading into the house. As she was trying the handle, it opened and a girl of about her own age looked round it into the rain.

'Bloody hell,' she said, because Alex had made her jump. 'Come on.' Taking Alex by the sleeve, she pulled her into the house.

Inside, Alex wiped the rain from her face with a towel the girl had fetched from the kitchen. She giggled and looked Alex up and down. An uneven brown fringe nearly covered her eyes.

'You're the new girl,' she said.

'Yes,' said Alex and shrugged off her coat. The girl hung it over the banisters and waited, shifting her weight from one leg to the other impatiently while Alex dried herself.

'I'm Marjory,' she said as she led her along a corridor. 'We've been waiting for you.' Marjory stopped and pointed to a door. 'In there.' Then she turned and walked away.

Alex went inside and found she was in a dormitory. Another young girl, who looked about thirteen, was sitting cross-legged on her bed with a ball of sky-blue wool and a pair of knitting needles. Whatever it was she was knitting was long and thin and snaked across the blankets.

'Hello,' she said. 'Your name's Alex.'

'How do you know?'

'Because you're the new girl. I'm Doris. That one's free,' she said, pointing to the bed by the window. Doris was small with hair like curtains which swung in front of her face. Outside, the weather was getting worse. Big drops of rain slammed against the pane.

'Thanks,' said Alex and put her bag down. She looked around as if she half expected Rachel to spring out of one of the cupboards. She wondered where she was.

'What are you here for?' said Doris. The knitting needles clicked together quickly.

'Dressing up as a boy. And other stuff.'

'That's bad. I'm only here for stealing. What job did you get?'

'What do you mean? I only just got here.' She opened her case so she could get changed and peeled off her sodden clothes. She was too wet not to.

'Everyone has a job,' Doris said.

Alex slipped on her blue dress gratefully.

'I light fires with Marjory and clean the laundry room,' Doris went on, finding a dropped stitch and beginning to click the needles again.

'What does Rachel do?'

'Oh well, she goes to the library of course.' She began another row, wrapping the wool round her hand as she did so.

'Why?'

'The librarianship,' said Doris.

Alex didn't understand but she nodded anyway. 'Is that where she is now?'

115

'Yes,' Doris said conversationally. 'Mrs Brown isn't here. She's at the Old Vicarage visiting her daughter.' She looked at the window. 'She'll get caught in the storm if she tries to come up now. I hope she does get caught. She made me miss dinner yesterday. You'll probably have to cook because you worked in town in a bakery.' She said it all in a rush without pausing for breath.

'Who's in charge?' Alex asked, surprised that the young girl knew so much about her.

'Mrs Brown is.'

'You said she isn't here.'.

'I know I did,' Doris said, starting a new row. 'Rose is around somewhere. She's the chubby one who's got a thing going with the boatman.'

Alex looked out at the rain and then at the knitting winding its way across the bed. 'What are you making?'

Doris opened her mouth to tell her, but Alex never did find out, because a young woman with a sad pale face and a brown plait came in and stood by the door. She looked about nineteen.

'Are you Alex?' she said. 'I've got to show you round.'

They went into the lounge, where Marjory and another girl sat next to a glowing fire. Marjory had a radio in her hand and her friend was leaning in close so she could listen. Elvis was singing 'Don't' in her ear. As soon as they came in, she held the radio behind her back, where Elvis continued to sing. The rain was beating against the window.

'Damn,' said Marjory. Her friend got up, went round the table so she could yank the curtains closed, then she sat down at the piano and pretended to play. Alex noticed that her hair was wet. The discordant notes echoed around the room for a while, accompanying Elvis and the sound of the weather. Alex was so nervous about meeting Rachel again that she hardly heard what was said.

'You've been outside, Joyce,' said the sad-faced girl at last but the girl at the piano just blinked at her. 'And you're not allowed radios. Where did you get it from?'

'Don't tell Mrs Brown,' said Marjory. 'It's mine.'

The sad girl frowned at her. 'Next time I will. I'm showing the new girl round now,' she said and closed the door.

'What do we do all day?' Alex asked as they climbed the stairs which curved round on themselves so that the landing was at the front of the house.

'We have classes in the laundry room,' said the girl. 'In the afternoons.'

When they reached the landing, they listened to the wind howling around the house as if it was trying to scoop it up and carry it off.

'You haven't told me your name,' Alex said after a moment.

'Harriet. My name's Harriet. As well as jobs and classes, we do educational visits. You're lucky. We're going out to the light soon.'

'The light?' Alex said.

'Lighthouse,' said Harriet. 'You haven't been down to the quay, have you?'

'No. I just got here,' Alex said.

Harriet pointed to the doors on that floor. 'Mrs Brown sleeps there. The attendants next to her.'

At the top of the curving stairs, a door opened onto a large room. The window was wide open. The pale yellow curtains were blowing around fiercely and the rain had made a puddle on the bare floorboards. There was only a single bed inside, with a patchwork quilt and thin white sheets. Alex noticed an ornate metal headrest and dragon's paws for feet. The only other furniture was a chair and a bookshelf, although there was space for much more. They went over to the window together.

'This is the baby room,' said Harriet, trying to yank the window shut, but it was very stiff. Alex looked up at the sky. Dark clouds were hanging so low she wanted to put her hand out and touch them.

'Why's it called that?'

'It's where people have their babies,' Harriet replied, standing back from the cold wind for a moment because her arms were sore from tugging. She wiped the rain from her face. 'It used to be just pregnant ones who came here. It got changed.' They stood and thought about it for a while, leaning against the wall and watching the storm rush into the room.

'How long have you been here?' Alex asked.

'Ages. I was here before any of the others that are here now.' The window looked over the hillside and through it Alex could see the lake at the bottom of the hill. The trees which circled it were blowing this way and that in the same cold wind that caught hold of her hair. Alex took a deep breath and leaned right out into the rain, just as a burst of lightning juddered across the grey clouds somewhere out at sea.

'What are you doing?' said Harriet's voice behind her. 'Don't do that.' But Alex ignored her for a second. Her hair and face were so rain- and wind-blasted that she could hardly open her eyes. Thunder rumbled in the distance. She could just make out a horse chestnut at one end of the house and, below her, the front door and the green gate where she had entered. A home-less crow was calling to the rain clouds from the top of the tree as if it could stop the rain by shouting at it. She imagined she was watching the pastor's car arriving now, with her in it, from above, as if she was a bird herself.

1956 Renault Dauphine, Alex had thought automatically when she had climbed into the back seat that morning, the engine where the boot should be. The sky had felt so low, it had pressed down on her head as if she was in a saucepan.

Harriet pulled her back in and with a violent tug shut the window at last.

'Don't do that,' she said again, looking at Alex's glowing face. 'You're wet again now.'

'I don't care,' Alex said, rubbing her sleeve across her face.

'I'll show you something,' Harriet said. She went over to the bookshelf and handed Alex an unusually thick book. It had a brown spine sewn with leather thread-work and was made out of rough black paper. It looked like a cross between a scrapbook and an encyclopaedia. Harriet reached out and turned the page for her.

'There,' she said. On the first page was a black and white picture of a lighthouse at the end of a trail of rocks. The sea was right out and the long rocky pathway led right up to the door. Underneath the photo, in uneven type on a slip of faded paper, Alex read, 'Eade Village Lighthouse. First light: 1830. Height: seventy-six feet. Type: promontory. Reach of lamp: twelve miles.'

'Are we really going out to see it?' Alex said.

'When the weather improves,' Harriet replied, rolling her eyes as if the raging storm outside was a stupid excuse. She flicked the pages impatiently. On each double spread was a different lighthouse. Underneath were the facts and figures.

'Right up to it?' Alex said.

'Yes. Right up to the top.' Suddenly the solemn girl looked excited. 'John's taking us in his boat. I can't wait.'

Alex studied the book, wondering who John was. There were lighthouses from all over the country. Some that looked like churches or castles and others which were simply thin poles with a lamp, perched on cliff edges.

'Good, isn't it?' said Harriet eagerly.

Alex nodded. 'Where did you get it?'

'Rachel brought it from the library.'

To hide her anxiety at the mention of Rachel's name, Alex looked inside the front cover to see who had published it. 'The Lighthouse Foundation,' it said, 'for the protection and preservation of lighthouses and those who work in them. Published 1933.' Then there was the address of the foundation in gold letters underneath. The book was over twenty-five years old already.

'When does Rachel get back?' she said, trying to sound as if she didn't care.

'Oh, she will stay with the librarian tonight. She does it quite often.'

Alex's heart sank like a Yorkshire pudding, she was so disappointed. She had been saving herself up for seeing Rachel all day, working out what she would say to her and how she might get her alone. She would have to wait another day before she saw her. She handed the book back to Harriet.

'Mrs Brown will stay in the village too,' Harriet said. 'When she gets back, you have to see her.'

'What happens then?' Alex said. Her guide hesitated. She was solemn again.

'It's not so bad,' she said. She looked at Alex as if she suddenly felt sick.

'What isn't?'

'What did you do to get sent?' Harriet asked, avoiding the question.

'Dressing up as a boy,' she said with a shrug, trying to sound as if it didn't matter. 'And . . .' She didn't know whether to admit the rest, but there was something in this sad girl's face that was longing for her to tell her everything. 'And drinking and I kissed someone,' she said. 'A woman.' She watched to see how her guide would react. 'What did you do?' But Harriet turned on her heels immediately and wouldn't look at her.

'It's dinner now,' she said. 'Cold meat again.'

They made their way back downstairs. As soon as they entered the dining room, a round woman in a dress that was too small for her came up and shook Alex's hand. Another crack of thunder echoed outside.

'I'm Rose. One of the attendants,' she said. 'Now sit down, everyone,' Rose continued. 'Let's say grace.' They all looked at her expectantly except for Joyce, who put her hands together and closed her eyes.

'One, two, three,' Rose counted.

'Grace,' said everyone, apart from Alex who looked around at them all in surprise and smiled. A couple of the others started to giggle and she saw that a man in a mackintosh was peering round the door. Rose blushed, but she looked pleased to see him all the same.

'John,' she said in surprise. This must be the boatman who would take them to the light, Alex thought.

'I got caught in the storm,' he said. 'I can't go on in this.'

'All right,' said the attendant. 'Come in, come in. It's just me tonight anyway.'

He took off his mac and they shuffled along the benches to make room for him, while Harriet handed round the plates of cheese, meat and pickle.

While the storm roamed around the outside of the house looking for a way in, Alex spent her first evening at the Haven in the lounge with the other residents, feeling frustrated at the lack of Rachel's presence. Rose and her boatman friend sat on the sofa together, doing a crossword from a newspaper he had found under the coal scuttle, and drinking hot chocolate, with a bit extra poured in from a silver flask in John's big coat pocket, because, Rose said, in this weather you needed it. The young women were arranged in the comfy chairs. Some of the others were reading, so, for a distraction, Alex went to find the lighthouse book. She shuddered when she re-entered the baby room and saw the iron-framed bed with its colourful patchwork quilt and dragon's feet. She grabbed the book and ran back downstairs, suddenly frightened. But the lounge was warm and she was relieved to go in and sit down next to Doris, who was knitting.

Harriet was badgering John about the boat trip and Rose had turned to defend him.

'It's only like this when Rose is on duty,' Doris whispered. 'Make the most of it.'

'You said we could go soon,' Harriet said urgently.

'Yes, dear,' said Rose. 'But look at the bloody weather.'

'You said bloody,' Joyce pointed out unnecessarily.

'No dinner for you,' said Marjory. They both giggled.

'Shut up,' Harriet snapped at them and turned back to John. 'You said—'

'I know what I said,' answered the boatman. 'I said if it's fine.'

'As soon as it's fine we'll go?'

'Yes,' he said. 'Now leave me in peace.'

Harriet reluctantly picked up the sketchbook she had with her and her set of coloured pens and settled back into the chair. John and Rose returned to their crossword. Alex wished again that

Rachel would come back, while next to her Doris started another row. She looked up and waved a needle at her.

'Agree with what she says. It makes it easier.'

'With who?'

'Mrs Brown. And think about the words she gives you so you've got something to say.'

'What words?'

'Depends. For dressing up I don't know what you'll get. It's supposed to cure you. I got cured.'

'You don't steal any more?' Alex asked.

'Not much anyway. I stole a pencil.'

'When?'

'This morning.'

'Maybe you're not cured after all.'

'Yes I am,' Doris said indignantly.

'If you're cured, why are you still here?' Marjory asked, over-hearing.

Doris wouldn't say anything else. She stopped knitting so she could wind her blue wool round her fingers. But earlier at dinner she had described each girl to Alex in a whisper as they chewed their ham and pickle. Alex looked around the room at them now: Marjory was at the house for constant swearing. Compulsive, Doris had said, as if it was a disease like measles. Her friend Joyce with the auburn hair was backward. Alex glanced at Harriet who sat alone in the armchair by the fire with her sketchbook, trying to draw the flames. Harriet had killed her cat and the neigh-bour's cat and all the cats in the street, if Doris's story was true. She did it at night time, when the moon hung in the sky like a ball of Dutch cheese. Alex looked at her round blank face and wondered how many cats Harriet had really killed. Perhaps it was only one. Perhaps she didn't like it scratching and crying.

Alex turned the pages of the encyclopaedia and began to examine each picture in detail. Each time the wind rattled the door, she looked up in case Rachel had returned, but she went to bed disappointed.

16

'Sit down,' Mrs Brown said as she bent to pick up some papers which lay in an untidy bundle at her feet. When she found the sheet she was looking for, she smoothed it with her fingers before reading it. The senior attendant had greying hair and her glasses made her look surprised, as if someone had asked her a question she wasn't expecting. 'This is very serious,' Mrs Brown said and she read out loud from the paper in front of her.

After the conversation she had just had with Rachel, Alex felt as deflated as a popped balloon. She listened to the senior attendant's words despondently.

'Kissing, underage drinking, visiting a bar where gambling takes place, dressing up as a boy, disrespectful behaviour in the Lord's house, seduction by an older woman.' She paused and the silence was punctuated by the rain which was falling steadily outside. Mrs Brown shook her head and surveyed another piece of paper carefully.

'I don't . . . what I mean is . . . I . . .' Alex began, but she didn't know what to say.

'I hear you was doing a full-time job,' Mrs Brown said, fiddling with her necklace, 'and that's where it happened.'

'Yes, I worked at the bakery.'

'Disgusting,' Mrs Brown exclaimed suddenly, making Alex jump. Then, looking at her, 'It takes time to weed out these habits. Do you understand?'

Alex didn't say anything for a moment. She thought of Rachel, asleep on the bed, with the words that had just passed between them hanging in the air above her head. She had tears in her eyes.

'I asked if you understood?' Mrs Brown said, blinking at her and pushing her glasses along her nose.

'Yes,' she said at last. The word Mrs Brown had used, disgusting, was ringing between her ears like a bell. Alex made herself think about Rachel again and looked at the floor.

'We won't discuss the details. I hope your parents are dealing with the,' she studied the paper again, 'with the older woman concerned.'

Alex thought angrily of her parents in front of Hughie Green on *Double Your Money*.

'You don't want to disappoint them, do you?'

'No,' she said, concentrating on not letting the tears run down her face.

'Good. Let's hope we can avoid the embarrassment of speaking to a doctor.'

'A doctor? Why?' Alex was shocked.

'Sometimes there is something wrong physically,' said Mrs Brown calmly. Alex stared at her in horror. 'Or mentally. Let's hope it doesn't come to that. We require you to re-learn ladylike behaviour.'

This time Alex just nodded.

Mrs Brown's grip on her wrist was surprisingly tight. Alex was too shocked and unhappy to struggle as Mrs Brown pulled her towards the stairs. She was beginning to think that there was something wrong with her after all, like Mrs Brown and the pastor said.

Mrs Brown seemed reluctant to go into the baby room. She stood a few paces away on the landing and made Alex go inside. Then she locked it quickly and Alex heard her hurrying back downstairs. Inside, it was completely dark. The bulb had been removed from the light and the shutters had been drawn tight across the window. Alex felt her way over to the bed, imagining hundreds of unseen ghosts shifting along the walls only a few paces away.

As she lay down, the darkness piled on top of her as if she was trapped in a demolished building. She was frightened, imagining someone else was there, only inches away from her. She could see Mrs Brown's face and hear the words she had said coming out of her mouth. She was a monster spewing up bits of rubbish: old tin cans, bits of newspaper, toilet-roll holders, broken jam jars. Alex imagined the rubbish filling the lounge until there wasn't room for either of them, so that they were backed up against the wall. Soon it reached over their heads and they were in danger of drowning. She shook her head and tried to block out the senior attendant's words. If she brought her hand up to her eyes so that it was almost touching her nose, she could just make out the lines that crossed her palms. She tried to concentrate on her hand instead of Mrs Brown's words. But as soon as she let her mind wander, they rushed back into her head like dogs let off their leads.

'Once you get married and have a family and a home to think about,' Mrs Brown had said before she closed the door, 'you will be normal again. Deviant, married, normal. Those are the words I want you to think about today. Put them into a sentence for me.'

After a while, the darkness became comforting. Her fear subsided. If there was something there, it was watching her gently, or rather it coated her, along with the gloom, like chocolate coats your tongue when you suck it.

She couldn't stop herself from running over the conversation she had had with Rachel either, even though it made her feel like screaming at herself for being so stupid. Just thinking about it turned her hollow, like one of those dead tree trunks with nothing inside them but air and space.

The previous night, as Alex had fallen asleep, she had imagined she was dancing with Rachel next to the piano in the Memory Lane while Melanie played, and by the next morning she had decided to tell her why she had come. In the dark of the baby room, she curled up in a ball and wished hard that it hadn't happened, but her head was full of it anyway.

When Rachel came back from the library, Alex was sitting on

her new bed in the dormitory, thinking about what to say. Rachel stopped just inside the doorway.

'I remember you,' she said. Alex was shocked at how tired she looked and how thick her waist was getting. 'From the café. You look very different,' she went on when Alex didn't reply. 'It is you, isn't it?'

'Yes.' Alex looked right into Rachel's green eyes. Rachel took off her coat and undid her headscarf.

'You look pretty in a dress,' Rachel said. Alex flushed when she said it.

'Thanks.'

'Why are you staring at me? Is it my hair?'

Alex looked away. She felt awkward. 'No reason.'

'The rain stopped for a bit, so I made a run for it,' Rachel said. They looked out at the wet morning. The drizzle had begun again. Then they heard the front door bang.

'That'll be Mrs Brown.' Rachel wrinkled up her pretty face.

'What's she like?'

'Stupid,' Rachel said.

Alex looked into her face, wanting to tell her everything.

'Why did they send you?' Rachel asked her.

'Dressing like a boy, drinking and kissing Isabelle,' Alex replied, as if she was reading a shopping list.

'Really?' said Rachel. She seemed shocked. She bent down to pull off her shoes just as the rain began to beat hard against the window again. 'You kissed Isabelle?'

'Yes. In the bakery.' There was an uncomfortable pause while Rachel arranged her shoes next to the bed.

'Is that where you work?' Rachel asked, changing the subject. 'Do you make bread and cakes and things?'

'Not bread very often. Cakes mainly.'

'You'll have to teach me,' Rachel said mildly.

'Really?' Alex's eyes lit up but Rachel shrugged.

'I'm probably too lazy to learn.'

'That girl Doris told me you go to the library,' Alex said to try to keep her talking.

'Yep,' said Rachel. 'It's a tradition. If you're in the club, you have to work in the library.'

'Why?'

'God knows.' She yawned. 'I'm so tired I feel sick. I couldn't sleep last night because of the rain.'

Alex was worried in case Rachel fell asleep before she could tell her. She went and sat next to her on the bed and took a deep breath.

'I only came because of you,' she said.

'What?'

'I made them send me because I couldn't stop thinking about you.'

Rachel looked stunned. She put her hand across her heart as if she was protecting herself.

'Of course you didn't get sent because of me. Don't be stupid.'

'I did. I made them send me. I've been watching you at the café and I . . .' Alex trailed off, wishing she hadn't said anything.

'Well, I'm not queer like Isabelle.' Rachel lay down on her bed, closed her eyes and turned her back on Alex. 'I don't want to talk about it.'

Alex felt as if someone had kicked her in the chest. She wanted to run away but she stayed where she was in spite of herself because Rachel looked so beautiful. It was wonderful to be so close to her. She was watching her eyelids flicker and her chest as it rose and fell when the door opened and Rose came in. She was wearing her coat and had her bag hooked over her arm.

'I'm going now,' she said, sounding out of breath. 'Mrs Brown wants to see you.'

At first Alex thought that Rose had been out in the rain, but as they went along the corridor she could see that the attendant had been crying. Rose caught her looking.

'Mrs Brown thinks John shouldn't have stayed here last night,' she said, by way of explanation.

'But there was a storm,' Alex said.

'He left her some fish. If he hadn't left the fish, she wouldn't have known.'

Alex was suddenly worried. 'He's still going to take us out to the light, isn't he?' she said.

Rose laughed. 'You sound like the others already,' she said.

They stopped outside the lounge.

'She's in there,' Rose said. Then she added, 'Be brave.'

'What do you mean?' Alex asked her but Rose was hurrying back down the corridor to the front door.

Alex had gone into the lounge and found Mrs Brown perched on the edge of the sofa like a bird unsure whether to take off or not. And now here she was lying on the bed in the dark, trying to read the lines on her hands. She could feel the tears welling up in her eyes again, but she wiped them away quickly. She didn't want to cry. She felt angry.

After a while, because it was so dark, she became dislocated from the room around her. She could have been floating instead of lying on the bed and she didn't know how long she had been there. She didn't want to fall asleep. She opened her eyes wide to stop herself. 'Disgusting,' she heard Mrs Brown say in her head, and 'kissing'. She stared at her hand and imagined she was a palm reader, although she had no idea which line was which. She tried to make it up. This one means you'll live a long time and have three children. This one is good health, although you might break your leg when you are forty. You'll be very wealthy. And this one means happiness. But she couldn't keep it up. She wrapped her arms round her head and pulled her knees up to her chest as tightly as she could and moaned to herself. It was a low quiet moan that surrounded her like a cocoon. Eventually, in spite of herself, she fell asleep.

When Alex woke up, she felt as though the darkness should have vanished and morning light should have flooded the room by now. It was like waking up unexpectedly in the middle of the night and being convinced for a confusing moment that it was morning. She was very hungry and she needed a pee. As she licked the roof of her mouth, she wondered what time it was and how long she had been asleep. Slowly, she got up and inched her way along the wall to the window, but the shutters were sturdy and she couldn't find a way of opening them. She slid down to the floor

128

underneath the window and was leaning her head against the wall in despair when she heard a key turn in the lock. The door opened and unaccustomed light meandered into the room from the landing. Alex blinked as Marjory put her head round the door.

'Soap lesson's over.'

'What?' Alex stood up, rubbing her eyes at the brightness.

'In the laundry room. We're learning to make soap.'

'Oh,' Alex said, not sure if she understood.

'Mrs Brown says you can come down for dinner,' Marjory said grumpily.

'What time is it?'

'Dinner time,' Marjory said.

'Is Rachel here?' She didn't know if she could face her.

'She's at the library. Come on,' Marjory added impatiently.

Now her eyes had got used to the light again, Alex thought of something. She turned and looked all over the shutters for a way of opening them. She found the two bolts and pulled the stiff shutters back, letting the early evening into the room. She wondered if she would be able to find them again in the dark. She tried to remember them with her fingertips.

'Come on,' said Marjory.

As Alex went out onto the landing, Marjory was already descending the stairs, saying 'Damn' with each step as if she was walking down into the underworld. 'Damn, damn, damn, damn, damn.'

'What's wrong?' Alex asked, catching up.

'You don't care. You're new.'

'Yes I do. What's wrong?'

'I have to miss dinner for having a radio. I'm starving.'

'Did Mrs Brown find it?'

'No. She heard the music through the wall, but I won't tell her where it is.' She disappeared into the dormitory.

Doris, Joyce and Harriet were already sitting on the benches in the dining room. Bowls of soup and chunks of bread were laid out along the table. There was a young attendant at its head. Harriet was staring into her bowl as if she was waiting for something to jump out of it. Joyce had her hands together and her eyes closed.

'Now. Let's say grace,' the attendant was saying as Alex slid into her place. Doris waved at her.

Alex absent-mindedly counted to three under her breath, feeling light-headed from hunger.

'Grace,' she said, but no one else said it. Doris shook her head in alarm. Taken by surprise, the attendant stared at her while Joyce giggled, her fingertips still pointing to heaven. Harriet didn't take her eyes off her soup.

After a long pause, the attendant looked down at her lap and said, 'I have strayed from the path of righteousness. Have mercy on me, O Lord.'

The others all repeated it and said, 'Amen.'

Alex was halfway through her soup when Mrs Brown came to the door.

'Excuse me, Hazel-Anne,' she said to the young attendant. She came in, put her hands on the table and looked at them all.

'Today Marjory admitted to having a radio but has hidden it,' Mrs Brown said. 'There will be no trip to the light until it is found.' Harriet looked at her, eyes wide with disappointment.

'We can't go anyway in this bloody weather,' Joyce said happily, but Mrs Brown didn't hear her because Doris chose that moment to knock her glass over. Alex wondered if she had done it on purpose because she knew Joyce would get herself into trouble. Water ran all over the table.

'Clear it up,' Mrs Brown ordered and Doris ran for a towel.

'Stand, please, Alexandra.' Alex stood and the others watched her mutely, to find out what would happen. Doris reappeared and began mopping up the water energetically.

'Did you have time to think this afternoon?'

Alex didn't say anything.

'Answer me.'

'Yes,' she said quietly.

'What words did I ask you to think about today?'

Alex looked into her soup. The first word filled her head until it was so big there wasn't any room for the others. 'Deviant' was painted on the insides of her eyelids.

'Well?'

But Alex couldn't reply.

'No one is to talk to the new girl for the rest of the week,' Mrs Brown said. Joyce clasped both hands over her mouth to illustrate what the senior attendant had said.

'That's right, Joyce,' said Mrs Brown. 'She needs more time to think.'

'About what she's done?' Doris said eagerly, putting the towel on the window sill and slipping back into her place.

'Shut up, Doris,' said Harriet suddenly. It was the first thing she had said since dinner began.

'Anyone found talking to the new girl will miss dinner,' Mrs Brown continued. Joyce mimed buttoning her lips and then pretended that she couldn't open her mouth to eat her soup. Half a spoonful ran down her chin.

'Be careful, Joyce,' said Hazel-Anne. 'Use your napkin.'

'What about pass the salt? Can we say pass the salt?' said Doris.

Mrs Brown turned and blinked at her. 'I'll pretend I didn't hear that,' she said.

'Sorry,' Doris mumbled in reply and she made to pick up her bread, but Mrs Brown reached out and snatched it.

'Or perhaps you want to go and spend some more time upstairs too?' she said.

'No,' Doris said, and Mrs Brown left, taking Doris's piece of bread with her. Hazel-Anne got up to close the door and while her back was turned, Alex broke her own bread in two and passed half to Doris, who chewed it hungrily. The young attendant didn't comment on Doris's magically reappearing bread when she returned to the table. She looked frightened, as if she had been threatened herself.

'Well now, let's eat our dinner in peace,' she said, glancing round the table and attempting a tight smile.

Hazel-Anne announced phone calls after the plates had been cleared. The phone was in the office and residents were allowed one phone call a week. Alex went out into the hall with the others to queue up. Although they gazed at her, no one spoke. They were taking Mrs Brown's new rule seriously.

Alex asked for her neighbour's number, while Hazel-Anne stood behind the desk with a watch.

'No more than five minutes,' she said.

'What?' said her neighbour. 'Who?' When Alex explained, he shuffled off to get her dad. She had used up most of her time limit when he eventually picked up the phone.

'Hello,' he said, too loudly, because he thought you had to shout into phones to make yourself heard. 'I'll have to be quick, *Double Your Money* is on.'

She hesitated. She didn't want to tell him about the baby room and what Mrs Brown had said about her. 'We're going out to see a lighthouse,' was all she could think of to say.

'A lighthouse?'

'Yes.'

'How long do they keep you there for?'

'I don't know yet.'

'I see.'

Hazel-Anne tapped the watch.

'Will you be fixed up soon?' Alex imagined him scratching his knee like he always did when he was thinking about something.

'Why, what's wrong?'

'It's a bit difficult.'

'Time,' said Hazel-Anne, putting her hand out to press down the receiver button.

'Hold on,' Alex said to her.

'Your mum's calling me,' said her father.

'Why is it difficult?'

'It's Mr Bradley.' But before he could tell her about Mr Bradley, Hazel-Anne pushed the receiver button and her call was disconnected.

'Bye, Dad,' she said into the empty phone. Doris was hopping from foot to foot outside the door.

'Next,' the attendant said.

*   *   *

132

In the baby room the next day, Alex was plunged into darkness again as soon as the door closed. She edged over towards the window, bruising her leg on the bedstead before veering off in the wrong direction and groping the cold tiles around the fireplace. From there she felt her way along the wall, until the rough wood of the shutters was under her hands.

While they were washing that morning, she had been cloaked in silence. Rachel didn't even look at her. When Alex went into the washroom Rachel just slipped past her into the dormitory, wrapped in a towel, and left for the library without breakfast. Thinking about it, Alex got more and more desperate. Her fingers searched the edges of the shutters, but she couldn't find the bolts. Trying to remember what had seemed so simple the day before, she ran her fingers over the wooden trims again. Still nothing. She was about to give up when her hand brushed the small bolt on the underside edge. With renewed energy, she felt for its twin on the top, found it, and slid them both back. The shutters seemed even stiffer in the dark, but when she pulled them hard enough, they opened suddenly with a creak and she shielded her eyes as daylight flooded in.

She leant against the wall under the window all morning, studying the lighthouse encyclopaedia from the bookshelf, memorising the dates and figures. She thought about Mr Sabre and the kinds of questions he would ask her if he had a chance to read the book. How tall is the tallest lighthouse in Great Britain? When was the first lighthouse built? Partly to keep herself from thinking about Rachel and partly so that Mrs Brown's face wouldn't hover in front of her like a balloon, she tested herself on the reaches of the lamps and the heights of the towers, until she heard someone approach. It was about midday and she was very hungry. She leapt up and pushed the shutters to, so that the room was dark once more.

Marjory didn't speak this time. Clearly she didn't want to miss out on dinner again by being caught talking to Alex. She let the door swing open and simply waited for her to follow. Alex left the lighthouse encyclopaedia on the floor and went downstairs.

Marjory pointed to the open door of the office and disappeared into the lounge.

This time, she put Mrs Brown's words into a sentence for her: deviant behaviour, get married and have a family, be normal again. She said it so quietly she was frightened the words would sail away and that Mrs Brown wouldn't hear her, but she nodded sharply.

'There's a ham sandwich for you in the dining room,' she said. 'After lunch, your word is husband.'

Alex found some paper and a pen in the lounge and she smuggled them up to the baby room that afternoon while the others went out to the laundry room for their lesson. She wrote about what had happened in tiny letters so the paper would last. The paper gave her an idea but she had to wait until after dark to ask Doris about it.

Alex lay wide awake on her stomach, facing the window. The others were asleep all around her, including Rachel who had come back late from the library. She had simply slipped off her clothes and got into bed without speaking to any of them. When Alex was sure there were no other sounds, she whispered to the girl in the neighbouring bed.

'Doris.'

There was no response, although Alex could sense that Doris was awake. She tried again.

'Doris.'

'I'm not allowed to talk to you,' the younger girl whispered back. There was silence while they both considered it.

'How long do I get locked in for?' Alex asked.

'Depends how fast you learn what the words mean.'

'What other words do I get?'

'I told you. It depends on what you done. Some people get bible verses too. I got "the love of money is the root of all evil" but I never stole money.'

'Did Rachel get locked in?'

'No. She goes to the library, silly.' Harriet stirred in the bed on the other side of Doris. Alex lowered her voice even more.

'Why does she go there?'

'Don't you know?' Doris replied.

'Tell me.'

''Bout a hundred years ago a pregnant girl drowned in the lake.'

Alex was stunned. 'So?' she whispered at last.

'So her father gave the farmhouse to the church for unmarried mothers.' Doris's pride in her story meant her voice got louder. 'She was friends with the librarian so she agreed to train the pregnant girls.'

Alex thought about it. 'The librarian's a hundred years old?' One of the others rolled over and moaned to herself.

'No, stupid,' Doris said. 'It's a different librarian now. But they still do it. Only if you're pregnant.'

They lay in silence for a while. Alex thought about the pregnant girl under the surface of the lake, but she had to keep talking because she wanted to ask Doris about her idea.

'Doris,' she whispered again, after a while.

'What?'

'Can you get me a notebook from the office?'

'Why?'

'To write in while I'm up there.' She sensed Doris weighing up the proposition.

'What do I get in return?'

'I'll make you a cake,' she said.

'How will you do that?'

'Trust me.'

'What kind?'

Alex thought quickly. The wind howled outside like a lonely dog.

'Orange sponge,' she said at last. She was sure that she had seen some fruit in the kitchen.

'OK. I'll get you a notebook when Mrs Brown goes down to the village.' They heard footsteps. 'Shhh,' Doris said.

Hazel-Anne put her head round the door to make sure they were all asleep and after that Doris wouldn't talk any more.

For the next few days, Alex leant against the wall under the shutters in the room at the top of the stairs and either read the lighthouse encyclopaedia or wrote in the red notebook Doris had stolen for her, which she kept hidden under the mattress. When Marjory came to take her to Mrs Brown, she would give the senior attendant the definition of the word she was supposed to be thinking about: wife, duty, married. Sometimes, if she came up with a good meaning for a word, she was allowed to eat lunch, otherwise she was sent back upstairs hungry. In the dining room at the end of each day, the others watched her in case she did anything unusual, but none of them spoke to her. All the time she was locked in the baby room, the rain fell steadily outside. She wished hard for it to continue because she didn't want John to take them out to the light without her. She only saw Rachel at dinner time or in the evenings before they went to bed. She felt as if she was in a bubble all of her own, full of silence, entries in her notebook, lighthouses and creaking shutters. The words Mrs Brown made her think about roamed around her head like the hill walkers who went past the house sometimes: clothes, ladylike, husband, etiquette, hygiene, needlecraft, homemaking, housewifery. She was trapped in a roomful of words like she had been shut inside a book, or like a bird in a forest of leafy trees.

It was about two o'clock in the morning when Alex went into the kitchen and worked out how to turn on the oven. She didn't want to switch on the light in case someone went into the wash-room and noticed, so she cooked by the moonlight which was pouring in through the window. She found an old baking tin under the sink. She had to scrub it, but when she was finished it was fine, like an old tramp in new clothes. In another cupboard she found eggs. There was butter left out on the side in a dish and a bowl full of fruit next to the cooker. She pulled on an apron and began to pour ingredients into a bowl, one after another, not needing to measure them because she had made orange sponge so many times. She worked fast, pouring in a little more sugar and testing the mixture with a wooden spoon as though she was back at Mr Sabre's bakery. She made herself recite the recipe in her head, as if she was writing it down for someone. Sieve the flour twice with baking powder. Rub the sugar into the butter, mix with the flour, add vanilla pod if you have one. (She looked hopefully in all of the cupboards but was disappointed.) Add the eggs carefully. Squeeze in the juice of an orange, not too much. Grate a little of the orange zest. Pour in water. Stir gently. Let the mixture rest. Use two cake tins. (She only had one, but she could chop the sponge in half when it came out.) Make sure the oven is hot enough. Bake for twenty minutes and then test with your thumb. She had lulled herself with the words and the rhythm of the stirring, beating and pouring, so she started when she heard someone behind her. It was Rachel. She was leaning on the door frame. Alex turned away and wiped her hands on her apron. Rachel yawned.

'I couldn't sleep,' she said.

'Me neither.'

'What are you making?'

'Sponge,' said Alex, turning round again. 'Orange sponge.'

'Can I help?' The cake mix was ready, so Alex let Rachel scrape it into the tin and slide the tin into the oven.

'Let's go outside. It's stopped raining,' Rachel said. She yawned again.

'What? Now?'

'Yes. I need some fresh air.'

When they opened the door, the dark shapes of the courtyard were arranged like statues here and there. Alex shivered and followed Rachel into the walled garden. Rachel bent down and examined the gravestones along the wall. Most were in bits like large biscuit crumbs although the biggest had just one chunk missing as if someone had taken a bite out of it. The moon went behind a cloud for a moment and it was too dark to make out any words.

'It really used to be a church?' Alex said, going over to look at one of the lumps of grey ruin which had ivy clinging to it jealously.

'Yes. A long time ago. Then it was a farmhouse, built on the same foundations. Billy told me.'

'Who's he?'

Rachel laughed. 'She. Billy's the librarian.'

'What do you do there all day?' Alex said.

'Oh, book-binding, returning books to the shelves, rearranging the card catalogue, totalling up fines, that kind of thing.'

The moon came out from behind its cloud and shone into the garden, lighting up a tree with long dangling branches in the corner. There was a bench next to it, which was lit up too. Alex was gazing up at the sky which was full of stars as if someone had scattered a handful of salt across a table, when Rachel pulled her sleeve.

'I haven't seen that one before,' she said, and pointed to a stone which had collapsed under the tree with dangling limbs. 'I'm going to look.' She crossed the flowerbed, leaving Alex on the path under the salt sky, and ducked under the branches. Now the moon had reappeared, Alex could see there was something written on the stone. She went closer, past the bench, and crouched next to her companion. Rachel was tracing the yellowing words with her fingers. 'Almost Brown', the stone said, '1834–1849'. And that was all. If there had been any other writing, it was lost.

'Fifteen,' Alex said, working it out in her head.

'Almost is a strange name,' Rachel murmured to herself.

'Do you think she was the girl who drowned?' Alex said.

'Perhaps,' said Rachel.

In the moonlight, Alex could see that the bench nearby had turned lumpy from being outside. It looked as if it was made from the bottom of tortoises' feet, but they sat down anyway, feeling the damp beneath them. The moon rested on Rachel's face and Alex put out a hand and brushed her hair behind her ear, smoothing her cheek as she did so. Rachel pushed her hand away and jumped up.

'I told you I wasn't like that,' she said. 'Maybe the others are right. Maybe you are queer.' She turned and went swiftly back into the house. Alex saw her disappear down the corridor to the dormitory, but she couldn't call after her because she didn't want to make a noise. The smell of orange sponge was filling the kitchen. She took it out just in time and put it on the side to cool. Then she went back to bed herself.

17

When Alex went into the kitchen to retrieve her cake, Mrs Brown was already there. She was wearing her nightdress and leaning against the sink.

'Did I tell you to make a cake?'

'No, you didn't,' Alex replied levelly. Attempting to ignore the attendant, she found the grater in the cupboard and picked up an orange from the fruit bowl. She began to grate the orange over the cake.

'Stop that,' Mrs Brown said, but Alex carried on grating. The senior attendant came over and snatched the orange out of her hand.

Alex opened another cupboard and found icing sugar and a sieve, and began to shake on the icing. Mrs Brown picked up the sponge in both hands and broke it in two, scattering crumbs and orange rind as she did so. Then she threw it into the bin. Alex watched her in disbelief, the sieve still in her hand.

'Clear up this mess,' Mrs Brown said and left the room.

By the time Alex went into the dining room for breakfast, Rachel had left for the library and the others were sitting along the benches eating cornflakes glumly because Mrs Brown was eating with them, still in her nightdress. On the table in front of her was a bundle of clothes.

'Stay there,' Mrs Brown said before Alex could sit down. Everyone watched as Mrs Brown got up and went to the front of the dining room.

'What are these, Alexandra?' Mrs Brown said, pointing to the pile on the table. There was a pair of old men's trousers, a shirt, jacket and tie.

'Clothes,' Alex replied.

'Men's clothes,' Mrs Brown said, looking around the room. 'Go into the dormitory and put them on.'

'What?' Alex said. 'Are you serious?'

'Very serious,' she said, pushing her glasses along her nose. Everyone was staring at her and Alex felt suddenly embarrassed. She picked up the clothes, ran into the dormitory and sat on her bed clutching the bundle.

Alex had no intention of putting on the clothes. She didn't know what else to do, so she shook them out one at a time and inspected them. The trousers were brown and baggy. The shirt had no collar and was worn and yellow under the arms. They looked as if they had come from a jumble sale. The jacket wasn't much better. It was huge and faded and didn't match. She held up the tie. It said 'Eade Village School' on it in a circle, in the middle of which was a picture of a boat with a sail.

The door opened and Harriet came in.

'I told Mrs Brown I'd come and get you,' she said, looking at the floor. Then she sat down on the bed next to Alex and frowned.

'What's wrong?' Alex said, but the older girl didn't reply. They sat like that for a while, Harriet staring in front of her and Alex looking at the trousers she still had crumpled in her hand. The rain had started again and the sky was almost as dark as it had been when she first arrived. There was hardly any wind now though, so the rain didn't pound against the window as it had done then. It fell almost silently. She turned to her companion. Harriet dropped her head onto Alex's shoulder.

'What's wrong?' Alex asked again, putting her arm round her awkwardly. Harriet moaned under her breath, like a sleeping cat, but she didn't reply.

'Did she make you do something like this too?' Alex noticed that she could see their reflection in the mirror at the end of the room. She examined the blue dress she was wearing. It was one of the smart ones she used to wear in the bakery.

'It's better just to do it,' Harriet said suddenly.

'Why?'

'Otherwise you make it worse.' She moaned again and turned her face into Alex's shoulder.

'Will it make you feel better if I put them on?'

'It'd be over quicker.'

'Will it make you feel better?'

Harriet nodded. Alex rocked her a little bit and held her tight because she didn't know how else to comfort her.

'Doris said you killed your cat,' she said. 'Is that true?'

Harriet wouldn't answer, so Alex stood up and watched herself in the mirror at the end of the room as she pulled her dress off over her head and slipped on the trousers, shirt and jacket. Harriet watched her in silence.

'You're in here for the same things as me, aren't you?' Alex asked her when she was dressed.

Harriet nodded miserably.

Alex went over to the mirror to knot the tie. 'Ready?' she said when it was done.

'Yes,' Harriet said. She was examining the floor again. She got up and led the way back into the dining room. Harriet slid back into her place and stared into her cereal bowl.

'You took your time,' said Mrs Brown, adjusting her glasses. 'Now, take a good look at her, everyone. This is what a female homosexual looks like.' Alex took a step backwards at the words. Joyce gasped. Marjory, for once, didn't swear, she just stared with her mouth open, as did Doris.

'I didn't know she was like that,' Doris said. She sounded fascinated.

'She dressed up in men's clothes,' Mrs Brown continued, 'and went to a club with other female homosexuals. It's disgusting.'

Alex looked at her miserably. Maybe she really was disgusting like Mrs Brown said she was. She glanced at Harriet, but she wouldn't meet her gaze. Alex hung her head. The tears welled up in her eyes again and she didn't want to cry in front of them all. She swallowed, but it was no good. Mrs Brown was saying something about gambling and drinking when she made a run for the door. She knew she had to get out of the house. She shook the front door frantically before realising it was bolted. She slid the bolts back quickly, expecting Mrs Brown to come after her, but the hallway was silent. Nothing moved.

She went out of the driveway and down the hill, running blindly. She didn't stay on the path for long, but went across the grass instead. The rain was still falling and the ground was soft and wet under her feet, but she didn't notice. She was crying as she went past the trees which guarded the lake, through a gap in the low stone wall and out onto the road. She stopped for a second. There in front of her was a red brick building with a wide arch over it. 'Eade Village Library' was carved into the stone over the door. She wondered for a moment if she should go and ask Rachel for help, but then she looked down at herself; she didn't want to talk to Rachel looking like this. She ran further down the hill, past a hair salon, houses and a square with one or two shops in it.

She could hear the sea before she saw it and the seagulls which hung above it like high-up mobiles, calling out to each other. The tide was out, and it had uncovered rocks along the edges of the beach. She sat down on the edge of the promenade and realised it wasn't raining any longer. The cold air made her stop crying and wipe her face, and suddenly there was the lighthouse in front of her like a giant white matchstick. She looked up at it, astonished that something so round and icing coloured should be reaching up into the sky, or existing at all. It looked so smooth and perfectly circular that she could imagine hugging it, circling it with both arms or pressing her palms up against the curving wall to test its shape against her skin. In the encyclopaedia picture there had been a path of rocks, but no land was visible now between it and the harbour wall, only blue-grey sea. The light fell on the water in patches, but in other places there were shadows where the rain was still falling. The wind that blew her hair around her wet face was blowing the grey clouds around too. The sky above her was acting like an old man's face, wispy bits of grey hair twisting this way and that. The lighthouse stood alone on a brown rock, like a sudden tree on the edge of the harbour or a giant candle.

Alex pulled off the tie, jammed her hands into the pockets of the trousers and went down onto the sand. There were fishing boats resting in the water beyond the harbour wall, but no sign of any fishermen or any of the people who lived in the houses nearby. She walked along the sand to see if the lighthouse looked different closer up, but she couldn't get much closer unless she walked over the water towards it. She thought of Mr Sabre, in the jeans which were too small for him, shuffling into the bakery kitchen to ask her questions, pushing his feet into his battered slippers and his arms into his cardigan. How tall is it? What's its girth? How far does its light stretch? When was it built? And she knew the answers to the questions because of the encyclopaedia, but the questions weren't enough. She wanted to stand beneath the lighthouse, rest her back against it and look up at its branchless top. A sudden spray of water hit the brown rocks below and sent an arch of foam up against its walls. She sat down on the sand and thought about how it was built, brick by brick. How did the builders get it to curve so smoothly and how did they carry the bricks out to the rocks? She thought about how long it had stood there, hundreds of years, watching the beach and understanding everything that happened in Eade Village. It could even see what was happening at the house. Silently it watched, like a giant with his tongue cut out and his feet rooted to the seabed by a fast-tight spell. She couldn't wait to make the journey across the water in John's boat now. She imagined herself swimming instead, pulling herself up onto the brown rocks like a mermaid, her hair wet and her clothes sticking to her, and it was on the beach that Billy Burns found her later, her face still flushed from crying, staring up at the light.

The librarian tied the hood of her mac under her chin and left Rachel at the library. Fed up with letting the rain keep her indoors, she had gone out, one of her walking sticks in her hand. On her way back she decided to go past the harbour and the fishermen's cottages so that she could look at the beach before returning up the road to the library for hot coffee and bread. She was thinking about wrapping her hands around a warm mug and breathing in the steam as she got to the beach and saw one of Mrs Johnson's terriers dart down onto the sand, its ears flying as it went. It rushed up to a figure Billy didn't recognise, who was sitting on the wet sand, her hands round her knees.

When the dog leapt up to her, Alex held on to him and laughed as he licked her face. The librarian came up behind her.

'Is he with you?' Alex asked, smiling at the friendly animal, who leapt out of her grasp and bounded off over the beach.

'No. He must have escaped. It happens quite often,' Billy said.

'Where's he escaped from?' Alex said.

'Next door to me, in fact. You're from the house, aren't you?' she said.

'Yes,' Alex said, not wanting to talk about it.

'I'm the librarian,' Billy told her. 'Now, what's wrong with you?' The dog bounced up again and nearly knocked her over, before racing off towards the rock pools.

'We'll have to take him back,' she said when Alex didn't reply.

'I want to go home,' Alex said, and looked back out at the lighthouse again.

'I see,' said the librarian. 'You look wet. My name is Billy.'

'I'm Alex.' Billy sat down next to her and laid her stick on the sand. The terrier was playing at the water's edge, getting his feet wet and leaping away. 'It's amazing,' she said eventually.

'The light? Yes, it is I suppose. Haven't thought about it much,' Billy said, but the way she said it and the way she followed Alex's gaze made it sound as if she did think about it, a lot.

'Have you ever been out to see it? Inside, I mean?'

'No. Tried to once, but we had to turn back, my friend and I. That was a long time ago. You can walk, when the tide is low enough.'

'When does that happen?'

'Oh, it only stays out for long enough a couple of times a year.'

Billy pulled at Alex's shirt. 'Why are you wearing these clothes? Have you run away?'

'Yes,' Alex said and hung her head again. 'I mean . . . I don't know.'

'Knowing you don't know is a good place to start,' Billy said.

'Where's Rachel?' Alex asked her.

'Mending books in the library. Did they make you wear these,' Billy asked, 'at the house?'

'Yes.'

'It's chilly out here. Come on.' The librarian used her stick to help her stand up, dusted the sand from her clothes and waved a hand at the dog. When Alex stood up too, feeling very cold all of a sudden, the dog turned and ran towards them. Billy grabbed his collar.

'Do you think you can carry him? He'll wriggle a bit,' she said.

In reply, Alex bent down and lifted the dog into her arms. He yelped and tried to get free but she held him tightly. He warmed her up a little like a hot water bottle. After a glance back at the lighthouse, she climbed onto the promenade with Billy and they went up the hill together.

Lively music was coming from somewhere inside Eade Village library as the librarian took Alex through the wide arched entranceway. It was getting windy again and Alex could hear the gate of the Old Vicarage next door swinging to and fro. They were in a wood-panelled porch which had two doors leading off it, one to the right into the library, one to the left which was Billy's front door.

'I found someone you know on the beach,' Billy called. Inside the library, the music got louder. Alex recognised it as Gracie Fields. Rachel was sitting behind the issues and returns desk with a pile of damaged books in front of her. She stood up in alarm when she saw Alex in the strange clothes with the dog, drenched and still shivering.

'What happened?' she said. When Alex saw Rachel looking so concerned she felt brighter.

'I think they've both run away,' Billy said. Just then the dog yelped and finally managed to leap out of Alex's arms. He tore away, barking as he went, up one aisle then down another, as if he was a book borrower in a hurry. Billy closed the door quickly and the three of them tried to catch him. The little dog thought it was a game; he raced up to Billy, slipped between her legs and ran back round the children's picture books towards Rachel, who jumped out of the way instead of grabbing him. Finally he ran up to Alex in the geography section next to the atlases and sat at her feet wagging his tail. When she had a hold on his collar, she sat down on the floor and stroked his ears.

'He likes you,' Billy said, out of breath, coming round the corner to find her. He was licking her hand.

'Here,' said Rachel. She had brought some string from the desk to use as a lead. She held it out to Billy so that she didn't have to go near the dog. 'I don't like them much,' she said.

The librarian tied on the makeshift lead while Alex held him still.

'Now, Alex, we better get you into something warm,' Billy said. 'You're shivering.'

'What about him?' said Rachel. Trying to be brave, she stretched out a finger to scratch the terrier between the ears, then pulled it back again quickly.

'He won't hurt you,' said Alex.

'Rachel, could you bear to take this young man next door while I get Alex something warm to wear?' Billy asked. Rachel hesitated, looked from the librarian with the panting dog on a string to the shivering girl leaning against *The Times Atlas of the World*, and nodded her head.

'OK,' she said. She went to get her coat and headscarf, then held a hand out nervously for the lead. 'What do I do if he jumps up?' But Billy was already opening the door. Alex patted her new friend goodbye.

'Go on then,' the librarian said to the dog, clapping her hands to her knees. 'Show Rachel where you live.' The dog made a run for it, pulling Rachel after him.

'I'm not sure about this,' she said as she was yanked outside.

'See you in a minute,' Billy said cheerfully.

She put her arm round Alex's shoulder and led her into the librarian's apartment through another door next to the issues and returns desk. The sitting room was also full of books. The music was coming from an old wind-up gramophone on the side. Billy took Alex into her bedroom which was bright with daylight from a big arched window. A patchwork quilt covered the bed, just like the one in the baby room. The walls were painted in a colour that was either pink or purple, Alex couldn't work out which. It changed each time she looked at it. The librarian had gone over to a cupboard next to the door and was rummaging urgently through jumpers, socks and pairs of slacks.

'Put these on,' she said, throwing some over to Alex. 'I'm going to light the fire and make some coffee.'

'Thanks,' said Alex, stripping off the clothes Mrs Brown had made her put on that morning. She was almost lost inside Billy's jumper. She had to roll up the sleeves because they flopped over her hands.

Soon a fire was roaming around the grate and jumping over the log Billy added, as if it was getting ready to leap out of the fireplace and dance for them. When Rachel returned, Billy had warmed bread in the oven and laid out their breakfast on the little table in front of the sofa.

'He's home now,' Rachel said, taking off her headscarf and checking her hair in the mirror. 'It's cold outside. My face has dried out and my hair's a complete mess.' She turned round and looked at Alex's sombre expression. 'Have you been crying? Why were you out in the rain wearing those silly brown trousers?'

'Exactly what I'd like to know,' Billy said. Alex looked into her mug for a moment.

'Mrs Brown made me put them on,' she said. 'And stand in front of everyone. She said I was . . .' But she couldn't finish the sentence. 'Because of kissing Isabelle,' she finished quickly. Rachel put her hand up to her mouth.

'That's terrible,' she said. She sat down on the sofa and rested a hand on her thick stomach. Billy poured her some coffee.

'Now. Who's Isabelle?' she said.

'Comes to our café to play cards,' Rachel said.

'She used to come into our bakery to buy slices,' said Alex at the same time.

'Ah well,' said Billy, sounding a little lost. 'Kissing is fine. Not enough of it around. I've got something you might like, Alex,' she went on, changing the subject. 'Let me go and find it.' She went out into the library and they heard her footsteps echoing between the shelves. There was an awkward silence when she had gone. Rachel examined her chipped nails.

'Have you seen the lighthouse?' Alex said at last.

'Of course I have,' Rachel said. 'Billy took me down to the beach when I first got here.'

'It's amazing. I'd love to look inside.'

'I bet it's small and poky.'

'John's taking us in his boat,' Alex said. 'I can't wait.'

Rachel wrinkled up her face. 'I don't like boats. They make me sick. And the wind ruins my hair.'

When Billy came back in, she held out a small book to Alex. On the front was a picture of a brown-haired girl lying in what could have been a cave. Another girl with blonde hair was leaning over her. It was caled *Odd Girl Out*. Alex took it from her hand.

'Oh,' Rachel said, looking over her shoulder. 'I've seen it.'

'Can I borrow it?' Alex said.

'Of course.'

Alex remembered the look on Harriet's face when they had sat in the dormitory together. She suddenly wanted to make sure she was all right. 'Thanks for the book,' she said and stood up, 'and for the clothes.'

'Where are you going?' Rachel asked. She yawned widely.

'Back to the house.'

'Why don't you stay here for the day?' Rachel said. 'Help me with the repairs.' Alex looked at her pretty face and her heart warmed up like a bread roll in a toaster. She would like nothing better than to sit next to Rachel at the desk with the black tape, but then she remembered Harriet, who was sad and unsolved like a jigsaw puzzle.

'Easier to go back now than later,' she said.

'That's very brave of you. Looks like we're returning everyone home today,' said the librarian brightly as if Alex was a book to be put back on the shelf. She went into the bedroom and found her headscarf.

'I will come up to the house with you,' she said. 'To have a word with Pamela Brown.'

'What will you say?' Rachel asked.

'Don't worry about that.'

'Mrs Brown is scared of Billy,' said Rachel as she stood up and began to clear the plates away.

'What gave you that idea?' said the librarian vaguely.

When they got to the Haven, Alex took a deep breath and was about to go through the green gate into the walled garden, but Billy strode up to the front door. Alex watched her tug the handle sharply before pushing it right and left, and it swung open magically.

'How did you . . .?' Alex began but her companion didn't stop to explain. She marched into the house with Alex behind her and banged on the office door.

'Ah. Mrs Burns.' Mrs Brown blinked at Billy through her glasses. 'And Alexandra.'

'Listen to me, Pamela Brown,' Billy began, but to Alex's surprise Mrs Brown waved her hands to make her keep her voice down, then reached out and pulled her into the office.

'Go into the lounge, Alexandra,' Mrs Brown said.

'Goodbye, Alex,' Billy said, smiling at her. 'Come and visit me again.' Alex smiled. Then she heard Billy say, 'What do you mean by letting her get soaking wet like that? She'll catch a chill—' The door slammed shut. She could hear their voices going up and down inside.

Alex wanted to talk to Harriet on her own, but when she went into the lounge all the others were there too. She sat down next to Harriet.

'Where did you go?' Harriet asked, looking up at her. There was something in her eyes that Alex recognised from the way she herself had looked at Rachel in the Memory Lane.

'To the beach.'

'Are you all right?'

'Yes. You?'

Harriet nodded.

'Marjory got told off about the radio,' said Doris, her needles clicking.

'Shut your cake hole,' said Marjory. Joyce giggled.

Just then the door opened and Mrs Brown came in. 'Has Billy gone?' Alex asked. Mrs Brown ignored her. She seemed agitated after her conversation with the librarian.

'Today,' she said, 'I will find the wireless. And when I do, it will be disposed of.'

'Shit,' said Marjory, then clamped her hand over her mouth.

'Marjory,' said the senior attendant, leaning towards her, 'no dinner.'

Marjory hung her head miserably and said, 'Shit,' again so quietly that only Joyce heard her say it, making her giggle so much she blew saliva bubbles.

'Be quiet, Joyce,' Mrs Brown said.

Joyce put her head on Marjory's shoulder. From there she stared up at Mrs Brown. Alex heard Marjory murmur something gently in her ear, just as Hazel-Anne put her head round the door.

'It's your daughter on the phone,' she said. 'She's having problems with the dogs.'

Mrs Brown went out swiftly. 'Take Alexandra upstairs,' they heard her say, before she went into the office.

Hazel-Anne took Alex's arm and escorted her upstairs quickly. Alex heard the key turn, then she was alone in the darkness. She was still wearing the librarian's floppy jumper and she had smuggled *Odd Girl Out* up underneath it.

She opened the shutters and imagined she was sitting on the beach near the lighthouse as she read the book. It was about an American girl who falls in love with another girl who thinks she loves her too. It was an astonishing book. She found herself wishing hard that it was a true story because then she wouldn't be the only person in the world that had ever felt like she did about Isabelle, and Rachel, and now Harriet. The book made her feel as though she had made an igloo out of sand and was sitting in it, warm and safe. She stopped only once, when she heard the front door slam below her. She stood to see Mrs Brown hurrying across the drive.

She was about half-way through when she felt too hungry to concentrate on the words any more. She put the book down and went to retrieve her red journal from under the mattress. As she wrote she could feel the air growing cooler and the light dimming around her. She filled the pages with descriptions of all the things that crowded into her head: Rachel behind the issues and returns desk and Billy in her mackintosh, the little dog that had found her, the senior attendant's fingers as she fiddled with her necklace, what she had said at breakfast that morning, the clothes, Harriet's head against her shoulder and the way she had looked at her in the lounge, the gravestone in the garden, the one with the strange name, Almost Brown, Joyce's hair, the fire jumping in the grate in the librarian's apartment, the cake she had made at night lying in the dustbin, the Creature from the Black Lagoon above her bed at home, her parents dressed as a flamingo and a lion, Rachel with the multicoloured cocktails, the mixer, Isabelle pressing her against the wall, her dad's thick neck as he watched *Double Your Money*, the card game, Melanie at the piano, Mr Sabre's new clothes, her favourite brown bowl in the bakery, Edith Sabre's face, cracking an egg and beating it with a fork, the colour the lake had been on the day she had arrived, a drowned pregnant girl, and the astonishing book.

18

Alex didn't know how much time had passed when the key turned in the lock again. It took her a moment to realise who it was, because she had pushed the shutters to when she heard someone coming. Harriet closed the door behind her. She stood awkwardly in the dark. Alex scrambled up and let the light in again.

'What time is it?' she asked. She heard the front door slam again.

'Don't know. We just had dinner.'

Alex was disappointed. It must have shown on her face, because Harriet fished in her pocket.

'I saved you some,' she said, producing a napkin. They sat down on the edge of the bed. Harriet laid the napkin on the blanket for a miniature picnic: a piece of cooked ham, some bits of carrot, a couple of potatoes. Even a slice of sponge pudding.

'I couldn't get a fork,' Harriet said. 'Sorry.'

Alex was too hungry to care. She ate gratefully with her fingers.

'Thanks,' she said, in between mouthfuls. 'Where did Mrs Brown go?'

'To help her daughter with the dogs,' Harriet said.

'The dogs belong to her daughter?'

'At the Old Vicarage, yes. Next to the library.'

'I found one of the dogs today. On the beach.'

'She breeds them. Mrs Brown used to do it. What's that?' Harriet pointed at the book on the floor.

'I borrowed it from the library.'

Harriet picked it up and examined the cover. Her eyes grew wide.

'This is fantastic,' she said, in spite of herself. As she looked at the book, Alex finished her last bit of cold meat and started on the sponge, which was dry and stodgy and nowhere near as good as the cake Mrs Brown had destroyed that morning.

'Won't you get into trouble coming in here?' Alex asked.

'No one saw me,' she said, 'and Hazel-Anne's gone.' Harriet had the same mixture of longing and fear in her eyes that Alex had seen earlier.

Alex finished her sponge, suddenly feeling nervous although she wasn't sure why. She rubbed her hands together to get rid of the crumbs and they looked at each other for what seemed like ages. Then very suddenly Harriet leaned over and kissed Alex quickly on the lips. It was so unexpected that it took her by surprise and she didn't have time to respond before her companion pulled away again and hung her head.

'What did Mrs Brown do to you that made you upset this morning? You didn't tell me,' Alex said after a moment.

'Nothing,' said Harriet. Alex reached up and tucked a stray bit of hair behind her companion's ear.

'Tell me,' she said. 'Did she make you dress up?'

'Nothing,' Harriet said again, more sharply. 'I'm not the same as you.' But she stayed where she was. Then, just as suddenly as before, she kissed Alex again, and this time Alex responded. She put her hand to Harriet's face as she kissed her and held on to her hair. It was nothing like kissing Isabelle. Harriet was much less sure of herself. Her skin smelt fresh like pineapple and felt smooth and creamy under Alex's hand. After a moment, Harriet pulled away, got up and ran from the room, *Odd Girl Out* abandoned.

'Wait,' Alex called after her, but she had gone. After a moment, Alex followed her downstairs and into the lounge. She was clutching the book. The others turned to look.

'Hello, Alex,' said Rose, standing up to greet her. 'Chucking it down again.'

Rachel wasn't there. Harriet had already sat down next to the fire and had opened a poetry book upside-down. Her eyes were fixed on it and she wouldn't look up.

Alex went over to her. 'Harriet,' she began, but her friend still wouldn't look at her.

In the dormitory, Alex lay on her bed so she could think about what had just happened. She touched her lips where the kiss had been, feeling confused. There was thunder rolling around in the distance somewhere. It growled as if it was threatening moodily to come back. Alex pretended to be asleep when the others came in to bed, her heart beating fast as she heard Harriet's voice and sensed her stopping to look at her. When the lights were out she sat up again. The rain had stopped and the moon had come out from behind the clouds. She couldn't sleep. Her head was full of Harriet, Rachel and Mrs Brown's words, so she held the book up to the window and carried on reading. Alex couldn't stop turning the pages. She didn't sleep at all and finally finished the book when the sun was beginning to rise over the hill. When she put *Odd Girl Out* down, she could still see the characters moving around in front of her.

Before anyone else could wake up, she slipped out of bed and hid the book. She had decided what she was going to do. Still in the librarian's clothes that she had worn the day before, she went past the other beds and made her way silently to the little yellow office. She took the phone off the desk, sank down next to the wall with it and asked for her neighbour's number, hoping that he would be up. After a long pause he picked up the receiver.

'You again,' he said, when he heard who it was. 'I'll see if they're about.' He shuffled off.

Alex felt as if she was holding her breath for several minutes. The house was silent around her. The only sound was the birds waking up outside. It wasn't raining at the moment, although the sky had clouded over again. She could see that the ground outside the window was waterlogged and muddy. After what seemed like a very long time, her mother came to the phone.

'Hello?' she said.

'I want to come home,' Alex whispered. 'Will you get Dad to

154

borrow the car and drive over and get me?'

There was a pause.

'I thought you were getting fixed up,' her mother said at last.

'They lock me in a room, Mum,' she said, still trying to keep her voice down.

There was another pause.

'I hear they do all sorts of things,' her mum said mildly.

'What do you mean?'

'To . . . um,' she coughed, 'get rid of it.'

'Mum,' said Alex. 'What are you talking about?'

'All right, I'll tell you,' she said. 'Mr Bradley has been here to tell us that, well . . .'

'Tell you what?'

'He's heard about you from someone at the church and your dad's not to drive for him any more unless you get cured, that's what.'

'So what did you say to him?'

'He's very well informed, Alex,' she said. 'He says he knows someone with . . . well . . . what you've got. It took them a year to get cured.'

'A year? Mum! They made me wear funny clothes—'

'Seems you like dressing up, Alex,' her mum interrupted. 'Anyway, you've nearly lost your dad his job. Mrs Brown called us yesterday and she said that she was fixing you up.'

There was a pause.

'I've got to go now,' her mother said at last.

'What if I just came home? You couldn't stop me.'

'Your dad would get the sack, that's what would happen. I've got to get breakfast on the table.'

Alex didn't know what else to say. 'OK. Bye,' she said at last.

'Bye, love.'

Alex sat staring at the phone for a moment, suddenly feeling very tired and lonely. She got up and went back into the dormitory where the other girls were waking up.

Mrs Brown had stayed with her daughter in the village, so, before breakfast, Rose initiated another unsuccessful search for Marjory's radio. Harriet searched the hardest. But Alex had promised herself she would find a way to see the light whether the radio was found or not, so she slipped into the kitchen instead to make Doris her orange sponge.

When it was finished, Harriet was still arguing with Marjory about where she had hidden the radio.

'You must remember,' she said grumpily.

'I wouldn't tell you if I did,' the swearing girl replied.

'But I know all the hiding places and I've looked in all of them,' Harriet said.

'You can't have looked in all of them, can you?' Marjory snapped back, just as Alex came in to present Doris with her orange sponge. The young girl stared at it in disbelief. Joyce and Marjory came over to look but Harriet sat down on her bed with her back to them.

'Bloody hell,' said Marjory. 'Can we all have some?' Joyce clapped her hands.

'Why didn't you get us a knife?' Doris said.

'Use a knitting needle,' Marjory replied and Joyce giggled at Doris's indignant face. 'Harriet. Come and look at the cake, why don't you?' she said, but Harriet wouldn't move. Alex left the others to work out a way of dividing the orange sponge between them and went over to Harriet. When she sat down next to her and put a hand on her shoulder, the older girl jumped.

'It'll turn up,' Alex said. She glanced at the others to make sure they weren't paying attention before she spoke again. 'I liked it,' she said quietly. For the first time, Harriet looked up at her. She smiled quickly.

'What?' she said although she knew already.

'Kissing you,' Alex whispered. 'Can we do it again?'

'When?'

'Is the key always left in the lock upstairs?'

Harriet nodded. 'But it's Rose today. She won't lock you in.'

'Come and find me again tomorrow,' Alex said, as Joyce came over to hand them both a piece of sticky orange sponge cake.

156

19

It was very early when Alex slipped out of the house the next morning. None of the others were awake. The spring air was cold as she went quickly down the hill. As well as the librarian's clothes she had *Odd Girl Out* with her. The lake was shining in the early morning sun and the trees looked smart in their new leaves. When she got to the bottom of the hill, she went past the Old Vicarage, where the dogs were sleeping, and in through the wide arch of the library porch. She knocked loudly on the librarian's front entrance. At first all she could hear was silence from the closed books inside. Then she heard movement and the door opened wide. There was Billy Burns in her dressing gown.

'Alex,' she said in surprise.

'I brought back my library book,' Alex said, holding it out just as she had rehearsed. 'Have you got any more like it?'

'Come in. You're up very early. Rachel's still asleep.' Alex followed her into the apartment. 'I think we have the sequel to this one, as it happens,' Billy said. A couple of dogs barked loudly next door. 'Something must have startled them again,' Billy said. 'Such a storm last night. I could hear them over the wind.'

Even though it wasn't yet six o'clock, she went into the library. Alex waited nervously, listening to her wandering up and down the aisles. But the librarian came back empty-handed. 'Seems as though I've lent that one out already. To one of your attendants.'

'Really?'

'Yes. But while you're waiting for it we can fill in a form and send it to another library,' Billy explained. 'That way we can track down some more. It's like a treasure hunt, you see. If they haven't got anything, they pass the form on to the next library. It's the light blue forms. I keep them next to the late returns tray with the fine payable slips. Those are dark blue.' Alex was disappointed, but then she thought of Harriet's face when she had seen the book in the top room.

'I've changed my mind about *Odd Girl Out*. Can I keep it a while longer?' she asked.

'Of course.'

Alex hesitated, 'Billy,' she said. 'Is Mrs Brown really scared of you?'

The librarian smiled and shook her head. 'Not really,' she said. 'She's scared of the ghost.'

Alex's eyes opened wide. 'What ghost?' she said carefully.

'The house is supposed to be haunted,' Billy said. 'Did you see the gravestone under the tree?'

'Almost Brown?' Alex said. She shivered.

'She drowned in the lake.' Billy's eye's glazed over, as if they could have been lakes themselves. Then her face softened as she realised that her young companion might be frightened. Billy sat down on the sofa and looked into the distance like she was remembering something.

'You better get back,' she said, 'or they'll notice you're gone.'

Alex had forgotten about the time. She ran most of the way up the hill. The wind had got up again and the horse chestnut was knocking against the side of the house when she crept in through the back door and into the dormitory. She needn't have worried. Only Joyce was awake.

'Where have you been?' she said, sitting upright and staring at her wide-eyed.

'Nowhere,' said Alex. 'Shhh.' She took off her coat quickly. 'I went into the garden for some fresh air.'

'You're not allowed,' said Joyce, lying down again and kicking her feet around under the covers. The sky had clouded over again and the rain started falling once more.

'Keep it secret, OK?' said Alex. She took *Odd Girl Out* from her bag and pushed it under her pillow.

'Shhh,' said Joyce.

'That's right,' Alex said. 'Guess what?'

'What?' said Joyce, happy that she was being let in on a secret.

'Mrs Brown is scared of ghosts.'

Joyce smiled. 'Shhh,' she said again, as the others began to wake up around her.

Later, Harriet and Alex sat on the bed in the baby room just as they had before when Harriet had brought the picnic. They had locked the door on the inside. 'I found this.' Harriet held out a card. On one side was a list of rules. 'I agree to keep to these rules,' it said at the bottom and it was signed 'Jemima Faraday, 2nd June 1917'. Alex was sure she had seen the name before but she couldn't think where. On the other side was a prayer, 'The Prayer of Salvation'.

'Funny, isn't it?' said Harriet.

There was something about the card that made Alex want to keep it. 'Can I have this?' she asked.

Harriet nodded, so Alex slipped the prayer card carefully into her pocket. Alex looked at her friend for ages before they kissed again. It felt warm and soft like kneading bread dough. They lay down on the bed together and had to get very close because it was so narrow. Alex felt as if they were sailing away somewhere on a raft and had to hold on to each other so they wouldn't fall into the sea. She closed her eyes and imagined the choppy water all around them. All they could do was hold on to each other until they ran aground on a desert island.

After they had kissed again for a long time, Harriet bumped her head against something. She reached up and retrieved the novel from under the pillow.

'You can't keep it under the pillow, stupid,' she said, kissing Alex on the lips again playfully.

'I thought you might want to read it,' Alex said, holding it out to her. But when Harriet tried to take the book, she held it above her head and grinned. Harriet tried to grab it.

'Kiss me again first,' Alex said.

Harriet kissed her quickly and snatched the book from her hand.

Alex fought with her friend to try to get the books back and landed on top of her. They stopped struggling for a moment and smiled at each other. Then Harriet dropped the books and wrapped her arms round her. Alex could feel her pressed tight against her and was breathing in the scent of her skin when they heard feet on the stairs. They looked at each other and laughed, the idea of being caught locked in the baby room together suddenly funny. Alex held her friend even tighter and kissed her again, but when there was a bang on the door, she sat up.

'Shhh,' she said, because Harriet was giggling again.

'Alex? Where's the key?' a voice called through the door. It was Marjory.

'How should I know?' Alex lied. 'Must be downstairs.' She heard Marjory grumbling under her breath.

'You have to come down to the laundry room,' she said.

'Well, find the key then,' Alex called. When Marjory had gone away, Harriet opened the door quickly. She had Hazel-Anne's book with her.

Alex watched over the banisters as Harriet ran downstairs and went into the lounge. She came back without the book.

'Where is it?'

'The lining of one of the armchairs is loose,' Harriet said. 'I can get it out when I do chores in there.' She kissed Alex on the lips again and grinned.

'Stop it,' Alex said, laughing at her. 'What are we doing in the laundry room?' They heard someone in the corridor below.

'Harriet?' a voice called. It was Mrs Brown.

'Your first class,' Harriet said. 'They must think you are ready for the next stage.'

'What's that?' But her friend didn't have time to answer, because

Mrs Brown was at the bottom of the stairs. Alex pushed her out.

'Lock the door,' she said. After a moment she heard the senior attendant on the landing.

'What's going on? Where have you been?' Alex heard her say, just as her friend finally managed to turn the key.

'I'm letting Alex out, like you said, Mrs Brown,' Harriet replied.

'Let me do it. You're turning it the wrong way.'

Alex ran over to close the shutters as the key turned again. The room was cloaked in darkness just in time.

'Come on. Miss Du Bois is waiting for you,' said Mrs Brown. She peered into the room nervously and Alex remembered what Billy had told her.

'Is the Haven haunted, Mrs Brown?' she said. The senior attendant sickened visibly. She held on to the banister and looked from one girl to the other.

'Who told you that?' she said sharply.

'The librarian,' Alex said.

'She's got no business telling lies like that.' Mrs Brown turned on her heel and hurried downstairs.

Smiling at each other as they went, Alex and Harriet followed.

The Haven residents stood around the low brown tables in the laundry room with baskets of crushed lavender and rose petals in front of them, as well as a tub of what looked like bits of old driftwood and a bowl of cloves. The sky had been washed clean like a window. The door was open and the spring air that danced around their faces was pillow-like and sweet. A bee flew in and landed in the basket nearest to Alex, then zoomed off again. Harriet glanced up at Alex and smiled.

Mrs Brown stood at the top of the laundry room. On the blackboard, the words 'Learning how to be a young lady' were underlined twice. Next to her was Miss Du Bois, the retired Frenchwoman who taught crafts at the village school. Mrs Brown had been talking about the importance of smelling nice for the last five minutes, but Alex wasn't listening, she was watching the bee visiting one young woman at a time, Marjory, Joyce, Doris and Harriet, then back to Alex again, as if they were flowers. Her eyes lingered on Harriet. Mrs Brown had just finished her talk when they heard the sound of barking. She waved a hand at Miss Du Bois and walked out.

Miss Du Bois smiled at them kindly, turned round and underneath 'Learning how to be a young lady' she wrote: 'Pot-pourri. Ingredients: cut orris root, lavender oil, dried lavender flowers, rose petals, dried bark, muslin, ribbon, needle and thread.' Outside, the sound of excited barking got louder. Alex looked up to see a woman who looked just like Mrs Brown, but younger, in her coat and headscarf out in the courtyard. She had three small brown terriers with her. Harriet glanced over at Alex and raised her eyebrows. 'That's Mrs Johnson,' she whispered. Alex laughed. Their leads had become tangled, so Mrs Johnson was bending down to untie them. After a moment, they went into the house together. Muffled barking continued from inside.

'The root has already been mixed with the oil,' Miss Du Bois was saying. Doris had taken out a notebook and pencil similar to the ones she had given to Alex. She was writing down everything from the board. From under the sink the teacher produced a crate with several glass jars in it and began to hand them round. When Alex took the lid off hers, the smell of lavender was strong and musky.

'Now. Take some muslin and some ribbon. Gather the cloth together.' She turned and began to draw a diagram of a heart shape on the board to show them how to sew the muslin and secure it with a hanging cord made of purple ribbon. Suddenly they heard raised voices coming from inside the house, accompanied by frantic barking.

'If you finish,' Miss Du Bois said, producing a brown paper bag full of oranges, 'you can try one of these pomanders. Stud it with cloves all over like this one I've already done and I will show you how to make the tie. I'll write the steps on the board.' Next to where she had written the ingredients for the first pot-pourri recipe, she wrote 'HEARTS' in big letters. Then she wrote 'ORANGES' further down and began to record the instructions.

Doris picked up her pencil again and copied the diagrams slowly and carefully.

'Hearts and oranges,' Joyce said loudly. Alex watched as Joyce abandoned her muslin and rose petals and sat to prick cloves carefully into an orange.

Two of the dogs darted outside excitedly and began to chase each other around the twisted tree in the courtyard and in and out of the walled garden. Mrs Johnson came out after them.

'Come back here,' she shouted, but they were too excited to listen.

'Try to ignore them,' Miss Du Bois said, but everyone was watching now. Mrs Brown appeared, framed by the doorway, like an unflattering portrait of herself. The third dog ran past her to join its friends.

Alex went back to sewing her heart. Whenever Miss Du Bois turned her back, Harriet would look at her and smile, so she pretended to be concentrating on her sewing to tease her. Eventually the dogs were rounded up and they heard Mrs Brown's bird-like footsteps cross the courtyard.

'What's this?' Mrs Brown pointed at Doris's notebook and pencil. Doris picked them up quickly, but Mrs Brown's lips curved into a tight smile, while her eyes remained enlarged and fish-like behind her lenses. She dipped a hand into her pocket and pulled out three more pencils. Doris gasped.

'Found under your pillow by Hazel-Anne,' said the attendant. 'You stole them from my office, didn't you?'

'Really, Pamela,' Miss Du Bois began. 'The girls haven't finished their pot-pourri.'

'No dinner,' said Mrs Brown. She fished in her other pocket and took out the pair of scissors. Alex and Harriet exchanged glances. Doris didn't say anything. She began to write down the instructions for making the orange pomander as fast as she could.

'You stole the notebook as well, didn't you?'

Doris scribbled faster.

'I must interrupt,' Miss Du Bois tried, but the senior attendant ignored her. She plucked the notebook from Doris's hands, and sliced up her carefully written notes. The pieces fell on the table.

Miss Du Bois looked horrified. 'What will it take for you to learn?' Mrs Brown said, blinking at Doris. The silence was broken only by the bee banging against the window. The question hung in the air like the smell of lavender from the cloth hearts.

'Oranges?' suggested Joyce finally.

Mrs Brown re-pocketed the scissors and the pencils along with Doris's notebook as if she was an undercover representative from a stationer's shop.

'Now,' she went on, walking over to Alex, 'Mrs Johnson needs some help with her terriers. Mrs Burns has spoken to Mrs Johnson and recommended you, Alexandra.' The librarian's name seemed to agitate her. Alex could feel her breath on her cheek as she put a hand into her pocket and snapped the scissors together impatiently. 'You'll go down to the village tomorrow morning.' She was about to issue more instructions when Joyce interrupted her, indignant at being ignored before.

'Are you scared of ghosts, Mrs Brown?' she said, the words bursting out of her mouth like balloons. 'Is there a ghost at the Haven?'

Alex expected the attendant to snap at her but instead the colour drained out of Mrs Brown's face and she had to lean on the table to steady herself.

'What? What did you see?' she stuttered.

Miss Du Bois adjusted her glasses. 'Are you feeling quite well, Pamela?'

When Mrs Brown didn't reply, she went on, 'Perhaps the girls could finish their pot-pourri now.'

20

*M*y next word after duty was dress. When I was locked in again, that's what I had to think about. I remembered the Memory Lane and the fancy dress shop but I'm not supposed to so I put my hands over my ears to try to get rid of them. In my head, I made myself a beautiful dress instead. It was made of patches of different coloured material that shone when I turned round. It had a train that stretched across the room as if I was in a fairy tale. I lay on my stomach on the bed and made myself a dress out of rubbish: sweet wrappers, gravy boxes, custard labels, the paper that the butter comes wrapped in. I was like Cinderella.

'Have you thought about it?' she said later. I said, 'Yes,' so my next word is wife. I have to tell her the meaning of this one. I have a day to think about it.

Wife: pots and pans, carpet, Hoovers, washing machines, lipstick, toenails, hairdressers, sheets, aprons, houses, babies, dinner parties, shiny floors, toilets, schools, vicars, white dress, wedding ring, breakfast, cradle, ironing, laundry, setting tables, flowers, honeymoon, candlesticks, nappies, marmalade, fruit baskets, hair curlers, nightgowns, lavender, pillow cases, stuffing, Christmas pudding, lying in bed waiting for him to climb on top of me. What would it be like to feel his breath in the darkness and what if it smelt horrible, like old socks? I would have to turn my face away or hold my breath so I couldn't smell it. When she asked me, I said, 'Wife means socks and bad breath,' and she said, 'Yes,' and nodded as if I was very wise. 'Now,' she said, 'how do the three words go together?'

Duty, dress, wife.

1) A wife on duty outside a dress shop, wearing a smart green uniform and smoking a cigarette.

2) My dress made out of rubbish. I am on a platform marrying a man wearing a suit made out of the same wrappers and labels. Someone is taking our photo. We look into each other's eyes. He turns into Isabelle.

3) Soap and scrubbing myself all over in a bathtub. A man saying, 'Clean on the outside, clean on the inside.'

'Clean on the outside, clean on the inside,' I said when she asked me about the three words and how they went together and she said that was very good, but I'm not completely ready. Now I am the sponge cake again without any icing. I have to copy out recipes for soap-making. She gave me a pen and paper because she doesn't know I already have these from Doris. The main ingredient in soap is caustic soda. If you pick it up untreated it will burn your hands and make you cough. If you rub your eyes with it you could go blind. Yesterday I had to go into the garden to do the names of flowers – little violets and yellow pansies. She said that usually I would do cake recipes next but cakes were my undoing, as if I've got buttons down my front and could get opened up, one button at a time, and my skin could get laid out like a coat. What would I have in my inside pockets?

After the soap, I have to copy verses out of Genesis over and over without making any mistakes. So God created man in his own image, in the image of God he created him; male and female he created them and But for Adam there was not found an help meet for him and Therefore shall a man leave his father and mother and shall cleave unto his wife: and they shall be one flesh. 'What do you think help meet means?' she said. Meet sounds like mate and mate means friend or when animals breed. Help is the thing you shout when you're drowning, so I thought of mating and drowning animals. I imagined cows in a field. I thought of a drowning dog I saw in the sea once when I was small, being pulled in by the current. 'A friend who helps you,' I said when she asked me. I imagined a hand and rocks and water.

This morning I had to write: get behind me, Satan, until the letters mixed together like a recipe for coconut surprise. Get behind me, Satan: thou art an offence unto me: for thou savourest not the things that be of God, but those that be of men. They turned into one word: getbehindmesatanthouartanoffenccuntomeforthou-savourestnotthethingsthatbeofGodbutthosethatbeofmen like that. I came up here by myself so I could write. She hasn't locked me in this time. She thinks I am writing about what Jesus said to Peter but I am writing this. Doris said she had to do the same for stealing, only different bible verses. She showed me the ones she had copied out when we were supposed to be sleeping. She says sewing helps too. I have to practise stitches on handkerchiefs and then unpick them all over and start again: cross stitch, blanket stitch, tacking, darning.

I had to put the book back because Eve was shouting up the stairs. 'I could do with some help,' she called, as I came into the almost finished kitchen. 'Can you clear up for me?' I looked around. Eve had been finishing off a vanilla turnover and a raspberry roulade.

'I was hoping you'd do this with me,' Eve said, wiping her hands.

I nodded in what I hoped was a knowledgeable way, looking at the red sauce dripping over the handsome custard sponge. The vanilla turnover seemed hideously complicated, like a lady in an old-fashioned dress who wouldn't give away her secrets. 'Got those references yet?' Eve said. I turned my back on the cake, without replying, and filled the sink with Eve's washing-up.

Maybe I should just leave, I thought, as I stirred the water round and round. I could feel Eve's eyes fixed on the back of my head. By the time I got back to the library I had half made up my mind to go, but Rachel was waiting for me. She waved a small green book as I came in. *The Eade Village Hauntings*, I read from the spine.

'A whole chapter about the house,' Rachel said. The expression on her face suddenly made her look as if she was a ghost herself, haunting the library. She looked at me steadily and I shuddered.

'Do you believe in them?' I said, but for a moment it seemed as though I was asking her if she believed in herself. She grinned at me and the spell broke. I took out the tub containing Eve's vanilla turnover.

'This looks lovely,' she said, when I'd filled our bowls. 'And of course I do.'

The way Rachel spoke was so compelling that while I was eating my second helping of Eve's impossibly complicated pudding, I believed in ghosts too, like some kind of new religious convert. I wanted it to be true and it was, just as true as the creamy vanilla custard that dissolved on my tongue as if my mouth was made of quicksand. As soon as my bowl was empty, I turned the yellowing pages and read while Rachel banged around in the kitchen. Then I saw that she had left her box of papers next to the sofa. I put down the book and rooted through it.

I don't know what I expected to find. There were newspaper reports, advertisements asking for donations, mortgage deeds, inventories, prayers, house rules, menus, even a list of what one girl had had with her when she arrived, on a torn piece of card: *pair of black laced pumps, locket on a silver chain, brown bottle containing tonic, tin of boiled sweets.* I pulled out a handwritten card with a description of a uniform: *pinafore (grey), apron, black stockings, flat black pumps, white cap.* There was no date on it but it had a name on the back: *Wilhelmina Dearing.* Rachel hadn't said anything about a uniform, but Wilhelmina Dearing had to wear one, I thought, whoever she was. The hundreds of girls whose names I had seen in the notebooks, the ones who crowded the house in my imagination, the garden, the driveway, the stumpy stone wall outside, now I saw them in their grey dresses and caps. Then I suddenly remembered where I had seen the name before. I found the 1917 notebook with the crossed-out name, Sally Worthing. Then I read the list: *Mavis Free, Jemima Faraday.* She was the lighthouse researcher. *Elaine Brooks, Doreen Hutchinson, Amanda (sixteen, runaway)*, and over the page: *Wilhelmina Dearing.* I could picture the women in their uniforms, as if I had seen a photo.

I tried to work out the years in my head, guessing how old they would have been in 1917. Maybe they were still alive. It was too hard so I grabbed a scrap of paper and scribbled on it. What if one of them had been twenty in 1917? That would mean she was born in 1897. She would be a hundred and seven. I tried making her younger. What if she had been fifteen when she was at the home? A hundred and two. Amanda was sixteen. A hundred and three. I stared at the paper and the pencil marks. I had seen the oldest woman in the world on the telly and she had been a hundred and twenty-something, but she was in *The Guinness Book of Records* and I was sure none of these women were. I thought about going to get it off the shelves to check, because suddenly I desperately wanted them all to be alive, but I told myself not to be stupid. They were almost certainly dead. Jemima the lighthouse researcher was, Rachel had told me. Wilhelmina Dearing, the crossed-out girl, the runaway and the others would be too: Mavis, Elaine, Doreen, whoever they were.

When Rachel came back in from the kitchen I was staring at the piece of paper as if it had grown a mouth and started speaking to me.

'What are you looking at?'

I showed her the 1917 book with the name of the lighthouse researcher and the others.

'Billy was the librarian before me,' Rachel said, tapping the page.

'Wilhelmina Dearing,' I said, looking up and suddenly realising. 'She was Billy Burns the librarian? I saw her stone in the graveyard.'

'Yes. Billy's short for Wilhelmina. Mrs Wilhelmina Burns. She married her childhood sweetheart. He worked here too, until he died. Get me one of those jam fingers and I'll tell you about it.'

When Rachel had told me all about Billy and her husband Jim, she leant forward, her hand hovering over her cake. 'She found him face down on the enquiries desk. Only it was called issues and returns in those days.'

'What happened?'

'Heart attack.'

I shuddered as I imagined a man slumped forward over the books waiting to be stamped or re-shelved.

'And Billy died in the library on a Sunday afternoon with a copy of *Wind in the Willows* in her hand. I found her stretched out in the children's section as if she had just fancied a nap and had gone to sleep.'

'Really?' I was leaning forward too now, entranced by these people who had inhabited the library before me. After that, whenever I rounded the corner into the children's area where Rachel had arranged bean bags and colourful pictures for story time, I thought of Mrs Billy Burns, stretched out across the floor inside one of those chalk lines the police draw around bodies on the telly.

'Yes, really.' Rachel took a bite out of her cake and relaxed. '1986. Nearly twenty years ago.' She didn't say anything else until her cake was gone. I was worried that her story was over. I flicked the page of the notebook over again.

'What about this one?' I said, pointing to the name at the top of the list. 'Who's Sally Worthing and why has she been crossed out?'

'What? Where? Oh. Billy told me all about that. Sally was the one everyone liked. She was very beautiful apparently. Blonde curly hair and skin like cream.' She paused as if she was reminiscing about a friend. 'She ran away. They never saw her again.'

'But it says that Amanda ran away. She's not crossed out.' I frowned at the fading letters in front of me.

'No. She was a runaway when she arrived.'

'What? That doesn't make sense.'

'Yes it does. They found her half dead from cold in the church. She had run away from home because she was pregnant. It's probably written down like that because she wouldn't give her surname.'

'They were all pregnant in those days, weren't they?'

Rachel hesitated and I realised I might have offended her, but after a moment she carried on telling me about it, businesslike and cheerful.

'Yes. Not when I was there though.'

'When did it change?'

'I don't know for sure, but I think they just started letting in the odd miscellaneous wayward girl if she turned up or if her parents asked. Then there were fewer pregnant girls around for some reason so they made it official. They were all sent to libraries, you know.'

I listened to her like a fish caught with its gills on a hook.

'What for?' I said.

'To work. Billy said that sometimes girls stayed behind after their babies were born if their families didn't want them back, waiting for a library place to become free. Sometimes there was a problem if they couldn't read and write very well.'

'So we might be able to find out what happened to them? If we knew which library they were sent to.'

'Hmm. But we don't know where they were sent.'

'Rachel,' I said, because the question had suddenly occurred to me. 'What kind of stuff did you do while you were there?'

'I used to come to the library to work, like they all did.' She waved a hand at the notebook. 'How I got the job.'

'And you're still here.'

Rachel looked down at herself as if she was checking. 'Looks like it,' she said, grinning at me. 'I expect you're bored of talking about it now, anyway.'

'No. I like hearing about it.'

'I'll tell you about my first day and the boy I was in love with if you like.' She saw my surprised face. 'Oh yes. I was very good-looking, you see.' She patted her short hair as if she was remembering it.

And that was when she first told me stories about the Memory Lane Café, falling in love with Gabriel, Alex French and the cakes, a trip out in a boat to see the lighthouse, and the time Mrs Pretty cut all her hair off. After listening to Rachel's stories for the first time, I lay in the spare room and hugged myself to sleep with her words ringing in my ears.

The next morning, eager to hear more, I picked up the silver case from beside the fireplace and opened the clasp with my thumb.

I had come in from the spare room with a blanket round me because it was cold and I was only wearing an old T-shirt. I had to turn the case upside down to shake the cards out, because they fitted exactly into the black velvet lining inside. I began to look through them. The first was a picture of a pixie playing a flute. It was called the nine of music. There were four different coloured suits, and the cards all had exotic-sounding names: the blue spider, the green devil, the golden crown, the queen of grass and the sea of mirrors, which was blue and shiny. The cards bore their numbers in Roman numerals along the bottom. I shuffled them, wondering how the game was played. I hadn't seen anything like it before. I dealt a handful out in front of me: the red feather man, the nine of paper, a yellow hen, which was a one, the trick of mirrors, a seven, and the blue jackdaw. The bird on the last one was painted in vivid colours, as if it was going to fly out of the card and zoom around the apartment. It had a string of pearls in its beak. I was about to deal again when Rachel came in from the library. I looked at her guiltily, with the cards spread out on the coffee table in front of me.

'Ah,' she said, waving a blue interlibrary loan form at me. 'Playing Scrummage by yourself, are you? Not easy.'

I began to put the cards away quickly, feeling embarrassed at being caught.

'I was bored, that's all,' I said.

'Quite a story attached to them, you know.'

'What kind of story?' I slotted the cards back into the case and examined the silver tree branches engraved on the front. I pretended not to care about Rachel's story but I desperately wanted to hear it, so much so that I was surprised by how excited it made me feel.

'I've got to go up to the house,' I said. 'I'm late.' But Rachel ignored me.

'It was Billy who gave me the cards,' she said proudly. She shuffled the pack absent-mindedly and stared out of the window at the sun which was peeping round a cloud like a hesitant book borrower.

172

'Why?' I said, to prompt her. I hated it when she stopped before she had started.

'Present,' she said simply. 'She taught me to play, same time as she taught me the library.' Then she lapsed into silence again.

'You said there was a story behind them.'

'Yes, I was getting to it,' Rachel replied. But then she suddenly seemed worried.

'What?' I said. I followed her gaze. My blanket had fallen down. Rachel was staring at the lines of white scars. I pulled the blanket over me again.

'I thought you said you got those scratches gardening,' she said.

'Yes,' I lied. 'That is how I got them.' She reached out and pulled the blanket away again.

'Those look deliberate to me.'

'Get off,' I said, just as Eve came in, rubbing her hands together from the cold.

'You're not even dressed,' she said.

'So?' I said automatically.

'I'm not paying you to sit around chatting. You were supposed to be up at the house an hour ago.'

'My fault,' Rachel said. 'I kept her talking.' Rachel looked at me steadily but I could only return the look for a moment.

'Don't just sit there,' Eve said. 'Go and get ready.'

'You were going to tell me about Billy's cards,' I said quietly.

'Another time,' Rachel said, still looking at me.

I jumped up and ran to the bathroom. I left for the house without saying anything else to her. I was thinking about the cards: the nine of music, the blue spider, the green devil, the golden crown, the queen of grass, the sea of mirrors, the red feather man, the nine of paper, a yellow hen, the trick of mirrors, and the blue jackdaw. I imagined someone had thrown them up into the air in front of me and now they lay scattered around my feet.

21

November 2004

> Sin-stained and weary, hopeless and friendless,
> Outcast and scorned by the whole world around;
> Soon to pass on to that life which is endless,
> Misery here by a fearful death crowned,
> Fetters of darkness these lost ones have bound.
> But there is hope, for Calvary's story
> Makes no exceptions, for Jesus has died!
> Sight out of darkness comes, and the full glory
> Shines on Salvations Sea, boundless and wide,
> Still in God's mercy, a limitless tide.

The card was propped up above the fireplace in the library. I read it, fascinated by the old-fashioned curly letters and the decorated border. There was a note from Rachel waiting for me next to it: 'Have gone to see Eve's new flat. Monica is in the Kitchen with the silver surfers. P.S. Thought you'd like to see this.' I turned the card over. 'The Rules of the House', it said at the top. Then:

1. Girls must keep their uniforms clean.
2. Girls must take part in the work and schedule of the house.
3. Girls must attend church on Sundays.

4. Girls must not discuss their circumstances with others.

I agree to keep to these rules.

It was signed in neat black handwriting: 'Jemima Faraday, 2nd June 1917'.

I took the card with me, reading it again as I went down the ramp to the extension, meaning to go online and see if I could find out anything else about the house. In the Millennium Kitchen, Monica was washing up cups and two people, a man and a woman I recognised from the over-sixties book club that met in the library on Friday afternoons, were writing emails slowly and deliberately. There was one computer free. It was already on and the search engine was filling the screen.

I slid onto the stool in front of the computer and propped up the prayer card next to me. I had no idea what to type. Jemima Faraday, the Haven, Eade Village? I was sitting and watching the cursor blinking at me when I saw that an email had been left open at the bottom of the page. I was too curious not to read it.

Hi Eve. No luck so far. Will keep trying, was all it said. Eve must have been here checking her emails and had forgotten to shut down. I was about to go back to the web page when I realised that because it was a reply, Eve's original message might still be at the bottom. I moved down the page and found it.

Hi. How are you? I'm trying to find out some information on someone. Previous employment, any criminal record etc. Can you do a trace for me? Her name is Erica Priestly.

I felt so angry I wanted to reach into the screen, screw up the email and throw it across the room, but I couldn't. The whole story I had woven together, including the library, the Millennium Kitchen and the rubbish house on the hill, was shattering into tiny pieces. I was staring at it in horror when Rachel came in behind me. I jumped.

'Did you see the card?' she asked me.

'Yes,' I said. I clicked quickly and got rid of the email.

'Closing up now,' she said.

Monica and the silver surfers were leaving. It was a clear blue night outside. The moonlight poured in through the glass roof, like an angel was tipping silver liquid from one cup to another, one in the sky, one on the ground.

I shifted in my seat uncomfortably. Rachel sat smiling cheerfully at me, and I decided to leave before I was found out. When she had gone back into her apartment, I put Jemima's card in my pocket and ran up to the house.

My car was parked outside the Haven, so I began to climb the hill, not thinking properly about what I would do. I just wanted to get away from Eve and Rachel and the village and the unfortunate and feeble-minded girls that kept crowding into my head. I never wanted to come back.

I reached my car and felt inside my coat for my keys. Then I swore to myself because I had left them on Rachel's coffee table. My eyes filled with tears of frustration and for a moment I thought madly about walking away up the road which led into town instead, just so I wouldn't have to go back to the library.

It was cold and the night was getting thicker. Soon I realised that the mist that had been hanging over the lake earlier was swarming up the hill and surrounding me and the car with its icy fingers. I was freezing. I ran over to the house and went in through the back door which Eve always forgot to lock. Once I was inside, I felt calmer. I closed my eyes and the silent house was full of the delinquent girls in grey pinafores peering round door frames and banisters at me.

I sat cross-legged in the top room in front of the fireplace. I lit match after match and watched the flames glow and die. The anger I had felt for Eve in the library subsided for the moment, enough so that I could try to sleep.

I spent that night in one of the rooms that still had a bed. I decided I would go back to the library the next morning, sneak in and get my keys and leave without speaking to anyone. As I huddled under an old patchwork quilt and some coats, I closed my eyes and saw tiny flames flying through the air.

As the sun was coming up the next day, I went to find the penknife, and brought it upstairs. The cuts turned red first and white, and then there was a little bit of blood, not much, in a row as if I had been planting seeds and was waiting for them to sprout and grow into flowers. I stood and looked at my arm, feeling more steady. The window was open and cold air was rushing in. I stared out, like I was gazing into a magic mirror which was telling me my future. I felt wonderfully light, as if I had flown up to the clouds. I dropped the knife and lay down on the bed, letting the feeling cocoon me or wrap around me like a blanket. For ten seconds, ten, nine, eight, seven, six, five, four, three, two, one, like a rocket going off, I felt safe. Safe in someone's arms, I was rocked to and fro, wrapped up like a present, like the bananas my mum used to wrap in bits of cold ham when she wanted to cook posh. Then I felt the pillow underneath my head and the air from the window. My arm stung like bees had swarmed up my sleeve and were arguing with each other angrily. I wanted it to go away again: ten seconds, enough time for a rocket to go off, wasn't long enough.

I decided to write my initials because then I could pretend it was a tattoo and people get tattoos all the time. I knew it was stupid, unhygienic, unsafe, dangerous, all the words I had heard Eve use when she was talking about the old cooker from the rubbish man's kitchen, but I didn't think about that. Instead I tried to decide where the best place would be. My sleeve was still rolled up. I held the knife tight in my left hand and halfway along the back of my arm where the smooth brown hairs were, a hand's width from my knuckles, I pressed hard and drew the first line of an E. My eyes watered straightaway. There wasn't much blood, only a little bit, like flowers again. When I did the three horizontal lines I couldn't feel it any more. They were small anyway. That's what I thought to myself, that's why I couldn't feel them. They were small lines. For the P, I was concentrating, as if I was carving a piece of wood. Then there it was, my tattoo, finished. I had written my name on myself and underneath my name was everything that had ever happened to me, so I wouldn't forget.

I closed my eyes and sank back into the pillow again. It lasted longer than ten seconds this time. It was more like five minutes.

It was like when you go to the dentist and have that horrible stuff that makes your mouth go numb. I went like that all over. I imagined covering myself with pictures and decorations as if I was a tree carved with beautiful patterns or one of those illustrated books with all the colours. I imagined flowers and bees and heart shapes.

When I started to feel the bed underneath me again and the low autumn sunlight on my face, I felt worse than I had for ages. I didn't want to float off any more. I looked at the red marks on my arm, like a secret thing written where anyone might notice. I pulled my sleeve down and held on to the cuff as if it were a rope that would stop me floating off again like a hot air balloon. I looked at the knife and felt a sinking feeling as if I had swallowed something really heavy or something had swallowed me. I held on to my cuff tighter and listened carefully in case Eve or Bernie had arrived, but there was only silence. No one was around. It was too early. I grabbed the knife and without looking at it went downstairs. I cleaned it at the sink, pretending to myself that I was just washing up like a normal person. I washed it again and hid it at the back of a cupboard. After that I sat down on the stool and watched the morning sunlight play in the garden like a kid with a dog. Even though I couldn't see the marks on my arms I knew they were there under my sleeves. I could feel them biting into me like an apple must feel when it's eaten, so I got out the prayer card again and examined it. I gazed at it as if it might take me back to 1917. Looking up, I half expected the house to have been transformed around me and for Jemima herself to come walking down the corridor towards me, but she didn't.

As I left the Haven that day, my face cold, hugging my coat, I heard each footstep echo around inside me as I went. I thought about what I would do next. Get the keys, go back to the car, drive away, keep driving till I ran out of petrol. I forced myself to think it like a mantra, but any hope I had of sneaking back into the library evaporated as soon as I went in through the brown porch. Eve and Rachel were both waiting for me, wide-eyed, like two owls on a perch.

'Did you stay at the house last night?' Rachel said.

'Yeah.'

'Why?' said Eve.

I shrugged in reply and picked up my car keys. 'I'm leaving,' I said.

'What's got into you?' Eve said.

'Ricky, at least tell us where you're going,' Rachel said.

I shrugged again. I was nearly at the door when I remembered something else. 'Can I have my wages?'

'Give us an explanation first,' said Eve, folding her arms. I really needed the money but I didn't want to talk about it.

'Fair enough,' I said and turned to go.

Rachel had come up to me and now she put a hand out to grab my coat. I remembered about her and the lesbian cake teacher. That's all I need, I thought, the librarian's got a crush on me. I shook her off angrily. But all she said was, 'Who's going to help me with the display if you're not here?' as if she was really upset. I looked into her face. Her eyes were wet. I was confused. She didn't really want me to stay, did she?

'Well?' she said.

'No one,' I said.

'The glass case has arrived.'

I looked up in surprise. 'You didn't tell me.'

'Came this morning.' I knew Rachel had managed to borrow a long glass case from a museum in town. We were going to put the things from the house inside.

I sank my hands into my pockets as I always did when I was annoyed. Eve sighed impatiently. My hand rested on Jemima's prayer card, and I pictured Jemima with Billy next to her. I really did want to know what had happened to them. I couldn't help myself. Rachel was still staring at me as if she was trying to persuade me not to jump off a cliff.

'I do want to find out about them,' I admitted, hesitating before I said it, in case I sounded stupid.

'About who?' said Eve impatiently. When no one answered

her, she changed the subject, sounding as businesslike as ever.

'Stop being stupid, Erica. I need you at the house. Take your coat off and have some breakfast. You've got forty-five minutes and then the sofa for the tearoom is arriving and you're going to have to help me shift it.'

'She can help you this afternoon,' said Rachel firmly, still staring at me. 'We've got a display to finish.'

There was something about both of them that made me want to stay. I shrugged off my coat, knowing it was only a matter of time before Eve found out about me and I would have to leave anyway.

That morning, Rachel and I laid out the things in the museum case: a menu, Jemima's prayer card, the list of an anonymous girl's possessions, the rules of the house, the postcard and all the newspaper articles and adverts. Eve had found a sheet of piano music, a small white cap and a pair of flat black pumps, which looked like dancing shoes. They stood on their own with Billy's uniform card.

We included some of the notebooks, although Rachel kept the one with her name in next to her bed and wouldn't let anyone touch it. I still hadn't finished the journal but I hadn't told anyone about it. I had been keeping it to myself, snatching the next bit of the story whenever I could and watching Rachel curiously afterwards.

We put the mortgage deeds and the other legal documents in big frames and hung them on the wall near the enquiries desk and in the Millennium Kitchen. The bequest with the words 'for the upkeep of unfortunate or feeble-minded girls in memory of my daughter' ambling playfully across the page was by the door with a caption card Rachel did called 'A History of the Haven', with dates and facts and figures.

22

April 1959

Alex went down the path with the dogs skipping around next to her. She was about to head for the harbour so she could look at the lighthouse again when she saw that a car had pulled up outside the church. A 1957 Ford Thunderbird, Alex thought straightaway, imagining *The Modern Motor Car* open on the table in the bakery kitchen. She tried to remember where she had seen it before, but she couldn't. One of the dogs barked at her, impatient to go on its walk, but she went over to look at the car instead, taking the four terriers with her. Then she remembered. It was Rufus Immanuel's car. She had seen it parked outside the Memory Lane. Rachel's father was here.

She heard a door bang inside the church somewhere and felt curious. She went up the steps, trailing the leads behind her. The dogs skipped up too, sniffing carefully because this walk was new and unusual. She went over to the porch, which she passed through when Hazel-Anne escorted them to the church service on Sundays. She hadn't paid very much attention before. The inner door was banging in the wind. The outer one had been left open. She read the faded notice on the wall as she entered: 'Please close this gate and door lest a bird should enter and die of thirst.' She tied the dogs to a railing and stepped into the church itself. She stood still for a moment, to let her eyes get used to the gloom. It was very quiet inside and it smelt of hymn books.

Gradually, objects took shape: glass stars, candles and a gold cross. She expected to discover Rachel's father sitting in a pew, but there was no one there.

She picked up some lilac blossom that had flown in through the door and noticed how cold the stone floor was, as cold as the inside of a marble statue would be. Then she heard a noise, a chair scraping and footsteps, coming from a small lady chapel on one side of the church which she hadn't noticed before. Out of the stone entranceway came Rachel's father, with his black moustache and his worried eyes darting around him.

'Hello,' Alex said. 'Sorry to disturb you. I was just walking the dogs and—'

'Which way is the library?' he asked abruptly. She pointed and he hurried past her down the steps. Alex watched him go in through the brown archway of the library as she untied the dogs.

'Come on,' she said to them, because they were looking at her expectantly. 'Let's go and see the beach.' She set off down the hill, feeling cold with worry for Rachel.

By the time Alex returned the dogs to the Old Vicarage, Mr Immanuel's car was gone. When she went into the library, Billy was pacing up and down in the sitting room and Rachel was flicking through a book on puddings.

'What happened?' Alex asked them.

'My dad says he doesn't want me back,' said Rachel, still turning the pages of a chapter on semolina, trying to hide how upset she was. 'He doesn't want to see me again.'

'That man made me so angry, I . . .' Billy stopped herself, seeing Rachel's face. 'I've asked Rachel to live with me here. After the baby is born.'

Rachel picked up another book randomly, called *Things to Do with Apples*, as if Billy had said something uninteresting about card cataloguing, and began to leaf through it too fast.

'Are you going to?' Alex said.

'Yes,' said Rachel. 'I'll be the library assistant.'

'Well, I need one,' Billy said. 'Look at all these books. I'm glad

you're here. I can't bear this room any longer. You can both help.'
She began to throw the cushions off the sofa. She said she wanted
to turn it right round, so Alex went over to lift it, while Rachel
stood at one end and pretended to help. The sofa toppled piles
of books as it swung. After it had been reversed and the cushions replaced, Rachel slumped down into it, but Billy stayed on
her feet.

'Billy?' Rachel said. 'What do you think of this dress?'

Billy glanced at her. 'I love it,' she said. She paced to and fro,
taking in the new layout of the room.

'What about my hair?' said Rachel.

'I love it. I also love your hands, your feet and your nose.' Billy
pushed the wooden coat stand behind the door to the tiny kitchen.
Alex had never seen her so worked up before.

Rachel looked at her hands. 'Really? I don't like my hair any
more. I want to cut it short.'

'Well,' said Billy, 'Mrs Pretty is due to bring back *Pride and
Prejudice* today. And that book I found her on dog training. She's
had a puppy from Mrs Johnson. Why don't you ask her?'

Rachel got up to examine her hair in the mirror above the
fireplace.

Finally the whole room had been reversed and almost every
pile of books had been scattered in the process. Billy sat on the
edge of the sofa tapping her left arm with her right hand, looking
around her at the new arrangements.

'Better,' she said. 'But not perfect.' She got up and began to re-
pile the books, making the stacks neater and straighter, pushing
some of them against the wall.

'Can't you just get rid of these?' Rachel said. She bent to pick
up a torn copy of *The Wind in the Willows*.

'I can't bear to,' Billy said. They both seemed so unhappy and
agitated that Alex wanted to do something to cheer them up.
Then she remembered what she had been planning to ask them.
She took the lighthouse encyclopaedia out of her bag.

'Do you have any more of these?' she said, putting the book
down. 'More recent ones.'

'Oh, those,' Rachel said. 'They come out every five years.'

'Yes,' said Billy. 'We have a few, I think.'

Rachel found the right box and Billy came up with three more encyclopaedias made in the same way with leather thread-work, but these were a little newer and smarter. Alex was pleased. She arranged the books in front of her on the coffee table, so that they were all open on the first page. As the books got newer, so some of the information had been updated and better photographs had been taken. More lighthouses were covered in the later editions too.

'Why is Eade on the first page?' Alex asked.

Billy studied the books for a moment and smiled to herself. 'Do you know what a home lighthouse is?'

'Is it a lighthouse that someone lives in?' Rachel said, sitting down again. If that was true, Alex thought, then the bakery should be called the home bakery and the Memory Lane Café was the home café.

'Not exactly,' said Billy. 'It's the first lighthouse you visit. Sometimes it's in your home town, if you come from the seaside. But not everyone does, of course.'

Alex studied the photographs of the Eade Village light. The photo was the same in all of them. It hadn't been updated.

'The person who wrote these books,' said Billy, and her face went serious for a second, 'well, Eade is her home lighthouse.'

'You don't smoke, do you, Billy?' Rachel asked suddenly.

'No, I don't. What makes you say that?'

Rachel had seen what looked like a silver cigarette case by the fire. When she picked it up, Alex saw that it was decorated with tree branches.

'Don't touch that,' Billy said sharply. Alex noticed the S shape on the back of the top card before Billy took the case from Rachel's hand.

'Sorry,' Rachel said. 'Are they Scrummage cards?'

Billy looked surprised. 'Yes,' she said. 'How did you know that?'

'People play it in the café.'

'I see.'

'Will you teach me?' Rachel said.

'I taught someone once,' she said vaguely. 'Maybe.' They heard footsteps.

'Cooee,' someone said from the library next door. Rachel got up. 'That's Mrs Pretty,' she said. 'I'll go.'

Alex was still examining the lighthouse books. 'Who wrote them?' she asked. 'Does she still live here?'

'Look on the back.'

She turned one of the books over. In very small, neat, gold lettering at the bottom of the cover was a name: 'Compiled by Jemima Faraday.'

'No, she doesn't live here,' said Billy. 'I don't think she's been to Eade for a long time.'

Alex felt inside her pocket for the prayer card Harriet had given her. 'Look,' she said. 'I knew I'd seen her name before. Do you know her?'

'I used to. She's a full-time researcher now.' Billy took the card. 'Where did you get this?' she said, examining it as if it was a photo of a friend.

'One of the others found it.' Billy stared at the card for so long, Alex thought she might have forgotten she was there.

'Well, now it seems she updates lighthouse books,' Billy said at last. 'I only knew about it myself when I saw her name on the back.'

'Did you used to be friends?'

Billy didn't reply. Alex noticed she had tears in her eyes.

'You should write her a letter,' she said.

'She wouldn't want a letter from me. It would make her sad. It would be like getting a letter from the bit of you that you want to forget about,' said Billy. Alex tried to imagine why someone would be sad after getting a letter from the librarian, but she couldn't. Two tears had escaped from Billy's eyes and were travelling across her cheeks like little streams.

'I would like to be a lighthouse researcher,' Alex said, to change the subject.

'I should think it's hard work,' said Billy, wiping her face with the back of her hand. She stood up and Alex could tell she was embarrassed about crying in front of her. 'Let me introduce you to Mrs Pretty,' she said too cheerfully.

They left the pages open on the table and went into the library.

The woman who was browsing amongst the books was in her forties and wore a lot of powder on her face. So much that Alex could smell it when she came over to them. She had a terrier with her.

'Hello, Mrs Pretty. This is Alex,' Billy said brightly.

'She says she can't fit me in,' Rachel said glumly.

'Hello, Mrs Burns,' the woman said. 'Hello, Alex. No, I can't. I've got a week of perms ahead of me.' She and the terrier disappeared down the aisle where the novels sat waiting to be read.

'Mrs Pretty has the hair salon on the corner,' Billy explained.

After a while, the hairdresser and the terrier approached with a copy of *Jane Eyre*.

'Reading it again?'

'Yes,' said Mrs Pretty. 'I can't help it.' She talked about the book as if it were a secret habit, like eating raspberries in the middle of the night. Rachel took her ticket and stamped the date slip and Mrs Pretty and the terrier went back out into the morning.

'I'd better go,' Alex said.

'Have you brought *Odd Girl Out* back yet?' Billy asked her.

Alex blushed guiltily. 'No. Sorry.'

'Oh, well, we can renew it for you. Hazel-Anne hasn't returned *Women in the Shadows* either.'

'It was Hazel-Anne who borrowed it?' Alex smiled.

'Yes. Now would you like something else on lights?' Billy said, scanning the shelves. 'I have one in history about the first ones. Where they were built. That kind of thing. It has maps.'

Rachel stamped *Keeping the Lights: A History of British Lighthouses and Their Keepers* and Alex stuffed it into her bag quickly. When she left them, they were listening to Billie Anthony singing 'This Ole House' on the wind-up gramophone. The librarian liked it because they had the same name.

'I need to tell you about request forms,' Billy was telling Rachel as Alex left. 'Don't let a borrower request a book if they are uncertain whether they want it. It saves a lot of inconvenience.'

In the baby room that day, Alex finished copying out the bible verses Mrs Brown had given her. Then she went over to the bed and took out her red notebook. Using a page torn from it, she began to write a letter as neatly as she could. 'Dear Mrs Faraday, I enjoyed reading your books.' She wondered what to say next and chewed the pen for a while, but because there were so many things she could say, she couldn't think of anything in particular. It seemed to her that if only she could get to meet the lighthouse researcher, she might be allowed to help with her work and it might not matter any more who she had or hadn't kissed.

Several sentences came into her head at once. She lay on her back and stared at the ceiling, the wrong way round on the bed so her feet were on the pillow. She let the words fill her head like the smell of a chocolate cake cooking: I'm in the home because I kissed Isabelle but really I wanted them to send me because of Rachel and now I've kissed another girl and I wish I was a lighthouse researcher like you though I'm not sure if I am disgusting or not or if I've got something like my mum and Mr Bradley say I have. My mum says I can't come back or my dad'll lose his job. Maybe you can tell me if I'm like the characters in *Odd Girl Out*. Mrs Brown said I'd make someone a good wife. When I saw the lighthouse for the first time, I thought it was one of the most beautiful things I had ever seen (not kidding) and I wanted to go and look inside straightaway. Next door to the library they breed dogs and Mrs Brown's daughter lives there. I took some of them for a walk this morning. John's probably taking us in his boat but you could take me if you came to see the librarian.

But she couldn't say any of that. She took her pen from her mouth and rolled over. She wrote quickly, 'Billy Burns, our librarian, says that she once knew you. I am sure that Mrs Burns would like you to visit her.' She heard footsteps on the stairs and signed off quickly, 'Best regards, Alexandra French', and ran over to the shutters.

In the office, while Mrs Brown found something in a filing cabinet, Alex slipped an envelope into her pocket. Then the senior attendant adjusted her glasses and examined the bible verses Alex had written out neatly: *Therefore shall a man leave his mother and his father, and shall cleave unto his wife: and they shall be one flesh. Therefore shall a man leave his mother and his father, and shall cleave unto his wife: and they shall be one flesh. Therefore shall a man leave his mother and his father, and shall cleave unto his wife: and they shall be one flesh. Thereforeshallamanleavehismotherandhisfatherandshallcleaveuntohiswifeandtheyshallbeonefleshthereforeshallamanleavehismotherandhisfatherandshallcleaveuntohiswifeandtheyshallbeonefleshthereforeshallamanleavehismotherandhisfatherandshallcleaveuntohiswifeandtheyshallbeone*

'Now,' said Mrs Brown, interrupting her thoughts, 'dinner please, Alex.' Alex had just taken some rock buns out of the oven and had replaced them with a fish flan, when Rachel came in. She seemed excited but when she came closer Alex could see that her eyes were red from crying. She was holding Marjory's radio.

'Oh my God! Where did you find that? Everyone's given up looking for it,' Alex said.

'Never mind where I found it.' Rachel sniffed and wiped her face on her sleeve.

'What's wrong?' said Alex, putting the buns on the window sill to cool.

'Nothing,' Rachel said.

'We can't go out to the light until Mrs Brown gets that radio,' Alex said, feeling annoyed with Rachel for the first time. It was a strange feeling, like realising your favourite dress doesn't suit you.

'I know and I don't care. I'm putting it back where I found it when I've finished with it.'

'Tell me what's wrong,' Alex said.

'Mrs Pretty won't do my hair for me. I went to ask her again and she said she still couldn't fit me in. I hate my hair like this.' The tears started tumbling down her face.

'She'll fit you in eventually,' Alex said.

'It's because I'm like this.' She looked down at her pregnant stomach. 'She doesn't want me in the salon.' Rachel sniffed again and began fiddling with the radio. There was a fuzzy noise and then they could hear Fats Domino singing 'Blueberry Hill'.

'Billy likes this one,' Rachel said.

'Let me give Mrs Brown the radio, Rachel. I really want to go on the lighthouse trip,' Alex said, reaching for a bowl to make a pudding.

'The weather's too unpredictable anyway. You heard what Rose said.'

'It hasn't rained for ages,' Alex retorted. 'It's gorgeous outside today.' She waved a hand at the sun streaming in through the window. The hissing sound from the radio continued behind Fats' voice.

Rachel turned to Alex and pretended to cheer up, even though the tears were still shining in her eyes. She looked into her face.

'You're very pretty, you know,' she said, trying to change the subject.

'Really?' Alex said. It was the second time Rachel had called her pretty. She remembered how happy she had been the first time and felt so confused she thought she might turn on Rachel and get angry with her.

But then Alex saw how beautiful her eyes were and she couldn't help but smile. She swayed to the music as she stirred. Rachel swayed too and smiled back. Then she picked up Alex's pudding mix and began turning round and round to the music, as if the bowl was her dancing partner and Melanie was playing the piano. She went right the way over to the sink and back again. Alex laughed, and Rachel put the bowl down, took Alex's hand and danced with her, rocking from side to side and holding her arm up so Alex could twirl underneath it.

It felt lovely holding Rachel's hand and feeling her clasp her waist. Fats finished and 'Summertime Blues' began. They carried on dancing with the smell of fish flan and rock buns all around them. The door opened. Harriet came in and gazed from Alex to Rachel with her mouth open.

'You found the radio,' was all she could say, but she didn't manage to hide the pain in her voice.

'Yes,' Rachel said. 'And I'm putting it back afterwards.' She handed Harriet a rock bun from the window sill. 'Try one.'

'They're not really ready yet,' Alex said in alarm. But Harriet took a bite and her eyes opened wide when she tasted it.

'Lovely,' she said with her mouth full. Her face softened. Behind her, the music still played.

Rachel reached out suddenly and pulled Harriet towards her.

'What are you doing?' Harriet said. 'Where did you find the radio?' Rachel began to pull her to and fro to make her dance.

'I'm not telling,' she said loudly, dancing far too energetically. After a couple of minutes, she collapsed onto the stool, exhausted. She had just rested her hand on her wide stomach when Doris ran in. She had something behind her back. She stopped short when she saw them all with the radio. 'You found it.' she said. When no one replied, she went over and stood in front of Alex. She addressed her solemnly.

'Are you really one of what Mrs Brown said you was?' she said, revealing the book she had hidden behind her back.

'I don't know.'

'Why did you dress up then?'

Alex felt Harriet and Rachel watching her. She shrugged. 'Don't know,' she said again.

'I'll show you this anyway,' Doris said. She pressed the book into Alex's hand. Then she noticed the rock buns. 'Can I have one of them?' she asked.

'They're not—' Alex began, but Rachel was already passing one over.

'Sure,' Rachel said. Alex examined the book.

'Where did you get this?'

'It was in the attendants' room,' Doris replied with her mouth full.

Alex gazed at the book. It was *Women in the Shadows*. 'Which attendant does it belong to?' she asked, though she knew already.

'Hazel-Anne. It was in her underwear drawer.'

'You went through her underwear?'

Doris nodded and grinned, while Alex inspected the summary of the story on the back.

'That's a library book,' Rachel said.

'The sequel to *Odd Girl Out*,' Alex murmured, almost to herself.

'It's a book about,' Doris hesitated, 'what Mrs Brown said you was. Is Hazel-Anne one as well?'

'How should I know? Can I borrow it?' Alex put the book down next to the mixing-bowl.

'Yes.' Doris went over to the radio and turned it up. *Comes A-Long-A-Love* was half way through. She began to dance.

'Dance with me,' Alex said, sliding Harriet's fingers into her own.

'You were dancing with Rachel,' Harriet said into her ear. 'You like her better than me, don't you?'

'No, of course not,' Alex said quickly, but she wasn't sure.

'Where did she find the radio?' Doris asked them as Rachel watched from the stool.

'Don't know,' Alex replied.

'We'll never get to go to the light unless we hand it in,' Harriet said.

'Come on then,' Alex said and Harriet flashed a smile at her. They both tried to grab the radio at the same time, but Rachel got there first, her energy returned for a moment. She lifted it above their heads and Kay Starr sang down at them. Doris tried to snatch it from her, but collided with Alex instead. Rachel was too quick for them. She ran out of the kitchen, flicking Marjory's radio off as she went. By the time the others untangled themselves and came out into the corridor, there was no sign of Rachel. They went into the lounge and found her sitting in the armchair by the fire, pretending to read a book. The radio was nowhere to be seen.

'It's in the lounge,' Harriet said. 'I knew it.'

'Has it been in here all along?' Alex asked.

'Yep,' said Rachel. 'And I'm not telling you where. I don't want to get in a boat and I don't want to go out to the light.'

'You don't have to,' Doris said, 'you can stay in the library.'

'Everyone has to go on educational visits,' Rachel snapped back. 'And I don't want to.'

She stuck her nose in her book and wouldn't say anything else. Harriet went over to her and looked like she might take her by the shoulders and shake her. 'Tell me where you've hidden it,' she said.

Just then, Marjory and Joyce stuck their heads around the door. 'What's going on?' Marjory said. 'We heard music.'

'And we found this in the kitchen,' Joyce held up the library book. There were footsteps in the corridor.

'Hazel-Anne's coming,' said Joyce happily.

Harriet had gone over to Marjory now. 'Tell me where it is,' she said. She grabbed hold of the young girl's arms.

'Leave her alone,' said Joyce in surprise and she pushed her away. Alex peeled Joyce's fingers from the book and stuffed it inside the torn lining of the armchair, just as Hazel-Anne came in.

23

Tumble forward in time like someone rolling down the grassy hill over and over towards the lake, roly-poly like an acrobat turning head over heels on the beach, cartwheel along the sand then jump up into the sky, up above the lighthouse, the shops, the library, the church, and back to the house, fly past three baskets of lavender, four pot-pourri hearts and one orange pomander as if you are a bumble bee going from basket to basket, leap over hundreds of books stamped and returned and eighty-six fines issued, dart around the hair salon and watch four hundred and fifteen trims, fourteen perms and three peroxides, creep into the dog shed behind the Old Vicarage and zip in and out of the cages, dive past three weeks the colour of saucepans and countless blossom petals blowing round the walled garden, until the sky is washed clean like a window and Eade Village plunges headlong into summer like a bather jumping off the rocks into the sea, swim idly through the hot air and watch all the stolen kisses between Harriet and Alex, the dinners on long benches and the lemon surprises, somersault down the road to the harbour like a jester set loose from a pack of cards and four months later if you floated lazily above the house and looked across the hillside you would see: one, Hazel-Anne walking up the hill on her way to do her shift, twisting her hands, wondering again what had happened to the book she had been reading, praying so hard that her lips are moving, please don't let her find it, over and over again; two, a pottery demonstration in the laundry room; and three, a car pulling up by the grey wall next to the lake. A white 1956 Citroën DS 19, Alex would think the first time she saw it, but that wasn't until later.

The woman who got out of the car and walked into the library a few moments later was so powdery white that she could have been a ghost in proper clothes and a hat. Her hands were perched one on top of the other in front of her so that they wouldn't take off and fly away, and her face was the texture of marshmallow, with two quick, darting eyes. Billy found herself thinking that the woman framed by the library entranceway should have been fat and round like a Buddha and that the eyes that darted from her face to the books behind her should have been laughing and her hair should have been amber and not grey. She thought all of these things in the bottom of her stomach and in her hands and feet. In her head, she felt an empty space, like a piece of the black empty universe. In her head she found words like, do come in, are you new to the library, you look tired can I fetch you a chair, would you like a cup of tea, have you visited Eade Village before. But neither of them said anything, they just looked at each other.

'I remember you fatter,' the woman said at last and just for a second her eyes lit like candles and then died again.

'Come in,' said Billy politely, feeling confused. 'Have you visited Eade before?'

'Fat like a pig,' the powdery marshmallow woman said under her breath as she came into the library and looked around at the books as if they hurt her eyes. The part of Billy that thought of tea and cake and chairs and new library tickets decided that the powdery woman must be old enough to speak her thoughts out loud and thoughts didn't always make sense. She knew that because in the mornings she thought of her little boy, the one she had lost, his head appearing and reappearing on her pillow like the Cheshire cat.

'Of course I have,' said the woman, looking at her sharply. Billy fetched a chair but the woman ignored it. She held out one of her vein-mapped hands instead. Billy grasped it but made no effort to shake it or let go. She held the soft hand in her own.

'I'm Mrs Billy Burns,' said Billy.

'It's me, you silly old woman.'

Billy let go of the marshmallow hand and sat down in the chair herself with a bump. Jemima Faraday walked up one of the aisles of books slowly and let Billy sit and watch her.

'Can I make you some tea?' said Billy at last.

'Tea would be very nice,' said Jemima. When she spoke, the sides of her mouth folded up like someone folding a napkin, and her eyebrows darted up and down.

When they were sitting on the sofa with cups and saucers and slices of the cherry cake Alex had made the day before, Billy looked at the old woman who had appeared in her library that afternoon and she smiled.

'What are these?' Billy picked up a brown pill bottle which was poking out of her friend's handbag.

'Oh, nothing.'

'Are you ill?'

'Getting old.' Then Jemima saw Billy's silver case by the fire. She looked at her and her eyes lit up again. 'May I?' She picked up the silver box, undid the clasp and took out the top three cards. They were worn around the edges, like old cigarette cards.

'I've got something for you,' Jemima said when she had looked through them. She reached into her handbag and took out a card which said 'The Six of the Sea' across the top. It was more weary than the last time Billy had seen it and a little faded. Jemima handed it to her. The words Billy had written still ran across the bottom as if a spider had crawled over it: 'I promise' it said.

'I was going to write to you,' Billy said. 'I hadn't forgotten. I'm not old yet.'

'Well, I got old before you did.' She delved into her handbag again. This time she took out a letter and showed it to Billy. 'Dear Mrs Faraday, I enjoyed reading your books.'

'Alex wrote to you,' she said and smiled. She was turning the Scrummage card round and round in her hand.

'I haven't replied. I wasn't going to come and then, well, I had some news which changed things.'

'What news?'

'I'll tell you later.' Jemima tapped the letter. 'Who is she?'

'One of the girls at the house.'

'Really?'

'Friends with Rachel who works here.'

'And who's Rachel?'

'Pregnant girl from the Haven.'

'Shit,' said Jemima.

'Yes. Quite,' said Billy. The two women sipped their tea.

Jemima picked up the brown pill bottle from her bag and took two of the tablets. 'I want it to stop now.'

'What?'

'The house,' Jemima said quietly. 'I didn't come back before because I was frightened, but now ...' She looked at the pill bottle.

'But now what?'

'Nothing to lose, I suppose.'

Billy stared at her in alarm. 'I don't understand,' she said, but Jemima didn't reply. 'What are you going to do?'

'Don't know really,' her friend said. 'Now I'm here, I'm not sure. I'll stay until I can sort it out, if it's all right with you.'

'Do you still play?' said Billy, picking up the card again.

'I've won a few hands in my time. You?'

'Not here.'

'Why not?'

'No one to play with.'

'We could organise a few games. Here. In the library.' She waved her teaspoon around the room.

Billy laughed and after that they swapped stories, opening each other up like books and fitting forty years into a late afternoon full of tea and cake.

*   *   *

'Where are you staying tonight?' said Billy, putting her cup down.

'With you of course.'

Billy smiled and patted her hand. 'You can have the spare room.

'Can we go and look at the house? Can we go now?' Jemima said.

The lake shone like a mirror as usual. As Billy and Jemima approached it, the Haven squatted on the side of the hill, like a cat about to jump.

After breakfast Alex had sensed something was wrong, but it wasn't until she went over to her bed that she realised someone had gone through her things. Her clothes had been hastily refolded, but she could see that they had been tampered with. Her bag, too, was hanging open next to the window. 'Hazel-Anne, looking for her book again,' she told Harriet, later.

'She'll never find it,' Harriet said.

Odd Girl Out and *Women in the Shadows* sat side by side under the torn lining of the armchair, keeping each other company. Alex had read both books over and over again, and Harriet liked to read her slices from each, like she was eating slices of cake, when they locked themselves in the baby room together.

At the moment the two friends had set out for the house, Billy with the big brown key to the library in her hand, Jemima tying on her headscarf, Alex was delving into the back of the armchair for *Women in the Shadows*. Hazel-Anne was supervising after-dinner reading, so she hid the book inside a big copy of *Literary Verse for the Young Reader*. She leant into the crock of the couch so her book couldn't be seen. The fire was lit even though the day had been hot. As soon as Alex had started reading, Doris ran in.

'She wants to lock me upstairs again, but I won't go,' she said. She stood in the middle of the room and folded her arms. They all looked up in alarm as Mrs Brown came in and grabbed hold of her wrist.

'Upstairs,' she said, attempting to drag the young girl out of the door.

'No,' Doris said and tried to prise the attendant's fingers from her arm. Mrs Brown made another effort to pull her away but her hand slipped. Almost falling with the momentum of the struggle, Doris flung herself into the armchair next to the fire. She landed hard and nearly sank right through the chair. Suddenly music began loudly from underneath her, as if she had turned into a human musical box. It was Frankie Lymon and the Teenagers. Doris sprang up again in alarm.

'Oh no,' Rachel said, trying to suppress a giggle.

'Shit,' said Marjory and she put her hands over her face. Mrs Brown marched over and lifted the armchair cushion. Underneath a broken wooden bar and flimsy piece of material which had torn from Doris's fall, there was a hollow space. She reached in and retrieved the radio. The Teenagers were still singing. Mrs Brown glared at them all, but Joyce clapped her hands in delight.

'Can we go in John's boat now, Mrs Brown?' she said.

'You said we could,' Harriet said very quietly. She put her sketch pad down, gazed into the fire and watched the flames playing hopscotch with the logs. 'It was in there all the time,' she whispered to herself. 'Why didn't I think of it?'

Mrs Brown flicked off the radio. 'Let's see what else is hidden in here,' she said. She felt around inside but didn't find anything, so she walked round the back of the chair and lifted the lacy antimacassar.

When she saw that the lining was torn, she glanced around at them all with a triumphant look in her eyes. She put her hand inside the lining. Now Harriet had her head in her hands. To Alex's horror, Mrs Brown removed *Odd Girl Out*. Alex felt Hazel-Anne tense. Mrs Brown held the paperback in her finger and thumb and dangled it in front of her nose where it swung like a pendulum, just as if her face was a clock with numbers. Its yellowing pages fluttered in fear.

'This is a homosexual novel,' Mrs Brown declared, waving the frightened book around. 'Is this yours, Harriet?'

Harriet shook her head and looked away.

'Alexandra, is this your book?' The others watched silently. When Alex didn't reply, Mrs Brown opened *Odd Girl Out* and began to rip the pages from it. The young attendant didn't say a word.

'You can't,' Rachel said. She stood up, her fledgling librarian's instincts getting the better of her, but she didn't know what to do next.

'Alexandra,' Mrs Brown was saying, 'you do realise that your father may lose his job?'

'That's a library book,' Rachel shouted, and as if to back up what she said, a date slip with 'Eade Village Library' stamped on it fluttered down and landed at her feet. Mrs Brown hadn't stopped tearing the pages, but then she glanced down to where Alex had let the poetry book fall open on her lap. She snatched up the exposed copy of *Women in the Shadows*.

'Stop,' Alex shouted. 'It's not my book. It's not mine.'

'Whose is it?' Mrs Brown said, the light of the fire reflecting off her thick glasses.

'It belongs to the library, they both do . . .' Alex trailed off as she saw Hazel-Anne stiffen even more. Doris looked at her in fear.

'You're lying,' Mrs Brown said, against all the evidence. 'They both belong to you.' She threw *Women in the Shadows* down into the middle of the room as if it was hot. Joyce picked it up and began to flick through it, with Marjory and Doris leaning over either shoulder.

'Hazel-Anne,' Mrs Brown said suddenly, making the young woman jump almost clear of the sofa. 'Go and see if there are any more.'

Hazel-Anne ran out of the room without looking back. They heard the dormitory door open as Mrs Brown stuffed the torn pages into Alex's hands.

'Now,' she said. 'Throw them on the fire.'

'No,' Alex said, standing up to confront her, holding the pages in her fist like a strange bridal bouquet.

'Stop it,' Rachel said but Mrs Brown wasn't listening. She

grabbed *Women in the Shadows* from Joyce, ripped it up too and pushed the damaged chapters into Alex's hands.

'Throw them on the fire,' she said again.

'I can't.'

'Do it,' Mrs Brown said.

Alex went over to the fireplace. She was feeding the first few pages into the flames when the door flew open wide and banged hard against the side of the piano, sending out a deep clamour of notes. The draught from the door caught some of the pages and blew them to the side of the grate. There was a series of loud bangs from upstairs.

'What's that?' Mrs Brown said. It sounded as if someone was jumping up and down in a tantrum.

Hazel-Anne came running back in.

'No more books,' she said.

At that moment, the front door opened: a sharp tug of the handle, then a quick twist right and left, although no one heard because of the noise from upstairs, which stopped just as suddenly as it had started.

'Was that you, Hazel-Anne?' Mrs Brown asked. She had turned pale. 'Banging upstairs?'

Hazel-Anne shook her head.

'It was probably just the wind, Mrs Brown,' said Harriet, calmly meeting the senior attendant's gaze. No one said anything for a moment.

'Maybe someone left the window open,' said Hazel-Anne, unable to look at Alex who stood by the fire, most of the torn books still in her hands.

'Go and see,' Mrs Brown said, but the young attendant wouldn't move.

'Is it the ghost?' Joyce said happily. Doris and Marjory both told her to hush at the same time as Harriet stood up and began to collect the pages that could be saved from the side of the grate. It was too late for those in the middle. They burned like witches on the pyre. Harriet fished out the ones she couldn't reach with a poker.

Alex took in the scene: the words sparking and fraying in the fire, Rachel with her hands on her hips, Harriet hooking out singed sentences like a fisherman, Mrs Brown still holding part of *Women in the Shadows*, the white-faced attendant next to her, and Marjory, her arms round Doris and Joyce, whispering, 'Shit, shit, shit,' under her breath.

'Go and see,' demanded Mrs Brown for a second time.

'I'll go,' said Alex, putting the torn pages down on the sofa. She ran upstairs before Mrs Brown could object.

At that moment Billy and Jemima stood next to the low grey wall at the front of the house, looking up at the windows. The librarian reached out for her friend's hand and clasped it tight. They were both remembering a bright Sunday morning, and the eight young women who had lined up outside, when the grassy hill had been white with frost.

When Billy opened the front door, Jemima peered into the hallway with an odd look on her face, like people do when they go into churches with painted ceilings. An instant later she stood framed in the entrance to the lounge.

'What's going on?' Billy said, coming up behind her.

When Mrs Brown saw them in the doorway, she backed towards the fireplace, nearly knocking Harriet into the flames. Harriet moved out of the way, still holding her poker like a guard on duty, and began to stamp on the saved fragments to put them out.

'Billy,' Rachel said.

'Good evening,' Hazel-Anne said politely. 'Perhaps you would like to wait in the office.' But Jemima ignored her. She walked into the room and stood directly in front of Mrs Brown.

'Hello, Pamela,' she said, just as Alex ran back in.

'The window was open. I've closed it. I think there might be a storm . . .' Then she looked at the two newcomers in astonishment.

'It's all right, Alex, we're just . . .' Billy said grimly, but then she saw the torn pages on the sofa. 'What's been happening here?' she demanded angrily, inspecting a piece of *Odd Girl Out*. 'This is a library book.'

Jemima's eyes darted around the room like tiny spies.

'I saved these,' said Harriet. She picked up the blackened remnants but rather than showing them to the librarian she came over and gave them to Alex.

'Thanks,' Alex said, meeting her gaze. The chaos in the room around them froze for a moment and she felt as if Harriet was giving her a present rather than the singed pages.

'It's Jemima, isn't it?' Mrs Brown was squinting at the woman in front of her.

'That's right.'

'What do you want?'

'I think I've seen enough and heard enough about what goes on here these days,' Jemima said firmly.

'What do you mean?' said Mrs Brown, sounding really frightened.

'It's time for it to stop now,' Jemima replied.

'You can't come in here like this and threaten me,' Mrs Brown said, glaring at Jemima.

'What are you talking about?' Hazel-Anne said quietly.

'I'm going to get this place closed down if it's the last thing I do,' Jemima said.

Marjory, Doris and Joyce were staring at her open-mouthed.

'And it might be,' Jemima added. She prodded Mrs Brown in the chest with a white finger. 'In the meantime, I think you've promised these girls a boat trip.'

24

Alex climbed unsteadily into the boat and sat down next to Harriet. Rachel was opposite her, round and uncomfortable, her hands across her lap. John made room for Rose next to him inside his cabin, started the engine and turned the wheel.

'I don't like boats,' said Rachel. She looked unwell already.

'Shut your bloody mouth,' said Marjory, because she was nervous too. Rachel glared at her and she bit her lip. Rose didn't notice. She was laughing at something John had said. Joyce smiled widely and trailed her hand in the water. In the distance Alex could see the lighthouse like a flagpole at the end of the ridge of brown rocks which meandered into the bay. When she turned round again, Rachel was staring straight at her, with a queasy boat-sick expression on her face.

'Go to hell,' said Marjory, because Joyce had flicked a handful of water over her and was laughing to herself.

'I don't feel so good,' Rachel said. She moved her knees apart to make herself more comfortable. She leant forward and put her head in her hands.

'Do you feel sick?' said Doris.

'Yes,' said Rachel. 'Are we nearly there?' Doris looked out over the bay and back at the harbour to judge the distance, while Joyce threw some more water at Marjory.

'We're halfway,' Doris said. 'Look.' Rachel kept her head in her hands.

'If you're going to be sick,' called Rose, 'lean over the side.'

Doris dipped her hand in the water and rubbed the back of Rachel's white neck. Rachel shivered and looked at Alex again.

'I meant what I said before, you know. You're pretty.'

Alex blushed. 'So are you,' she said quietly. Rachel smiled.

'Am I pretty?' said Harriet suddenly. They all looked at her, even Joyce, who stopped throwing water.

'Yes,' said Doris after a while. 'You're pretty.'

'We're all pretty,' said Joyce. Alex gazed at Harriet and she smiled back. She looked beautiful. Then she watched Rachel and realised that none of the things she had thought about would ever happen. She felt as if she had woken up suddenly. Harriet reached out and squeezed her hand.

'Damn,' said Marjory, because the spray from the boat had caught her, as if the sea itself was throwing water and laughing. She bit her lip again.

'Harriet and Doris,' Joyce said, slowly and carefully, 'Marjory, Alex, Rachel and Joyce,' she pushed her flat hand against her chest, 'we're all pretty.'

Rachel knelt up on the bench, leant over the side of the boat and threw up into the sea. As the boat turned and the lighthouse loomed above them, they watched the trail of sick as they left it further and further behind.

When they got to the place where the boat could sling its rope and moor, John helped each of them up the step and onto the rocks as if they were princesses. Rachel went first, stumbled the short distance to the steps and sat down on them. The others arranged themselves on the rocky platform and waited for the lighthouse keeper to open the door. John and Rose stayed in the cabin, rocking up and down gently, with a newspaper and a flask of tea arranged between them.

In the first room there was a huge machine taking up most of the space. Alex stood and wondered what it was for, while the lighthouse keeper found Rachel a chair.

'I'm one of Eade's three lighthouse keepers,' he said as Rachel sat down. Then he began to hop up the winding stairs which curled away above them into the sky.

'Bloody hell,' said Marjory, looking up after him. The stairs could have climbed all the way to heaven for all Alex knew. Harriet stood next to them and gazed upwards too. Alex smiled at her and squeezed her hand. A few minutes later the lighthouse keeper returned with a cup of something that smelt of peppermint.

'Drink this,' he said. Rachel sipped it gratefully.

'What does the machine do?' asked Alex.

'It pumps air for the foghorn,' said the keeper.

'Are you all right?' she whispered to Rachel.

'Yes,' she said. She smiled but she still looked pale. The keeper spread out his arms and waved them all towards the stairs.

'The talk will take place in the lamp room,' he said.

'At the top?' asked Joyce happily.

'Yes,' said the keeper.

'Wow,' said Doris, and Joyce clapped her hands in delight.

They left Rachel next to the foghorn pump and climbed up to the next level, then the next, then the next. Alex went up the stairs carefully one at a time, holding on to the rail, feeling the muscles in her thighs pull and her heart hurting in her chest. She felt like she was inside a pencil, climbing the stairs inside it to where the tip for writing was. They passed a room with a red light, a round kitchen with chairs, and a place where bunk beds hugged the walls. On each level there was a window, which they took turns to peer through. Each time they looked, the rocks and the sea below were further away. The final part was a steep metal ladder. They stood in a queue waiting to climb. Doris, who was the smallest, gazed up to the hole at the top and looked frightened.

'Hurry up,' said Joyce impatiently behind her. They went up one by one, taking a deep breath first and tucking their skirts between their legs. Alex felt like she was climbing up into someone's head, into a dream land where wild and fantastic thoughts lived. Up at the top, they stood around the giant lamp with the lighthouse keeper and watched the lenses and mirrors as they spun round slowly.

'The light from the bulb is refracted by the lens,' the keeper began the talk. Doris pulled out a notebook from her pocket and wrote down what he said. Then she drew a picture of the light. 'The signal is made up of several pulses of dark and light,' he said.

The slatted windows were too high for them to see out, but there was a step which they climbed onto one at a time after the talk had finished. Alex was the highest up she had ever been. She could see the beach where the sea ended and Eade Village started. It was a line of yellow sand fringed with white breaking waves, like a scarf with a lace edge. She could see the fishing boats in the harbour, small enough to be toys. She could see the brown rocks below them where the waves crashed and dived. She wished that Rachel could see it. She wanted to look out of the window for ever.

'Bloody hell,' said Marjory behind her, whose turn it was after Alex.

'Next,' said the lighthouse keeper.

Alex reluctantly got down from the step. Now she could no longer see the tiny beach and harbour or the rocks. She could only see Marjory with her face against the high-up windows and the plain white walls. She walked around the narrow passageway that led in a circle past the giant lens, until she found Harriet leaning against the wall.

'Have you seen out of the window?' Alex asked her.

She nodded. 'We're so high up,' Harriet said as if she almost couldn't believe it. They held each other's gaze until Alex had to look away because she thought she might kiss her in front of everyone.

25

December 2004

Eve came downstairs just as I was about to go into the kitchen to inspect the new tea and coffee machine which wasn't out of its box yet. I should have known something was wrong because of the way she narrowed her eyes at me.

'This kitchen's about ready for some more cooking,' she said mildly. 'Wash your hands and let's see what you can do.'

'I was going to help Bernie with the floorboards . . .' I trailed off.

'Bernie's not here. Anyway, I want to see what you can do,' she said again, smiling at me curiously.

I stood in the hallway without moving for a moment, even thinking about dodging past her and running out of the door so I wouldn't have to make a fool of myself. There was a beautiful smell of baking coming from the oven already.

'I've made a couple of sponges for a lemon surprise. Make me a lemon mousse and a raspberry sauce and whip up the cream. I'll do the meringue for the top.'

I looked at her in horror. I suddenly thought that if I kept her talking I might come up with a way out.

'Have you got the recipe?' I said at last. That was the worst thing I could have said.

'What do you need a recipe for?'

'Oh, I don't,' I said. 'Of course I don't.'

207

'Why did you ask then?'

'It depends which kind of lemon mousse you want.'

'Does it really?'

'Yes. And then there's the raspberry sauce. There are so many ways of making raspberry sauce.'

'You'd know about that, would you?'

'Yes, and I thought you might be following one of the recipes from the scrapbook in the library.'

'Rachel showed you that?' Eve went into the kitchen, reached down and lifted the sponges from the oven.

'Yes.'

'I suppose you know how to make a lot of the recipes in there, with your NVQ Level 2 and everything,' said Eve in a flat voice. She was making me feel uncomfortable.

'Er,' I said, in a strangled sort of way. 'Some of them. Can you make them all?'

Eve carried on staring. 'Of course I can,' she said. Her voice was angry, but it was still low and calm. 'Do you want my whole bloody CV? Ex-cookery teacher, that kind of thing?'

'No,' I said sulkily.

Eve calmed down for a moment. 'We'll have tea at four, OK? Set the table properly in the tearoom. Eggs are in there and I bought some more raspberries. You know where everything else is.'

I grabbed some forks and serviettes and a tablecloth and set up a table in what was to be the tearoom, to give myself time to think. The renovations at the house were progressing fast. The builders had knocked down some of the corridor walls so that now when you walked in through the front door you went straight into a long room. It was going to have lots of tables and chairs so that people could come and try the cakes that the students would make. Monica would sell them in the Millennium Kitchen too. I stood examining the new room, trying to work out how I was going to make a lemon mousse. Meanwhile, Eve made the meringue. When I went back into the kitchen, she was expertly scooping the fluffy egg whites into their baking dish.

I arranged a bowl, fork and wooden spoon in front of me. Eve had mentioned eggs and raspberries, so I found them and I knew lemon mousse must involve lemons. I also found the lemon curd in case that helped.

'Sugar?' said Eve, waving a packet at me.

'Oh. Yes. Thank you,' I said. 'I was looking for that.' I was about to break an egg into the mixing bowl when Eve put a hand out to prevent me from doing it. I don't think she could stop herself.

'Aren't you going to separate the eggs?' she said.

'Thanks,' I said, not sure what she meant.

'I'll leave you to it then.'

I tried mixing the eggs with some sugar and lemon juice and stirring them together with a fork, but I ended up with a sticky mess. I poured it over the sponges anyway and mashed up the raspberries with some water, because how else was I going to make them go runny? The sauce didn't look very good so I decided to heat it up in a pan. It was what I used to do in the flat with my Dad when I was making chocolate sauce out of a packet to go with dessert.

An hour later, Eve came to take the meringues out.

'Where's the lemon mousse?' she said. 'Have you let it set?'

'I already put it on.' I wondered what she meant by set. She looked at her soggy sponges but didn't comment for the moment.

'Put it all together. Meringue, fruit, sauce, cream,' she said, still strangely calm. 'You know the kind of thing, don't you?'

I didn't reply.

I arranged the sponge on the plate with the meringue, followed by the cream, more meringue and lemon curd. I also sprinkled some almonds on, which were my special touch. I hoped Eve would like it. It was all slightly lopsided so I tried to compensate with more cream and poured on the sauce. I cut two slices and carried them into the future tearoom, placing them carefully on the table. Then I made tea.

By the time Eve came in to inspect, the slices had begun to sink like submarines.

'What did you use almonds for?'

'Extras,' I said hopefully.

'You didn't let the sponge cool,' Eve said, poking one of the lemon surprise slices so it sank even more. 'You don't know how to make mousse, do you?'

'Er. Kind of,' I said.

'Only I got this.' She waved a piece of paper. I saw that it was a copy of an email. 'Theft and arson. That's pretty serious,' she said.

'How did you find out about it?' I said, even though I knew already.

'I traced your name.'

'Oh.'

'You don't know anything about catering, do you?'

'No. Not much.'

She waved a teaspoon at me. 'How long did you think you'd be able to keep it up?'

There was a loud knock at the door, making us both jump.

'Find out who it is,' she said irritably. But I didn't move, so she went herself. I wiped my arm across my face and ran upstairs so I could get away from Eve and her cakes. As I went, I heard a voice but I couldn't see who it was.

'Hello,' Eve said, sounding surprised.

'Hello,' said the new voice. 'I thought I'd come and see how you were getting on.'

'You said you weren't coming till it was finished.'

'I couldn't wait any longer.' The conversation trailed off as I went into the top room.

I sat on the new bed with the matches from next to the fireplace and played the see-how-long-you-can-stand-it-for game with myself, tears running down my face. I tried to tell myself that I didn't care about the stupid lemon mousse, the delinquent girls, Rachel's Scrummage cards or any of it, but I did care. I waved out a match and struck another one, watching it flare then die. I didn't hold my hand over it this time, I just watched the flame like I used to when I was younger and had candles by my bed.

I could hear Eve moving around downstairs, showing whoever it was around. I struck another match and flicked it over and over itself so it landed next to the door and went out, like I did when I was a kid and like I had done in Mr Jeffers' flat. That was the bit of my story I hadn't dared to tell myself yet, the bit I kept tucked away so I couldn't see it. I hadn't gone over it since I had shared with the woman who had the *Alien* postcard.

I went over to where the match had fallen, sat with my back against the door and looked around at the room I'd cleared. I had painted the walls peach and white. Some of the new furniture was in already. It was going to be lovely. The smell of cooking had wound its way up the stairs. I was imagining the cake students falling asleep to the smell of vanilla sponge cake, when I heard Eve's voice below the window. They were outside.

'Let me show you what we've done to the courtyard,' she said.

I searched around in the drawer next to the bed and found a carpenter's pencil. I scratched some lines on the back of my hand. It hurt but I carried on doing it, because it took my mind off the story I didn't want to tell myself. But eventually I had to stop, because the cuts stung too much. This was the picture that went with the story: a hospital bed, brown floral drapes, a box of coins and a basin full of dirty dishes. Finally I put the pencil down, closed my eyes and let myself sink into the story as if I was a lemon mousse on a warm sponge.

26

After my brother left home and it was just me and my dad, I started doing overtime at the hospital. I volunteered for all the extra shifts. My supervisor loved me. With double time on Sundays, it meant I earned a little bit extra. At the hospital my days spun round like wheels. I did the same thing over and over: bay one, bay one toilets, bay two, nurses' room, sluice room, bay three, bay four, day room, again and again.

One of my jobs was to clean the tops of the lockers by each bed. I didn't bother too much to make conversation, I just moved the cards and presents and chocolate out of the way and gave them a quick wipe over, though sometimes, if I was halfway along a bay and found a patient with just a jug of water and no flowers or cards, I used to sit and talk.

I was shagging a bloke called Chris when it happened. He was one of the other cleaners.

'Other lad not with you today?' said one man as I went past.

'Chris? No, he's doing an early shift.'

'Work you hard, don't they?' He coughed. Then I realised that the man was Mr Jeffers, our next-door neighbour. He didn't recognise me at first. He was one of the patients with just a water jug and no cards. I sat down on the edge of the bed.

'They work us hard enough,' I said. I thought about all the times I had passed Mr Jeffers' door and heard him muttering to himself or shouting. I realised that I knew nothing about him. He had always been old, ever since I was a little girl.

'Pour me some of that, will you?' said Mr Jeffers. He waved his hand at the water jug. I poured some water into a plastic cup and handed it to him. He gulped at it.

'Thank you,' he said.

'Anything I can get you?' I said, not knowing what to do next. My floor polisher sat next to me idly. Then I looked up and saw the supervisor coming down the corridor. I got to my feet.

'I wouldn't mind one of them books,' he said. 'You know. From the trolley that comes round. They always go by so fast I never get a chance.'

I smiled at him quickly. 'OK,' I said.

When the supervisor came towards me, I put my hands back on the polisher. 'He wanted me to get him a drink,' I said, but she didn't care. I was her star worker at the moment.

'Tomorrow's early shift,' she said.

'Sure,' I said, thinking about adding a bit of money to my savings and how I could go back to Chris's mum's house afterwards, rather than how tired I felt.

Later on that week I caught the WRVS woman before she set off on her library trolley round.

'Yes?' she said suspiciously.

'I want something for a patient. I said I'd take him a book.'

'Why can't he get it when I go round?'

'He's a bit ill, you know.'

'They're all ill. What sort of thing does he like?'

'I don't know.'

'War, crime, science fiction, biography, non-fiction, romance.'

'Probably not romance,' I said, thinking of how Mr Jeffers used to shout at the postman.

'Try crime. If he doesn't like crime, bring it back and I'll change it over.'

'OK.'

Mr Jeffers loved the crime book.

'How did you know?' he said when I gave it to him.

I shrugged. 'Lucky guess,' I said.

213

'You live in the same block as me, don't you?' he said, looking at me carefully.

'Yeah.'

'How's that brother of yours?'

I was surprised that he remembered. Then I realised that he must have seen us coming and going just as much as we had seen him and laughed at him behind our hands.

'In the army.' I saw Chris coming down the corridor towards us.

'Oh. I see. Army, eh?' said Mr Jeffers. Chris came over to the bed and smiled at me.

'This is my next-door neighbour,' I said.

'Hello, Mr Jeffers,' said Chris, reading his name from the board above the bed.

Mr Jeffers held up his book. 'I like a good detective story.'

'When you've finished that, there's some others,' I said. Mr Jeffers was studying Chris and me with his watery eyes.

'Are you two courting?' he said in a sly voice.

I felt embarrassed for a second but Chris said, 'Yes,' and put his arm round my waist. Mr Jeffers put his hand into the drawer where he kept his personal things and took out fifty pence. He gave it to Chris.

'Get her some chocolates,' he said in a mock whisper and chuckled to himself. Then he opened his book.

Mr Jeffers got through the books quickly. He was on his third already. I sat down next to him.

'How are you feeling?'

'Good,' he said. 'Nearly better. If it wasn't for them making you wash all the time. They wake you up to wash. How stupid is that? A man needs to sleep. But the doctors say I can go home soon.'

'That's great,' I said.

'Yes. Now can you get me another one of these books?'

'Yes,' I said, but when I went to see the library trolley woman she didn't have any more.

214

'That's it on crime,' she said. 'I can do biography.' She showed me four or five hardbacks.

'No. He likes crime,' I said. So I went to the shop at the end of our road where they have books on one of those plastic stands that turns round and I found him something, though I didn't tell him that I'd paid for it.

'Here's your book, Mr Jeffers,' I said. 'And I brought you some tea as well.'

'I can't stand tea. Pour me some of that water.' He took the book and examined it. I looked at his lumpy hands with the pronounced blue veins and brown liver spots. Then I looked down at my own hands and tried to imagine them old. Mr Jeffers' watery eyes scanned the summary of the story on the back.

'Looks new,' he said.

'Yep. Looks like you're the first person to get that one,' I said. I poured him some water.

Mr Jeffers opened the first page of the book and began to read. Then he looked up again.

'I was wondering,' he said. He reached into his drawer and took out a key. He handed it to me. It looked just like the key to our flat. I realised it must be his door key. 'There are some things in my flat. Can you sell them for me?'

'What things? Sell them? You're going home soon,' I said cheerfully, giving his bedside cabinet an extra wipe.

'Yes, I know. But I won't be able to get out and about for a while. There's a desk in the front room. They're in there.' He coughed and waved me away impatiently. Then he folded his hands in front of him again, the book forgotten about for the moment. 'You couldn't get me some biscuits as well, could you?' he said with his eyes closed.

'I'll try,' I said.

I finished off the floor and did the toilets before I looked for the biscuits for Mr Jeffers. There was no one at the nurses' station and I knew that a grateful patient had given them a big box of shortbread. I looked down the corridor. No one was about, so I leant over the counter and picked out a few biscuits and put them in my pocket, but when I turned round, the staff nurse was right behind me.

'Mr Jeffers, is it?' she said.

'What?'

'Asking you for biscuits. I've seen you talk to him.'

'Um. Yeah. I guess. Sorry.'

'It's nice of you to bring him books. Only he's not allowed to have sweet things. He's on a special diet because of his heart. He asks everyone.' I felt the biscuits in my pocket. 'You have them. But you won't give him any, will you?'

'No. Is he really ill then? He's my neighbour.'

'Oh, I see. Hasn't he told you?'

'No. He said he was going home soon.'

She smiled and rubbed my arm. 'He's not going to be going home,' she said. 'The floor in bay two needs doing again, I'm afraid. Have the biscuits on your tea break.'

I didn't give Mr Jeffers the biscuits. I shared them with Chris instead when we went out onto the concrete balcony with our tea. I told him about Mr Jeffers being ill, but I didn't mention the key for the moment.

'You should be allowed biscuits before you die,' Chris said philosophically. I flicked my match absent-mindedly after I had lit my roll-up. It spun over in a wide arch before snuffing itself out by his feet.

The door to Mr Jeffers' flat swung open. Inside, it smelt of old socks and undone washing up. I had a look round first. The layout was exactly the same as ours, up some stairs and then straight on into the front room which was the kitchen as well. There were two bedrooms off the passageway and a bathroom, but no box room like we had. It was like coming home and finding our flat had been changed and that my room had disappeared.

I went and found the drawer in the front room that Mr Jeffers had described. I unlocked it and searched around inside. There were lots of bits of paper, old keys, bits of string, receipts, a crossword torn out of a newspaper and old tokens torn off a packet of Rice Krispies. Underneath them all was a cardboard box, about half the size of a shoe box. I lifted it out and sat down on Mr Jeffers' sofa. Inside, I found a collection of old coins. Some of them I recognised as foreign money, but there were other coins in the box too. They were smaller and green with age. They had strange designs on them. There were loads of them. I wondered if they really were worth anything. I turned one of the largest over in my hand. On one side I could just make out a head, but it was worn away so that I could hardly feel the indentations when I ran my fingers over it. The edges were quite smooth. On the other side there was a picture of a bird of some kind.

I put the box back where I'd found it, filled the sink with hot water from the kettle and left the washing-up, which had grown mouldy from days of waiting for Mr Jeffers, in the water to soak. I decided to come back when I could to tidy up a bit. Just in case he did get better like he said he would.

Chris and I were outside with our tea. I had nicked some more biscuits from the nurses' station. Chris was lying on his back on the concrete looking up at the autumn sky and I was sitting on the wall.

'Mr Jeffers gave me the key to his flat,' I said.

'What? Why?'

'He said he wanted me to sell something for him, but all I found was a box of funny coins.'

Chris looked excited. 'What if they're worth something?' he said. 'Did he say you could keep the money?'

'No.'

'Maybe you should ask him about it.'

'Do you want to see them?'

'What?'

'The coins, stupid.'

'Yeah. OK.'

'Come round tonight about seven. Only don't let my dad see you. I'll wait for you inside. Number eight.'

That night, I let myself into Mr Jeffers' flat again. I went to look at the washing-up. The crusts of food and mould had started to break down, so I found a sponge and did the dishes. Then I cleaned up the rest of the kitchen. I found an old-fashioned Hoover in Mr Jeffers' bedroom, which was cold, with a yellow cover on the bed and a large dark cupboard lurking in the corner. I suddenly felt as if there were people in there waiting to jump out at me and accuse me of robbing an old man while he was in hospital. I slammed the door and went to do the front room.

Half an hour later, I opened the door to Chris who was hopping from foot to foot.

'I've been outside ages,' he said.

'Sorry. I was hoovering,' I said.

'Have you cleaned up then?' he said, coming up the stairs.

'A bit.'

We sat down on the sofa. Chris tried to put his arm round me but I felt a bit awkward. I wondered if Mr Jeffers had ever put his arm round anyone on that sofa.

'Want to see them then?' I said. I went over to the drawer and got out the box.

'This is just foreign money,' he said, rooting through the box as I had done a few days before.

Then he stopped and picked out one of the small coins.

'Shit,' he said and held it up so he could see it better.

'See. I told you,' I said. 'Do you think they're worth something?'

'No,' said Chris but he didn't sound sure. He turned it over and looked at the picture of the bird. 'An eagle or something,' he said.

'Maybe,' I said. 'Will you help me tidy up a bit more now? He might be coming home soon and I want to make it nice.'

'He's not going to come home. You said. About the biscuits, remember?'

'Yeah. But what if he does? What if there's a miracle or something and he does come home?'

'Don't be stupid. Do you think we should touch his stuff?'

'He gave me the key, didn't he? I mean, he probably wanted me to tidy up a bit. He knows I'm the cleaner.'

So Chris helped me to do the front room and the bathroom, though I didn't go into the bedroom again.

'Are you going to ask him about it?' Chris said. 'Tomorrow?'

'Yeah,' I said. 'We can both ask him.'

Mr Jeffers had his eyes closed when I came into his bay with the floor polisher. I had another book with me in case he had finished the last one. I had bought it from the hospital shop. This time I had bent the spine so that it didn't look too new. I didn't want him to be embarrassed. Chris came in from doing the sluice room and stood next to me. I sat down on the bed. Just then the staff nurse walked past. She saw that Mr Jeffers was asleep and looked at us both as if she wondered what we were doing, but then a woman in another bay rang for a bedpan.

'Mr Jeffers,' I said softly. He opened his eyes.

'Can't a man get some sleep?' he said. 'Pass me some water. I'll be glad to get out of here tomorrow.'

'Did the doctor say tomorrow?' His hand shook as he drank the water.

'Tomorrow or the day after,' he said when he had finished.

'Sorry we woke you up,' Chris said.

'Oh, it's you two. I thought they'd come to wash my privates again.'

'Er. About the things you asked me to sell, Mr Jeffers,' I said slowly.

'Things? What things?'

'Coins.'

'I don't remember no coins.'

'You gave me the key to your flat, remember?'

'What would I give you the key to my flat for?'

I looked at Chris. I took the key to the flat out of my pocket and showed it to Mr Jeffers.

'Oh,' he said. 'Yes. I remember now.' He closed his eyes again as if it was an effort for him to think.

'Good,' I said. 'Mr Jeffers, I cleaned up your flat for you a bit. For when you go home.'

'Good girl,' he said. 'I'm hungry. Can you get me some biscuits?'

'Listen,' I said. He seemed more ill than he had been. I was worried. 'Maybe I should tell the nurse that you're not ready to go home yet.'

He opened his eyes. 'No. Don't do that,' he said, looking straight at me. I was shocked by how wide and blue his eyes were. 'Did you sell the coins for me?'

'No,' I said. I looked at Chris for help. The staff nurse walked past again.

'The toilets in bay four need doing,' she said.

'OK,' I said.

'We wanted to ask you about them first, Mr Jeffers,' Chris said.

'Don't let them take my stuff away,' Mr Jeffers said.

'No one's going to take your stuff,' I said.

'What sort of coins are they, Mr Jeffers?' Chris said.

'Coins? What coins?' he said and then he closed his eyes and his chest began to go up and down slowly. Chris looked round and I followed his gaze. We could see the supervisor talking to the staff nurse at the end of the corridor.

'He's asleep,' Chris said. 'Come on.'

'What shall I do with this?' I said, opening my hand quickly to show Chris the key. 'Do you think I should put it back?'

'He definitely gave it to you, didn't he?'

'What? Do you think I'd nick it? You heard what he said. He asked me if I'd sold the coins.'

Before I had a chance to put the key back, the supervisor came into the bay where we were standing.

'Toilets please, Chris,' she said sharply, but she smiled at me. I was still her favourite.

'We was talking to Mr Jeffers but he fell asleep,' I said awkwardly, slipping the key back into my pocket. She looked into his wrinkled face.

'Bless him,' she said. She said that about all the patients, even the loud ones. We moved away from the bed. 'Can you do a late tomorrow?'

'Yep,' I said, trying to think about the bit of extra money and not about how there were some days when I had to drink plastic cups of coffee every hour to stay awake.

'Another split shift?' Chris said. 'You'll be knackered.'

'You volunteering?' said the supervisor. He shrugged.

'I said, toilets please, Chris.'

He pretended to salute and went to find a bucket.

'You might as well go for your break,' she said to me and pottered off to make sure the sluice room had been done properly. I left my floor polisher by the wall and went outside to the balcony to think about it all.

Chris and I stood in the antiques shop. The man behind the counter eyed us suspiciously.

'Where did you get these from?'

'My granddad,' I said. Chris looked at me but he didn't say anything.

'I'd need verification, but I believe they're Roman,' the man said.

'How much?' I asked him.

'It's just an estimate,' the man said seriously. 'But probably ten to fifteen.'

Chris laughed. 'Is that all? Ten quid?'

The man looked at him in surprise. 'No. You don't understand. Ten to fifteen thousand. For the collection.'

'What?' I said. 'Just for these?'

'It's very unusual to find a group of them like this. Keen on the metal detector, was he, your granddad?'

'Er. Yeah,' said Chris. His eyes had lit up.

'If you can leave a few with me, so I can authenticate the date, it's likely that we can come to some kind of arrangement. As long as you don't show them to anyone else,' the man said. He took a few of the coins carefully out of the box and passed me a pen and form with 'Name and address of seller' at the top.

'OK,' I said. I scribbled my name and, after a second, the address of the hospital. I took Chris by the hand and picked up the box of coins. 'No, we won't tell anyone else. Thank you very much.'

*　　　*　　　*

I opened another account to pay the cheque into. I was going to tell Mr Jeffers about it that afternoon, but something stopped me from doing it. I got him another book and poured him some water instead.

After that, I started getting a little bit of money out of the account, telling myself he wouldn't mind. I bought some new clothes and some for Chris too. Then Chris pulled me into the travel agents, just to look at the brochures, and before I could stop myself I had booked us on a holiday, which we never even got to go on in the end.

'It's not much,' I said to Chris afterwards, trying to convince myself. 'He won't even notice.'

After that I decided I had to stop. I cut up the bank card so I couldn't get any more money out. I decided I would tell Mr Jeffers the next day. I would tell him about the clothes and the holiday and say I would pay him back and he wouldn't mind and it would all be all right.

How do you want this bit of my story to end? How much do you want me to tell you about Mr Jeffers and how he got hold of the coins? What do you need to know? How big his shoes were? The colour of his wallpaper? The date it first began to peel off the wall, the exact day the flats will be demolished, what will be built there instead? Do you want to know about the bits of pizza crust that floated in the washing-up water and got stuck in the plughole when the cold water drained away? Or the smell of smoke that curled around the flat? Do you want to believe that it was all a mistake and I never meant to do it or that I only did it because I was fucked up? Sometimes, I think that this story clings to my neck like a small red monkey and I can't shake it off. The monkey laughs a lot, in my face, and won't let go. He just laces his leathery fingers tighter and goes with me everywhere.

This is what happened. There's me on Mr Jeffers' sofa, waiting for Chris after rowing with my dad. Chris doesn't come but the sofa cushions feel good under my head and I like the musty smell in the air and the quiet of being all on my own with the curtains drawn, so I spend the night there. There's Mr Jeffers with the brown flowery drapes pulled round his bed the next day so I knew something was up. All the other drapes round all the other beds were drawn fast while they wheeled him out with a sheet over his face and there's me still with his door key in my pocket, watching, with my floor polisher in my hand.

What do you want to know about next? Do you want to know about the beans that were still stuck to a plate next to the sink? Or the Yellow Pages he kept in the front room with biro scribbles on it and a piece torn off the cover as if he'd got hungry and had taken a bite?

There's me going round his flat to tidy up a bit more, but then the council never come to sort it out, so then I start going round there to think sometimes. Do you want to know all the things I thought about? Do you want me to lift the carpet in one corner and roll it up until all the floorboards are exposed like a naked body? There's me going round the flat and lying on the floor staring at the ceiling with my matchbox in my hand, thinking about the dancing angels twisting their hips on the candlewicks. There's Chris phoning the flat and my dad telling me later that fucking Father Christmas had been on the phone for me and Chris telling me he didn't want to see me any more and me telling him he was a crap shag anyway and crying on my bed.

What order do you want it in? Do you want it chronological or in bits like a jigsaw or like someone picking up scraps of paper on an island? What's next? Me spending more time round Mr Jeffers' flat because of the yellow colour when the curtains were closed and not going back to cook my dad's dinner and not doing anything apart from lying on the sofa and getting up to go and do an early or a late shift. Chris phoning our flat again and my dad calling him a fucking Nancy boy so he started mouthing off to the supervisor and the staff nurse about coins and a key. The police going round to see the antiques man. Me with my back against the sofa, flicking the matches just like my dad had shown me ages ago, so that they tumbled over and over, wishing I could dance like that in the air, like an angel on fire and turning somersaults, something catching, the room full of smoke and someone banging on the door and I wanted them to shut up because all I wanted to do was lie down on the floor and sleep and I was so tired all of a sudden and the banging went on and on, even though I put my hands over my ears to try to shut it out and then the window got smashed and then police and questions about keys and money and a holiday. I said Chris would back me up but he never and I had to see a shrink with a clipboard and my mum not coming because she was in Spain on easyJet and seeing my dad in a suit in court with a flower, like he was at a wedding and I thought if I closed my eyes really tight and opened them again, me and Chris would be getting married instead and there would be a big wedding cake but then the judge said three years which the lawyer said meant two years and feeling car sick in the van and seeing plastic blue chairs when I went in and thinking about the dancing angel with the twisting hips who got me into trouble, walking up the corridor with a hand on my back and thinking about a pig chef biscuit barrel as I climbed the metal stairs for the first time.

How much more do you want to know? Do you want to know about the letters Neil wrote every week? Do you need to know where in Spain my mum and Kevin went on holiday or what the man in the antiques shop said to his wife after he saw Mr Jeffers' coins or what the staff nurse had for tea or whether the other cleaners cared or what the woman in the service station shop with Barry Manilow and pick 'n' mix thought about before she went to sleep at night, as she gazed at the dark blue sky outside her window or how many times the toilets she worked next to had won the cleanest toilet competition and whether the security guard was suffering from depression and whether the woman who made my coffee on the bridge above the motorway was secretly bisexual and fancied me over the Danish pastries in the plastic wrappers but didn't say anything, even though, after she had pressed the buttons on the till, she thought about how nice it would have been?

A hundred other things could have happened, like pages in a

book. Do you need to know how much I had in my savings from working extra shifts? Do you want to know about the hotel I stayed in for a night after I got out or the people who worked there and how much they got paid? Do you need to know the details? How my feet moved across the floor in the hotel bathroom? How my coffee spoon sounded in my mouth when I sucked it? I pulled this story out like a man who sinks his hand down his throat and pulls out flowers. I pulled it out like someone rummaging around in a sandpit or mixing up the bits in an impossible baked-bean jigsaw. These are the pieces: tablecloths, blue chairs, Kevins, flowers, service stations, angels.

27

I had picked up the pencil again when I heard Eve on the landing outside. I just had time to scramble up from the floor as she opened the door.

'What are you doing?' she said. Then, 'Oh my God,' because she had seen my hand. I looked down too. The scratches were bleeding and I hadn't noticed. 'What have you done?' The pencil was still dangling from my fingers and the matchbox was on the floor. She grabbed my hand and turned it over, but I pulled away from her.

'Nothing. I haven't done anything,' I said. I ran out of the room and down the stairs and out of the front door.

'Erica,' Eve called after me, but I didn't turn round. I ran down the hill towards the lake, my hand still bleeding. The ground was icy as I ran and the light was fading. I didn't stop until I reached the tree with spreading arms and a thick trunk. I hid under the branches and leant against the tree, exhausted. The giant roots around me were hard and cold from the frost. I turned round but Eve was nowhere to be seen. I pulled my jumper off so I could wrap it round my bleeding hand and I got cold straight-away. In just my T-shirt, the goose bumps rose on my arms and I shivered. I sat staring at the lake, getting colder and colder. I must have passed out because when I opened my eyes again it was dark and I was shivering so much I thought it would never stop. Someone I didn't recognise was leaning over me. I could hear branches moving and Eve's voice.

'We couldn't find you,' she said. She sounded anxious. 'We've been looking for ages. Rachel and Mrs Pretty are down by the harbour looking for you.' I tried to say something but my words wouldn't come out properly.

'We've found you now,' said another voice. Then I was half carried out from under the tree and lifted to my feet. I felt a blanket being dropped round my shoulders. When the jumper fell away from my hand, I heard exclamations. I think I passed out again. The next thing I could hear was Eve talking into her mobile.

'Rachel? We've found her. Under a tree by the lake.' My eyes had gone blurry and I couldn't see the figure next to me properly, but she was very close. She put her arm round me and I leant against her.

'OK now?' she whispered.

'Yes, I'm OK,' I said into her coat, which smelt of strawberries. I let her lead me back up the hill to the house. I sat in the half-finished tearoom with the blanket still wrapped round me and things started to come back into focus again. The two slices of lemon surprise and two cups of cold tea were still sitting on the table. The woman who had brought me back to the house was tall with short brown hair and she was wearing a blue shirt and black trousers. She was plunging my aching hand into a warm bowl of water which had been perfumed with something herby.

'Look at her arms,' I heard Eve say. I felt the blanket pulled away and I wanted to grab it back to hide them, but I couldn't move. My limbs felt like lead all of a sudden. They stood and looked at me in silence.

Once my hand was bandaged and I had started to warm up, the tall woman appeared in front of me. I noticed how fiery her eyes were.

'Hello,' she said, 'I'm Alex.'

'Erica,' I said, feeling stupidly embarrassed. I could hear Eve outside the door, on her mobile again.

'Pleased to meet you,' Alex said as if we had just met. Then she looked around at the tearoom like she was seeing it for the first time. 'Wow. I can't believe what you've done to this place. When I was here, this was the dormitory.'

'I know, Rachel told me.'

'Did she? Well, I used to sleep just about here,' she said, going to stand over by the window and stamping her feet.

'What was it like?'

'There were eight beds. Four here,' she marched up and down as she said it, stopping like a soldier coming to a halt when she got to each imaginary bed, 'and four here.' I tried to picture it.

'Were there eight of you?'

'Six of us. Let's see. There was Rachel and me,' she counted on her fingers, 'Harriet,' she went on, smiling as she said the name.

'I know,' I said. 'Doris, Marjory and Joyce.'

'Yes, you're right. Rachel must have told you that too.'

'No, we found it in . . .' I began but my hand hurt suddenly and I stopped. Alex wasn't paying attention. She was looking at the two pieces of lemon surprise, sitting side by side on the table. I felt embarrassed again, but then she grabbed her coat and pulled a brown paper bag full of strawberries out of the pocket.

'Snack for the train. Supermarket, I'm afraid,' she said as she took out several and wedged them into the middle of my wonky cake slices. 'But this time of year, what can you do?' The strawberries propped up the cakes beautifully. She got a teaspoon and scraped away some of the excess cream. Then she lifted the bowl of brown sugar and gave them a dusting.

'Now,' she said wiping her hands on her trousers. 'Are these for us, do you think?' She picked up one of the plates and grinned at me. She didn't wait for me to reply. She used the teaspoon and ate the slice of lemon surprise. I wasn't sure if she was enjoying it, but she kept going till it was finished. Eve came back in from making her phone calls just as Alex put the plate down and dabbed her mouth with the napkin.

'Right,' Eve said. 'Let's get you back to the library, Ricky.' Her anxious voice was gone and she was businesslike again. 'Alex, you'll stay with me, of course. Have you seen Rachel yet?'

'No, no, I came straight up here,' Alex said and it was the first time I heard her hesitate.

When Alex put her head round the library door, she had a nervous look on her face, almost as if she was frightened Rachel wouldn't be there. But the librarian was waiting for her and I noticed she had put on her blue dress with the flowers round the collar and had sprayed herself with the perfume Monica had given her for her birthday. They looked at each other without saying anything.

'Just a flying visit,' Alex said, while Eve put several cake tins away in Rachel's kitchen.

'Right,' said Rachel.

After a moment's pause, Alex went over to her, and they hugged each other for ages. I sat on the sofa feeling awkward. Then Rachel turned her attention to me. 'Are you OK now?' I nodded. 'We were really worried about you. What have you been doing to yourself?'

I couldn't answer. I just looked at the floor.

'Well,' said Eve. She shook her head at me.

'What's wrong now?' Rachel said, looking at our faces.

'Oh, only that she's not a cook and she's just got out of the nick.'

'Ah,' said Alex. 'Yes, you told me about that.'

'What were you in for?' Rachel asked when no one said anything else. She said it cheerfully as if she was talking about tennis or shopping. Eve answered for me.

'Theft and arson. Jesus.'

No one knew what to say for a moment. We all looked at each other. Then Alex began to walk up and down, taking big strides across the library sitting room so that she walked from the bookshelf to the fireplace in a couple of steps and had to turn round and start again.

'Why did you do that to yourself?' Rachel said, suddenly serious. She nodded at my bandaged hand.

I shrugged. 'I don't know.'

229

'No, not good enough, I'm afraid,' she said. All three of them were waiting for me to answer.

'Come on,' said Eve impatiently.

'Stories,' I said. There was silence again. Alex stopped pacing. I wriggled out of my coat so they could see my arms. I held them up and showed them the marks. 'They're stories about stuff that happened.'

'Aha,' said Rachel as if she had suddenly solved a murder mystery. 'Like books.'

'Only reading books isn't a bloody stupid thing to do and books don't hurt you and make you ill,' Eve said.

Rachel shook her head. 'Some books do,' she said.

'How about a contract?' Alex said suddenly. 'Eve teaches you in your spare time. And you don't run off any more. Every time you want to hurt yourself you tell someone a story about it instead.'

Eve looked from Rachel to Alex with her arms folded.

'All right,' she said, to my surprise. 'I'll teach you some basic stuff. If you can do it OK, you're in and I'll teach you the rest. Otherwise I'll pay you what I owe you when the first lot arrive and that'll be it?' She sounded as if she was talking about assault course training at army camp instead of cake-making. I thought about the picture Neil had sent me of himself in his army uniform. 'And I'm taking you to see the doctor tomorrow morning, you know.'

'Right,' Alex said. 'That's decided then.' She sat down on the sofa next to me and rubbed her hands. Her eyes were glowing. 'Now. What's for tea?'

'I'll let you two catch up,' Eve said. 'Here's the directions to the flat.' She put a piece of paper down on the coffee table. 'Go and have a bath, Erica, and leave them alone. They haven't seen each other for a while.' But Rachel followed me into the bathroom to pour Radox in my bath and fuss around me.

'Any stories you want to tell me now?' she said, her eyes shining, as if she was story monitor instead of keeper of books.

I shrugged. 'I don't know.'

'What are your stories about?'

'Stuff that's happened.'

'I see. What kind of stuff? What you did to get put in prison? I'd like to hear that one.' She grinned at me as if she was excited about it.

'That and how I got here, and how I started doing this.' I rubbed my arm to show what I meant.

She nodded. 'Why do you think that was, I wonder?'

I shrugged again.

'Whenever you feel like telling me about it, come and find me,' she said. 'I am the librarian, after all.'

When I finally climbed into the steaming water, I could hear her and Alex talking and laughing, their voices rising and falling in the sitting room and it was comforting, like listening to soft music.

'Don't think I've been sitting in the library like a lonely old woman,' I heard Rachel saying. 'I've had plenty of boyfriends.'

Alex laughed and I imagined Rachel with her arms round some bloke on the sofa that I had slept on when I first arrived.

When I wrapped myself in a dressing gown and went to see if there was anything to eat, Rachel was holding Alex's face in her hands and pressing it as if she was learning one of those weird massage things off the telly.

28

Flour, butter, sugar, eggs, vanilla essence, baking powder, icing sugar. Preheat the oven to 190 degrees. Eve had pinned the instructions to one of the cupboards in Rachel's tiny kitchen. We were having our first cake lesson at the library because the builders were doing something complicated at the house.

We started with basic sponges: lemon, coffee and walnut, over three days, while Monica mixed up lattes and Rachel scanned bar codes next door. Eve made me write things down on a pad, which made me think of the crate of notebooks with the lists of names. She would dip a wooden spoon into a bowl viciously as if the flour and eggs had offended her and shout out headings. I had to scribble quickly: *basic equipment, staple ingredients, common errors, care of eggs.*

'Write it down,' she'd say if I stopped, so I wrote faster: *choosing the right cake tin, managing the oven, mixing, folding and sieving, correct cooking times, checking that your cake is cooked, weights and measures, greasing versus lining.*

On the fourth day she said she was going to see how much I had learnt so far.

'Is it a test?' I asked reluctantly.

'I just want to see how much you've taken in,' she said. 'There's no point in us carrying on if you're not learning anything.'

I had to wait in the library, listening to Rachel and story time. The children were sitting on the bean bags and the mums and dads were murmuring to each other in the Millennium

Kitchen. Parents of story-time children got a hot chocolate and a doughnut for 99p for bringing them. The smell of coffee from Monica's machine wafted amongst the books like incense. I leant against a shelf near a poster of a worm wearing glasses, with 'Reading is fun' in a speech bubble coming out of his mouth. Rachel was halfway through the story of Midas and his golden touch from *Classical Children's Tales* and she had the children doing sound effects, clapping their hands, banging the floor and saying 'oooh' and 'ahhh' at the right moments. I was engrossed in the story myself when Eve came out impatiently to tell me she was ready. Monica saw me going past the enquiries desk. Mrs Pretty, one of the silver surfers, was leaning on the counter talking to her.

'Bring us a slice when you've finished, love,' Mrs Pretty said.

'Ha,' said Monica from behind a cappuccino she was holding, but I ignored her.

The dessert Eve had made in Rachel's tiny kitchen looked beautiful.

'It's lemon surprise, isn't it?' I said. Eve nodded. It had layers of meringue, lemon mousse and cream, with a sponge base full of black and red berries, which made it seem as though it was encrusted with jewels. I had no idea how I was going to make anything that perfect. I felt sick.

'Remember the lemon surprise you tried to make at the house?' I nodded. How could I forget it?

'This is what it's supposed to look like.'

I tied on my apron as Eve slid a piece of the dessert onto a plate which she had already decorated with streaks of homemade lemon curd and sieved icing sugar. There was a pan of bright red raspberry sauce on the hob.

'Pass me that,' she said, so I handed it to her and watched as she tipped it carefully over the end of the cake. The red sauce merged with the yellow like raspberry blood on the sand.

'Your turn,' said Eve.

I didn't move.

'What's wrong?' said Eve.

'Nothing.'

'Good. Go on then.' There was nothing to worry about, I told myself. The mousse and the meringue were already made. The lemon curd was out with a spoon already in it. The cream was ready in a bowl to be whipped. Eve had made the sponge. All I had to do was put it together. It was easy.

'Cream first,' said Eve, lifting the bowl and pushing it into my hands. The whisk clicked against the side of the bowl as Eve watched me critically. After just a few seconds she grasped hold of my wrist, said, 'No, not like that,' and started to move my hand for me, but soon she got fed up.

'I'm going for a cigarette,' she said. 'Finish it by the time I come back.' It had stopped raining and the winter sun was shining. She stalked off so she could smoke outside.

I tried to make the cream go stiff like Eve had shown me but I was so nervous it just stayed the same thin milky consistency it had been when I started. I began to get angry with it and to whisk it erratically, so that splashes of cream hit my apron and my arms. I got faster and faster, but still the cream wouldn't go stiff. Eve returned smelling of damp leaves and cigarette smoke. She wrinkled up her face.

'Pathetic,' she said, dipping a nicotine-flavoured finger into the bowl. She took the whisk from my hands and within a couple of minutes the cream was peaking like she was God and she had just created a mini mountain range for her mantelpiece.

'Now spread it on the base,' she said. I slopped cream untidily over the cake. Eve sighed.

'Concentrate,' she said. 'Don't just stare at it. Scrape some of it off.' She handed me a palate knife.

'Now meringue, and more cream. Then the lemon curd.' When I spooned on the lemon mixture, the meringue sank into the cream below it and tilted slightly like a sinking ship.

'Now lemons. You can at least slice a lemon, can't you?' said Eve. She gave me a lemon from a bag and put it down firmly on a chopping board in front of me. I began to chop the lemon into thin slices. My hands were covered in lemon juice and when I lifted my fingers to my face they smelt fresh and new. Stupidly, I rubbed my eyes with my hand and they stung with the juice.

'Ow,' I said.

'What have you done now?'

'Nothing.' Tears rolled down my face, but I was determined to carry on cutting. I sliced more savagely, so that the last few pieces of lemon were chunky and misshapen because I couldn't see what I was doing. When I had finished I splashed my face in the sink.

We stood back and looked at the two lemon cakes. Eve's, with the perfect slice cut out of it, looking regal and full of tiny burst bodies and mine which was drunk with love, and dishevelled, like someone who forgets to get dressed properly because she's thinking about some bloke she has fallen for. Eve cut a slice, just as she had done with her own, and I felt like she was dissecting the body of the dishevelled love-sick woman, as if she had died and Eve was trying to find out what colour her heart had become. It had turned yellow as the sun and sharp as a lemon. Eve made me sprinkle icing sugar and pour on the raspberry sauce. The pieces of the dead woman's heart sat side by side.

'I normally serve it with lime sorbet,' said Eve after we had looked at my sinking cake for a while.

During the next two weeks, before leaving for the house or after work in the evening, or on days when the builders had the Haven to themselves, we covered: cupcakes, butterfly cakes, rock buns, biscuits, scones, flapjacks and fruit loaves, Christmas cake, meringues, pastries and mousses, followed by icings, toppings and sauces. Eve demonstrated, I made notes and tried out the stirring, folding, rubbing and beating until I was dizzy with it.

After that, I learnt a different recipe one day and had to jot it down on my pad and try it out the next. When I had tried out yesterday's cake, Eve would demonstrate another, holding her spoon aloft at the end and looking at me with narrow eyes. I barely had time to finish one before she would grab the flour and we would start again.

Over the month that followed, we made mascarpone and apricot bites, cherry tart with orange and chocolate sauce, kumquat sherbet sponge and summer fruits, lime cheesecake with rosemary butter, coconut tea bread, spiced apple dumplings with fig yoghurt, passion fruit sorbet on chocolate chip brownies, lemon cream snaps, caramel crunchies with orange curd sauce, oat and pecan slices, apple and almond Charlottes, tropical fruit delights, date bread and zabaglione icing, lemon mousse tartlets, fruit strudel with a poached pear and flaked almond roof, and finally sticky chocolate muffins. We carried on baking as Christmas got closer and closer, like an eavesdropper trying to learn our recipes. Rachel and Monica decorated the bookshelves with tinsel and there was holly and ivy on the door. The council sent Rachel a giant bookworm to stand by the enquiries desk and we gave it a Santa hat and put presents around it to be given out at story time. I spent Christmas Day on the sofa at the library eating fig roll, mince pies and the cranberry and Dutch cheese tartlets I had made, which Rachel said weren't bad if you closed your eyes.

My cakes were overcooked, undercooked, lopsided, soggy in the middle and dry on the outside. They sank or rose too much; one of my fruit breads glued itself to the top of the oven and I had to yank it out so hard I nearly fell over. My pastry went brittle and my icing melted, the flapjacks wouldn't stick together and Eve had to rescue them with more flour and butter. She would only let me sample a tiny bite of each creation. She would take a couple of teaspoons herself, acting as if it was a scientific experiment, criticising the presentation, taste and texture, before I had to deliver the plate to Monica in the Kitchen, where the mums and dads waiting for their children, the silver surfers, the book borrowers, Rose and John who did the boat trips and the girl from the hairdressers would come over to the counter and rub their hands.

'. . . making cakes. There's a lighthouse and a library. Rachel is the librarian. Eve owns the house. It used to be a home for delinquent girls.' On a frosty day at the end of January, I stood in the tearoom, reading the words I had just written. Then I stuffed the letter into my pocket and looked around me. We were going to paint the tea room pink and yellow later, but at the moment the walls were still scratched and dirty. If I concentrated hard, I could still smell the sick smell and see the sacks of rubbish with sticky liquid oozing out of them from when I had first arrived. I went over to examine the old sign. We had scrubbed it up and Bernie had varnished it and now it was in a case waiting to go on the wall.

Eve drove up and started to get cans of paint out of the boot of the car. I wandered around from room to room, looking at everything we had done. I poked my head into the old dining room and downstairs bathroom, which were both empty, painted pink and ready for beds. In the new kitchen, there was a big electric oven and the cupboards were waiting for cake-making ingredients. There was an archway through into what used to be the lounge which the builders had finished at the weekend but hadn't painted yet. I had cleaned up the fireplace. Now the room was much bigger and Bernie had begun to make separate workstations for the students and the plumber was halfway through putting in more sinks.

Upstairs, the bedrooms and the bathroom were almost finished. We had even put a picture of a haystack on the wall in the top room, because Eve said that we had to have a theme. The others were going to be Hedgerow, Horse Chestnut, Ploughed Field and, downstairs, the Millpond and the Old Barn. Eve had been to look for more pictures already. When she was talking to the bank manager on the phone, I heard her say that people liked to have a theme almost as much as they liked to feel they were in the countryside, so the extra expense served two purposes, but I secretly knew it had been Rachel's idea.

I went over to the window that had been broken when I arrived and watched Eve sorting through the tins of paint and wondering why I wasn't helping her. I could see Bernie arriving with one of the builders. Eve shouted at me.

'What are you doing?'

'Nothing.'

'I'm not paying you to do nothing. We need to get the tearoom painted today.'

I went outside to help her with the cans.

Later I felt in the pocket of my jeans for the biro and the letter I was writing to my brother, so I could add a couple more lines. After that, I sat and scanned it, drew an arrow next to the word 'cakes' and wrote: 'sponges, gateaux, meringues, that kind of stuff' in the margin, before reading it all the way through again. I signed it and scribbled two phone numbers underneath: the library and Eve's mobile. Then I went to find an envelope.

29

I picked up Rachel's silver card case from next to the fire and played with it, running my fingers over the tree branch patterns. As I undid the clasp and took out the first few cards, Rachel came out of the kitchen and saw.

'Pudding,' she said, pushing a rock bun towards me across the table. 'I never did tell you about the cards. Want to learn?'

'Yes.'

She grinned at me.

We started with the four hens laid out in front of us: yellow, blue, green, red.

'These are ones,' Rachel said, 'but they're not aces.'

I studied each card. An identical chicken, except for the colours, strutted across each card like Chicken Licken from the book I had when I was a kid. There was something medieval about the way the hens were drawn, as if they had been etched with a quill. Their eyes were dark and heavy. I rubbed my crumb-covered hands on my trousers and picked up the yellow one.

Rachel wheeled herself closer to the table so she could put down her empty plate and reach her cup of tea. She waved a hand at the hens on the table.

'These are useless. Only good for making a family.'

'What's a family?' I said, picking up the cards.

'Don't jump ahead.'

'Sorry.'

Next, Rachel laid out the twos. Two sandcastles, two figures rowing across the sea, two green hills, and what looked like two running goblins, grinning over their shoulders, with red paper clutched in their fists.

'Got any stories you want to tell me today?' Rachel said.

I picked up the red goblin card. I shrugged. 'Maybe.'

'Come on. You promised.' The librarian's eyes shone.

'OK. What happened to my dad when I was a kid, and my mum and the Kevins.'

'Who are they?' she said, sounding alarmed.

'Don't jump ahead,' I said and smiled.

'Sorry.' Someone had scribbled something on the card with the rowing boat, but if Rachel was annoyed, she didn't say anything.

'I'll tell you about Billy and her cards and you can tell me one in return. Like a swap,' she said.

'Maybe later.'

'OK. Now, the yellow and the green twos are just low cards, like the hens.' She pointed at the card with the boat. 'But the blue is the Friendship Card and the red is the Nab of Twos. I'll tell you about those another time,' she said, because she could see I was about to ask. Someone banged on the library door.

'That's Monica,' Rachel said. 'She said she'd pop in to get ready for story time tomorrow morning. Get me another one of those rock buns and find the threes.' She pushed the pack of cards towards me and wheeled herself into the library, where I heard her pick up the keys from the desk. I took two more of the buns out of the plastic tub in the kitchen, went back into the lounge and sorted through the pack.

The yellow and red three were decorated with men who had feathers in their caps and in their hands. They both looked as if they had jumped in the air. Their arms were spread and their legs bent. The green three was a similar-looking figure, but this time he was standing on a hillside, had a Robin Hood hat and piercing eyes. He held a pink flower. Finally, the blue man sat on the edge of a steep bank looking out at the sea. He had his back turned. I heard Monica banging cups about. When Rachel wheeled

240

herself back in, I was gazing at the threes and each one looked back at me with a shining face.

'What's this one called?' I said, tapping the blue three.

'The Prince of the Sea.'

'I wonder what he's looking at.'

'Dancing fish, probably,' Rachel said. She took a big bite out of her rock bun and waved her hand. 'Pretty to look at but also useless,' she said dismissively.

I chewed my cake while I looked at the pictures. She began to gather the cards together, like a fortune teller.

'Enough for now. Tomorrow we'll do the nabs and the mirror cards.'

She leant back in her chair instead and smiled at me.

'Now,' she said. 'The story of Billy and her cards . . .'

30

January 1917

It was the winter of 1917 when Billy stood at the end of the dormitory and saw the eight iron beds which guarded the walls like soldiers. As she looked at the row of identical jugs on the bedside chests and the white cupboard in the corner, she remembered the salt wind which had blown her hair last time she walked along the coastal path in her home town. She wondered what the beach at Eade was like. She had heard there was a harbour. She listened to her footsteps on the polished stone floor and imagined she was walking along a jetty which jutted out into the ocean. If she closed her eyes she could keep going until she stepped over the edge. There was a murmur of voices outside the door. They were talking about lunch. Somewhere in the house, someone began to play the piano. It was ragtime. It sounded like the music Billy had heard at the fairground once when she was small.

She sat down on her new bed. There were two picture post-cards on the chest but the backs were blank. One had a dog on it. The other was of a lighthouse. 'Eade Village Light' it said in white letters along the bottom. There was also a handwritten prayer on a piece of card, like a message from a bottle. On the other side of the prayer card were the rules and the name of the home in curvy letters: *The Haven, founded 1849.*

Billy took her silver case out of her bag and held it in her hands. She stroked it for a moment, before pushing it under her mattress. Her head was full of Jim in his uniform: his fingers as he caressed her scalp and held onto her hair and the green and red fishing boat bobbing in the sea just far enough out from the harbour so they couldn't be seen. The boat had rocked up and down on the water. She had lifted her skirts. She had had a feeling inside her like when she really needed to piss, but lower down. Her breasts and her thighs and the patch between her legs felt full of life, as if someone had a jug and was pouring warm water into them. She had lowered herself onto his lap after he had unbuttoned his trousers. She had held his face in her hands and kissed him. The fishing boat had rocked one way then the other and water had come over the side. Her thighs were wet and cold afterwards as she lay in the bottom of the boat looking up at the sky while he rowed her back to the beach.

'Will you marry me?' he said as he took her hand and helped her down onto the sand.

'Yes,' she said and she felt happy right down into her legs.

She liked to think of that moment over and over again: taking his hand, stepping out of the boat, feeling the sand under her feet. She liked to think about how alive her thighs had been and his kisses and the way the water had come over the side of the boat as it rocked this way and that.

It was all a stupid mistake. She didn't even take off her hat and coat, because by the end of the day Jim would arrive to take her home. She was so tired, she could hardly keep her eyes open. She lay down, telling herself it was only until Jim came to fetch her. It was all a silly misunderstanding and he would straighten it out.

Later, an attendant found her curled up on her bed with her coat still on. Her hat and bag had fallen to the floor.

'Wake up,' she said. 'And take off your coat.' The attendant had a flat, serious face. She laid out a grey dress, a white apron and white hat on the bed. 'Put these on,' she said.

'This is all silly. I'm not supposed to be here,' Billy began, but the attendant interrupted her.

'Put them on and we'll sort out where you're supposed to be.'

She stood and watched as Billy lifted her dress over her head, revealing her baggy white chemise and her swollen stomach.

'Can you read and write?'

'Yes.'

'Good. These are the rules,' said the attendant, picking up the small card from the chest next to Billy's bed. 'Read them.'

'I read them already,' said Billy. 'Honestly, I won't be here long because—'

'Read them out loud.'

'The Rules of the House. Girls must keep their uniforms clean,' Billy read. 'Girls must take part in the work and schedule of the house. Girls must attend church on Sundays. Girls must not discuss their circumstances with others. I agree to keep to these rules.' There was a space for her signature and the date to be added underneath.

'Write your name please,' the attendant said. Billy took the pen she was offered and signed her name. She turned the card over. 'The Prayer of Salvation', it said at the top.

'You needn't read the prayer,' the attendant said. 'Have you seen the doctor?'

'Yes.'

'Good. Do you have a date yet?'

'I said I would think about it.'

'Make sure you do.'

She took Billy out of a door at the back of the house and across the courtyard, where a new tree had been planted in a round earth bed surrounded by bricks. They went into the outbuilding which was full of washing equipment. The smell of bleach and soap hurt Billy's nose as soon as they went inside. Large silver washing tubs full of hot water were arranged along low tables and an array of copper-coloured irons and wicker baskets were lined up along one wall. When the attendant left her, Billy went over to peer into the baskets. They were full of dirty clothes.

'Is it your first day?' said a thick voice behind her. Billy turned round. A woman with a ginger plait right down to her waist had come into the laundry room and was standing by one of the tubs. She was fat and round like a big ginger melon, and much bigger than Billy.

'Yes,' she said. 'But I won't be here long. Jim has promised to come and get me.' Billy moved over to look at the baskets under the wide shelves at the back, where clean clothes had been neatly stacked, with paper tags attached to them on pins.

'I'm Jemima,' the woman with the plait said.

'Do you work here every day?'

'In the afternoons. Except Sundays. People from the village pay to have their clothes done.'

The door opened and more pregnant young women filed in, followed by the serious-faced attendant who stood at the top of the room with her arms folded and watched them as they worked. They positioned themselves around the washtubs. One woman, who had greasy hair and a flat stomach, brought over an armful of dirty clothes. Jemima stood next to Billy and showed her how much soap to pour in. Once the scrubbing had started, the women began to talk in low voices to one another.

'What's your name?' Jemima said.

'Billy.'

'Hello, Billy.' She dunked a cream-coloured shirt into her tub. 'I'll tell you the names. That's Mavis Free. This is her second time in here,' she said, nodding at a small round woman on the far side. 'Elaine Brooks. I don't like her.' She waved a wet shirt sleeve at the greasy-haired woman who had fetched the clothes. 'And that's Sally. Everyone is fond of her.' Sally had blonde curly hair and her face shone as if she had scrubbed it really hard. Elaine Brooks was next to Sally now. She was talking quickly and gazing at her in admiration every so often.

'Mavis is the oldest. She's twenty-three.'

'How old are you?' said Billy.

'Seventeen,' said Jemima.

'Same age as me,' said Billy.

'Amanda plays the piano,' Jemima went on. 'She's the youngest.' The piano player was on the other side of Billy. She glanced up and smiled. She had a face like a pixie.

'Hello,' Amanda said. She looked about sixteen years old and was stirring baggy white knickerbockers round and round with her hand, not paying attention to how clean or dirty they were.

'There's Doreen. She's holy,' Jemima continued. Doreen had her head down, concentrating on the red dress she was washing, lifting it out of the water from time to time to see if it was clean yet. She had auburn hair which clung to her face as if it might fall off otherwise.

'Doreen's man used to take her to a boarding house in Blackpool on weekends,' Amanda said. 'And Jemima's an aristocrat.' She laughed to herself, her pixie face wrinkling up as she did so.

'No I'm not.'

'She's got a big house but her parents told her not to come back.'

Jemima went red. 'Well, Amanda's a runaway,' she said quickly. 'They found her curled up asleep in the church.'

Amanda pretended not to care and went back to her knickerbockers. She began to hum as she stirred her washing round and round. The greasy-haired girl Elaine was talking without pausing for breath. On one side of her, Mavis was listening carefully with her small face tipped towards her shoulder. Sally was listening too and staring into the bowl of dirty water in front of her as if it might reveal her future.

'What happens the rest of the time?' Billy asked.

'Breakfast, wash, exercise,' said Amanda quickly, stirring the knickerbockers in time with her words. 'Chores, free time, lunch, laundry room, or nap if it's Sunday, reading, free time, dinner, prayers or sewing or education depending on what day it is, sleep.'

'Doreen is usually at the library,' Jemima said, 'but it's closed today.'

'Jemima's annoyed because she was there before her,' said Amanda, looking sideways at the ginger-haired girl.

'No I'm not.'

'Are you pals with the old librarian?' Amanda laughed as she said it.

'No. Shut up about it.'

'Why should I?' They were about to argue but Billy interrupted them.

'Why did you go to the library?' They both looked at her in surprise.

'Don't you know?' Amanda said. 'Maybe you're stupid like Jemima,' she added under her breath.

'No I'm not,' Billy said. The attendant looked over at them so they lowered their voices.

'Everyone goes to the library to train,' said Jemima.

'Train for what?' She thought of Jim setting off for the training camp in his uniform.

'To become a librarian, stupid,' Amanda said.

'Oh.'

'Everyone is sent to a library when they leave if their family don't want them back,' said Jemima. 'Apart from me. I'm going to live in my own house.'

'With servants,' said Amanda. 'You said.' She giggled again. 'The Eade librarian is very old. She's probably going to die soon.' She put her hands up to her neck and pretended to strangle herself and fall into her bowl of water. Billy laughed and looked to see if the attendant would tell her off, but she was busy examining a stain with Mavis Free.

'I don't know how I'm going to get it out,' Mavis said and when she said it, Billy heard her soft Scottish accent for the first time.

'You have to like books or you won't get a good library and you might not get to be a proper librarian, just a skivvy,' Amanda said.

'I don't know if I do like books much,' said Billy.

'Don't tell the librarian that,' said Jemima. 'She's the one who gets you a good library.' The holy girl Doreen went past with a handful of pins and heard what they said. She looked at Billy gravely. Amanda pretended to cross herself and Doreen hurried off to find a pincushion.

'She's taking her new job very seriously,' said Jemima, looking after her.

'Jim's coming to get me anyway,' said Billy. They both looked at her.

'Just in case he doesn't,' Jemima said quietly.

After the laundry, when Billy's hands were raw from the soapy water, they had to go into the sitting room. She gazed at the front door for a moment.

'You have to choose a book,' Amanda said from behind her, giving her a little shove. The room was large, with a fire jumping in the hearth and a sofa and chairs around it. There was also a piano, a table and a small bookshelf. Jemima looked exhausted. She was the fattest of all of them. She flopped down on the sofa before anyone else could steal her favourite place and pushed two cushions behind her back. Sally was already in a comfy chair with an almanac. The woman with the flat stomach called Elaine had sat down on the arm and was gazing at her fondly, but at the table a young attendant with a copy of St Mark's Gospel beckoned to her. She got up reluctantly and Mavis Free took her place.

Billy sat down next to Jemima.

'I don't see why I should start a book when I'm not going to finish it,' she said.

'Suit yourself,' Jemima said. They watched Doreen, the holy girl, as she hovered by the shelves trying to choose. She studied the spines carefully and then removed a book from the shelf.

'And he entered again into the . . .' Elaine began to read with effort.

'Synagogue,' said the attendant.

'And there was a man with a . . .' Elaine said slowly.

'Withered,' said the attendant. Amanda was on the piano stool. She arranged her grey skirt and lifted the lid.

'Hand,' said Elaine.

'Try this one,' Doreen said seriously, handing Billy a dusty copy of *Illustrated Ovid*.

'Thank you,' said Billy in surprise. Jemima leant over her shoulder so she could share it. She was too tired to go and choose her own book. When Doreen finally turned away from the shelf, she had five books in her hands. She came over to Billy again.

'Try these too,' she said, putting most of them on her lap, like an enthusiastic preacher giving out religious tracts. Billy looked at them. *A Child's Book of Myth, A Pictorial Wordsworth, Journey with Odysseus,* and *A Pilgrim's Progress (Abridged).*

'Are you holy too?' Jemima asked suspiciously. She lifted *Illustrated Ovid* from Billy's hands and curled her feet underneath her.

'No,' Billy said, glancing over at the door as if she expected Jim to stride in at any moment and take her hand.

'Doreen's practising at being the librarian,' Jemima said. 'She probably wants to be your pal.' She stared darkly at Doreen, who was already lost in a big book of romantic poetry and didn't see. They turned to watch Amanda flicking through some sheet music.

'She's the only one who can play,' Jemima whispered. 'But she'll only do it when she's bored. It's no good asking her.' The music Amanda had arranged in front of her was Scott Joplin's 'Maple Leaf Rag'. The tune began.

'She has to play in church sometimes, when the pianist is sick. She doesn't like it,' Jemima said.

Amanda struck the keys faster and faster as the tune progressed, her fingers racing through the notes. Next she played 'The Entertainer' even more quickly. Everyone was watching now, apart from Doreen who wrinkled her brow in annoyance, hunched up her knees and held her book closer to her face. Elaine started reading again, more loudly to compete with the music.

'And He began again to teach by the seaside: and there gathered unto Him a great ...'

'Multitude,' said the attendant. 'There gathered unto Him a great multitude.'

Later on that evening Billy lay on her bed, reached under her mattress and found her silver case. It had a clasp which opened with a click when she pushed it with her thumb and finger. The cards inside were larger than normal playing cards and there were more of them. The case was lined with soft black fabric and was just big enough to hold them. As she took out the cards, she imagined that she was sitting in her boat in the middle of the ocean. She felt the weight of the cards and studied the backs, which were crimson and carried an identical S shape, drawn to look like a curled sleeping woman with her arms raised. Billy turned over the top three cards. The first was of a crown on a golden chair. The card was marked with the words 'Yellow Throne'. The second was a young woman with red feathers in her hair. She was holding some white flowers. The words said 'Red Feather Woman'. The third was the Six of the Sea. It showed two people in a boat rowing across a stormy sea towards blue hills beyond them, which were touched by the sun. Billy pushed the three cards into the centre of the pack and breathed in the smell of her grandmother's scent which still hung around them. She thought about her grandmother, who could sit on her hair when it was loose, in her black dress, reaching into her drawer to give the cards to her. The drawer was in a mahogany tallboy in the corner of the sitting room at her grandmother's house. It had a lace cover spread over it and a blue vase. The old woman reached in her hand, took out the case and gave it to her. Billy held the cards to her mouth and smelt her grandmother's front room again and the tallboy with the lace cover and saw the old woman's creased, quilted face.

The door opened and Jemima came in. She swayed from side to side as she walked.

'You're next to me,' she said, sitting down on the neighbouring bed. She sounded pleased.

Billy smiled.

'What have you got?' Jemima came over and examined the silver case, and the S-shaped women on the back of the crimson cards. Billy could see how astonished she was. 'Where did you get them?'

'My grandma gave them to me.'

'Are they really yours?'

'Yes. She's dead now.'

Jemima sat down carefully and the bed sank under her weight. She shuffled around to get more comfortable. Then after she had taken the cards in her hands and looked at the pictures for a while, she pointed to each empty bed in turn and told Billy where the others slept. Billy wanted Jemima to be her friend, because she liked her long ginger hair which was plaited down her back like a strong piece of rope. She imagined that Jemima was Rapunzel and that she had witches climbing up it.

Jemima put her hands behind her head. 'I would like to go on a picnic right now,' she said.

'What would you have?'

'Little sandwiches and pork pies and champagne.'

'Lovely,' said Billy, feeling hungry.

'I don't suppose you'll be here for a church picnic,' Jemima said.

'What do you mean?'

'There's two. One at Easter and one on midsummer's day. I came just before the summer one. There were strawberries.'

Billy shuffled the cards and thought about the picnic. 'I won't be here because—'

'I know. Jim's coming to get you,' Jemima interrupted her.

'Do you know how to play?' Billy said after a while.

'No. What's it called?'

Billy closed her eyes and saw her grandmother sitting tall in her chair, dealing the cards to her friends, picking up her hand with a twist of her wrist and smiling to herself.

'I'll teach you,' she said. She looked at Jemima to see whether she wanted to or not.

'All right,' said Jemima softly and she moved closer. Billy could see how round her stomach was and how pale brown freckles darted around her nose, like her face was a field with brown poppies in it. When she laughed her milky-smooth face creased up like a discarded napkin.

'You start with three,' said Billy, dealing them out. 'I'll go first.'

'But I don't know how to play.'

'You'll see.' Billy laid down a card which said the Queen of Grass across the top and had a Roman V at the bottom. The picture was of a woman in a green hat. She sat on a throne in a field and held a big bunch of pink flowers. She had eyes which shone like silver drops of rain.

'That's a green five. Now I can pick up another card and you can lay down any green card higher than a five.' Billy looked at Jemima's cards and showed her which one to play. The card she chose depicted an empty green hillside stretching into the distance, like they were looking through the window of a farmhouse. It was the Green of Sixes.

'My turn,' Billy said and laid the Trick of Mirrors, which was a seven. The trick card had a green border and its shiny blank centre gleamed silver in the light.

They were each looking at a bit of their own face, distorted by the scratched surface of the card, when they heard someone coming along the corridor. Billy gathered up the cards and slotted them inside their case. As she did so, Jemima waddled over to her own bed and lay down on it uncomfortably. The door opened. It was a young nurse Billy hadn't seen before. She walked across the room quickly, as if she was frightened to look at their swollen bellies in case she began to balloon out herself. She went over to the cupboard without speaking or even looking in their direction. The nurse was pink and white and she wore glasses which made her look constantly surprised. She collected a tablecloth from inside the cupboard. Then she left again quickly. Billy heard the midwife's voice outside the door.

'Did you get it, Pamela?'

'Yes.'

'You didn't speak to the girls?'

'No.'

As soon as they had gone, Billy dealt the hands again.

'She's young for a nurse.'

'She's a novice,' said Jemima. 'We could get her to bring us food.'

'How will we do that?'

'I'm going to think of a way. We'll have to get her to talk to us.'

'I shan't be here for very long, anyway,' Billy said. 'Jim said I should wait for him and . . .' But she never finished the sentence because Jemima reached over and held her face, one hand on either side. Billy was startled.

'Everyone says it when they first come,' Jemima said. 'Every girl thinks a man's going to come and get her. Even Amanda said it and she stowed away for hundreds of miles. Or that's what she told us anyway. That's why every girl signs the papers.'

Billy shrugged Jemima's hands from her face and looked at her in bewilderment. 'Did you sign them too?' she said, looking at Jemima urgently. Her friend looked into her lap.

'Everyone does. Then everyone pretends that they didn't.'

'They said they wouldn't let me stay if I didn't sign them. I didn't think it would matter.'

'Every girl says it doesn't matter. It doesn't matter that we've signed our babies away because our heroes are coming back from the war to find us. None of it matters. Ask Elaine and Mavis, they'll tell you.'

'Why should I ask them?' When Jemima didn't answer, Billy turned away. 'I don't know what you're talking about. I haven't signed my baby away. It was just so I could stay here for a while.'

Jemima turned one of the crimson cards over and looked at the sleeping woman on the back. 'You didn't tell me what the game is called,' Jemima said quietly. 'It must be something beginning with S.'

'Scrummage,' Billy said.

'Every girl says it doesn't matter,' Jemima went on, playing with the card. 'And every girl signs the papers and gives up her baby. Some of them want to. Not me. I won't give him away. I'm going to have a big house with servants. I don't care about the papers.'

'He *is* coming,' Billy insisted angrily. She lay down on her bed with her face in the pillow and cried. Jemima didn't argue. She let her cry.

'He *is* coming,' Billy said again. She fell asleep like that, dreaming of the boat bobbing in the harbour and Jim's face the last time she saw him.

31

Billy had been at the house for almost a week when she went into Eade for the first time. She had decided she would have to be patient and that there must be some kind of hold-up. Maybe it was hard for Jim to get leave to come and find her.

They lined up outside the front door before they left for church because there wasn't enough room inside for them to walk in twos along the corridor. No one was allowed to stand with a pal. The attendant who supervised in the laundry room was going with them. She didn't smile. Jemima was in front of Billy next to the greasy girl with the spotty face. She noticed that Jemima waited until the last moment before holding Elaine's hand, and then she held her too tightly round the wrist so that she winced.

'I'll have to stand with Elaine,' Jemima had told her as they washed that morning.

'You hate Elaine.'

'That's why,' she said. 'I don't like to hold her hand. It makes me sick. She's never clean.'

'Who will I go with?' Billy said and, as she watched the soap sliding across her friend's white shoulders, Jemima explained that she was the one the others had to go next to if they tried to get with a pal.

'Usually it's Doreen, but you're new,' she said, leaning over to rub her hair with a towel, so that her breasts hung in front of her like bells. She sighed and looked over to where Sally was scrubbing her face with soap and a flannel. 'Everyone wants to go with Sally because she's beautiful.'

Billy knew it was Amanda's turn to walk with Sally today, because it had been arranged in the dormitory earlier. Amanda had a thin tin of cigarillos under her pillow, which were part of her plan. She had promised a smoke to the small round Scottish woman called Mavis Free in return for pretending to be her pal at breakfast. Billy had watched while they had tried to brush each other's hair during the grace.

Now they were outside, Sally was nowhere to be seen. Billy stood awkwardly on her own, her breath turning cloudy in the cold. When she glanced behind her, she saw Amanda swinging Mavis Free's arm backwards and forwards. The two of them looked like an odd pair of housemaids in their grey dresses and white caps, with their skirts inflated like tents in front of them, and Billy knew she must look the same herself. She wondered why Elaine's stomach was so flat and why Jemima had told her to ask Elaine and Mavis about whether the babies were given away. She couldn't imagine anyone wanting to take a baby from its mother. The whole papers business must be some kind of official nonsense.

Doreen was alone at the back, staring at her bible as if she was expecting it to grow a mouth and speak. It was her treasure and the only thing the married man who took her on holiday to Blackpool had given her, apart from the curled-up child she carried round in front of her. She could have been the Magdalene, made to bear the weight of her sin but ready to wash the Lord's feet with her hair and cry and cry.

Amanda put her arm round Mavis Free's shoulders and grinned like a pixie. The attendant looked at her as if she had gone mad.

'Amanda. Move next to the new girl,' she said.

'I'll go,' said Mavis quickly, thinking of her cigarillo. She hurried over to Billy.

'Hold hands,' she whispered and held out a red hand for her to grip. Her palm felt damp and warm. The attendant saw Mavis whispering and stared at her coldly just as Sally came out of the house, her skin fresh and creamy from washing and her blonde hair perfectly curled. It seemed as if a light was coming from inside her, but it was just the winter sun, sliding through the clouds and onto her face.

Doreen looked at her fondly but she turned up her perfect nose at the holy girl and her black bible and slotted in next to Amanda who was the only other woman without a partner. Amanda grinned to herself, because her plan had worked. She stood as close to Sally as possible, leaning on her arm, nearly pressing her face into her shoulder. Elaine turned and glared at her jealously but Sally looked as though she had glazed over like an ice-skating rink in the frost, and didn't seem to notice Amanda's pixie face next to her.

Now the women were paired up, it was as if Noah's ark was calling them. Billy imagined the line of pregnant women entering a vast wooden boat in twos to sit in rows next to tiny portholes. It would smell of elephant dung and straw, like the zoo.

When she saw how the light played with the surface of the lake, she felt like running down the hill with her arms spread open wide. The frost had touched the grass and the dead stems that remained in the beds. It had painted the tree branches and filled the air. The cold made her feel suddenly alive. She felt like there were things in the world: trees, grass, water. Here was the sharp cold world alive in front of her and not dead. She lifted her head up and felt the blue sky around her face. She looked at the trees lifting their hands up, saying yes, yes, and she wanted to lift her hands too and say yes, yes in reply.

'Keep your head down,' Mavis said as they started to walk. Billy saw that the other women had their eyes fixed on the ground, as if they were searching for lost rings or clues.

'Mavis Free,' said the attendant. 'Talking out of turn. No lunch.'

Billy tightened her hold on Mavis Free's hand and turned her eyes downwards. She watched the path under her feet as she walked, her grey skirt moving quickly, and Jemima's skirt in front of hers. She watched the yellow dust and stones of the dirt path turn to a road and become steep as it went round the side of the hill. All she saw were the swinging skirts and black-shoed feet for the rest of the journey.

Only when they reached the bottom of the hill did she look up again. The village shone in the frosty morning and dipped down towards the beach The air was still and cold. She could smell the sea and hear gulls crying. To her right where the houses ran away from her, she could just see the top of the lighthouse from the postcard by her bed, in the distance above the rooftops. It looked magical, as if a magician had planted his wand there and she could see the tip of it. Billy wished she could go down the hill to the harbour to watch the waves and study the light-house properly, but they turned left instead and stopped at the bottom of the steps up to the squat brown church. Billy saw the gravestones with frost playing across them and the bumps of grass around them as if they were pregnant too, bursting with dead people who had come to church to lie down outside and enjoy the cold earth under their white backs and had been buried there. She saw the thatched roof of the church and the wooden cross and the five steps up to the path which led through the stone porch.

They waited for the rest of the congregation to enter first. A woman in a pink coat and a matching hat looked at her and her eyes were hard as metal. Billy looked away. Once the congregation were inside, they walked up the steps and in through the cold doorway, like a strange funeral procession with no coffin or a blas-phemous group of grey brides without veils. Billy noticed how much colder and quieter it was as she went through the porch. She saw a sign on the wall in blue letters which read, 'Please close this gate and door, lest a bird should enter, and die of thirst.' She thought of a bird with sun on its wings, flying into the porch, and the door closing behind it. She thought of it turning to a skeleton slowly. She wondered how long it took for a dead bird to turn to a skeleton and if a cat would come and take it before it had had time to turn, before the bones were white. She was thinking about the bird skeleton when she let go of Mavis Free's hot hand and they shuffled into the pew. When she looked up, she could see other people's heads. Doreen had sat down next to them and was praying already. Jemima, Elaine, Sally and Amanda were in front, Jemima's ginger plait curling round her shoulders. The air smelt holy, like God must smell: of cassocks, old books, cold wood and stone. There was the vicar in his robe at the front lifting his arms for the blessing. She would know if she ever met God, because he would smell like this, holy, old and still.

Billy looked down at her lap and the child that grew inside. It was a strange alien thing, getting bigger, gaining fingers and toes and eyelids, getting stronger and heavier. She stared at her red hands which she clasped in front of her so that it looked as if she was praying. She let the words of the liturgy wash over her as if Noah had left her behind and the flood waters had come suddenly and had swept over her head. Now here she was under water seeing the grey cold shapes for the last time before she opened her mouth and took in a lungful of salt water instead of air.

She was thinking about the bird skeleton again when she realised the hymn had been announced but there was no one at the piano. The vicar coughed and people shuffled nervously in their seats as the attendant pushed Amanda up the aisle, her hand firmly on her shoulder. Everyone watched them until they reached the piano stool. After some scuffling with the music book, Amanda began to play the twenty-third psalm so fast that the congregation had to skip words to keep up. Billy recognised the tune but she didn't sing. She watched the attendant slip back into the pew in front of her and close her eyes.

But then Sally cried out suddenly and clutched her stomach. Billy looked up. The young woman's face was almost blue with terror. Several heads turned round to stare. Elaine held Sally's elbow and watched her with a mixture of love and fear. The attendant turned to her sternly.

'Your confinement isn't due,' she whispered. 'Not for another three months.' Sally sat with her hands wrapped round herself in a hug, her face still and pale. Elaine tucked her arm round her friend's waist.

'Perhaps it's coming too early,' Billy heard Elaine say very quietly.

'Unless you guessed the date wrong,' Jemima said under her breath, but Sally shook her head hard from side to side.

'No,' she said as if she were trying to convince herself. 'No, I didn't.'

'Be quiet,' said the attendant. 'Sit still.'

Gradually, Sally's face cleared again, but Elaine didn't move her arm away.

During the final hymn, which Amanda played as though she was in a race with pianists in other village churches to see who could finish first, the congregation filed forward for Holy Communion. The women from the home went last, in twos as if Noah had called them again, although Mavis didn't get up to go with them. Billy looked at her in confusion.

'Roman Catholic,' she mouthed.

Billy saw the slabs of cold stone which showed the names of the people who had been buried under the floor. 'Here lies', she read, before she watched her feet move over one of them. She imagined the skeleton underneath. She wanted to lie down on the floor, press her hands and face to it and feel how cold it was. She wanted to call down to the dead man below to ask if he minded the sound of her footsteps above him, if it comforted him to hear them. She wanted to know if he was a friend of the bird that died in the porch and if their souls kept each other company around the font and rested on the step before the altar rail after the people had gone.

Billy knelt down and lifted her eyes. She waited for the wine and the wafer, but the vicar pressed his hands down hard on her head, as if he was trying to push demons out of her.

'The Lord bless you and keep you,' he said. He worked his way along the line of women as he did so, pressing as if he was washing clothes in the laundry, so that Billy only had 'and keep you' to herself. Amanda had joined them again. She and Sally had 'The Lord bless you' between them. Both their faces were turned downwards, like twin moons watching the water, and

Billy could see that Amanda was clasping Sally's hand tightly. Jemima had 'and make his face' and Elaine had 'shine upon you', although the vicar didn't push his hands into her greasy hair. They hovered over her head delicately, shaking the blessing over her like flour in a bakery. He moved quickly on to Doreen who had the whole of 'And give peace unto you' because he had run out of fallen girls to bless. She crossed herself and said, 'Amen.' When they rose and turned round, Billy saw that they were the only ones left at the front so the whole congregation watched them as they walked slowly back to their places.

As they left the church, Mavis Free grabbed her hand again and Billy kept her eyes on her shoes as they climbed the hill back to the Haven. Halfway up, she stopped for a moment and allowed herself to glance back at the frosty village and the top of the lighthouse. Amanda and Sally almost collided with her and Doreen walked into them, as if they were playing at dominos.

'Be careful,' said Amanda sharply, because she was still angry about the piano-playing.

'Come on, why don't you?' said Mavis, looking up to make sure the attendant hadn't seen, but Sally doubled over in pain and stood with her hands on her thighs, making wrenching sounds as if she was being sick although nothing was coming out. Amanda put her arm round her and glared at the holy girl. The attendant noticed and stopped. Soon they were all grouped around Sally, who was still holding her thighs and gasping for breath.

'Your confinement isn't due yet,' the attendant repeated, as if saying it would make it come true.

Slowly, the pain passed and Sally stood upright again.

'Is she having her baby?' asked Doreen.

'It's probably nothing but sickness,' said the attendant, but she didn't sound sure.

'How are you feeling?' Elaine said, pulling her arm out of Jemima's grip and hurrying to the beautiful girl's side.

'When we return, Sally will sit in the front room by the fire. Elaine, go and fetch the midwife.'

Elaine left them and they began to walk again. Billy watched the road as it grew steep and her footsteps fell away behind her.

By the time lunch was ready, Elaine had returned and the midwife was examining Sally by the fire and searching her face as she questioned her about dates. The young women stood along the benches for the grace and Billy looked at the solemn picture of King George who gazed at them all. They sat down and spoons began clattering hungrily while the king watched them. The midwife came in and said the words which would stay in Billy's head for years afterwards: past the months at the Haven, past the time spent with the old librarian, past the time when Jim came back, past the hundreds of thousands of cards she would file, the years (over sixty) full of books to be categorised, arranged on shelves, recommended, stamped and collected again three weeks later, past the fines she would issue after a month had gone by, past all the excuses she would listen to. What she remembered was the flipping over of those words like a pancake in a pan: how relieved she was to hear them and how they turned out to be untrue.

'She is not in danger,' said the midwife. 'The baby isn't coming.'

'As I thought,' said the attendant, laying down her spoon.

Billy laid a hand on where her own child lay curled inside her. Their words seemed far too sharp and hard. She suddenly felt she had to protect him from them.

'I shall call later,' said the midwife.

When the attendant had gone to see her out, Billy pushed some cheese inside the front of her dress for Mavis Free. It made her breasts look bumpy, as if they had turned into rocks suddenly. Elaine had two slices of cold ham wrapped round her own breasts.

Mavis was by the dormitory window, with her elbows on the sill.

'Where's Sally?' she said as soon as they came in.

'In the front room,' said Elaine.

'No one is to go in there,' said Amanda, taking bread from under her skirt. They were supposed to have an afternoon nap because it was Sunday. Doreen was already under the covers with her eyes closed and her bible open on the blankets when Billy put her hand into her dress and pulled out her share of Mavis Free's lunch. Jemima passed her an apple and lay down on her bed, wrapping her long ginger plait round her wrist. She was so big she could have been made queen of the house. She made Billy think of the Queen of Grass and her shiny eyes.

'Look,' Mavis said. Billy looked up and saw that the midwife and the attendant were outside in the frost talking gravely. They stood quite a way from the house, near to where the path turned into the road. There was only one attendant on Sundays. The cook wouldn't work on the Lord's day. She went back down the hill in her coat on Saturday evenings, leaving cold food behind her in the kitchen, which meant that with the attendant out on the road, they were alone in the house. Amanda looked at the others with a spark in her eyes. She didn't say anything. She just fished under her pillow for the tin of cigarillos. Mavis was eating her lunch which was spread out on her bed like a picnic.

'I hope Sally is better soon,' Mavis said. The others murmured their agreement.

Billy could see the attendant and the midwife were still talking, their breath forming patches above them as if they were horses waiting for riders. Jemima lay on her side with her back to them all.

'You're not going to smoke those in here,' she said in her thick voice, which was so much richer than the voices of the other women. It was as creamy as custard and smooth like silk sheets.

'Why not?' said Elaine. Her face was resting against the wall now. She had already taken a match out of the box. Elaine hated Jemima for being cleverer than her and her wrist still hurt from church.

'She'll smell it.'

Elaine glared at her but Amanda looked worried.

'Jemima's right,' she said.

'Where then?' Elaine said.

'The laundry,' said Jemima quietly, still with her back to them.

'She won't smell it above the bleach and she won't go there again until tomorrow afternoon. She's no need.'

Elaine stood up. Mavis Free had finished her lunch and had brushed the crumbs under the bed.

'All right,' said Elaine. 'We might look in on Sally on the way.'

'Who'll watch?' said Amanda.

'We will,' said Jemima, who still hadn't moved and certainly couldn't see the window with her face turned into her pillow.

The attendant and the midwife were talking faster now. Billy wondered why they didn't come inside again, but they showed no sign of it. The women hesitated for a moment longer and then went quickly out of the room. Billy kept her eyes on the window.

'They're deciding what to do with the baby,' said Jemima when they had gone.

'What do you mean?'

'They've been caught out because Sally mistook the dates.'

'Is she having her baby after all?'

'Of course she is. The midwife is going to fetch the doctor.'

'What do you mean, deciding what to do with it?'

Jemima looked at her steadily. 'You signed the papers. You know what I mean.'

'I told you. I needed somewhere to stay until Jim comes to find me and then we can get married,' said Billy. She was surprised that Jemima really believed the babies could be given away like Christmas gifts.

Jemima wouldn't say anything more about it. Billy heard the other women opening the door to the front room and enquiring after Sally's health one after the other and imagined the beautiful blonde curls reflected in the firelight.

Jemima rolled over. 'Let's play cards,' she said.

'We can't. I'm watching.'

'I don't care about Elaine Brooks and the others.'

Billy looked into Jemima's face and smiled. Then she got out her silver case and found the Queen of Grass. She held it up so that she could see if it really did look like her new friend.

'What are you doing?' said Jemima.

'Nothing,' said Billy.

Doreen sighed to herself and tossed from side to side. Her face held a sudden painful expression. She said 'fish pie' to herself under her breath and wriggled to and fro as if someone were forcing her to name food and then eat it. 'Boiled egg,' she said anxiously. 'Apple tart.'

Jemima and Billy watched Doreen have her nightmare for a while, then Billy looked out of the window again. The conversation continued. The midwife was talking now and the attendant listened to her, nodding sharply like a woodpecker from time to time, with her hands on her hips. Billy dealt Jemima's cards face up so that she could tell her which ones to play. The Boy of Mirrors, the Crown of Water and the Yellow Four. Jemima stayed on her side. She picked up the Crown of Water.

'What does this one do?'

'It beats any lower blue cards. Most of them because it's a fourteen. That's all.'

'It looks like it should do more,' said Jemima.

'The Ghost Card, the Red Rose and the Nab of Fours,' Billy said as she dealt her own cards and let Jemima see them. They played for about half an hour, Billy occasionally glancing up at the window to check that the two women were still there. She had just shown Jemima how to win a hand with the Trick of Mirrors when she saw that the midwife was gone and the attendant was hurrying back towards the house. Billy pushed all the cards and the case onto Jemima's bed. 'Hide them,' she said and she ran into the corridor. She was almost at the courtyard door when she heard the attendant stamping her feet in the hallway from the cold.

'Wilhelmina. What are you doing?' said the attendant.

Billy turned round. 'I want some water,' she said. She came back down the corridor towards the attendant, trying to think of an excuse which would stop her from going into the dormitory and discovering the other women gone.

'Where is the jug from beside your bed?'

Billy stood between the attendant and the door, not knowing what to say next. The attendant reached out to turn the handle.

'Move aside,' she said.

Billy held her breath and closed her eyes as if she were about to be thrown into the lake for the witch test. The handle moved in the attendant's fingers and the door opened a crack, but just then Sally came out of the sitting room. Her dress was wet. She was paler than ever and her eyes looked icy cold. Her face was wrinkled with pain. She held her middle and stumbled forwards so that they both had to hold her up, one on either side.

'Upstairs,' the attendant said. The two of them pulled Sally round the bend in the stairs, into the room at the top and sat her down on the bed. 'I thought we had a few hours yet. Tell Elaine Brooks to run after the midwife and then fetch the doctor herself.'

'I can run after her.'

'Tell Elaine to do it.'

Billy left the room and hurried towards the laundry. She found the others crossing the courtyard on their way back. When Billy told Elaine what had happened, Elaine ran out of the front door and let it slam behind her. As they went quickly back towards the dormitory, they heard Sally cry out.

'Why didn't you come and warn us before?' said Amanda. She slid her tin of cigarillos into her pocket.

'No time,' said Billy.

Jemima sat up as they came in. 'Was that Sally crying out?'

'Yes,' said Mavis Free.

'She's in the top room,' said Amanda.

'She came into the corridor when I went to warn the others. Her dress was wet,' Billy said. 'I had to help her upstairs.'

Sally cried out again. The women lay on their beds looking up at the ceiling, trying to see through the floorboards to the bed above them. Doreen was still asleep, tossing from side to side, the moaning from above making her dreams more vivid. 'Marmalade,' she said and turned her face into her pillow.

'Why did she send Elaine and not me?' Billy asked.

Jemima didn't take her eyes from the ceiling. 'She is more able to run.'

Mavis got in under her blankets and pulled them round her. 'Why?'

'Because Elaine already had her baby,' Mavis said quickly. They all stayed still and listened for a while.

'Where is it?' Billy said eventually.

'Where's what?' said Jemima.

'Elaine's baby.' Billy had a creeping cold feeling like she had when the vicar pressed his hands on her head and said the blessing instead of giving her Communion, even though she had been confirmed when she was twelve.

No one answered.

Elaine came back in an hour later, out of breath, and lay down on her bed with her hands over her ears.

Only Billy had her eyes open when the attendant came to fetch them for reading. The others pretended to sleep. The attendant stood in the doorway and breathed in the air which smelt of Doreen's nightmares, and Billy thought she might be able to smell the tobacco that clung to the dresses of the secret smokers, but she said nothing about it.

During reading, they were all supposed to study the bible because it was Sunday. Amanda sat on the piano stool automatically but she didn't lift the lid. The other women were arranged around the room in the comfy chairs and Jemima was in her favourite place on the sofa. The attendant had taken the doctor up to the top room and now they were waiting to find out what would happen next. Doreen was the only one with the New Testament open in front of her, but even she didn't have her eyes on the pages. Mavis was telling her what had happened while she had been asleep. Elaine had gone to listen by the stairs. Mavis paused and took a breath. Then because she knew everyone was listening, she pretended to lower her voice.

'Sally told Elaine that she loves her.' Billy shifted position and watched Mavis Free's face grow wide and confident with the story she was telling. 'After breakfast on Wednesday. In the garden.'

266

Doreen gasped.

'That's never true,' said Amanda indignantly.

'I suppose Elaine Brooks told you that, did she?' said Jemima, yawning lazily.

'So what if she did?' said Mavis.

'Sounds like a made-up story to me,' Jemima said. 'I think Elaine is a liar.' They all looked at Mavis Free to see what she would do.

'She's not a liar,' said Mavis.

'Elaine's got a rough mouth and everyone knows it,' said Jemima.

'Better than being stuck up,' said Mavis.

Jemima blushed. 'I heard that this is your second time in here, Mavis Free,' she said. 'Can't get any of them to marry you, can you?'

'So what if it is?' Mavis said quietly.

Elaine came through the door and the room went quiet. 'I can't hear nothing,' she said, but then she stopped. Billy saw that tears had welled up in Mavis's eyes and were now spilling down her cheeks.

'What's wrong?' said Elaine.

'It's Jemima Faraday.'

'You've got a wicked tongue, Jemima,' said Elaine.

'Better than a rough one.' Jemima and Elaine glared at each other. There was another moan from the room above them. Mavis was still weeping. She couldn't help herself. Big fat tears kept coming.

'So what if it is?' Billy heard Mavis say under her breath a few times over. 'What's it to you?'

Later, as they went to bed, they heard a baby crying.

Billy fell asleep that night thinking about the day her father had been round to Jim's house to arrange things and what Jim's mother had said about her. She could see her father's worried face as he repeated the words and she heard them in her head as if Jim's mother had said them to her face. Jim was going away to fight and heroes didn't marry loose women. She had cried then because she thought she would never see him again.

'He's joined up already,' her father said. 'He's due to go any day.'

But a week later she had been writing at her desk when Jim knocked on the window. They walked down to the beach together and he held her hand.

'It'll be all right,' he said. 'They won't send me away before we're married. I won't have it.' Billy had believed him then. The sun was shining and everything suddenly seemed safe and right. They had sat down on the sand together and he had picked up a pebble for her to examine.

'We'll have a house with a garden and I'll be back before he's born.'

Billy smiled and touched his face. 'If I had a ring, I could show it to people and they'd believe me,' she said.

'You'll have one,' he said. 'I'll talk Mother round. She'll have to like you.'

'Only, my father said that you were leaving any day. I thought you had already gone.'

'Would I go without saying goodbye?' Jim said and kissed her.

'Ma's written to a boarding house. She won't tell me where because she thinks I'll tell you.'

Jim's face creased into a frown. 'A boarding house? Why?'

'A place where babies are delivered out of marriage,' Billy said, looking him in the face. 'And your mother said I was no better than a—'

'Don't even mention letters to boarding houses,' he interrupted. 'We'll be married soon and everything will be all right.' He stood and they went to stand closer to where the waves were breaking gently across the pale sand.

'Ma says people are talking already,' Billy said quietly. 'She says she can't stand to look at me.'

He smiled and lifted her face in his hand. 'There's no sense in that,' he said. 'You're beautiful.'

The next day he was gone. When she tried to call on him, his mother would only open the door a fraction.

'You should be inside,' was all she would say.

32

A few days later, the crying from the room upstairs stopped abruptly after lunch. The women each found different things to do to ignore the silence which filled the spaces that it left behind. Amanda played ragtime on the piano. Doreen helped Elaine with her letters. Mavis Free collected leaves in the garden. Billy and Jemima went into the dormitory to play Scrummage.

Jemima rested her back gratefully against the metal frame of the headboard. Billy's first card had a picture of a carved wooden chair, floating above a wave in the middle of an ocean. At the bottom was the number XIII. She turned the blue thirteen round so that her friend could see it.

'The Throne of the Sea,' she said. The next had a picture of an empty blue ocean, with a blue sky, and no chair or wave this time.

'Both high cards,' she said. The third had a picture of a fox wearing a green suit like Robin Hood. It was the green nab card.

'The Nab of Eights,' Billy said. 'Do you remember what the nabs mean?'

'You can steal other people's cards.'

'Or?'

'Take more cards from the pile.'

'Yes,' Billy said, putting the nab card down. 'Why has Sally's baby stopped crying so suddenly?' she asked. 'I haven't heard her cry since we went into the laundry this morning.'

Jemima looked at her carefully. 'A man came,' she said. 'I saw him in the hallway.'

'Perhaps he and his wife are looking after her,' Billy said, 'until Sally is feeling herself.'

Jemima put a hand on her swollen stomach. She seemed paler than ever. 'You're probably right,' she said.

'I don't want to talk about it anyway,' Billy said. She picked up one of the picture postcards from beside her bed. 'Have you been down to the beach?'

'No. Only as far as the library.'

'Look,' Billy said, holding up the postcard. 'It's the lighthouse in the village.'

Jemima stared at the picture. 'I'd like to go there.'

'So would I,' said Billy, thinking of the frosty road through the village which led down to the harbour. 'I come from a town near the sea, but it doesn't have a lighthouse.'

'Is it a long way away?'

'Yes. Miles and miles. Jim asked me to marry him on the beach.' She put the postcard back.

Jemima could have been a planet waiting to explode into lots of other little planets, she was getting so big. Billy wondered how she would feel when she grew as large. She noticed how the smooth fingers of Jemima's left hand curled round her cards. Her right hand rested softly in her lap. Billy reached over and held it in her palm so she could stroke it gently. Jemima yawned and let her do it.

'He's going to come and find me soon,' Billy whispered. She carried on stroking Jemima's hand.

Jemima smiled. 'You told me already, remember?'

'Yes.'

'When I leave here,' said Jemima, 'I'm going to live in a big house with servants and a nanny for my baby.'

'And you told me already. Can I come with you?'

'Yes, if you like,' she said. Then she thought for a moment. 'How will Jim know where to find you?' The door opened as she said it and Pamela the young nurse came in to fetch something from the cupboard. Billy let go of Jemima's hand, gathered up the cards and sat on them.

270

'Hello,' Billy said. Pamela's glasses made her look like someone had punctuated her face sideways with the two dots of a colon and she had forgotten what the rest of the sentence was supposed to be.

'Hello,' said Jemima. The young nurse looked at them nervously round the cupboard door.

'I'm not supposed to talk to you,' she answered. Billy gazed at her.

'I should like to be a nurse,' said Jemima.

'Well. You won't ever be one now,' said Pamela sharply. She touched the gold cross round her neck.

'Why not?'

'You know why not.' Pamela took the glass jar she had been looking for out of the cupboard and hesitated.

'I shall if I like,' Jemima said.

The young nurse came over and picked up the lighthouse postcard from next to Billy's bed and held it close to her face.

'Frederick Brown's father is a lighthouse keeper,' she said.

'Who is Frederick Brown?' Jemima asked her. Pamela put the card down. She pushed her glasses along her nose and looked at them carefully.

'I'm not supposed to talk to you,' she said again. 'My aunt and uncle are dog breeders. They've got dogs in cages.'

Jemima listened carefully and half a smile fell across her face. 'What kind of dogs?' she asked. She yawned and flicked a white hand over her mouth.

'I'm not telling.'

'What happened to Sally's baby?' she said suddenly. Billy stared at her in surprise.

'You're not allowed to say anything about that,' Pamela said.

'Pamela.' It was the midwife calling from the end of the corridor. Billy heard her voice echo and for a second none of them said anything.

'I can see the Haven from my front window,' said Pamela. 'I don't like to look at it.'

'Why not?' said Jemima, but the young nurse didn't answer.

'Pamela,' the midwife called again.

'Do the dogs bark in the night?' Billy said.

'Yes. I have to cover my ears with my hands.' She looked from one woman to the other and her eyes seemed even bigger. Billy thought of the story her grandmother used to tell her about the dog with eyes as big as saucers.

'What happened to Sally's baby?' Jemima said again.

'Pamela.' The midwife was in the doorway now. 'What are you doing?'

'Nothing,' she said and walked across the dormitory quickly holding her glass jar, without looking back again. Billy and Jemima followed her with their eyes.

'Were you talking to the girls?' Billy heard the midwife say as they went along the corridor together.

'No,' Pamela said, before their voices trailed away.

Jemima reached over so she could look at the postcard the nurse had left behind. 'We could go there together,' she said as if nothing had happened.

'How would we do that?' Billy said. She thought of the frosty village again and the magical tip of the lighthouse tower she had seen in the distance.

'We could walk. Do you think Frederick is her sweetheart?' Jemima had a goblin-like shine in her eyes.

'Who?'

'Frederick. She said his father was the lighthouse keeper.'

Just then the bell rang for dinner. Billy put the cards away and they slipped out of the dormitory together.

'Will we really go down to the harbour?' said Billy quietly as they went.

'Yes,' said Jemima. 'We'll have a picnic,' and Billy could see that she had made up her mind to go.

No one had seen Sally since she had had her baby. Two nights after the crying from upstairs had stopped, Jemima lay on her bed looking up at the ceiling, so Billy did the same. They stayed still, while the other women got into bed and snuffed out lamps.

Billy kept her eyes wide open for as long as she could to stop herself from falling asleep. She felt as if they were conspirators with the sound of dreaming around them. The curtains weren't drawn and she saw Jemima watching the dark shadows of trees outside the window, so her eyes rested on the window too. It was intoxicating to look at the night and yet not feel the cold air close around her face. It was like being asleep and awake at the same time. Billy imagined that they were outside the window, with their backs to the house, holding hands. Eventually she saw that Jemima had fallen asleep, so she turned her face into her pillow and slept too.

A few hours later, Billy woke suddenly as Jemima sat upright, as if she had seen an owl or a fox through the window and wanted a better view.

'I heard someone on the stairs and the door opening,' she said in a whisper.

'Did it wake you?'

'There's someone there,' she said.

'What do you mean?' said Billy, looking around the dormitory at the sleeping women.

'Outside the window. A shape,' she said.

'A walker?' she said, but she knew a walker would be unlikely to pass the house on a cold night like this.

'No. Someone from the house. Running,' said Jemima, still looking intently. 'There. I saw it again.' They both got up quietly and went over to the window. There was someone there, just as Jemima had said, a small figure in the distance, running across the curve of grass which led down to the lake.

'I heard the door,' said Jemima again. She pulled Billy by the hand out into the corridor. The front door was open.

'Come on,' she said and even though they had nothing on their feet, Jemima took her across the drive and onto the grass, to the place where the lake came into view. The moon was bright as there were no clouds and its white light reflected on the surface of the lake, but for a moment they couldn't see anyone.

'Let's go back in. I'm cold,' said Billy, but just as she said it, they saw the figure again. It was still running. When it got to the edge of the lake, it stood for a second on the bank.

'It's Sally, isn't it?' Billy said but her friend stood still as if she had been hypnotised. Billy shook her arm. 'We'd better fetch someone,' she said.

As they went back inside, one of the attendants came downstairs carrying a light. She caught Billy and Jemima in the dormitory door, their faces lit up as if they were sudden ghosts.

'We saw someone go down towards the lake,' said Jemima, moving over to the window again.

The woman didn't reply. She turned and ran. Within a few minutes they saw the flat-faced laundry attendant with the first one, crossing the driveway, holding lights. They both wore cloaks. Billy saw the lights glow and then disappear round the brow of the hill. The other women had begun to wake up now and were coming over to the window.

'What's wrong?' said Doreen.

'We saw someone down by the lake just now.'

'It's Sally,' said Jemima, staring through the window. Elaine was already out of the dormitory by the time she had finished speaking. They heard the front door slam and watched as she went out to join the others. She had no lamp so she ran like a shadow and soon her black shape was lost in the night.

After half an hour of watching the darkness, waiting for them to return, Billy felt tired and went back to lie on her bed again. Jemima also climbed into bed and wriggled under the covers and one by one the other women fell asleep too. Only Elaine and Sally's beds were empty.

In the morning Elaine sat against the headboard with her knees drawn up and a blanket wrapped round her.

'What happened?' said Mavis Free, but Elaine shrugged her away. Her face was blank with grief.

At breakfast, most of the attendants who worked at the house were there. One of them stood and announced that Sally was a runaway.

'You are not to talk about her again,' she said. She looked as

274

though she had not slept at all. 'Any girl found talking about the runaway will be asked to leave.' The gentle reading tutor who helped Elaine with her letters had arrived and was also having breakfast with them. She rose to her feet.

'Surely, we must . . .' she began, but the flat-faced laundry attendant motioned at her to sit down and Billy never found out what the reading tutor thought they must do.

They washed in silence. Amanda usually scrubbed herself enthusiastically, dunking her head into the big tub of water as if she was baptising herself, but today she just splashed her face to make it look as if she had washed and squatted next to the wall. Doreen didn't even go into the washroom. She sat on her bed looking out of the window. Even when they had all wriggled into their dresses, she was still in her nightgown. The others had already been gone for ten minutes before she finally made her way outside for exercise.

They each found a reason for going alone to a different part of the garden, to examine fallen leaves or bare branches, or to look at winter flowers. Billy went past the crumbled old gravestones and sat on the bench in the walled garden under the tree with spreading branches. She imagined that each woman's movements around the grounds of the house were traced with a roaming chalk line. Jemima came over and sat down next to her. She had the lighthouse postcard in her hand and began to talk about going down to the harbour, although Billy couldn't listen properly.

Where they were all positioned, Amanda, Doreen, Elaine, Jemima, Billy and Mavis Free, they might make a five-pointed star if you joined each of them together with the same chalk lines. Billy wondered where the runaway was now, although having Sally in it too ruined the star pattern.

She imagined Sally in the top room and the man Jemima had seen in the hall, like a shadow, entering the room. She imagined Pamela handing over the baby while Sally cried. Then an unthinkable thing happened. Gradually she realised that she was seeing herself in the bed instead of Sally and the shadow was taking the baby from her own arms. She felt so angry with Jim, she wanted to stand up and shout. He isn't coming back, she thought to herself, closing her eyes tight and seeing the shadow man again. Even then, when she heard the gate creak, she looked up in case it was him, but there was no one there except Jemima next to her on the bench, still talking about lighthouses and picnics.

'He's not coming back, is he?' she said quietly, feeling frightened of the words in case saying it made it true.

Jemima stopped halfway through a sentence about rocks and tides. She put her arm round her. 'If you pretend that he's coming, it makes you feel happier about things,' she said.

'That's just stupid,' said Billy, wiping her eyes.

'No it's not. I like to pretend things.'

'About the house with the servants?'

'No. That part's true.'

'They took Sally's baby and Elaine's and Mavis Free's. Where did they go?' Billy leant on Jemima's shoulder and stared wide-eyed at the garden as if the flowers might move and the infants might suddenly be revealed in the foliage. It seemed to her at that moment that the world wasn't big enough to hide three babies.

'Ssh,' Jemima whispered, stroking her hair.

'I signed the papers, so they'll take mine too.' She lifted her palm and caressed her stomach as if she might be able to hold on to her child that way.

'Jim's coming to get you, remember?' Jemima whispered.

'You know he isn't,' Billy snapped ferociously. She got up angrily but a moment later she was sorry for lashing out at her friend. She stood by the tree next to where she had been sitting, feeling embarrassed. When she turned in order to make amends, she noticed a shape beneath the branches. She wiped her face on her apron.

'Look,' Billy said.

Jemima leant forward so she could see. 'Another gravestone. It's got writing on it.'

Still red-eyed, Billy crouched down by the tree.

'1849,' she read. 'Isn't that when the house was founded?'

'What's the name?'

'A something Brown,' she said, trying to work it out. 'Almost.'

'Almost what?'

'No. That's what I think it says. Almost Brown.'

'Are you sure?' Billy was going to move the ivy aside and have a closer look, when Amanda came into the walled garden and stood by the gate.

'Are you two pals now?' she said.

'What's it to you?' said Jemima sharply.

Amanda shrugged. 'I wondered about it, that's all.'

Doreen brushed past her, went straight along the path and pushed the other gate open so that they could see the driveway.

'Do you think Sally will come back?' she said anxiously.

'No,' said Amanda.

'Where did you see her running?'

Neither of them answered.

Slowly, Elaine and Mavis came in too, wrapping their coats round themselves for protection from the wind.

'Show us,' Doreen said, so Billy led the way out onto the hillside. The six of them stood in a huddle on the grass. Jemima pointed.

'There. She ran past the window and down the hill.'

'We went out onto the grass with no shoes on,' said Billy. 'She was already at the lakeside.'

Doreen was looking out into the distance, beyond the trees and into the clear winter sky.

'Did she have the baby with her?' she asked urgently.

Mavis and Elaine turned away, unable to look at each other.

'No,' Jemima said.

'Don't be stupid,' said Amanda.

Doreen's face crumpled in confusion. Suddenly, she took off across the grass. The lake glimmered as they watched her run round the brow of the hill, just as Sally had done in the nighttime. Billy tried to go after her but Jemima held on to her arm.

'She's only going to the library. Watch,' she said.

277

Billy saw Doreen go through a gap in the trees, walk along by a shallow wall and disappear through what must have been a gate.

After lunch that day, Billy was supposed to be doing chores but she ignored the dustpan and brush put out for her and half-heartedly wiped a cloth over the pictures in the lounge. When she turned to dust the bookshelves, she saw that all the books were missing. She wondered why for a second, decided that the room was clean enough and tucked the cloth in her pocket. She wandered back out into the walled garden by herself so she could sit on the bench under the tree and think.

When she came back into the dormitory later, the other women were grouped around her bed. At first she thought someone was sick, but then she heard Amanda giggling. An attendant she hadn't seen before was on duty. She turned round.

'What is this?' she said.

Billy stood in the doorway and looked at all of them in confusion. She noticed that Doreen wasn't there. As Jemima watched her, a mixture of pity and admiration hung on her face like a mask.

'Whatever do you mean?' said Billy.

'You know exactly what I mean,' said the attendant. She stood aside so that Billy could see her bed, or rather what was on top of it. It was covered in books. A mountain of books roamed around the headboard and tumbled over the pillows and the sheet and blanket, as if someone had been planning a bonfire. Some of them had spilt onto the floor. She walked forward and picked one up. *Midas Has Asses' Ears*, it was called. She wondered what it was about, opened it and began to read the first page. 'After Dionysus lifted the curse of the golden touch from Midas, the king wandered around the forests.' Suddenly she felt she would like to sit down next to the fire and carry on with the story, but the attendant snatched the book from her hands.

'Now is not the time for reading,' she said. 'This is a wanton act.'

Billy picked up another book. *Fairies and Other Little Folk* it said on the cover. It was a children's book. There was greaseproof paper between each of the pages to protect the illustrations. She put it down and picked up another, but didn't see what it was called because the attendant snatched it away from her once more.

'It's a wanton act,' she said again. Billy looked from the bed to the attendant. She opened her mouth to say that it wasn't her and that she had been in the garden, but then she thought of Doreen handing her books and knew who it was who had made the pile on the bed. She must have done it during exercise before she ran off down the hill. Billy thought of the way her face had crumpled that morning and didn't want to get her into trouble.

'Sorry,' Billy said. Jemima laughed and put a hand over her mouth.

'Explain yourself,' said the attendant, but Billy wouldn't say anything more. She had to put the books back. She carried armfuls of them into the sitting room and Jemima wasn't allowed to help. She looked at the words on the spines as she arranged them along the shelves and wondered again what they were about. The attendant found her later with a pile of books around her, leaning against the half-filled bookshelves with a volume of poetry open in her hands and said that she would have to do without her meals the next day and paint the laundry room because of it. But Billy kept one of the books, *Fairies and Other Little Folk*, and read it while the others were asleep. She kept *A Christmas Carol*, too, and couldn't stop turning the pages.

Doreen reappeared just before dinner. She had been at the library all day.

'Did you find the books I brought you?' she said to Billy as she came in. The other women looked at her in disbelief.

'Yes,' said Billy and couldn't think of anything else to say.

'It was you,' said Mavis and she giggled in delight.

'Billy is in trouble,' said Elaine.

'It was a wicked thing to do, Doreen,' said Amanda in a mock serious voice. 'You'll end up in hell.' She had arranged herself on

Mavis Free's bed so that they could take turns brushing each other's hair. She put the hairbrush down.

'Billy is without food tomorrow, because of you,' said Jemima coldly.

'And she has to paint,' said Mavis.

Doreen gazed from face to face. 'I didn't mean to cause trouble,' she said, looking confused.

'What did you think would happen?' Jemima said. Then they all began to laugh because they couldn't help it. The pile of books and the attendant's stupid face were so funny. Only Doreen didn't laugh. She sat on her bed with her knees hunched up.

'It was a good joke,' said Elaine, leaning over to her and patting her arm.

The bell rang for dinner, but none of the women moved.

'It wasn't a joke,' Doreen said and then silence hung around her head like a cloud. The others could see her eyes were damp. Billy was about to get up and go into the dining room when Doreen began to talk again.

'I wanted to be pals with Sally,' Doreen said. She twisted the corner of her blanket in her hand and then looked around the room at the faces of her companions to see how they would react. Elaine looked into her lap, but all the others stared at her. 'She was so beautiful. Now she's run away.'

'Everyone misses her,' said Jemima. 'You still got Billy into trouble.'

'She'll never get to go to a library and be all right again,' Doreen went on.

'Why did that make you put the books on the bed?' said Amanda.

Doreen turned to face Billy. 'You said you didn't like reading and I didn't want you to be a runaway too. We all have to go to our libraries and then we'll be all right.'

'You should tell the attendants it was you that did it,' said Jemima.

'She can't,' said Billy. 'She won't be able to go down to the village any more.'

'It's my turn next,' said Elaine.

'You can't even read, Elaine Brooks,' said Jemima. 'So shut up.'

'What did they do with her baby?' Doreen said. When no one answered, she began to sob.

Billy had to miss breakfast, lunch and dinner and paint the skirting in the laundry in thick white paint, which she found amongst a large pile of cans of different colours under the stairs. She received her meals from inside the dresses of the other women for the whole of that day, warmed next to their skin or wrapped around their breasts. The best food was from Jemima who brought her a piece of fruit cake and a bit of fish after dinner. Doreen was still lying on her bed and looked as if she hadn't moved at all.

Suddenly, just as Billy was beginning to eat her third picnic of the day, the holy girl reached into her dress and pulled out half a bar of chocolate.

'Sorry,' she said, throwing it onto the end of Billy's bed.

'Thanks,' she said in surprise, her mouth full of fish.

'Where did you get that?' said Amanda, her pixie face lighting up.

Doreen wouldn't answer.

'You have to tell us, Doreen,' said Amanda. 'Or it's the same as lying.'

'No it isn't,' said Doreen.

'Tell us anyway,' said Amanda.

'The cook keeps it in a drawer in the kitchen. Pamela showed me once.'

'Pamela the nurse?'

'Yes.'

'You stole it?' said Amanda.

'No. I brought it to say sorry. It's different.'

Mavis clapped her hands. 'Can you get us some more?'

'I don't know,' said Doreen and she looked confused again.

'Don't worry,' said Jemima, smiling at Billy. 'I'll do it.'

'Really?' said Mavis.

'You're a liar,' said Elaine. 'You won't.'

'I'll get enough for all of us,' said Jemima. 'See if I don't.' Elaine was about to answer back but Doreen interrupted them.

'I told the attendant that it was me who did the books. I'm not to go to the library any more.'

'That means it's my turn now,' said Elaine and she turned a satisfied face towards Jemima. 'And Sally wasn't your pal, Doreen. She was mine and don't make people think any different.'

Amanda had gone over to Doreen's bed.

'I'll walk to church with you on Sunday if you like,' she said quietly.

'What about me?' said Mavis sulkily.

'You'll be with Billy again, and you know it, so shut up about it,' Amanda said.

33

A few weeks later, on the day the vicar came to give a talk on varieties of tree bark, Jemima had a chance to keep her promise and steal some more chocolate. The attendant and the Reverend had taken the other women on a nature walk around the lake, but Billy and Jemima had pretended to be sick. The sound of the gentle reading tutor playing Ivor Novello on the piano echoed through the house, her thin church voice arcing above it like a fading rainbow, as Billy and Jemima set out their playing cards. But the door was open and Pamela was arranging flowers in the dining room opposite. Jemima had spotted a bar of chocolate in her hand in a shiny silver wrapping. Billy stood in the dormitory doorway and watched as her friend went over to talk to her. She tried to hide the chocolate bar as soon as she saw Jemima.

'What do you want?' she said suspiciously and pushed her glasses along her nose.

'Can I have some of that?' Jemima said.

'No.'

'You stole it from the kitchen, didn't you?'

'No,' Pamela said. She licked her fingers. 'I can't give you any, I've sucked it. You won't tell on me, will you?'

'I might not,' said Jemima. 'If you come and talk to us.'

'You and Billy?'

'Yes. We're sick.'

Pamela hesitated for a second, bit the end of the chocolate and followed Jemima past Billy and into the dormitory. The three of them sat on the end of Jemima's bed.

'It's my birthday soon,' Pamela said, too loudly, as if she was waiting for presents. Billy watched longingly as she peeled away more of the wrapping.

'Many happy returns,' said Jemima. 'How old will you be?'

'Fifteen.'

'Will you get a dog for your birthday?' Billy said, remembering about the aunt and uncle and the cages.

'Yes. A black one with a pink tongue.'

'Do you have a sweetheart?' said Jemima.

'Why do you want to know that?' Pamela said, chewing the end of the bar lovingly. Billy could smell its bitter dusty scent.

'I like listening to stories about sweethearts. It's romantic. Like going to the pictures.'

Pamela swung her legs to and fro and a light went on in her eyes behind her glasses. 'Oh I don't know why you want to know that. His name is Frederick. He lives along the road from me in the village.'

'Tell us about him,' said Jemima. Billy watched unhappily as Pamela sucked the final piece of chocolate.

'His father is a lighthouse keeper. He has to row out to the lighthouse in a boat and he stays there for a month.'

'No. Tell us about Frederick, not his father,' said Jemima.

'Frederick says he wants to be a lighthouse keeper too. Frederick says that you could walk right along the rocks to the Eade lighthouse if you wanted to when the tide is low and not get in a boat at all but he wouldn't let me do it. We went in a boat.'

'What's it like inside?' Jemima said.

'The walls are curved and painted white. On the second floor, there's a stove and a chair. If you want to get to the light you have to climb up to the top of the stairs.'

Jemima smiled. She took the postcard of the lighthouse from the bed and looked at it.

'I live in the house between the library and the church,' said Pamela. She jabbed a wet chocolatey finger at the postcard.

'There's the harbour and there's the harbour wall. There are lots of rocks.'

'What happened to Sally's baby?' said Jemima, so suddenly it made Billy and Pamela jump.

'You're not allowed,' Pamela said. Her eyes clouded over with worry.

'And Elaine's? And Mavis Free's? Her first one.'

Pamela shook her head and kept her mouth closed.

'Tell me,' said Jemima. 'Or I'll go and find the midwife and the cook and say that you talked about the runaway and you stole from the kitchen.'

Pamela put her head down and swung her legs again. 'Given away to good families,' she said quietly, as if she had been taught to say it but didn't quite dare to.

Jemima nodded sadly.

'No one knows where. It's a secret.'

Billy turned cold at the words.

'You sign the papers when you come in or you're not allowed to stay,' Pamela went on reciting.

Billy thought of the office by the door with its yellow curtains, which she had been into just once. She remembered the pen and the ink pot and how her eyes had filled with tears at the senior attendant's words.

Pamela blinked at them both. Jemima looked closely at the postcard of the lighthouse in the nurse's pink hand as if nothing had happened.

'Where's the path that you can walk along?' she asked.

The young nurse looked relieved. She glanced at the postcard and pointed to the gap where the sea was between the harbour wall and the lighthouse. 'Tide must be in,' she said casually. 'I know how the house got started,' Pamela added. Jemima and Billy looked at each other.

'How do you know that?' said Billy.

'It's a secret but Frederick told me. It was his great-aunt.'

'Was she a benefactor?' said Jemima, pronouncing all the syllables of the long word and giggling to herself at the way it sounded.

'No,' said Pamela. 'She drowned herself in the lake.'

Billy was shocked. She thought of the lake's dancing mirror-like surface and imagined a body turning slowly underneath it.

'She wasn't married and she got herself in trouble,' Pamela went on. 'Afterwards, her father gave the house to the church.'

'That's horrible,' said Billy.

'She was friends with the librarian. That's why the library takes girls to train.'

Jemima noticed the look on Billy's face.

'You mustn't tell,' said Pamela. 'It's a secret. Nobody knows about it.'

'The Haven's probably haunted, you know,' Jemima said slyly.

'Really?' The nurse was suddenly afraid.

'What will you call the dog you get for your birthday?' Jemima said, wanting to change the subject because she could see the mirror lake and the body turning slowly in Billy's eyes.

'He's called Albert. I've seen him already.' She fiddled with the chain which held her gold cross round her neck. 'When my aunt and uncle die, my husband will inherit their house.'

'How do you know?' said Jemima.

'They told me.'

'You're not married,' said Billy.

'Frederick held my hand when we went walking on the beach. He gave me a shell and held my hand so that he could give it to me.'

'Very good,' said Jemima, wrapping her long ginger plait round her wrist. Her eyes were shining.

Pamela got up. 'I have to do the flowers.' She gazed at Jemima for a moment. 'Are we friends now?'

'Yes, of course,' said Jemima.

'And you won't tell about the chocolate or talking about the runaway?'

'I might not, if you get us some next time.'

'All right,' she said and went back towards the dining room.

'When?' Jemima called after her casually.

Pamela stopped. 'When what?'

'When will you get us some chocolate?'

Pamela hesitated. 'I could get some tomorrow.'

'Enough for everyone?'

'Yes.'

'Good. See you later.'

Pamela left quickly.

Without saying anything, Billy began to look at her cards. Jemima lay down and closed her eyes. They stayed like that in silence for such a long time that Billy thought Jemima had fallen asleep, when suddenly she opened her eyes, sat up and snatched a handful of cards. She tucked them down the front of her dress.

'What are you doing?' Billy said.

'Come to the lighthouse with me or I'll go by myself and I won't give you your cards back.'

Billy looked at her. 'I never said I wouldn't come.'

Jemima lay on her back on the bed beside her and laughed so much that her face wrinkled up like a monkey's. She was so fat she looked like a reclining Buddha with a laughing monkey face.

'I'll tell Pamela to bring us some food for a midnight picnic.' She pushed herself along the bed and put her head on Billy's lap.

'Really?'

'Yes. But wait till we get the chocolate first. For a test to see if she'll do it. It's your turn in the library next,' she added.

'I don't need to learn the library. Jim's coming to get me anyway.'

'Just in case he doesn't come.'

'You're turning into Doreen. You can make a pile of books on my bed too if you like.'

'Will I have to be holy and go to church all the time?'

'Yes.' They both laughed and Billy touched her friend's face and thought about the chocolate they had been promised.

'We did it in a boat,' she said.

Jemima smiled. 'You and Jim?'

'Yes.'

'How many times?'

'Just once.'

'Was it romantic?'

'Yes. He asked me to marry him afterwards.'

'That's lovely,' said Jemima.

'The sand was warm because the day was so fine. He held my hand. Then he asked me.'

Jemima closed her eyes so she could imagine it. 'I did it in a field,' she said, her cheeks turning pink at the thought.

'Once?'

'No. More than once. At night-time.'

'Who with?'

'My fiancé of course.'

'Are you still going to marry him?'

'I'll probably marry someone rich instead.'

'My father tried to get Jim to marry me but his mother said that I was no better than a prostitute. Then my mother wrote to the Haven and I only saw him once after that.' As she told her story, she stroked her friend's hair. Jemima listened from her place on Billy's lap, so that when Billy began to cry, her tears fell onto her face.

'Don't cry. Elaine is in trouble at the library already,' said Jemima.

Billy wiped her eyes, then touched Jemima's face where it was wet. 'Sorry,' she said and sniffed. 'I thought you didn't care about Elaine.'

'I don't. I'm trying to make you happy.'

'How are you going to make me happy?'

'The library,' said Jemima. 'If she does one more thing wrong, she can't work there any more. It will be your turn. Instead of the laundry. Everyone else has been.'

'I told you. I don't care about the library.'

'You will. You'll like it. Just be careful that you get to stay there for a while.'

'I don't understand why Elaine's still here,' Billy said.

Jemima sat up so she could look right at her. 'She's nowhere to go. No library will take her because of her rough mouth and because she doesn't know her letters.'

'What did Elaine do to get into trouble so quickly?'

'She swore when the curate's wife was listening. She has to go to her after church and apologise. It's her last chance.'

Billy thought of Elaine's ill-looking face, with her deep mud-filled eyes and the spots around her chin. Then she thought of the curate's wife. She had thin hair. Her eyes were too big and her skin was too tight, as if she was turning into a fish.

'What did she say?'

'No one knows.'

'Do you think it's true?' Billy said.

'What?'

'About Frederick's aunt.'

'Great-aunt,' said Jemima. 'No. She made it up.' She kicked her shoes off, reached under her dress and wriggled out of her stockings. 'My feet hurt,' she said. She lay down again, on her back this time, with her head on the pillow and her legs over Billy's lap. 'Rub my feet for me.'

Billy held her warm bare ankles in her hands and felt how strong they were. She squeezed them gently. Jemima closed her eyes so she could concentrate on the feeling, and Billy moved her hands much more firmly, clutching at her friend's white and pink flesh as if she was kneading dough. When she had had enough, Jemima sighed and turned over onto her side like a child going to sleep. Billy struggled out from under her friend's heavy feet and shuffled up the bed herself so that she was lying next to Jemima with her stomach touching her back. There was only just enough room for both of them.

Billy looked down at their swollen stomachs. She wanted to run her hand over Jemima's round belly, so that she knew what it felt like and to find out if it was the same as when she ran her hand over her own swollen stomach. She hunched herself up for a moment and watched Jemima's face and how perfectly moon-like it was, how thin her eyelids were and how her eyebrows fitted exactly. She wanted to run a finger gently over each eyebrow to follow its arch and to feel how soft the hairs were. Jemima felt Billy watching her and opened her eyes. She searched her face for a second as if she was reading a map.

Then she reached out and took hold of her slim wrist. She guided her hand inside her wide dress and rested it on her stomach and Billy felt how smooth and hard it was under her hand.

'Pamela said they give the babies to good families,' Billy said quietly. She ran her hand over Jemima's belly button and down the other side.

'They won't take mine,' said Jemima. 'I won't let them. I heard of a girl once who was allowed to keep hers. She was only four-teen.'

Billy thought about the little office and the ink which had come out in blotches. Then she pulled up her friend's dress and her wide cotton chemise so that she could watch her hand move.

'What about the papers?'

Jemima didn't open her eyes again. She just shuffled slightly so that the dress moved more easily away from her thighs.

'Who cares about papers?' she said sleepily. 'I'm going to live in a big house like I told you, with a cook and a maid and a butler and a nanny. I'm going to eat little sandwiches in the garden and invite people to tea to look at the roses. I might have a parasol too.' She was nearly asleep now. 'Yes. A pink and yellow parasol. There might be a breeze when we take tea in the garden but it won't be very windy. I'll have a gardener to keep the grass short. He can put awnings up for me so we can shelter if the breeze gets up.' Soon she was dreaming about the big house with servants and the garden instead of talking about it.

Billy saw that she was asleep. She leaned over and kissed her dry pink lips quickly. Jemima murmured with pleasure and rolled onto her back. Billy pulled her friend's dress back down over her thighs and slipped off the bed, then she went and lay on her own bed and ran her hand across her own smooth stomach until she fell asleep herself.

The next day Billy found one of the books Doreen had put on her bed wedged between the iron bedstead and the mattress. *Midas*

Has Asses' Ears, she read across the top. She must have missed it when she was putting the books back. She stroked the cover. The letters were embossed in gold on the front. When she opened the pages, she thought about Jemima, curled up on her bed, shining like the Queen of Grass, and she remembered kissing Jim on the sand and wondered what it would be like to kiss Jemima on the sand, softly and gently, with the waves hissing behind her. She wondered if the strange hissing sea feeling was love, even though she wasn't supposed to love Jemima because she was a girl. She was going to get married when Jim came and found her and they could visit Jemima in her big house. She wondered if she was allowed to love two people at once. I love her. She tried the words out in her head as she turned the pages of the book about Midas. I love her. I love her. I love her.

'The Hairdresser's Secret', she read. It was the title of the first chapter and the words spun their way across the page as if a spider had been weaving them. Billy sat down on her bed and read the story. At the top of each new page, the spider had woven some of the words and had coloured them in with red and yellow paint.

After Dionysus lifted the curse of the golden touch from Midas, the king wandered around the forests, repentant and humble. While he was in the forests, he came across a sound so beautiful that he was completely enchanted by it. He followed the sound and discovered that the music came from the pipes of Pan himself. He sat at the feet of Pan and listened. Much later, there was a competition between Apollo and Pan to find out who was the greater musician. After the contest, Midas shouted for Pan but the crowd jeered at him. Apollo was declared the winner and he cursed Midas by giving him the ears of an ass. Everyone laughed at him. Even Pan could not undo the curse of the Sun God. Midas wrapped a turban round his head so that no one would see his ears. Only Midas's hairdresser knew the truth and she was sworn to secrecy. But the secret grew and grew inside the hairdresser and became so big that she was frightened she was going to shout out, 'Midas has asses' ears,' wherever she went. One day when the secret became too much for the hairdresser to bear, she ran out into the valley where the river flowed. There she dug a hole in the ground with her hands and put her mouth to it. She whispered, 'Midas has asses' ears.' But the bulrushes by the river heard her and that is why, when the wind blows through the rushes by the water, they whisper to themselves, 'Midas has asses' ears. Midas has asses' ears.'

Billy looked over to Jemima's empty bed and changed the last bit of the story so that it was only hers and no one else's. She pretended the spider had written the words in the book in invisible writing so that only she could read his footsteps. A woman had a secret that she had told to nobody, said the invisible words. One day the secret got too much for her and she was frightened she would spit it out and everyone in the world would hear it, so she ran down to the river. With her fingers, she dug a hole in the dark brown soil. Then she put her mouth to the hole and she whispered, 'I love her. I love her. I love her. I love her.' And the bulrushes by the river heard, so when the wind blows through the rushes by the water, they whisper to themselves, 'I love her. I love her. I love her. iloveheriloveheriloveheriloveheriloveheriloveheriloveheriloveheriloveheriloveheriloveheriloveheriloveheriloveheriloveherilove'

Pamela brought in a bar of chocolate later that day. As the three of them sat on the bed together, Billy saw her friend glance at the lighthouse postcard and she could see an idea falling across her face like the shadow of a tree. She realised what she was going to do.

'Now tell me,' Jemima said, 'has Frederick touched you here?' She put her hand on Pamela's knee and squeezed it.

Pamela looked from Billy to Jemima in alarm. 'Why did you squeeze my knee like that?'

'I was only trying to warn you,' Jemima said. 'About what might happen if you let Frederick touch you. Here, here or even here.' Jemima pointed to Pamela's shoulder, then her knee and then one of her round, apple-shaped breasts.

'I'm not supposed to talk to you,' Pamela said automatically.

'Or here,' said Jemima, pointing to the top of her legs, just to the left of Pamela's white apron pocket.

Pamela jumped up in fright and ran to the door.

'Just warning you,' said Jemima calmly. 'I was deceived that way, you know.'

Pamela watched her carefully like someone might watch a dog to see if it is friendly and then came back into the room.

'Sorry,' she said.

'I accept your apology but to make up for it, we need some lights and some food.'

Billy watched her friend silently and thought about the beach and the boats she would see when she got to the light, to stop herself from feeling guilty.

'What?'

'Some lights and some food,' Jemima repeated patiently.

'Why?'

'Well, all right, I'll tell you but you have to keep it secret. We're going to see the lighthouse.'

'You can't do that.'

'Oh? It was you who said that we should.'

'Did I?'

'You said we should go and see the lighthouse when the tide is out. You said Frederick had told you all about it. Don't you remember?'

'I think I remember.'

'I could tell the midwife what you said if you like, just to see if we can go to the lighthouse by ourselves, like you said we could.'

'No,' Pamela said, pushing her glasses up her nose. 'Don't tell her. I can get you some lights and food.'

After Pamela had gone, Jemima picked up the postcard and laughed. Billy watched her and thought about the frosty village.

'We're going to go and see the light,' Jemima said contentedly. She lay back on her bed with her hands behind her head.

'Do you think we were mean?'

'Yes,' said Jemima. 'I don't care.'

Later, when all the women were in the dormitory, Jemima broke up the big bar of chocolate Pamela had taken from the kitchen for her. Billy watched Jemima's soft fingers as she snapped the bar neatly and handed it round.

'I told you. Didn't I, Elaine?'

Elaine looked at her grumpily, but she took the chocolate she was offered without replying. Billy had to decide whether to put it all in her mouth at once and chew it hard so that it stuck in her teeth, or whether to suck a little bit at a time and keep the dusty flavour in her head for as long as she could. Jemima told the story about how she had persuaded Pamela to steal chocolate for her, but she didn't say anything about the lighthouse. As Billy was sucking the last bit of chocolate from her teeth, she knew that they had that secret all to themselves.

34

Billy was glad Pamela had got the lights. It was black outside the house. As soon as they stepped through the door, they were plunged into the night as if someone had thrown a cloak over their heads and it was so cold Billy felt as though she was breathing in ice instead of air. Her legs felt heavy, like they had water swimming around in them, as they made their way across the cold grass towards the lake. Jemima said they had to go that way because they might be seen on the road. When they got to the tree with branches like a witch holding up her skirts, they sat down underneath it for their midnight picnic. Jemima rubbed her back and Billy opened the little bag that Pamela had packed for them.

'Pork pie and cake,' she said, passing some to her friend, 'and apples.'

Jemima put the food in her lap and clapped her hands in eagerness. 'Save the apples for later,' she said. 'Now let's say grace.'

Billy closed her eyes automatically.

'Grace,' said Jemima loudly and she fell back on the grass in the darkness and laughed her monkey laugh.

When Billy had finished her pie, she sucked one finger after another so that she could savour the taste that was left there and swallow every crumb. The pickle inside was sharp and bitter and made her tongue tingle. Jemima moved closer to her.

'I'm cold,' she said and put her arm round her. Billy looked at her suddenly. Her skin was white and creamy like milk under the witch tree. Billy put her hand out to touch her friend's face.

She ran her pork pie flavoured finger along it from where her red hair sat messily at her temple, down to her chin. She traced it as if she were drawing it, with the pork pie pickle taste still in her mouth, but after a moment Jemima pushed her hand away.

'Come on,' she said, jumping up.

When they had rounded the hill and walked past the lake, they could see the village stretched out in front of them. At the end of the lakeside path they went through a gate. The nearest house was a pretty stone cottage with roses in the garden. Next to it was a stout building with a wide arched door. 'Eade Village Library' was carved into the stone above it.

'That's the library where you come to work,' said Jemima. Billy looked from the library to the cottage next door and pointed.

'Pamela's house,' she said. 'Remember?' Then they heard the sound of the dogs. It was a slow yapping, only just audible in the wind which ran its cold hands across their faces.

'Ready?' said Jemima in her soft clear voice as she turned to look down the hill.

'Yes,' Billy said. She linked arms with her friend and they set off into the night past the quiet squat houses.

They came to the small square with shops on two sides, then suddenly they were on the beach. The sand was grey under their feet in the darkness, and the sea, which was flat and hissing gently to itself, was a dark and frightening blue. For a while, they sat down on the sand and ate the apples Pamela had stolen for them, and listened to the sea creeping and retreating.

'There's the sea wall,' Billy said, pointing. 'The harbour must be on the other side.' Then suddenly there was a flash of yellow light. They both jumped. For a second they had a glimpse of the white shape of the lighthouse against the dark rock. It was a long way from the land.

'One day I shall marry a rich man who could buy this whole village,' said Jemima, waving her arm like a conqueror.

'I'm going to become rich all by myself,' said Billy. 'And one day when I'm rich enough, I shall buy the Haven and board up all the windows.'

'You won't be able to see out of them if you board them up,' said Jemima.

'I don't care about seeing out of them.'

'When we're old,' Jemima said, suddenly serious, 'can we meet each other and tell each other our stories?'

'Don't be silly. We'll always be friends.'

'Just in case we're not.'

'All right.'

'Promise?'

'Yes. I promise.' Billy laughed because it sounded so solemn. 'When we're old.'

'Come on,' Jemima said, as the light flashed again.

They went back onto the promenade and found the steps up onto the harbour wall, which curved out into the bay. They hurried along the wide path on the top where people walked out in the daytime to fish or watch the boats, frightened all the while by the thought that someone could be following them a few breaths away. Once Billy turned round and thought she saw someone in the shadows, but it was just the tip of a sail bobbing in the harbour beyond.

When they got to the end of the wall, they found a bench cut out of the stone and some steps leading down to the rocks which linked the lighthouse to the land. Jemima held up her lamp, revealing the first part of the path to the lighthouse, uncovered by the sea. The waves were a few feet below the wide rocky path but the sea was choppy and jumping about excitedly. Then the light flashed and the outline of the lighthouse suddenly appeared again in the distance. Billy wondered what they would do if the water came back in suddenly and covered the rocks while they were walking along it. She imagined swimming all the way to the lighthouse with her grey skirt streaming out behind her, holding her breath, diving under the water to look at the sharp brown rocks.

'Pamela says it stays out for hours,' she said, trying to reassure herself.

Slowly, she went down the steps and helped Jemima to climb

unsteadily after her. They linked arms again and stood on the path together. The first few paces were fine, just like walking along the pavement of a high street after it had been raining. Then Jemima held up her light and they could see that in front of them the path through the rocks dipped slightly. Only a short way ahead it was covered in thick green seaweed. They walked a little further, but the pathway was so slippery they had to stop again. When they were lit up by the beam of the lighthouse once more, the light seemed to Billy to be coming from somewhere far away, another country maybe. They took a few more steps. Just then a wave touched the top of the rocks near where they were standing and sent a trail of water along the path. Jemima slipped. Billy put her arm round her friend's waist to steady her. She had to use all her strength to stop her from falling over completely.

'We'll have to go back,' she said.

'I can't move,' said Jemima softly. She felt very cold underneath Billy's hand.

'Yes you can,' she said.

'I can't. I'll slip,' said Jemima and for a moment they stood together like a sudden statue, clinging to each other. Another wave sent cold water over their feet.

'You'll have to move,' Billy said. 'Turn your feet slowly.'

Jemima stood still for a moment longer and then began to turn her feet round, bit by bit. Billy did the same, as another wave sent a film of rushing water towards them and retreated again. They made their way back along the path, moving slowly. Billy could see that they had come further than she thought. The wind was getting stronger and was throwing her hair around her face. The cold air stung the skin on the back of her neck. Jemima held on to her tighter each time she lifted her feet.

Finally they reached the bottom of the steps again. Billy helped her friend to climb back up and followed behind her, lit up by the pulse of the lighthouse as she did so. She felt as though she had been holding her breath since she had first stepped down onto the rocks. She sat down on the stone bench and Jemima sat next to her. They didn't say anything for a while. They just watched as the beam of the lighthouse shone and retreated, shone and retreated, like a heartbeat, like the heartbeats they could hear inside their own chests or the kick Billy felt when her baby moved in her stomach.

Jemima stood and looked out over the harbour wall at the black sea and the boat shapes bobbing in the bay like strange ghosts, so Billy got up and stood next to her. After a second, Jemima turned and put her hands up to Billy's face to warm it by rubbing her palms up and down.

'You look frightened,' she said. She put her fingers at the corners of Billy's mouth and lifted it upwards into a smile. She started to laugh to herself as she did so. Her laughter sounded strange in the silence of the harbour night. Their faces were so close, Billy could feel her breath. Then Jemima leant forward and kissed her on the lips. It felt so soft and fresh and cold that she couldn't say anything for a second. She held Jemima's kiss in her mouth all the way back to the Haven like a sweet. But as soon as the kiss was over, Jemima's face wrinkled up in pain. She put her hand to her stomach and sat down on the bench hard. She looked surprised. Billy put her arm round her friend's shoulder.

'We have to go back now,' she said but neither of them got up.

The pain subsided and Jemima looked at Billy steadily. 'I'm sorry I kissed you,' she said.

'I don't mind,' said Billy.

Jemima looked out over the sea. 'Did you mean what you said about buying the house?'

Billy thought about it for a moment. 'Yes,' she said. 'When I'm rich enough, I'll buy it so that no one else has to live there or sign the papers.'

'I don't care about papers,' said Jemima fiercely. Then she looked at Billy and her face was suddenly serious. 'We could almost fall in love with each other if we were a boy and a girl and not two girls. We could get married and live in a house with a big garden and flowers and servants.'

'How many servants?' said Billy.

'Ten and a big bathtub.'

'Made of copper.'

'Yes. We can't though.'

Billy put her hand out and stroked her friend's hair. They didn't talk for a while.

'I thought about kissing you a lot,' said Billy.

Jemima looked at her quickly. 'But we mustn't do it.'

'Why not?'

'Because I'm going to live in a house with awnings to shelter under when it rains and sandwiches and fizzy wine.'

'You said I could live there with you.'

'Well, you can't because you're going to marry Jim and I'm going to marry a rich man and have lots of children.'

'What names will you call them?' Billy moved her arm so that it hung round Jemima's neck and they sat close, keeping each other warm.

'Frederick, after Pamela's sweetheart, Billy after you, George, after the king.'

'Will they all be boys?'

'No. Not all of them. There will be Victoria, Mary and Elizabeth too,' Jemima said, resting her head on Billy's shoulder.

'That's only six.'

'Bernard, Eunice, Beryl. And I'll think of more. It depends what they look like.' Jemima sat up and shifted her weight and Billy watched as the lighthouse lit up her face. She leant towards her so that their faces were close together.

'I nearly kissed you again,' said Billy after a moment.

'I said we mustn't do it. What about Jim and the rich man I'm going to marry?'

Billy didn't reply, so Jemima put her head back on her shoulder and let Billy hold her more tightly.

'Arthur, Anne, Sybil, Rebecca,' Jemima said. 'Those are good names.'

'I almost held your hand too,' said Billy.

'Holding hands might not matter.' She lifted her white fingers and played with Billy's left hand as it rested in her lap.

'But holding hands makes me want to kiss you again.'

'You could almost kiss me,' Jemima said softly.

'How do you mean?'

'I could screw my mouth up tight like this and you could kiss me then, because you wouldn't be kissing me on the lips. Or you could kiss air just before my face and I could do the same. Kissing the air probably doesn't matter.'

'When you live in the house with the awnings and the sandwiches, can I come and kiss you? If your husband doesn't mind?'

'No. I will have my children to look after. But you can come on Wednesday afternoons and play cards.'

'And if we almost hold hands and nearly kiss on Wednesdays, it won't matter?'

Jemima looked at her. Then she held her middle and bent over in pain.

'On Wednesdays it doesn't matter,' she said when the contraction had passed.

Billy helped her to her feet. 'We have to go back now,' she said, and this time they moved back along the harbour wall together, holding hands as they went.

'Will you do it really?' Jemima said. 'The thing you promised?'

'Coming to find you when I'm old, you mean? I thought I was going to come on Wednesdays.'

'Just in case.'

It was midnight and the moon was round and full in the sky as they climbed back up the hill. They were nearly there when Jemima cried out in sudden pain as another contraction began and subsided, like the flash of the lighthouse, advancing and retreating. She stopped for a moment, then they crept across the sleeping driveway and up to the front door. Jemima gave the handle a sharp tug, then turned it right and left quickly and the door swung open.

'I'll fetch the attendant,' Billy said as they extinguished their lights.

'No, not yet,' said Jemima and she pushed open the dining-room door and sat down on one of the benches. Billy sat next to her and they watched each other's faces in the shadows.

'Elaine broke a commandment at the library,' Jemima said, putting her elbow on the table and leaning her head on her hand.

'Which one?'

'She took the Lord's name in vain twice and the curate's wife heard her. She's done it now.' She smiled at Billy.

'How do you know?'

'Mavis Free told me. She said "Jesus" and "Jesus Christ". She isn't to work in the library any more.' Jemima suddenly held her hand to her mouth and looked down at the bench. Billy could see a dark water mark forming on her friend's skirts. She put her hand out to touch it. It was warm.

'I'll fetch the attendant,' Billy said again.

'No. Not yet.' Jemima was so tired that she didn't even move away. She just leant forward and rested her arms and head on the table.

'Will we go to the lighthouse one day?' she said.

'Maybe,' said Billy. She laid her arms and head down next to her friend's on the table and put her hand out to touch her hair, until Jemima cried out again. She was shivering. She held on to Billy's hand tightly.

'They're coming quickly now,' said Jemima in a whisper.

'I'll fetch the attendant,' Billy said yet again. This time Jemima just nodded, so Billy ran upstairs and banged on the door to the nearest attendant's room. It was the one who had made her paint the skirting because of the books. She rose from her bed without a word. She didn't say anything about the grey dresses and aprons they were wearing, which they should have taken off hours ago in favour of wide white nightgowns, she simply put her arm round Jemima's waist and took her towards the stairs. Billy tried to follow but she wouldn't let her.

'Go to bed,' she whispered. Then she led Jemima away, while Billy stood in the hallway and watched. When they reached the landing, Jemima turned round and looked at her for a second. Her face was white and frightened.

Back in the dormitory, Billy slipped on her nightdress, lay on her bed and stared at the ceiling, just as they had both done before Sally ran away. She began to think about the pulse of the lighthouse and what the inside might be like, but then she heard Jemima scream. She turned her face into her pillow and tried to lift it around her ears so she wouldn't be able to hear, but it didn't work. The front door opened and from her bed Billy saw one of the attendants moving swiftly towards the path. Half an hour later, she returned with the midwife and someone else, Billy couldn't see who. As they came in and their footsteps moved along the hall and upstairs, Jemima screamed again. Billy could feel the other women waking up silently around her. She got out of bed and walked over to the window. For a little while, she watched the place where she and Jemima had walked only a few hours ago and realised she was crying. She put the back of her hand up to her face and wiped her eyes. She gazed out at the night through the window for a while but Jemima screamed again and she couldn't listen any longer. She went to the door and climbed the stairs to the room where her friend was. Pamela was outside, guarding the room like a soldier. She had a smug expression on her face. Billy tried to go straight past her and push open the door but Pamela put her arm out to stop her.

'Go back to bed,' she said, but Billy was big and fat so she just pushed Pamela's arm out of the way and went into the room.

The midwife turned to look at her in horror, like a ghost who had been disturbed in its haunting. Jemima was half sitting, half lying against the pillows behind her. Her legs were spread and her grey dress was gone. She was wearing a nightgown which was drawn up above her stomach. There were no lights in the room, but the moon shone in through the curtainless window and in the moonlight, Billy could see a look of surprise and terror on Jemima's face. She would have gone over and held her hand, but the midwife pushed her back out of the room.

'Take her downstairs,' she said and closed the door.

Billy's head was full of the picture of her friend on the bed with her nightdress drawn up. She was sure she had seen blood on the sheets. She didn't resist when Pamela took her by the wrist and led her back to the dormitory, closed the door and locked it. She felt the eyes of the other women on her as she rested her head against the door.

Billy lay on her bed for an hour after the screaming stopped. After a while, she could see the new morning arriving across the clean grass of the hillside. The light began to turn the room a blue-grey colour. It was creeping in like a robber who wanted to break through the window, when she heard the key turn in the lock.

The other women around her got up one by one and slipped out to the washroom and breakfast, but she didn't move. When breakfast had started, she stole out of the room and waited below the stairs until she was sure no one was guarding the door.

Jemima was sitting up in bed with her new baby when she went in. There was still blood on the sheets but her friend's eyes were wide with surprise and love.

'A boy,' said Jemima, smiling.

'He's beautiful,' Billy said.

'Yes,' said Jemima. Then they heard footsteps on the stairs.

'You'd better go,' said Jemima, looking into her baby's face.

'What will you do?' Billy said, but the midwife was coming and Jemima didn't reply.

After that an attendant sat either inside or outside the room like a guard at Buckingham Palace. The next time Billy crept up the stairs to see Jemima, the new baby wasn't there any more and her friend's face had changed. She lay looking at the wall and wouldn't answer any of her questions.

35

The librarian put her hand on Billy's shoulder and pulled her inside like an evangelist rescuing a sinner. The library smelt of dust and was gloomy because the librarian kept the blinds drawn. She believed, in the same way that some people believe in God and the church, that the light damaged the books. It meant that the library was lit by brown sunlight which streamed in through the blinds anyway and was coloured by them. Amanda had been right about how old she was. She was the oldest person Billy had ever seen. Her face wrinkled up like a walnut when she smiled. She wore an old-fashioned pinafore dress and a high white collar.

'Take off your hat,' said the librarian. 'Those hats look like jam-jar covers.' Billy took off her hat and put it on the chair next to the desk. 'And the apron. Why do you need an apron in a library?'

Billy stood in her black shoes and stockings and her thick waist-less dress. She wondered for a moment if the librarian would ask her to remove those too.

'Better,' said the librarian, putting on her spectacles and looking at something on the desk. She looked for so long that Billy thought she had forgotten about her. She coughed.

'I can't stand coughing in a library,' the librarian said, without looking up. 'People do it instead of talking. Just because they are not allowed to talk, their mouths have to do something. They would eat and drink with the books for plates if I let them.' She looked at Billy again. 'Let me show you the shelves,' she said, standing up.

Billy could feel how magical the books in the library were as she walked along the aisles. She wondered if the librarian had put a spell on them. She showed Billy the sections: animals, astrology, astronomy, cookery, gardening, geography, handicraft, history, home-craft, magic, novels, picture books (for children), poetry and science.

'I don't like Melvil Dewey and his new systems,' the librarian muttered to herself as she went. 'Look at this,' she said, holding up a copy of *Robinson Crusoe*, with a large water stain on page fifty-three. She shook her head. Then she looked at Billy as if she hadn't seen her before. 'You're fat. We'll have to have you in the back.'

Billy picked up her hat and her apron from the chair.

'You would have thought people had never seen a pregnant woman before,' the librarian said as she picked up a box of books and took Billy into a sitting room which was also dim and smelt damp. 'These came yesterday.' She cut the string with a shiny pair of scissors. 'We'll see how good you are at letters. Sit down. You can sort them alphabetically.'

Billy sat down gratefully.

'There are novels, poetry and a few should be geometry,' the librarian said, peering into the open box. 'Now.' Her voice was suddenly bright and friendly as if Billy had just arrived and the instructions to remove clothes and not to cough had never been issued. 'Would you like tea? With sugar? Of course you would.'

The librarian went into a tiny room which served as her kitchen and Billy began to sort through the first pile. She was flicking through one book when the librarian came back into the sitting room with two cups.

'Charles Dickens,' she said, setting the cups down on the small table next to the settee. 'Have you read that one?'

'Yes,' said Billy. The librarian was surprised and smiled widely. She had met a lot of women who couldn't read.

'I would like to read these too,' Billy said boldly. She pointed at the pile of smart new books.

The librarian passed Billy her tea. Billy thought how lovely it was to drink sweet tea with milk in it. At the Haven the women took it black and bitter.

'This is a library, after all,' the librarian said, and she smiled.

'Put those other books in order and that can be your work for today. Then you may read.'

Billy looked at her in astonishment. She knew it would take her no more than ten minutes to order the rest of the books. She finished her tea and set the cup back down on the table.

'My friend Jemima worked here before me,' she said.

'Yes,' the librarian said. 'Before the religious girl. Then they sent the girl with the dirty mouth who couldn't read.'

'Elaine.'

'Yes. It's surprising how many they send to train as librarians who don't know their letters.' Billy thought of the curate's wife with her fish eyes and her skin stretched so tightly back across her skull that when she saw her in church she was frightened that her skin would break and would have to be patched with tape.

'Elaine was rude to the curate's wife,' Billy said.

'Yes,' the librarian almost smiled at the memory. 'And Jemima had pretty hands.'

'Did she read too?'

'Yes. All of the Brontës. And most of George Eliot. She was halfway through *Middlemarch*. I said she could take it with her but she said she would come back and finish it.'

'We aren't allowed to read novels at the house. Only the classics, the bible and romantic poetry.'

'I have heard,' said the librarian sadly. 'And she never came back.'

'She wasn't allowed to,' Billy said, about to tell her Jemima's story, but the librarian interrupted her.

'Now. What would you like to start on?'

Billy laid her hand on top of the pile of books. 'I'll start with A.'

The librarian found Billy a cushion and told her to rest her feet on the sofa because her ankles were probably swollen. She also told her not to tell anyone at the house about the reading in case the visits were stopped.

'Before you leave each day, I'll show you tickets, book-shelving, returns and renewals, cataloguing or book-mending,' she said. 'Now I must get back to the desk.'

Billy had just finished sorting out the poetry and the geometry when she heard the librarian opening the wide arched door so that people could come in and choose. She picked up the next book on the pile and turned the pages. For a moment, before the words formed themselves into sentences, she saw the sections in the library dancing in front of her: astrology, astronomy, gardening, cookery, magic, animals. Then she began the story. It crept over her, ghostly, with prickly fingers. She sank into the book like she was burying her feet in wet sand.

A week later Billy saw Jemima for the last time. It was nighttime and Jemima was asleep, but she opened her eyes wide as soon as Billy came in. Billy got onto the bed and lay next to her. They lay like that in the dark for a while, breathing together. Then Billy put her hand out to touch her friend's face and it was wet.

'She came and took him,' Jemima said quietly.

'Who did?'

'She just picked him up while I was asleep. I woke up but she wouldn't let me kiss him goodbye. She just walked out.'

'Who walked out?'

'Pamela. The nurse.'

Billy stroked her face again.

'I'm going away,' Jemima said.

'When?' said Billy.

'Soon.'

'Where are you going?'

'To a library.'

'Where?'

Jemima didn't answer. Billy wrapped her arms round Jemima's flat stomach. The place where her own baby was pressed against her friend's back.

'Tell me where,' she whispered.

'No,' said Jemima, wiping her eyes with the back of her hand. Then she rolled over and Billy had to hold on to stop herself from falling off the bed. Jemima pressed her face into hers.

'It's funny,' she said, touching Billy's cheek with her hand. 'I feel I could marry you.'

'Why don't you then?'

'Don't be silly. If you were a man, I mean. You're going to marry Jim.'

'Tell me which library.'

'No. I've got to go away and not think about anything any more.'

'Why?'

'Because the midwife said so. I've got to go and never ever come back and never ever see anyone again.'

'Even me?'

'You as well. Apart from – you remember the thing you promised? About when we're old?'

'Yes.'

'We can meet then. Will you come and look for me?'

'Yes,' Billy said. 'I promised I would.'

Jemima smiled. 'So will I,' she said. 'You'll be really old like the librarian. Ninety-nine or a hundred and then you'll forget.'

'No I won't.'

'When you're old you'll have lines here and here.' She pressed her fingers into Billy's face next to her eyes, on her forehead and next to her mouth.

'And you'll have lines here and here.' Billy stretched Jemima's cheeks and pushed her thumb into her chin.

Jemima laughed. 'You'll have lines here and here and here.' She ran her fingers all over Billy's face as if she was playing a piano. Then she put her hands over Billy's ears and kissed her.

'Sorry,' she said. 'I'm not allowed to do that.'

'Don't go,' Billy said softly, but she could already feel herself zooming forward in time to the moment when Jemima wasn't there any more and all the moments afterwards that went on and on for ever. She had one of her cards in her pocket. She slipped it out and put it in Jemima's hand. It was the blue card with the two figures in a boat out at sea.

'It's for you,' said Billy.

'You won't have a complete set any more if I keep this.'

'I don't care.' Billy sat up so that her legs were over the edge of the bed. Jemima went over to the window and held the card out so that she could see which one it was. Time was still zooming forward quickly to the moment when Jemima would be gone. Then Billy took the card from her hand, picked up the pen from the ink stand next to the bed and wrote on it.

'What does it say?' said Jemima.

'It says I promise,' said Billy. 'It means we promise to find each other when we're old.' She put the card down on the bed and put a hand out to touch Jemima's face again, but her friend pulled away.

'You shouldn't do it. You have to forget all about it,' Jemima said, so Billy got up and went out of the room without looking back.

The next morning, Jemima was gone and, as the sun streamed in through the window of the baby room, the bed had already been stripped and neatened. The air smelt of clean sheets. The promise that had been made there was a secret as invisible as the wind that dashed around Pamela's head as she shook the pillows.

The night after Jemima left, Billy didn't sleep at all. She stood and looked at the dark night through the window. Through it she could see a cloudless sky full of stars and a tiny piece of moon hanging in front of the house. It was frosty blue and cold.

Slowly Billy began to hate the house. The feeling crept over her like water or sleep, gradually, until she woke up one morning, when the sun was shining white and clean into the dormitory, and she hated everything in the Haven, the beds, the floorboards, the cupboard, the window, the courtyard, the laundry room, the fireplace in the sitting room, the benches she sat on at breakfast, the curling texts on the walls, and the gravestones. She shivered when she opened her eyes, but she felt hot with anger. She wanted to smash everything, throw everything on the floor. She wanted to board up the windows and it would be just like poking out its eyes. She wished she could put out the fires, turn the beds on their sides, let the garden get overgrown so that it spilt into the courtyard and swallowed up the laundry room and all the tubs and soap and water.

36

It was a year after the end of the war, a year before a new decade would start, like a fresh sheet on a line. On a sunny spring day, Billy was working at her desk in Eade Library, a pile of broken and returned books in front of her. She had the door propped open and she was breathing in the fresh air of daffodils and salt water that spring brings with it. She was repairing book covers, cutting strips of cream-coloured tape and sticking them back together. She carefully pulled the tape straight with her long fingers and made sure it didn't cover the words on the spines. Then there he was silhouetted in the doorway. She couldn't see his face and wasn't sure whether it really was him, or just a ghost of him, until he came over to the desk where she was sitting, a broken book still in her hand.

'Two years,' she said softly, after she had stood, walked round the desk and held onto his arms just to check that he was made of flesh.

'I didn't know where you were.' He put his hand up to her face. 'I've been back for a year, but they wouldn't tell me where you were.'

She looked deep into his eyes and felt as if she was digging into thick muddy clay, pawing it with her hands and clawing at it. Then she hit him. She hit him with her fists, angrier than she had ever been. She hit him and screamed at him and he let her do it until she was exhausted. He took her wrists and she leant forward and pressed her cheek against his and they held on. Billy

311

felt something like a river in her stomach, swollen with rain and pulled away.

She turned her back awkwardly and told him about the day the old librarian had died because she didn't know what else to say. Then Jim said the same words he had said on the day of the boat, when he took her hand and led her down onto the soft sand.

'Will you marry me?'

Billy closed her eyes as her boy sang a song about leaves and trees in her ears. 'How can you expect me to marry you now?' she said.

When she opened her eyes again, she saw Jim looking around him, like people searching for books do sometimes, as if the book they are fated to read will fall from a shelf and land at their feet, pages open like legs ready to be entered, like a loose woman. He looked around him and she knew why he was looking. He was waiting for his child, he didn't know if he was a boy or a girl, to run round the bookshelves and declare himself, arms open, ready to be loved. Billy's little boy whispered to her from her shoulder, two now, able to walk and sing. Billy was proud of him, and his first words, which she imagined she had heard, and his first steps, which she had thought of while returning children's books to the shelves one Saturday morning and knew it must have been then that he walked for the first time.

Jim looked at her.

'He's gone,' said Billy simply and she heard the words echo around the library. Jim's eyes looked angry, like they had the last time she had seen him, when he swore that he wouldn't join up without getting married first, whatever his mother said about her. They flicked across her face, reading it quickly, like they had done when they had walked on the sand for the first time.

'Is he dead?' His eyes creased in the corners at the word, cowering as if they were afraid of it.

'Adopted,' said Billy. The words should have been giant waves beating against the side of rocks and a lighthouse. Instead her voice was absorbed by the library walls and by the listening books waiting to be repaired and returned to their shelves, as she explained about the Haven and the papers she had signed and not knowing where Jim was or whether he was dead or alive. 'What kind of life will you have?' the midwife had said.

Jim sat down on the floor with his back against the wall near the door and stared out at the rows of books in front of him in case they might hold the answer. Billy went and sat next to him and looked too and after a moment she laced her fingers through his. Her two-year-old walking and talking boy sat very still on her shoulder. The spring breeze came in through the door and wove itself round the three of them, binding them together, not like a vicar does but like a beautiful carpet which can't be undone without being destroyed. The breeze cast magic over them, soft as breath.

Later, a man came in wanting to borrow a book about kites and found them like that, leaning against each other as if they'd been tied to a mast and were waiting for the sea monster.

37

They waited till the day of the summer picnic. There was no one around. The village was deserted, like a haunted place that the residents had left in fear. After they had climbed up the hill, Jim banged on the front door, just to make sure. When there was no answer, Billy opened the door. The house was silent. A breeze raced about from a window which had been left open, because it promised to be a hot day. Billy shuddered as she went inside. She could hear all the voices from two years before, still there, echoing around her head. She expected Doreen and Mavis Free to come out of the dormitory and Elaine to go into the kitchen to fetch water before her reading lesson. She saw Jemima at the top of the stairs, turning to look at her, her face white with fear.

'Are you all right?' Jim asked her, putting a hand on her arm.
'I'm fine,' she said firmly.

They went into the little office with the yellow curtains and set about doing what they had come to do, feeling like spies all the while. Jim began with the cabinet in the corner and took out one piece of paper at a time, carefully, so that he wouldn't miss anything. Billy went through everything on the desk, letters enclosing donations, letters asking for admission for wayward daughters, letters from libraries asking for staff. Then she went through the chest under the window, one file at a time. After a couple of hours, they had looked through everything in the office twice and had found nothing. The only pieces of paper bearing

Billy's name were the letter from her mother asking for her to be admitted and the list of libraries that the women had been sent to. She sat on the floor and looked at the letter and the list. Tears began running down her face when she saw her mother's handwriting. Jim reached out his hand.

'Come on,' he said and pulled her to her feet.

They put the papers back where they had found them, but before Billy closed the drawer, she looked down the list of libraries again. At the bottom, she found the name she was looking for: Jemima Faraday, and the library she had been sent to next to it.

'What's that?' said Jim.

'Oh. Just the list of libraries.' She put it back and closed the cabinet drawer.

Billy led the way up the stairs. They stood in the room where their baby had been born and looked at the bed and the window and the bare floorboards. Billy wanted to take a hammer and destroy the picture she had in her head which filled the space in front of her: the picture of a young girl on the bed, the midwife, Pamela's face behind her eyeglasses, waiting for instructions, to fetch water, draw the curtains, clean up the blood, the young girl with her legs spread wide. Billy knew that the young girl was thinking about the boat rocking, thinking of the boat hitting rocks and sinking, imagining that she was drowning, imagining that a man would come with a saw, like the magician she had seen once, and cut her in half so that the pain would stop. Billy wanted to smash and smash until the picture was broken into tiny pieces. Each of the pieces would depict a fragment of the whole if she bent and held it up to the light, but each of them would tell the whole story too.

Jim saw a different picture. He saw Billy and their baby son in bed together and in the night a nurse came and stole him away. He saw himself in the doorway, blocking her exit, taking back his son, and climbing into the bed beside Billy, falling asleep on her chest, with their child between them. He would close his eyes tight, but before he fell asleep he would wish them forward to the moment they were in now. He would wish the three of them forward and the bed would be a magic bed and would send them through a tunnel. They would wake up and find themselves married, the nurses gone. They would wake up and see themselves watching, rise from the magic bed, walk a few paces, disappear inside their future selves and there would be their child safe in their arms, delivered through time from the place where it was born. Jim was the hero of the story, come back in time to save their son. But he looked at his arms and his legs and saw that he was himself and not a hero. He had not come in time.

Billy went and sat on the edge of the bed and Jim sat down next to her. She had her silver case in her pocket. She got her cards out and put them down between them. It was the only spell she could think of for healing. That and paint, and one other thing, which Jim was thinking about too. She cut the pack.

'Deal,' she said.

He looked at her, smiled, and shuffled the pack. Then he dealt three cards each.

He had the Nab of Eights, the Yellow Jackdaw and the Nine of Glass. Billy had two queens, the Queen of Grass and the Queen of the Sea, and the Red Feather Man. Jim put down the nine and took another from the deck. The Crown of Water, the blue fourteen. Billy smiled. She laid her blue queen on top of the nine. He reached over and kissed her, his three cards still in his hands. He tried hard not to let the tears form under his eyes, but that was where the picture was of the hero coming back just in time and blocking the door. She tried to stop herself from crying again too, but she was thinking of the magician with the saw and the smashed-up picture which covered the bed like shards of glass, so they both cried and pushed their faces together as they kissed. He put his cards down and held her head. His face was rough because he hadn't shaved that morning. Hers was smooth like a stone from the bottom of the sea. Their kisses tasted salty because of the crying. They lay down on the narrow bed with the cards underneath them and wrapped their arms round each other like string round a brown parcel. They lay like that for a long time, kissing sometimes, resting their heads on the pillow sometimes. Then Billy opened her eyes and looked around the room.

'What colour shall we paint it?'

'What?' said Jim. He turned and laughed at her.

'Let's paint it blue. Let's paint the sea and the sun and a boat.'

'How will we do that?'

'I know where the paint is kept.' They both laughed then and Jim looked at her face creased into a smile and he wanted to keep it like that for ever.

'We don't have enough time for painting,' he said.

'Yes we do,' said Billy, imagining the walls and ceiling deep blue, like it might be under the sea if she was thrown over the side of a boat and opened her eyes wide. 'They won't come back until after dark.'

'What if you're wrong?'

'I'm not wrong.'

Jim rolled on top of her and kissed her again.

'My cards,' said Billy, but she didn't move them.

Afterwards, most of the Scrummage deck had been scattered across the floor and one corner of the blue fourteen was bent. The cards that had remained underneath them were warm when Billy held them to her face, and they still smelt of her grandmother's hands. When Jim went outside to smoke, she put her clothes back on, gathered up the cards and returned them to their silver case. Then she took another look around the room and ran downstairs to join Jim in the walled garden. He was looking at the crumbling gravestones which lined the walls. She crouched down next to him.

'Are these real?'

'Yes, it used to be a church.'

He shuddered. She took him by the arm and showed him the laundry where she had worked and then they went across the courtyard and inside to the cupboard where the paint and tools were kept.

They carried the paint up the stairs to the baby room and began in one corner. Billy started with three thick strokes of blue and a streak of white along one wall, for a wild blue ocean. She filled it with fish and added a pretty boat with a sail, while Jim painted a sun with fiery pointing rays, in orange and red. The paint was all over their shoes when they had finished. They stood in the middle of the room and looked. Then Jim dipped his brush in the white paint and drew a thin tower at the edge of the sea for a lighthouse.

'It's beautiful,' said Billy and she put her hand over her stomach where her two new babies grew. Their older brother perched invisibly on her shoulder and laughed at the painting his mother and father had made in big sweeping strokes across the walls.

38

August 1959

Rush forward in time like the wind blowing along the High Street, through the public cemetery, past the men's outfitters, the florist, the butcher, the bakery, the chapel, the fancy dress shop, like the breeze that lifts rubbish and leaves into the air in a spiral, twisting out as far as the Rio and gusting on towards a café which stands silently with its blinds drawn on a street with no other doors. Burrow forward in time forty years, like a mole under the grass, its tiny pink hands working quickly in front of it, its soft flat feet kicking behind, burrow forward past twenty-year-old Jemima in her library filling in an application to the Lighthouse Foundation, attaching a letter from her librarian, rush past seventy-five lights updated in the first year, on rocks, inside stone towers, rigged up at the top of steeples, balanced on cliff edges, in towns, in barrels on harbour walls. Meanwhile the old Eade Village librarian dies with a stained copy of *Robinson Crusoe* in her hand, Billy and Jim get married, have twins, work at the library together, stamping, collecting, mending, filing, recommending, retrieving, fining, until one fine autumn day Billy comes back from chopping wood in the scrubby patch of land behind the library and finds Jim dead, face down in his newspaper which he had spread out over the issues and returns desk. She walks into the tiny kitchen, makes herself cinnamon tea, goes past him out into the back yard again, and drinks it, the sound of yapping dogs creeping over the wall from next door, her grey hair twisting round her head, the auburn leaves circling around her feet. She drinks her tea and watches the hills above the village.

Fling yourself further forward in time another five years, like a monkey leaping between high trees, until you reach the late summer of 1959. It's hot. At the moment Alex steps down onto the sand in Eade Village and Billy unclasps her silver Scrummage case, Mr Sabre the baker is in the back room in his best jacket with the woman from Carling Street, Mr Immanuel is washing dishes in the kitchen at the Memory Lane, while Henrico the barman sweeps the floor and Evan the waiter wakes up next to a beautiful man with long curling eyelashes. Isabelle is at home shuffling her cards, Miranda is watching her from the sofa with laughing eyes, Alex's mother is turning the television on while her father slips into his chauffeur's uniform and screws his hat onto his head, Mr Bradley looks out of the window, waiting for his car and he can see the start of the graveyard next to the house, yellow and pink garlands and a gate where the paint is peeling. Mrs Rodgers is brushing her daughter's ice-cream-coloured hair, the manager of the fancy dress shop is putting his key in the lock, Melanie is practising Chopin in her dressing gown. Gabriel is dressing his hair carefully in front of the mirror. Up at the house, Mrs Pamela Brown has given the residents a room each to clean, and handfuls of flowers for the vases: Doris has the laundry room, Marjory has the top room, Joyce has the lounge. Harriet is sweeping the floor in the dormitory and every time she stops and sits back on her heels with the dustpan and brush in her hand, she thinks of kissing Alex on the bed upstairs. Mrs Brown is in her office frowning over a pile of letters, the yellow curtains fluttering at her window. Hazel-Anne is going into the church to arrange some flowers. Rose is with John sharing a steaming cup of tea and he is making her haddock for breakfast. Mrs Pretty has opened up early for Miss Du Bois the crafts teacher who wants a permanent wave. Mrs Johnson is in her wellington boots and her nightie, scooping dog biscuits into bowls and sensing the keen eyes following her around the dog shed, while her daughter July is on a chair at the kitchen table, spreading jam on her toast. Her feet don't reach the floor.

All of this happened just at the moment Alex stepped down onto the sand and stood next to the lighthouse researcher who was waiting in the sun, watching the Eade Village light with her hands perched one on top of the other, and just as back at the library Billy grinned and held out the silver case with the engraving of the tree so that Rachel could see it.

'You said you wanted to learn,' said Billy.

Rachel looked up eagerly as Billy opened the clasp.

'Yes,' she said.

Billy took out the cards and played with them thoughtfully. 'I've had a reply to my letter. From the council. You're officially my new assistant.'

'That's fantastic.' Rachel's face glowed.

'Jemima's staying with me for a while. Can you bear to stay here in the house? Just until the baby's born, and then you can both come and live with me like we said.'

Rachel nodded. 'Of course,' she said.

The August sun shone lovingly through the window as Rachel moved right to the edge of the sofa and hugged the cushion to her swollen chest. Her wild blonde curls, twisting out from her head, were like coils of thread waiting to be cast out into the sea or wound round a spinning wheel in a story. Her face looked soft and curious and rounder than ever. She leant over so that she could see the cards moving in Billy's hands and the sleeping woman stretching into an S shape on the back of each one. Billy looked at Rachel's fat stomach and her wide hips. She reminded the librarian of Jemima. Rachel fidgeted in her seat impatiently. Billy took a deep breath, held the cards in one hand and passed them to her.

'You shuffle,' she said.

Rachel shuffled clumsily at first because they were bigger than normal playing cards, but then her fingers got used to it and she let them rise and fall as easy as breathing. Billy watched her and when she put her hand up to her face she realised that her eyes were wet. She had been remembering the time when her own cheeks were as soft as ice cream and it was almost a surprise to touch her face and find it creased and wet and in need of ironing.

321

'Now deal,' said Billy. 'Three each. That's right. Turn them over so I can see what you've got.' She smiled at Rachel in encouragement, and her eyes shone with love because the cards were like a part of her own body, like a hand or a foot.

Rachel leaned forward and her hair tumbled forward too. Her feet were spread to take her weight as she did so. She turned the cards carefully, like someone drawing up a plan or consulting a complicated map. Billy moved closer so that she could see them properly. She looked at them expertly.

'Look at this one,' she said. 'Look at the picture.'

Rachel picked up the card Billy had pointed to and looked carefully. It was a picture of a fox in a green hat.

'It's a thief,' Billy said. 'That means something taken and returned.'

Rachel looked at the librarian, who had suddenly started to act like a fortune teller, and wrinkled up her nose to show she thought she was talking rubbish.

'Yes,' she said impatiently, 'but can you teach me to play? Like Isabelle does.'

'I was just about to,' Billy said, turning over her own hand of three. She became businesslike and the lesson began properly. She pointed at the cards and explained the different suits to Rachel, who soaked up Billy's words like they were blood which she needed to fill up her toes and her feet and her legs and to pour into her hips and into her stomach. Blood which she needed to fill her heart with, to pump into her arms and fingers, her neck and shoulders and head, and finally she needed it to drip into her coiled hair to turn it red. Billy's words were like that and Rachel loved them.

Meanwhile, the lighthouse researcher stood on the beach next to Alex, her thin grey hair blowing about her face. It was a hot day and the sun was melting in the sky like one of Mrs Rodgers' ice creams. They looked out at the light. Mrs Faraday's eyes were narrow and serious as if she knew a joke Alex didn't but had stopped laughing.

'What's happening about the house?' Alex asked. 'You said it was going to close.'

Jemima looked at her sharply. 'It will,' she said.

Alex felt suddenly anxious. 'What will happen to everyone?'

Jemima didn't answer for a moment.

'A man called Mr Keel is writing a report,' she said, so quietly she could have been talking to herself. 'He's collecting evidence.'

Alex opened her mouth to speak but she didn't because Mrs Faraday put a hand on her arm.

'Let's not talk about it,' she said. She gazed out at the light again. 'I need to check the dimensions of the lamp. It hasn't been updated. And a few other things.'

Alex gazed at the high windows that she had looked out of only a few days before.

'Now?' she asked. She dipped her hand into her pocket for her headscarf, because it was breezy on the beach, even though everywhere else the air was still and thick as honey.

'I thought you might be interested in helping.'

Alex's face lit up as she knotted her scarf under her chin. 'Yes,' she said.

Her companion turned round to face her and jammed her hands into her coat pockets as if she had suddenly made up her mind about something.

'Shall we go for a walk?' Without waiting for an answer she hurried off up the beach, away from the harbour wall in a direction Alex hadn't been before. Mrs Faraday walked quickly, as if she needed to walk because she couldn't bear to stand still and watch any longer.

'We can ask one of the keepers,' Alex said, catching up with her. They came to some more rocks which divided this part of the beach from the cove beyond. Rough steps had been cut into them and they climbed up together.

'Billy says that Eade is your home lighthouse,' said Alex as they came down the other side. 'Is this where you come from?'

'She talks too much.'

'It's my home lighthouse too.'

Mrs Faraday looked at her sideways. 'All the better that you help me check it then.'

They walked round the edge of the cove, talking about what Alex used to do at the bakery and the films she saw for free at her dad's cinema. They stopped from time to time to examine a shell or to look back at the light which seemed impossibly far away now. They took the promenade path back again and sat at the end of the harbour wall for a while, watching the bobbing fishing boats.

'Where do the keepers live?' Mrs Faraday asked eventually, taking a notebook out of her bag.

'Oh, that's easy,' Alex said as if she was answering one of Mr Sabre's questions. 'They have bunk beds in one of the cottages over there. I don't know which one.'

Mrs Faraday nodded her head. 'Let's give it a try then.'

They went towards the fishermen's cottages together. The air smelt thickly of seaweed and old rope. A bronze sign by the door of one of the cottages told them which was the right one. It was made of thick grey stone like the Haven.

'So that's what I do,' said Mrs Faraday when they finally emerged from the keepers' cottage. 'We're about to go annual, so it's a lot of work.' She pushed her notebook back inside her bag.

Alex nodded and looked up at the Haven. She was supposed to return to the house straight after meeting the researcher but something made her hover on the pavement. Sensing her indecision, Jemima addressed her cheerfully.

'I'd like to see inside the church again while I'm here. Shall we?' She gave Alex her arm and they went back up the hill to the thatched church and through the porch.

'Don't you ever go inside the lighthouses?'

'Sometimes. Sometimes not. It depends how accessible they are. There's no point going out to a light for the sake of it, especially if the weather is bad.'

'Have you been out to the Eade Village light?'

'No, I haven't, as it happens.' She picked up a glass candlestick and examined it.

'Billy said you used to be a librarian too.'

'Yes. Then I got the job at the foundation. One led to the other really.'

'Did your husband work there with you?'

'I never married,' Mrs Faraday said.

'Why do you call yourself Mrs?'

'I don't. Other people do. Do you still do laundry? At the house?'

Alex looked at her in surprise. 'No. A van comes from town to take the laundry away.'

They sat down in a pew together so they could carry on talking. The light shone through one of the windows and made a warm patch for them to sit in. 'What do you do all day?' Jemima asked her.

'We're supposed to do ladylike activities,' Alex said. It sounded strange saying Mrs Brown's peculiar words to the lighthouse researcher. 'Like flower arranging, cleaning, soap making, pot-pourri, reading, gardening.' Mrs Faraday listened with her hands jammed into her coat pockets.

'Shall I tell you a secret?' Alex said.

'If you like,' she said, 'it depends. Why do you want to tell me?'

'You seem like a good person to tell,' Alex said.

Mrs Faraday looked pleased.

'I made them send me because I love Rachel.'

'The pregnant girl who helps Billy?'

'Yes. I got drunk on purpose and made them tell my parents. But now I'm not sure if I've got something like my mum says I have.' She looked at Mrs Faraday sideways. She decided not to tell her about Harriet.

'You probably haven't. Loving someone isn't like catching a cold. I'll tell you a secret now.'

'Really?'

'Yes. Really. One that I've only told Mrs Burns.'

'What is it?'

'I'm dying,' said Mrs Faraday.

Alex put her hand to her mouth and looked at her. She didn't know what to say. 'Only really slowly. I've got one of those things where it takes you a long time to die. So it's me who's got something, not you.'

'That's your secret?'

'I'm dying. Slowly. Yes, that's my secret.'

Alex thought about it for a moment. 'Everyone's dying slowly really,' she said. 'If you think about it. Most people very slowly. Mrs Sabre died. She taught me cakes. She died more quickly though, she didn't know she was going to, like you.'

'I'm nearly sixty anyway,' Mrs Faraday said. 'Maybe I'll die of old age before I die of what I've got.'

Alex looked at her in surprise. Mrs Faraday looked older than sixty.

'Is that why you came back?' Alex said.

'Well, I had your letter too, of course.' She smiled. 'We're looking for new researchers at the foundation, you know.'

'Really?' Alex looked excited and her companion patted her knee.

'So now we've both heard each other's secrets, are we friends?' Mrs Faraday turned to Alex and held out her hand.

'Yes,' said Alex and shook it.

'Now we're friends, I have a proposition for you,' Mrs Faraday said. 'I have to check a few of the other lights in the area while I'm here. Would you like to come with me?'

'I would love to,' Alex said.

'I almost forgot, I've got something for you. I left it at the library. Come on.'

She got up and Alex led the way out of the church, through the graveyard and down the steps. When they got back, Billy had returned from her walk and was at the top of a stepladder helping someone to find a book.

'Where's Rachel?' Alex called.

'By the lake with a couple of the terriers,' Billy replied. 'Now, here's *Treasure Island*, Mr Jones,' she said, turning to the borrower.

Mrs Faraday and Alex went into the lounge.

'There, by the sofa,' Mrs Faraday said. Alex picked up the bag she had pointed to. Inside were rolled-up clothes. 'For the house,' Mrs Faraday explained. 'A donation.'

'Thank you,' Alex said politely, although she had hoped it would be something specially for her. She put the bag over her shoulder. 'I'm supposed to cook lunch. I had better go.'

'I shall do another light on Tuesday. I'll pick you up.' Her powdered face turned soft and friendly then.

'Thank you,' said Alex.

Rather than climbing back up the hill straightaway, she wandered around the trees by the lake. She was wondering if she would see Rachel just as two of Mrs Johnson's dogs came running up to her. She went round a group of willows and there was Rachel, sitting with her feet in the water. It took a moment for Alex to realise what she was doing: with a pair of bookbinding scissors, she was cutting off her bouncy hair.

'What's going on?' said Alex.

Rachel put the scissors down and moaned to herself, rocking backwards and forwards slightly. Alex reached out and took the scissors away.

'I thought Billy was teaching you the cards,' she said gently as she sat down.

Rachel couldn't speak for a moment. She carried on moaning to herself. The damage she had done to her hair was terrible.

'She was,' she said when she had taken a big breath. 'It was good. Then Mrs Johnson came round with the dogs.'

'Didn't you ask Mrs Pretty again?' Alex said, trying to calm her down. 'About fitting you in?'

'Yes, but she's so busy.' Rachel shifted uncomfortably, her dress ballooning out in front of her.

'What happened?' Alex asked.

Rachel fished a hand into her pocket and pulled out a letter. 'I saved it till I was on my own,' she said, wiping the back of her hand across her face. 'It's from my dad. I thought he'd changed his mind when I saw it.'

Alex took the letter and read it. The dogs both tried to push their heads under her arms as if they wanted to read it too. It was a short note saying that Rachel should send for her things and not come to collect them herself. Alex slipped it back into its envelope. They looked at each other awkwardly, both remembering what had happened between them.

'I liked it when we danced in the kitchen,' Alex said and looked at her.

Rachel looked back. 'Oh,' she said, sniffing. 'Well, we're never going to kiss properly or anything.'

'I know,' said Alex. Rachel leant forward and kissed her on the cheek, then she held her hand.

'You need to find someone else the same as you,' she said, putting a hand on her swollen belly.

'Like in Snap?' Alex imagined two queens, side by side.

'Yes.'

Alex thought about Harriet and smiled to herself.

'But we're friends, right?' said Rachel.

'Yes,' said Alex. They sat looking at the water. 'I'm sorry about your dad.'

Rachel nodded.

'I think we should go and see Mrs Pretty now,' Alex said. 'Here. Put this on.' She got her headscarf out of her pocket and gave it to Rachel. They took the dogs back to the Old Vicarage first, then they went down the road together and into the salon.

'I'm sorry, girls,' said Mrs Pretty as the bell jangled. She was holding a comb and a can of hairspray above Miss Du Bois' head. 'I've got them lined up.' There were three other customers waiting their turn on black chairs along one wall. They were looking at Rachel's large belly and shaking their heads.

'But can't you . . .' Alex began. Mrs Pretty reached for a brush.

'Maybe Tuesday,' she said. 'Maybe. I've got someone coming for a bob, three perms and a couple of peroxides.' She turned away, expecting them to go. One of the waiting customers was staring at them from over the top of her magazine, her painted eyebrows raised.

'Well, go on then,' said the hairdresser when she saw they were still there. Rachel reached up and took off her headscarf. Mrs

328

Pretty dropped her comb and opened her mouth wide. If she had been smoking a cigarette, it would have fallen onto the floor and set the clippings of the craft teacher's hair alight and a spark would have caught the pile of newspapers nearby and the whole salon would have gone up in flames, the hairdresser and her customers just escaping in time, but Mrs Pretty wasn't smoking a cigarette, so that didn't happen. She just stared at Rachel in surprise and so did everyone else: a heavily pregnant girl from the house on the hill, the one that helped Mrs Burns in the library, with beautiful bouncy hair in places, in others bare patches as if someone had been practising topiary on her and had lost the design.

Mrs Pretty's face changed into a mask of professionalism. She clapped her hands.

'Right, everybody, out,' she said. 'Miss Du Bois, you're done. Come on. You heard what I said.'

'What about my shampoo and set?' said the woman with the painted eyebrows, putting down her magazine.

'Come back later,' Mrs Pretty said, hurrying them out of the door. When they had gone, she turned the open sign to closed and pulled down the blinds. 'What happened here?' she said.

Rachel looked at the floor, so Alex showed her the bookbinding scissors.

'Trying to do it yourself,' Mrs Pretty said, narrowing her eyes. Now she did take out a cigarette and lit it thoughtfully, so that smoke spiralled up towards the ceiling with her hairdresser's thoughts. 'One of the worst cases I've seen of someone trying to do it themselves,' she went on, 'and I've seen several.'

'I have to cook lunch,' Alex said, suddenly remembering. 'Will you be all right?'

Rachel nodded and Mrs Pretty led her over to a spinning chair and tucked a bib round her throat while she gazed at herself in the mirror.

'Nice and short,' Alex heard her say as she went out of the salon and into the summer's day to climb back up to the Haven, where she would leave the bag of clothes on her bed and quickly mix up a salad with orange segments and almonds, tear up some bread and toss it with herbs, so that when the others sat down to eat it they thought she must have been in the kitchen for hours.

When she had finished the dishes, Miss Du Bois had arrived wearing a headscarf over her new hairdo and had taken the others into the garden, to pick flowers for pressing.

Alex was amazed when she went into the dormitory and looked inside the canvas bag. Instead of the jumpers and dresses she had assumed it would contain, she pulled out a brand new gentleman's suit. She held it up. It was made of beautiful material. She examined it in astonishment and wondered how the lighthouse researcher had known. It was so smart. Alex took off her black shoes and, barefoot, pulled on the trousers from the bag. She stood by the window. If anyone had seen her, they would have noticed the shadows from the fast moving clouds outside passing over her face. She pulled the curtains quickly. She shrugged off her sky-blue dress and her bra and stood topless, feeling the warm air around her shoulders like a cloak. Then she reached down and found the white shirt. She buttoned it carefully. She had no other shoes or any socks so she kept her feet bare. She felt sad as she remembered what Rachel had said by the lake about never kissing properly and the way she had leant forward and pecked her on the cheek, softly, so that Alex could still feel the touch of her lips. She put her hand up to her face. It was as if she had a tattoo there.

Delving into the bag, she took out the tie and the jacket and put them on. She liked the rough feeling of the material pressing on her thighs and the sturdy white cotton next to her skin. She took two steps forward. She thought of Harriet in the boat on the way to the lighthouse and how she had squeezed her hand. Then she danced. She only stopped when she was out of breath and sank back on the bed with her feet dangling off the end. She lay there for a while, until she heard Miss Du Bois calling her.

'Alex, where are you? We're nearly ready to start pressing. You haven't picked any flowers.'

She got changed quickly, hid the clothes and headed off into the garden.

Later, when it was time for telephone calls, Hazel-Anne stood behind the desk with the watch and wouldn't meet her eye.

'I've met the lighthouse researcher I told you about. I'm going to see another lighthouse soon. The house is going to close, Dad. The lighthouse researcher said—'

'I see.' He sounded worried.

'Nearly time,' said the attendant.

'What's wrong, Dad?' She heard her father take a deep breath and imagined him scratching his leg.

'Your mum wants to let your room out. Now we're not getting any money from Mr Sabre. She says she fancies doing a spot of bed and breakfast.'

'Oh, I see,' said Alex, suddenly homesick. She imagined a stranger staring up at the posters above her bed before going down to eat bubble and squeak with her parents.

'Time,' said the attendant.

Alex held up a hand to stop her. 'But I think I'm better already. I could come back and work in the bakery again.'

The attendant frowned and looked down at the desk.

'Good,' said her father. 'Only, didn't your mum tell you?'

Alex could see Marjory hovering outside, eager for her turn. 'Bloody hell,' she said, but quietly because Hazel-Anne was there.

'Time,' said the attendant again.

'Tell me what?'

'Mr Sabre's got the woman from Carling Street living with him.'

'What?'

'She's doing the cakes and that now. And Mr Bradley insisted about you getting cured. He said—'

Without looking at her, Hazel-Anne put her finger on the receiver button and cut him off.

39

Dash forward in time like the wind that chases its tail down towards the beach in Eade Village, past the Haven and down the hill, around the lake, in and out of the trees like children playing, past the church and the Old Vicarage with its shed full of dogs, past the library and the hair salon, past the harbour and out towards the light, where the breeze twists and turns round the giant white candle: someone with a birthday is trying to blow the candle out.

Jemima was still staying at the library and Mr Keel was taking a long time to file his report. Autumn arrived. The trees became sudden bonfires. They turned golden as if Midas had touched them. It was a cold autumn day and Alex had just come back from visiting Billy at the library.

When Alex came in, Harriet was sitting on the stairs. Alex climbed up and sat on the step below her. She still had some of the ginger biscuits she had made earlier wrapped in a napkin in her pocket. She took them out.

'Are you hungry?' she said. 'Have one.'

They both ate the biscuits, watching the way the other's mouth moved. Alex felt suddenly shy. She was about to get up when Harriet leant forward, almost knocking her off balance, held her face in her biscuity hands and kissed her. She looked into her face and smiled for a second afterwards before turning her head away.

'Come on,' said Alex suddenly. She got up and pulled her

friend up the rest of the stairs. She opened the door of the baby room and took her over to the bed. They sat together on the edge of the patchwork quilt, not knowing what to do for a moment.

'Still hungry?' Alex said. The last ginger biscuit was still in its napkin. She broke it in half and crumbs fell onto her lap as she ate. Then they giggled and this time Alex started the kiss and they did it for ages. They both tasted of ginger. She held on to her lips like a bee clutches on to a flower. Alex felt as if someone had set her on fire. After a moment, Harriet pushed her hands into her friend's hair and held on to it. Soon they were entangled in each other like nets. They stayed like that for a long time, kissing and laughing, and then Alex pushed Harriet back onto the bed and climbed on top of her. She ran her hands over Harriet's blouse gently at first and then Harriet grabbed at the buttons and undid them, revealing breasts like cupcakes. She gasped as Alex touched them, before taking off her own T-shirt. When they were naked, they lay down side by side like two crayons in a box, waiting silently to be drawn with, close together and breathing into each other's faces. Orange and green, or purple and yellow, waxy and dark inside their case. Alex looked into her friend's face and saw how blue her eyes were for the first time. It was as if she had new blue eyes freshly opened wide, as if the sea had rushed over the sand and left them behind. When Alex kissed her again and ran her hand gently along her thigh, Harriet cried out.

'Shh,' Alex said and she laughed.

'No one's here apart from Rachel,' Harriet said, her new blue eyes shining. 'She wasn't feeling well. The others went on a nature walk.' Her eyes were like rock pools with crabs, brown spiky sea urchins, anemones and star fish which had fallen out of the night sky.

Alex hesitated for a moment at the sound of Rachel's name, then moved her hand to Harriet's other thigh, feeling the way it curved under her palm. Harriet smelt musty, like the trees around the lake smelt after the rain had been falling. It was a warm earthy smell. Alex pushed her hand between Harriet's legs and she cried out again, pushing her head into the pillow. Alex thought of the times she had stood in front of her mirror at home, dressed in the clothes from the fancy dress shop, and had run her hand inside her own shirt. Now she was doing the same to the girl with the rock-pool eyes, but with no clothes to feel inside, only warm skin. She kissed Harriet's neck and closed her eyes, and for a moment she couldn't remember whether she was touching herself or someone else. She felt as if smoke, teased by the air, was curving around their bodies, joining the two of them together. When Harriet reached out a hesitant hand and pushed Alex's legs apart, it turned into a plunging, swirling feeling, as if they were two glasses of water being poured into a jug together. Alex felt as if she was drowning, swimming to the surface again, then falling back under the water. Then they both heard the back door open and footsteps coming into the corridor.

They sat up quickly. Harriet was still kissing her friend's shoulders while they pulled their T-shirt and blouse back on. They heard the stairs creak.

'Harriet?' It was Hazel-Anne.

'Shh,' said Alex and they sat as still as they could, only half dressed. But then Harriet leant forward to stop her skirt from sliding off the bed and as she did so she knocked a pillow, which hit an alarm clock, sending it onto the floor with a clunk. The door opened and there was Hazel-Anne. She looked in horror at the two girls, arms round each other, almost naked, and backed out onto the landing again. The two of them quickly pulled on the rest of their clothes. They ran out after her. Over the banisters they could see the others coming in, clutching their beach finds.

'I'm surprised at you. I will be phoning your parents,' the attendant said.

'No,' said Harriet in horror.

'Unless you tell me that it was Alex's fault. Well?'

Harriet hesitated for a moment.

'No,' she said, looking Hazel-Anne in the face, opening her

eyes wide again so that the sea in them shone and the sea creatures danced. 'It was both of us.'

'Then you will both leave the house at once.'

'You can't—'

'Alex, go downstairs and make lunch.'

Alex looked into her companion's eyes. Harriet squeezed her hand.

'No,' Alex said. 'I'm staying here.'

'Go on,' Harriet whispered. 'It's OK.'

With a final look back, Alex ran downstairs.

In the kitchen, Alex stood still for a moment, breathing quickly. She was worried about what was going on upstairs. Maybe the attendant was persuading her that it was Alex's fault after all. But most of all she felt shiny as if someone had washed her in silver water. The feeling like diving under water with Harriet was wonderful. She closed her eyes and tried to hold on to it. She pushed herself against the oven which was warm from the potatoes cooking inside and held on to her breasts, her hands crossed against her heart, then she ran one hand between her legs. The sound of someone coming downstairs startled her. The smell of crisp potato skins was getting stronger, so she turned and opened the oven door quickly. After she had hooked them out with a cloth, she stuck her head inside a cupboard to look for the cheese grater, thinking all the while about what it had been like to lie on the bed upstairs with her friend.

What else was happening at that moment, as Alex put a hand out to move a saucepan? Mr Bradley was talking to his operator in the projection room at the Rio. At the moment Alex reached into the cupboard he opened his mouth to say, 'Cold,' in answer to a question about the weather, while in the foyer Mrs Rodgers was making a walnut sundae for a man about to see *It Came From Outer Space* and had just added a final cherry. In the bakery, the woman from Carling Street put her hand to her heart, because Mr Sabre, his hair slicked back with Brylcreem, had presented her with a posy of flowers. At the Memory Lane, Rufus and Melanie sat down at a silver table with an Uncle Arthur as the dancers came in to start rehearsing. Evan and Henrico were in the kitchen talking about a film they had both seen. Mrs Pretty had been sweeping the floor in the salon and was leaning on her brush and wondering whether she should start selling make-up as a sideline when Miss Du Bois came in for a chat. Mrs Brown was helping her daughter feed the dogs in the dog shed at the Old Vicarage. Rose was about to make her way up to the house. She pushed an arm into her coat. John had set off to do some fishing and had called in to the shop by the front to buy some bait. At the moment Alex leant into the cupboard, he was looking into a tub full of maggots. Out at the light, the keeper who had shown the Haven residents round was polishing the lamp and adding more grease to his cloth, just as Erica's grandmother pulled her brown curtains closed to shut out the daylight. She was about to slip into bed with Erica's grandfather and three months later she would discover Erica's mother growing bigger inside her. Erica's dad was three already and was on his way to nursery school. Bonny the Alsatian's great-grandmother, seven generations removed, the only surviving puppy of her litter, took her first breath. Kevin and all three little Kevins were still just a figment of the imagination, like a breath of wind blowing in through the keyhole of the council flat they would live in, where a builder was applying a last coat of paint. As he put down his brush, Mavis Free was hanging out her washing on a line which stretched across her long back garden in the Highlands. She stopped for a moment, a peg in her hand, and looked out at the mountains in the distance where she liked to think her two sons lived, just the other side. As Mavis Free sighed, and wiped her hands on her apron, Sally was looking out of a window on holiday somewhere. She could see boats and thick blue sky. Her husband brought two cocktails back to the table and put one in front of her, but she didn't look round. Amanda had her hands poised above the piano in a community hall and twenty-four ladies in leotards were getting ready for the fitness instructor to begin. As Amanda brought her hands down for the first chord, Doreen was going in through the doors of her church two hundred miles away with a basket of flowers and looking up at a tapestry of the most famous unmarried mother, who gazed down at her kindly just as Elaine Brooks shouted, 'Ham and tomato,' in her café and a woman in a brown coat sent her son to collect the sandwich from her. 'Go on,' she said. 'Fetch the plate from the nice lady.'

All of that happened as Alex reached round the colander for the cheese grater in the kitchen at the Haven. She found it just as Harriet slipped down the stairs, because she wanted to go into the dormitory and lie on her bed and think. Alex opened the kitchen door but stopped when she saw Hazel-Anne go into the yellow office a moment later. She realised what the attendant was going to do. A minute after the door closed, Alex went after her and stood, cheese grater in hand, with her back pressed against the wall, listening. The conversation had already started.

'I'm calling from the Haven,' Hazel-Anne was saying. There was a pause while the person at the other end of the line spoke.

'About Harriet, yes,' Hazel-Anne said. Alex could hear her taking a deep breath. 'Well, it seems that she . . .' The attendant was interrupted by the other speaker again.

'She has made very good progress and is ready to come home,' Hazel-Anne said. 'We're all extremely pleased with her.' There was a click as she put the receiver down.

Alex was astonished but at the same time she had a plunging feeling like a stone falling into a pond inside her because it meant that Harriet was leaving. She was about to run back to the kitchen to avoid being caught, when Harriet came out into the corridor.

After Harriet had gone into the dormitory she found Rachel, white as frost, on the edge of her bed. She was clutching her middle. She looked at Harriet with a mixture of pain and bewilderment on her face. Harriet held out a hand for her to hold and she gripped it so tightly she left nail marks in her palm. Harriet got up to find help.

'Don't go,' said Rachel. They sat together for a moment, but when Rachel moaned as the pain gripped her again, Harriet pulled her hand free and ran into the corridor. She nearly collided with Hazel-Anne who was emerging from the yellow office.

'I think Rachel's having her baby,' she said.

40

L ate that evening, Billy and Jemima left the library behind and walked down the hill so they could look at the sea in the moonlight. The lighthouse researcher took her friend by the arm as they went along the harbour wall, walking slowly until they got to the stone bench where they had sat forty years before. They fitted into their own outlines as they sat down carefully. Jemima unscrewed the bottle she had in her bag, and if there had been a message inside, it escaped before Billy could read it. Her friend poured a little of the drink into a mug and passed it to her. She looked at it for a second and then drank, shuddering as the warm liquid travelled down her throat like a train while the night was cold around her face. The boats bobbed in the harbour at their backs and in front of them the beach curved out into the evening. Jemima took a drink too and then they gazed out towards the lighthouse which stood like a dark giant against the night sky at the end of its trail of rocks.

When Billy looked down she half expected their stomachs to be swollen, but instead her son sat between them on the bench, laid a hand on each of their shoulders and disappeared again.

Jemima closed her eyes and Billy imagined that the little boy she had once seen in her friend's arms danced above them, naked and unafraid.

The yachts' masts knocking together in the harbour sounded like uneven drums. Billy imagined a band of out-of-time drummers on the quay behind them, unable to see two women on the jetty. After two more mouthfuls of whisky Billy stood up and lifted her arms. She concentrated on the air on her face and how alive she felt. She peered down at the dark sand and the water.

'You mad old thing,' Jemima said.

Billy looked round. She could see the young girl's complexion underneath the powdery one. She looked at her friend's face full of riverbed lines, like a rocky place which water had chiselled out and then left behind. But it wasn't so much like rocks, she thought, because it was cushion-soft too. Her friend's face was made of soft rocks.

'Stop staring at me and come and sit down,' Jemima said, and poured another drink into the mug and offered it to Billy, but Billy put her hand out and touched Jemima's face. Jemima tipped the drink down her own throat and then looked suddenly serious. Billy leant forward and kissed Jemima softly and smoothly on the lips. She smelt of powder, raspberries and whisky.

'Silly,' Jemima said when she had stopped kissing her. They both sat and listened to the waves playing on the beach, where children ran with spades during the summer. Jemima put out her hand for Billy to hold and they sat like that, holding hands and looking at the invisible children running.

After a while, Jemima got up.

'What are you doing?' said Billy, but her friend had already started to climb carefully down the steps to the lighthouse rocks. She got her coat stuck under her foot as she went down the second step and she swayed slightly like she was on wheels. Billy rose and followed, putting her arms out so she could hold onto Jemima's thin hip bones. Her friend turned round and grinned at her.

'I'm going to walk along the rocks to see the lighthouse,' said Jemima.

'But the tide's turning,' Billy said. She wasn't sure if Jemima was joking or not. 'Don't be silly. Let's go in the boat with Rose and John tomorrow. I'll ask them.' She held onto her friend's arm and tried to pull her back but that only made her sway more and Billy almost stumbled back onto the steps.

'I've been to hundreds of lighthouses,' Jemima said. 'But not this one.' Billy let go of her friend to stop them both tumbling over.

Jemima took a step forward onto the slippery rock. 'Hold this,' she said, turning around, almost losing her balance, and handing Billy the bottle. She took a few more steps forward. 'Come on,' she said. 'It's wonderful.'

'It's cold,' Billy said. She could see that ahead of them, the water was just beginning to wash over the lighthouse rocks every so often. It swirled around the way bath water does when you first turn on the taps, and retreated again. Even though she was drunk, Jemima stopped when she saw it too. She turned round and walked carefully back towards her friend.

'You're right,' she said. 'It is a bit cold. Let's go in the boat with John and Rose.'

'Tomorrow?' said Billy.

'Yes.'

They walked back along the harbour wall, arm in arm again, their coats wrapped round them against the cold. They helped each other down the steps so they could sit on the edge of the promenade with their feet dangling over the sand. Billy kicked her legs.

'More?' said Jemima.

Billy looked at the bottle. She could see her little boy inside it, and July, Mrs Johnson's little girl, and Rachel, leaning over the cards on the day of her first lesson, her hair still bouncy. She saw Alex too. They were all crowded into that bottle. Mrs Pretty was there, Mavis Free, Sally, Jim, the twins in Australia, all inside. If she drank from it she would be drinking all of the people and all of their stories.

'You did it then,' Billy said. 'The house is closing.'

'Soon as that Mr Keel files his report.'

Billy turned away, slid carefully down onto the sand and walked towards the black and white waves. Jemima took another sip of whisky. Billy imagined the stories swirling around inside her friend and suddenly her legs gave way underneath her and she sat down on the sand. She was like a little girl waiting for an ice cream or watching her father build a sandcastle. The beach felt wonderfully cold underneath her, as if a cold hand held her up. She had discovered that the hand of God really did hold her after all, but it was cold and grainy and smelt of salt. She waved to Jemima to come and join her and together they watched the sea coming in without saying anything for ages. They looked out over the sea and saw the lighthouse send its beam across the surface like a fast yellow ghost.

'Rose and John will take us tomorrow, won't they?' Jemima said.

'Yes,' Billy said, holding Jemima's hand and stroking it.

'Promise?' said Jemima, her eyes glinting at her.

'Promise,' said Billy.

41

The next day, the trees by the lake let go of their leaves suddenly, like weeping genteel ladies dropping a thousand handkerchiefs, and Rachel's baby died with the umbilical cord round her neck. She drowned and turned blue, unable to breathe like a fish on the beach as she lay on her mother's stomach. Rachel held her baby for no time at all. She wouldn't come back to life no matter how much she kissed her forehead and told her she was sorry. Her eyelids were see-through like petals. Rachel wished she had died too. The midwife secretly thought she was going to and had made Hazel-Anne call for the curate as well as the doctor. When the curate arrived, he baptised Rachel's dead baby there and then in the room at the top of the stairs, so that she would have a name.

Alex had gone out to wait in the walled garden on the tortoise-foot bench, next to the tree whose branches arched out over the flowers, lunch forgotten about. Just as if she had been locked in the top room in the dark again, she didn't notice how much time was passing. The sun started high in the sky like a lost balloon and gradually sank lower. Her insides had turned as pale as the frosty grass. After a while, she got up and went over to the bush near the high black gate to pick some lavender. She took it back to the bench with her and sat with the fragrance twisting round her head, imagining her friend in the room at the top of the stairs where she had had to leave her. Harriet came to join her for a while but Alex couldn't talk much. They held hands and the feeling of palms pressed together was as delicious as cake.

'She'll be all right,' Harriet said as if she was trying to convince herself.

Alex nodded. 'Hazel-Anne called your parents yesterday,' she said. 'But she didn't tell them. She said you were better and could go home.'

'I know. I spoke to them. What about you?'

'I'm going to work for Mrs Faraday.' Alex could see her companion had tears in her eyes.

Harriet got up and wandered out onto the hillside where she sat and watched the lake until the sun began to sink behind the sea.

When Doris came out to tell her what had happened, Alex felt as though someone had used the Hallowe'en biscuit cutter on her, the one Mr Sabre bought to make pumpkin-shaped cookies in October.

She ran inside, stumbled up the stairs and pushed open the door to the baby room. The midwife, who was sitting on a chair next to the bed, looked at her kindly and said that Rachel needed to sleep, but Rachel's eyes were wide and awake. Her face was white with shock. She wouldn't speak to Alex. She rolled onto her side, lay very still, and stared at the wall. Alex put the lavender she was still clutching on the quilt at the foot of the bed. The purple scent filled the top room like a magic spell, but Rachel still didn't turn to look at her.

Alex went back out into the walled garden. Angrily, she wiped her eyes with the back of her hand and went past the biscuit-crumb gravestones and the big leaves so she could sit down on the tortoise-foot bench again. She could see Doris telling Harriet the news out on the hillside and sitting down next to her to watch the sun glowing through the trees.

When Alex had dried her wet face on her dress, she remembered the old gravestone hidden behind the thick green tree trunk, next to the wall, which Rachel had found months ago. It was only just visible amongst the ivy which had spent the summer roaming across it. She pulled the white and green leaves away, so that the name and date were exposed again: 'Almost Brown 1834–1849'. There was a buzzing honey bee nearby, and it came over to fly busily round the top of the stone in a circle, as if it had got lost and was travelling the same path over and over again.

Alex never spoke to anyone about the stone. She kept it hidden inside her, in the same place she kept the way Harriet, with her new blue eyes, had held her on top of the patchwork bedspread. Sometimes, when she was unhappy, she would go down to the quayside and look out at the light. Then she would take her treasures out from inside her and turn them over in her hands: Rachel's new haircut, apple slices, the feeling like crayons, the magic she felt the first time she opened Jemima's lighthouse book, and the gravestone under the tree.

A few days later, Harriet was waiting by the window in the lounge, looking out for her parents' car, as Rachel went into the little yellow office. She picked up the phone and told her father that his granddaughter was called Annabel and that she had see-through eyelids and a dusting of hair the same custard colour as her own. She told him that the librarian was going to pay for the stone. She told him that she wasn't ever coming back. He put the phone down as soon as he realised who it was. Rachel heard the familiar heavy breath and then a click, but she spoke into the disconnected phone anyway because then she could feel that she had told him all about it.

Rose and Hazel-Anne had asked everyone to meet in the lounge. They came in and began to arrange themselves around the room.

'There's going to be a . . . thing,' said Joyce, forgetting the word she wanted to use. She was sitting on the floor with Marjory and Doris. Harriet came away from the window and sank into a chair.

'Announcement,' Alex said for her and sat down on the arm next to her friend. Rose entered. Doris had taken out her knitting needles and was clicking them backwards and forwards quickly.

'Mrs Brown is retiring,' Rose said. She paused and looked around the room. 'And the Haven will be closed,' she added at last. Doris stopped with half a purl stitch completed in front of her.

'Temporarily,' Rose went on. 'Alex and Rachel both have jobs.

You three will go to a different home.' Marjory slipped her arms round the girls on either side of her, so that she looked as if she was about to have her photograph taken by the pool at Butlins.

'Bloody hell,' she said softly into Doris's hair. Her breath made it flutter. 'Fucking hell.'

A week later Marjory was squashed into the back seat of a Morris Minor, with Joyce on one side of her and Doris on the other, off to start another story somewhere else. A honey bee darted in through one car window and out of the other before they set off, and buzzed round Alex's head as she waved goodbye.

Rachel had already moved into the library when she watched the arms take her daughter and the soil was wrapped around her like a blanket to keep her warm. She saw the carved words on the stone: 'Annabel Immanuel, born and died 17th November 1959'.

Afterwards, Rachel whispered something to Billy who nodded. Alex saw her going down the church steps and made to follow but Jemima held her arm.

'She wants to go on her own,' Billy said, coming over to them. The three of them watched her as she climbed quickly up the hill to the empty house.

Ten minutes later, Rachel stood in the doorway of the top room. Through the window, she could see the golden trees and the mist hugging the lake. She went over to the bed and sat down on the colourful quilt, so she could remember holding Annabel for the first time. She put her head down on the pillow. When she closed her eyes, she could feel her daughter in her arms. She stroked her soft skin, brushed her small toes, and put her finger into her tiny palm, which no one would ever read.

A tap dripped in the bathroom nearby. Rachel imagined she heard someone walking around in the kitchen below. In her head, she could still hear the other girls coming and going. She heard Marjory say, 'Bloody hell,' and Joyce laughing. She heard Doris's knitting needles clicking and Harriet's feet scuffing across the floor as they danced to the songs on the radio. The noises churned around in her stomach until she felt hypnotised by them. She thought she might have to get up from the bed and go and be sick in the bathroom. She stayed completely still, hoping the feeling would go away, staring at the uneven surface of the wall. Then she lifted her fingers and touched the wall nearest to her. It felt rough under her palm. She put her other hand between her legs. She cupped it protectively, trapping the material from her skirt there. It was the first time she had touched the space between her thighs since Annabel had been born. She lifted her skirt and cupped her hand inside her underwear. It felt hurt and frightened, but she sensed how soft it was with her fingertips. She was surprised by how beautiful her fingers felt there; she had expected them to be horrified and to have to pull them away again and yank her skirts down quickly, but she didn't. Carefully, she curled her fingers round further and pushed her palm down so that she could feel the dark hair against her hand. She felt as if she was touching a place deep inside her, a place she wasn't normally allowed to go, like the inside of a bone. She rested one of her fingers between her lips, left it there and went back to looking at the rough wall and imagining the sounds downstairs.

Rachel concentrated. She closed her eyes and went right inside where it hurt and wished hard that the pain would stop and as she did so she moved her finger very slightly, so it was hardly moving at all. After a while, she felt the soft feeling move over all of her. Then the torn places between her legs became alive with pain again as if the tearing had only just happened, and for a second she thought she was going to scream out loud, but she couldn't move her finger away. The pain went and was replaced by a feeling as if someone was throwing logs on a fire inside her and was putting them out with hissing buckets of water. It went on for a long time. It was half an hour later when she finally moved her finger away very slowly so as not to hurt herself. She stayed still and kept her eyes closed because she didn't want to feel sick again. Sleep came over her like a pillow, although when Alex came to look for her much later, she found her gazing out of the window in the top room, with the yellow curtains fluttering around her.

42

March 2005

On the day the house was officially finished, Rachel and I were looking at the Scrummage cards when Monica dropped a plate and swore.

'I've got to open up now,' Rachel said as if the breaking plate was a sign. She had a book in her lap. When she had snapped the silver card case shut, she grinned and passed the book to me.

'If you're bored, read the bit on the nab cards, but don't read the rest, it's better to learn slowly.'

I still had a bit of time before Eve wanted me. She was in town buying curtains. I pulled on my jacket and stuffed the book in my pocket. Halfway up the hill, when I could see the lighthouse in the distance, I sat down and opened the chapter Rachel had told me to read. The grass smelt damp and I could feel my trousers getting wet. Down by the lake, the trees were very still.

I looked down at the book. 'Nab Cards', it said at the top of the page in pretend old-fashioned writing. I felt vaguely pissed off at the book for having curly writing and a bit cold. I shifted around to get more comfortable, bent the book round so I could hold it with one hand and hugged myself. I looked at the first paragraph and screwed up my forehead to concentrate. 'There are four nab cards. They allow the player to say "Snatch" and to pick up half the number of the nab in unseen cards. The suit changes to the colour of the nab card and the hand begins again

347

at that number.' The words started to blend into each other, so I gazed out over the lake again. There were grey clouds coming in behind the trees. I tried to remember what I had just read but I couldn't. I glanced behind me at the house. It looked back with solemn eyes. The sky seemed lower than usual. I turned back to the chapter on the nabs and tried again to concentrate. 'A player may lay a nab card in front of another player and snatch one of his or her families, placing them at the top of the unseen pile, in order to bring them back into play.' There was a picture of the Nab of Sixes. It showed the same goblin-like creatures I had seen on Rachel's nab cards but this time there were six of them and they were coloured bronze. The design in the book was slightly different. These goblins were more evil-looking and didn't smile.

Behind the lake, the grey clouds were getting thicker. I flicked the pages so I could look at the pictures. 'Queens and Feather Girls (fives)', it said at the top of one page in the curly writing. There were illustrations of all of the fives. The Queen of Grass was tall and thin with a long robe and the colours were bright so the illustration shone. It began to rain. Big drops started to fall onto the queen's picture. Just as I stuffed the book under my sweatshirt so it wouldn't get any wetter, Eve's car appeared round the side of the hill. I scrambled to my feet. She stopped when she saw me and wound the window down.

'What the hell are you doing out here? Get in. It's going to chuck it down.' She had Bernie with her. As I ran over to the car and dived in, thunder started rumbling as if the sky was hungry. Eve began to pull away before I'd even reached out to yank the door shut. The book fell out from under my jumper as I landed uncomfortably on the seat on top of a couple of CDs Eve had chucked there.

'What's that?' said Bernie. Then he saw the cover of the book. 'Oh,' he said and laughed. 'Is Rachel teaching you?'

'Yes,' I said, pulling out a CD from under me. *Robbie Williams Live at Knebworth* it said on the front. Eve glanced over her shoulder as she rammed the car into third gear.

'Lucky you,' she said. She put her foot down hard and we zoomed through the rain.

There we are driving round the hill through the beginning of a storm. It's been muggy for days now, the air has clung to us like an enthusiastic friend. The rain is a relief. It smells cold and blue. There's the book on the car seat that I will forget about and find days later, the weekend the first students arrive, still bent open at the page headed 'Queens and Feather Girls', with the picture of the tall green Queen of Grass with food at her feet. Rachel will frown at me when I hand it back to her because the pages will be curled and rain splattered, and she'll make me put it under three encyclopaedias to straighten it out, but I will be thinking about the solemn queen in her cloak and how she looks a bit like Alex.

We listened to the thunder for a while before we got out of the car. Then we grabbed the things Eve had bought and ran to the house with our coats over our heads. Bernie began to hang the curtains in the tearoom and I dried my hair on a tea towel, while Eve made coffee for us all.

'I'm cold,' I said when we were sitting on the stairs clutching our mugs.

'You shouldn't sit on the bloody grass in the rain,' said Eve.

When the curtains were up, we stood and looked at each other. All we could hear was the rain on the windows and the thunder rattling around the sky. The house was finished.

That afternoon, I was standing in the pink and yellow tearoom waiting for Alex, when Eve came in, rubbing her hands.

'I'm going to get Rachel,' she said.

'Really?' I said, because Rachel hadn't seen the house yet.

'When Alex gets here, wait out the back for us,' she said. It had stopped raining. Garden tables were arranged around the old twisted tree in the middle of the courtyard. I went outside to wipe down the seats with a tea towel so we could all sit down and when I came back Alex had arrived. She was turning round on the spot so she could take everything in, with a small black case in her hand.

'It's amazing,' she said. Then she put her case down and ran around the house looking into all the rooms like an excited school kid. I went into the kitchen and got out a teapot. I was nervous but when I heard her go outside, I followed.

'Would you like a cup of tea?' I said. She didn't hear me for a moment, because she was staring into the walled garden.

'The gardener still hasn't been,' I said, because it looked scruffy. Bernie had cut away the brambles from the path but it was still wild and I liked to think that if I stood by the bench in the corner, the weeds would twist round me and hold me up so I could lie there as if I was in a hammock.

'What?' she said after a moment. 'Oh. Tea would be lovely.' She put her hand to her forehead. 'I've forgotten something.'

She went along the path and out of the repainted green gate. I followed her and as I stopped to examine the untidy garden, I heard her feet crunching across the driveway. I had seen the crumbling grey stones along one side before, when Bernie had first cleared away the rubbish, but they were still covered in brambles. I stood just inside the gate and looked through the weeds to see if I could make out any words. There was one that hadn't completely crumbled and I could read the words 'safe, arms, peace', but the only stone that was still whole had collapsed under the tree in the corner, where the broken bench was blocking my view of it. I almost missed it completely because it was covered in ivy. I tucked my jeans into my socks so the nettles would find it harder to sting me and climbed carefully over the thorny branches towards the dilapidated bench. The thorns stuck to my clothes as if they were trying to stop me going any further, but I managed to lift a couple of pieces of rotten wood out of the way and peer under the tree. I couldn't get close enough to see what it said. I gave up and went back to the path just as Alex was coming back through the gate.

'Exploring?' she said. She had a picture in her hand. She turned it round to show me. It was a photo of the Eade Village light. 'For the house,' she said.

'Wow,' I said as we walked back to the courtyard together. 'Have you been to look round? You can go out on trips in the summer.' Then I realised I was being stupid, because she was the lighthouse researcher and she had probably been there loads of times.

'Oh yes,' she said, grinning at me and sitting down at the table. 'Only once. But I went right up to the top. We usually get whoever's responsible to email the photos these days.'

I propped the picture up inside and we sat waiting for the others, sipping our tea. I felt a bit embarrassed because of what had happened the last time she had seen me.

'I hear you're an expert now,' Alex said.

'Not really.' I looked into my tea. I knew there was something I had to do, but I was worried in case she was going to get angry with me.

'That's not what Eve told me,' she said. I could see she was trying to make me feel better.

'She's letting me stay anyway.'

'Practice makes perfect,' Alex said. She began rummaging in her coat pocket and pulled out a brown bag. 'Macaroons,' she said, handing them to me.

'Thanks,' I said.

'How's the contract?' she said.

'The stories?' I asked.

She nodded and looked at me with bright eyes. 'Stories instead of. . .' She rubbed her arm to show me what she meant.

'I'm not perfect at remembering,' I said. 'Sometimes I get angry.' Alex nodded. 'But I'm telling Rachel all about it. And she's telling me some stories back.'

'Ah,' said Alex. 'Good.'

'Did you see the display on the house at the library?' I asked her. I knew she hadn't seen it yet, I was just trying to make conversation so I could put off doing the thing I was going to do.

'I've got something for you,' I said at last.

'Oh good,' Alex said. 'I like presents.'

'It's not a present. It's, well, I'll get it.' I went inside and back into the kitchen. I had already rescued it from upstairs. It lay wrapped in a carrier bag at the back of a cupboard. I took it outside for her.

'I found this,' I said awkwardly and handed Alex the red journal. Her eyes widened. She looked at me and didn't know what to say for a moment.

'I read it,' I said. 'I'm sorry. I know it's your diary and everything.' I closed my eyes waiting for her to be angry, but nothing happened. When I opened them again, she was staring silently at the unopened notebook in her hands.

At that moment, we heard Eve's car pulling up and went out to meet them.

'I thought you said it was finished,' Rachel said. She waved her hand at the green gate that we had left open. Through it Rachel could see the scruffy garden.

'It's finished inside,' I told her, wishing hard that she would like it, as if it was my birthday and I was blowing out candles.

'Where's the laundry room?' Rachel said as soon as we went into the courtyard. I had arranged more tea on a tray with a plate of Alex's macaroons.

'You mean that old shed?' Eve replied. 'It had to be taken down. It was falling apart.'

Rachel looked at Alex in disbelief.

'I know,' Alex said, raising her eyebrows.

Eve insisted that we had tea before Rachel could look round. After all the macaroons had gone, they inspected every inch of the tearoom and both downstairs bedrooms, Rachel saying, 'I can't believe it,' over and over. She looked at the new archway, the fireplace and the kitchen workstations and ran her hand over the table, while I demonstrated how the new coffee and tea machine worked.

Eve and Alex helped Rachel go slowly up the stairs so that she could see the bedrooms, but after I had carried the chair up, Eve made me go and do the dishes. I heard them pointing things out to each other as they went from room to room. Then they positioned themselves around the courtyard again and I brought out more tea. Eve arranged cakes and sandwiches on a three-tier tray and stood up solemnly to propose a toast with her china teacup, because the house was officially open for business.

When I watched the first students arriving with their suitcases, I felt so excited I thought I was going to have to run into the kitchen and shout out of the window. The Haven was no longer our secret, although the bin bags and the smell we had covered up was still ours to keep. No one else knew about that. I sat at one of the tables in the tearoom next to Eve. Alex sat on the sofa grinning at them all as they came in while I ticked off their names and directed them to the seats at the round tables where there were pots of tea waiting for them. As I did so, I thought with a smile about how I had watched Eve open the window with her jumper over her mouth on my first day at the house. I was daydreaming about it when I realised Eve was addressing them all.

'Welcome to the first Absolute Beginners Cake-Making Weekend,' said Eve. That was my cue. I lifted a large white plate from the sideboard which Alex had filled with cupcakes early that morning. While Eve talked, I handed them round, one each, for the students to try. They were made with crumbling sponge surrounded by delicate pink marzipan, with cream and a raspberry on top.

'By the end of the weekend,' Eve was saying, when I had put the plate down, 'you will be able to create these yourself. In a minute, Erica will show you all where your rooms are. At twelve thirty, lunch will be served in the courtyard, then we will move into the kitchen where you should wash your hands and put on one of the aprons hanging behind the door. If you have long hair, please keep it tied back.'

Eve's mobile started to ring. She rooted in her pocket for it, embarrassed.

'So sorry,' she said. She pushed it into my hand. 'Erica. You answer it.'

I went outside into the driveway. 'Hello?' I said as I went.

'Ricky.' It was Neil. I wandered through the gate and into the walled garden as I spoke to him. The gardening company had been and tidied it up. Now we had Japanese gravel and circular paving with patches of flowers here and there.

'What have you been doing with yourself?' I said, going over to the newly restored bench under the tree in the corner.

'First the basic sponge,' said Eve, after lunch, when the students were gathered around their workstations. 'We have the oven on at one hundred and ninety degrees already. Now flour.' She held up a bowl into which I had poured exactly the right amount of flour earlier. I had already sieved it, but Eve sieved it again, showing them how to tap the side.

'And now your turn,' she said and they turned to find their own separate stations, with bowls, sieve, scales and flour laid out for them. When everyone had sieved their flour, Eve went on to sugar, vanilla essence, butter and eggs.

'Use fresh free-range eggs at room temperature,' Eve said, motioning me to the front. While she talked, I demonstrated the egg mixing part next to her.

'Crack the eggs into a cup first. These are large eggs so we are using two.' I cracked the eggs, feeling like a magician's assistant. 'Now. Using a fork and wrist action, lightly beat the eggs.'

When I had finished, she held up the cup for them to see and they all gazed into it as if they expected a miracle to have happened.

'At this point, add a little milk. Now fold the egg slowly into your mixture, using a palate knife. OK. Now your turn.'

The students returned to their stations and Eve moved critically among them, showing them how to beat and fold and pour. I cleared up the demonstration table and got the baking tin ready. Eve showed the students how to grease their tins swiftly with a piece of wrapper from round the butter. Then the cakes went into the oven. Three on the bottom shelf, four on the top shelf, including ours although we had already prepared one as if we were on *Blue Peter*. The smell of baking sponges filled the kitchen.

'Go and get her,' Eve hissed at me while all the students gazed at us expectantly.

I found Alex with Rachel in the courtyard. They had the cake scrapbook from the library between them.

'We're ready,' I said.

'Oh, right, OK.' Alex got up.

'Look,' said Rachel, picking up a piece of paper from the table and holding it out to me. 'Alex found this earlier.' I took it from her. It contained a whole catalogue of places with names next to them. I looked from Rachel to Alex in astonishment. It was a list of libraries that girls from the house had been sent to.

'We better go,' Alex said. We left Rachel studying the list of names and made our way into the kitchen, where Eve had been talking about the importance of good cake tins.

'This is Alex French,' she said while Alex washed her hands and tied on her apron. 'Some of you will have heard of her as she has quite a reputation.' A few of the students nodded and smiled. 'You aren't going to make the fruit jelly today,' Eve said, 'because it is better to prepare it in advance. You'll be using some of ours. The recipe will be in your pack at the end of the weekend.'

We stood back and watched while Alex spread thick custard over the sponge. Then she began to slice an apple so thinly that the pieces were almost see-through. She painted them with lemon juice so that they wouldn't turn brown and arranged them on top of the custard so that they made a pattern like a clock with lots of hands. Next she did the same with a peach and an apricot. I handed her the fruit sauce we had made the day before which had cooled to a thick liquid and Alex poured just enough of it onto the cake. The apple, peach and apricot slices were caught in it like feathers in a paperweight.

355

Almost Brown

I am dead but I still like to take the train between the town and the city. I walk up and down the carriages pressing the button to make the doors slide open and sometimes the people who are drinking tea out of plastic cups feel me slipping past them like a cloud of mist. Then I sit down and look out of the window and I can see fields which roll like eiderdowns and a grey farmhouse tucked in the corner between two hills. A bit further on there are five fat trees. If you watch them as the train goes past, you can see that really there are eighteen thin trees standing in two lines. They open up like a fan.

I died in 1864, but I used to live in the stone farmhouse in Eade Village, which sits in the bend in the coast like a sulking child on a chamber pot. The house I can see from the train reminds me of it and makes me go through all the rooms in my head. I remember the kitchen, the bathroom and the bedroom at the top of the stairs.

The night before my first baby was born, Mr Brown was away and I was in the room alone. The lamps were out. I was used to sudden gusts of wind causing soot to fall down into the grate as I slept, but this time there were stones being tossed down the chimney, one after another, and it sounded deliberate. Even though it was the middle of the night, I was convinced someone was on the roof, so I put on my gown and my shoes and I went out into the garden with a lamp. I looked up to the roof. There was no one there. I told myself it was the wind and the soot and went back upstairs. Suddenly I saw a shape at the end of the corridor, like a hole in the darkness. It moved slowly towards me until it reached the landing and then I heard running as if someone was going down the stairs at great speed, then silence. I hurried back into the bedroom. After that night, the chimney in our bedroom was blocked and we could no longer lay a fire there, even after the sweep came.

It wasn't until we moved there that my husband told me the farmhouse was built on the ruins of a church, otherwise I would not have come, but because it was never deconsecrated, it meant that we could bury our daughter in the garden when she died. Sometimes I would hear banging, like a ball being bounced against the walls, or the sound of running water, or glasses chinking in a toast.

Mr Brown was standing by the window the following afternoon when my baby was born. He desperately wanted a boy. When the nurse looked between my daughter's new legs, she said the words before she realised her mistake.

'It's a boy.'

My husband clapped his hands and tears filled his eyes. Then the nurse looked again.

'No. A girl,' she said, and then to make up for it, 'A beautiful baby girl, with tiny fingernails and shiny blue eyes and a lovely smile and soft eyelashes and a curled nose. What will you call her?'

But my husband was looking out of the open window at the sun shining on the lake.

'Almost,' he said.

She was given another name. I've forgotten what it was. Maybe it was Angela, Angelica or Angelina. She was like an angel when I held her, so delicate I was frightened she would break. She had another name anyway, but she was called Almost because that was what my husband said when the nurse asked him, and that was the name the nurse spread around the village in a whisper, like floodwater, or child's piss spreading out in a thin yellow puddle over everyone.

'Her name is Almost,' she whispered in the library. 'Because he wanted a boy. I swear. He called her Almost.'

'Her name's Almost,' said someone else, passing it on in the post office, in the square of shops near the beach, down by the quay, out at the lighthouse, in the fishermen's shop on the front, at the school, outside the church.

'What?'

'Almost. That's what she's called. Like nearly, not quite. Like just missed. Like never did. Like something nearly begun but nothing happened.'

'Really? Almost Brown. He called her that? Imagine. Just imagine it.'

'Nearly, not quite, never, nothing,' someone repeated, with a shake of the head.

'Fancy,' said someone else. 'Almost Brown.'

Almost Speaking

When I was eight and still alive and breathing, I stood by the trees and watched the leaves bud and turn yellow-green, then dark green then gold then dead and I watched them falling. I met her in the trees when I should have been chasing the geese. She had pretty eyes and hair that hung like pearls around her forehead. I thought she was very beautiful. We knelt down by the lake together and laughed at our reflections. The girl, whose name was Miss Georgia Lacy, put her hand into the water and ruffled our reflections. Then we held hands and looked up at all the branches and pretended that stars grew on a big tree in the sky and the stars we can see are falling seeds ready to make more trees. We can only see the parachutes at night when it's black, I said, and we made a plan to come back at night and watch. After that I could call Miss Georgia Lacy George and she called me by my name which I can almost remember if I shut my eyes tight and think and think.

When we were ten, we had a picnic in the cabbage field, and my mother gave me a pot of tea and her mother gave her cake wrapped up in paper. When we were nearly fifteen we leant against the tree by the lake which we called the star tree because we remembered a bit of what we used to say to each other when we were small, only not all of it. We called the tree the star tree because at night it looked as if you could see the stars hanging on its branches. We sat under it together on long summer days and read books from the library together. I liked the librarian very much and she liked me because I knew the books almost as well as she did. George said she wanted to put her arm round me to see what it was like and so I let her and it felt very warm. George read me a story about how they used to kill witches by hanging them or setting fire to them. I said how did they know for sure they were witches. She said they had a mark on them somewhere, so I didn't tell her about the mark that I had in case she thought I was a witch. I looked at it at night. It was just above my belly button and was like a tiny palm. My mother said it was a birthmark but I liked to think that it was where a hand had touched me, a hand covered in mud or paint so that I got stained. I told George how my father wanted a boy so that was how I got called what I was called.

When George chased me the next day, I was exhausted. In and out of the trees we went, then we lay down but I felt as if we were going over the surface of the lake and up towards the horizon and in and out of the windows in the clouds, round and round and in and out, taking flower dust and stones with us into the sky. We were flying. It was the best time and for all of it we were lying under the star tree and she was making me feel like honey. No, not like honey, like a honey bee.

It wasn't long after that I got myself into trouble. I have forgotten what his name was. In the cabbage field where George and I had had our picnic, that was where it happened. It felt like someone tickling my feet, not like when George made me feel like I was yellow and black and flying into flowers. I laughed and rolled over, but later George said how could you and I thought we were special and I thought I was the one you liked and she cried. She wouldn't hold my hand any more or crawl under the low branches of the star tree to see if the leaves were falling or pretend that if they did fall they would bury us up to our necks and we would have to fight our way out. She said she never wanted to kiss me again and she agreed to marry a boy her parents liked.

After they got married, I knew I had something growing inside me but I couldn't stand to see George in her new garden with the boy she had gone with because of the cabbage field. Now I'm flying, it is hard to remember how angry I was when every day I saw them and she wouldn't speak to me. I ran round and round the trees myself but it wasn't the same as when I held her hand and did it because when I looked, she wasn't there. I hated to see them out walking by the quayside or on the sand. She gazed at me smugly and took his arm and held it tighter so even though I had the thing inside me, I put on my red dress and my matching shoes and went down to the lake and lay face down with my arms spread out so I floated. It wasn't so hard after I had taken the first mouthful. I felt like a fish. I felt the water swimming inside me. I think I was crying but I couldn't tell because the lake was all around me. I wished George was there to see me floating. I wanted to go so that I wouldn't have to see them walk on the sand together any more, but even though I wanted to I didn't go anywhere, I hung around and had to watch them haul my body from the lake. I had to watch George sit wide-eyed under the star tree and shrug her new husband away when he came to find her.

Afterwards they all said it was because of the cabbage field and the baby but they were wrong. It was because of George and the boy her parents liked. Apart from the librarian, she didn't say it, she stayed quiet. I liked her and I felt bad when I saw her crying between the books. I put my hand out to touch her hair and say sorry. Afterwards, my father was so full of sadness that he gave the farmhouse away so other pregnant girls could come and the librarian let them sit amongst the books and read. I've forgotten some of the things that happened now I'm flying. After the lake I felt as if I was sinking all the time. My feet, my knees, my thighs, my head, a hand, one bit of me was always sinking down further into the water. It would get covered in green weeds. I could taste the water in my mouth.

When I left for the last time, my feet hit the bottom of the lake, then I launched myself high into the air, over the surface of the water, between the branches of the star tree, up much higher so I could see the sea, out around the lighthouse and towards the horizon. Now I'm flying instead of sinking, I feel like I have six hairy legs covered in nectar. I go in and out of the windows in the clouds, carrying the flower dust with me into the sky.

Acknowledgements

Acknowledgement is due to The Lighthouse Society of Great Britain, Gravesend Cottage, Torpoint, Cornwall PL11 2LX, UK, who produce *The Lighthouse Encyclopaedia* CD ROM (www.lsgb.co.uk) and to Natasha Moskovici for help with the Spanish. Jane and Norman Latimer, former owners of the Waterside Bed and Breakfast, kindly provided me with historical information regarding the Haven, a home for unmarried mothers, which previously occupied the building. The text of Jemima's prayer card is taken from *Rules and Regulations for Rescue Officers* by Consul Mrs Booth-Tucker (1897). Permission has been sought from: The Salvation Army Archives and Research Center, The Salvation Army National Headquarters, 615 Slaters Lane, P.O. Box 269, Alexandria, VA 22313, USA. The text is quoted in Regina G. Kunzel's book *Fallen Women, Problem Girls* (Yale University Press 1993). Acknowledgement is also due to the staff at the Portland Bill Lighthouse, Portland, Dorset. Thank you to Ann Bannon for her kindness regarding *Odd Girl Out* and *Women in the Shadows*. And thank you to my editor, Mary-Anne Harrington.